THE
SECRET
DAUGHTER

ANNE GRACIE

BERKLEY ROMANCE
New York

BERKLEY ROMANCE
Published by Berkley
An imprint of Penguin Random House LLC
penguinrandomhouse.com

Copyright © 2024 by Anne Gracie
Penguin Random House values and supports copyright. Copyright fuels creativity,
encourages diverse voices, promotes free speech, and creates a vibrant culture. Thank you
for buying an authorized edition of this book and for complying with copyright laws by not
reproducing, scanning, or distributing any part of it in any form without permission. You
are supporting writers and allowing Penguin Random House to continue to publish books
for every reader. Please note that no part of this book may be used or reproduced in any
manner for the purpose of training artificial intelligence technologies or systems.

BERKLEY and the BERKLEY & B colophon are
registered trademarks of Penguin Random House LLC.

Book design by George Towne

ISBN: 9780593549704

First Edition: December 2024

Printed in the United States of America
1   3   5   7   9   10   8   6   4   2

PRAISE FOR
ANNE GRACIE AND HER NOVELS

"A confection that brims with kindness and heartfelt sincerity.... You can't do much better than Anne Gracie, who offers her share of daring escapes, stolen kisses, and heartfelt romance in a tale that carries the effervescent charm of the best Disney fairy tales." —*Entertainment Weekly*

"I never miss an Anne Gracie book."
—#1 *New York Times* bestselling author Julia Quinn

"For fabulous Regency flavor, witty and addictive, you can't go past Anne Gracie."
—#1 *New York Times* bestselling author Stephanie Laurens

"With her signature superbly nuanced characters, subtle sense of wit, and richly emotional writing, Gracie puts her distinctive stamp on a classic Regency plot."
—*Chicago Tribune*

"The always terrific Anne Gracie outdoes herself with *Bride by Mistake*.... Gracie created two great characters, a high-tension relationship, and a wonderfully satisfying ending. Not to be missed!"
—*New York Times* bestselling author Mary Jo Putney

"A fascinating twist on the girl-in-disguise plot.... With its wildly romantic last chapter, this novel is a great antidote to the end of summer."
—*New York Times* bestselling author Eloisa James

"Anne Gracie's writing dances that thin line between always familiar and fresh.... *The Accidental Wedding* is warm and sweet, tempered with bursts of piquancy and a dash or three of spice." —New York Journal of Books

*For the members and organizers of ARRA
(the Australian Romance Readers Association),
in thanks for all you do to support and encourage
Australian and international romance writers,
and especially for the support and friendship
given to me over the years.*

*And for the various beloved dogs who have kept
me company throughout my writing career—
Bessie, Chloe and Milly—
patiently watching or snoozing as I type, listening
to me muttering, helping with brainstorming
(though they rarely make suggestions other than
"I hope there's a dog in this one")
and dragging me out for walks.*

Chapter One

❧

France
Late autumn, 1821

The country house party had been a mistake, Zoë Benoît thought as she said her good nights and went in search of her bedchamber.

She had accepted the invitation, thinking there would be picnics, day trips, rides in the country and so on. It was, after all, what she understood people did at house parties.

Not this group. The guests were predominantly elderly people, and all they seemed to do was to sit and gossip, play cards, eat and snooze. So far the only exercise the ladies had taken was to stroll in the gardens or down to the lake, where they watched the gentlemen fishing—which was all they did, apart from eat, drink, play cards and shoot. It was most frustrating.

As for the handful of younger members of the party, she had very little in common with them. The girls were pleasant enough, but all they talked of was fashion—which was interesting enough—and gossip about people she didn't know.

And the three young gentlemen? They were cronies of

Monsieur Etienne, the son and heir—and the less said about him the better.

The only reason she'd accepted the invitation was that she was sure she'd finally have the opportunity to visit her mother's former home, which was about twenty miles away, or perhaps twenty kilometres—the new French system of measuring everything in decimals was confusing; people chopped and changed from one system to the other. But it was not too far away, she was sure.

Heavy footsteps sounded on the stairs behind her. Blast. She knew who it would be. She quickened her pace.

Behind her, Etienne, the spoiled, indulged, and deeply irritating heir of Baron Treffier, quickened his pace. She could hear him puffing.

Zoë's temper was at breaking point. Five days she'd been at the Treffiers' country house party, and Etienne had spent four and a half of them in hot and unwelcome pursuit of her. And not for the purpose of marriage, either—he was already betrothed to the unfortunate young woman who'd sat through the house party pretending she hadn't noticed her fiancé's appalling behavior.

Had Zoë been in her position, she would not for a moment have put up with it. Not that she would have accepted him in the first place, fortune or not.

She was fed up with Etienne's importunities, his sly, suggestive remarks and his even more infuriating surreptitious touches and squeezes, not to mention the persistent and unsubtle invitations to his bed.

And no matter how often and how firmly—even bluntly—she'd repudiated his advances, his self-consequence was so inflated that he took every rebuff as encouragement.

His parents must have known what he was like, but they'd done nothing, seeming to think it was natural for their beloved son to behave like a randy goat toward an invited guest. To him, all females were fair game.

Hurrying along, she turned a corner and found herself

in a dark, deserted corridor that ended in a wall. Curses. A dead end. She'd been heading to her bedchamber, intending to lock herself in, but the old château was such a rabbit warren of corridors, in her haste she'd taken a wrong turn.

The puffing came closer.

Very well then, it was time to make a stand.

Taking a deep breath, she turned and faced him. He bustled toward her, red-faced and breathing hard. Even in the dim light she could see his triumphant leering grin. "So, *mon petit chou*, you wait for me."

Zoë might speak French like a native, but she was English enough to dislike being likened to a vegetable, especially by this pig of a man. "Monsieur Etienne, I am *not* your little cabbage. I am not even your *chou de Bruxelles*!"

He giggled. "Ah, so witty, *ma belle*."

"I am not your belle, either. I am your 'touch me again and you will regret it' guest!"

"Ah, such fire, such passion, *cherie. Je t'adore*."

He hurried over to her, and she put up her hands to prevent the embrace that was clearly coming. "Monsieur Etienne—"

But before she could say a thing, he grabbed her outstretched hands and shoved them above her head. She struggled to free herself, but though he was shorter than her, to her fury, he was stronger. He pushed her hands together, gripping them in one hand, and shoved her hard against the wall.

"How dare you," she began, but seeing his mouth aiming wetly for hers, she jerked her head aside, and he slobbered on her neck instead.

He pressed her hard against the wall, holding her immobile with his body. His aroused body. She shuddered.

"*Oui, ma belle*, I am hot for you too," he muttered, and with his free hand he clawed at her skirts, dragging them up, muttering excited obscenities.

She could scream for help, Zoë thought, but in this part

of the château there was no telling whether anyone would even hear her, let alone come to help. Monsieur Etienne was indulged by all. No, she knew what to do. She'd never actually done it before, but if ever there was the time . . .

"I'm warning you," she said.

He giggled with glee and rubbed himself excitedly against her. A cool draft against her legs told Zoë her skirts had reached her thighs. Which gave her much greater ease of movement.

She took a deep breath and jammed her knee as hard as she could between his legs.

With a shriek, Monsieur Etienne released her and collapsed like a failed soufflé, rolling on the floor, moaning and wheezing.

She shook out her skirts, dusted her hands and said, "I said no, Monsieur Etienne, and I meant it." She stepped over his writhing body and walked away, leaving Monsieur Etienne in a crumpled heap, swearing and gasping out feeble threats.

Vile, disgusting, horrid little man.

She found the correct corridor, stepped into her bedchamber and locked the door behind her. She leaned against it, wishing it had a bolt as well, and realized she was shaking.

So much for being a lady. Three years of lessons in proper deportment down the drain.

One small difficulty and she'd reverted right back to the girl who'd grown up in the back streets of London. But what else could she do? She'd seen him bothering the other young ladies, and yet all they did was blush and move away and bleat at him, hoping he would stop.

Which he'd done once he'd spotted Zoë.

She poured herself a glass of water from the jug on the washstand and drank it down. She sat at the dressing table, removed her jewelry, pulled the pins from her hair and contemplated her reflection. Her hands were still shaking.

She'd done it now.

There would be a scandal. And she knew who would be blamed.

She kicked off her shoes, sat on the high bed and considered her options.

She couldn't stay here now. The house party was far from over—there were at least five days left to go—but she would have to leave. First thing in the morning for preference. She had no intention of staying to deal with the fuss that would erupt once Etienne informed his parents of what she'd done.

Though, would he tell them what she'd done, or would he keep quiet about it, too mortified to admit to defeat by a woman? She wasn't sure.

He'd deserved it, and more, but if he did make it public, he'd probably claim she'd attacked him for no good reason. The scandal might even reach Paris. Certainly it would deeply embarrass and upset Madame DuPlessis, her chaperone, who'd made it possible for her to attend the house party when Lucy, the friend and mentor with whom she'd been living the last three years, had been unable to travel.

It was regrettable—the motherly Madame DuPlessis had been very kind to her, and even if there were no scandal, Zoë had no doubt the good lady would be upset at Zoë's abrupt departure—but what else could she do?

She made up her mind. Whether the despicable Etienne told his parents or not, Zoë would leave first thing in the morning. She'd really only attended because of the locality, and after what had just happened, she doubted any of the guests would be willing to drive her anywhere.

She found some writing paper and ink in the little desk in her room and sat down to write some notes. At first she planned to tell both her chaperone and her hosts that she'd been called away urgently on family business and would apologize for the inconvenience.

But the moment she picked up the pen, she decided no,

she would not make things easy for her hosts. They must know of their son's unsavory habits, and yet they'd done nothing to curb them. She was a guest in their home and they owed her protection at the very least.

She dashed off a letter, which she hoped would leave them squirming with embarrassment. She described in detail the disgraceful way Etienne had behaved throughout the visit and what he'd just attempted. She'd added that she'd been forced to defend herself, but had her guardian been present, Etienne would be facing a duel. Not that she had a guardian, but they didn't know that.

Having expended a good deal of satisfying vitriol to the baron and baroness, her note to Madame DuPlessis was much shorter and more matter-of-fact. The kindly lady had been a delightfully lax chaperone, but Etienne's behavior wasn't her fault, so Zoë merely thanked her for her kindness and explained that Monsieur Etienne's behavior had made any continuation here impossible. She added that she would catch the *diligence* to Paris, which was why she was leaving so early, and hoped it would not be too much trouble for Madame DuPlessis to convey the remainder of her baggage back to Paris when she returned.

It was a pity she wouldn't get to see her mother's former home, but she could see no alternative but to return to Paris. She'd never learned to ride, and besides, she could hardly compound her disgrace by stealing a horse.

Feeling calmer, she rang the bell to summon the maid she'd been assigned to help her out of her dress, then began a letter to Lucy and her husband, Gerald.

A few moments later there came a soft knock on her door. She stiffened, then realized Etienne was incapable of knocking softly. It would be Marie, the young maid assigned to her for the length of her stay at the château.

"*Entrez,*" she called, then recollecting that she'd locked the door, she rose and unlocked it.

"Your hot water, mademoiselle," the maid murmured, and placed a large jug of steaming water on the washstand. "Shall I help you disrobe?"

"Yes, please, and perhaps you could—" Zoë broke off as the girl turned and the candlelight fell fully on her face. "Marie," she exclaimed. "What happened?"

The maid's eyes were red-rimmed and there was a nasty bruise on her face. Half her face was quite swollen and there was a cut on her cheekbone.

Marie dropped her gaze in shame. "It's nothing, mademoiselle."

"It's not nothing at all. Tell me who did this to you."

Marie lifted a hopeless shoulder and shook her head. "Shall I help you undress, mademoiselle?"

Zoë eyed the cut on her cheekbone. Made by a signet ring, she thought, a signet ring she'd seen very recently on a pudgy aristocratic finger. "Monsieur Etienne." It wasn't a question.

Marie nodded.

Zoë muttered something under her breath. "You resisted him?"

Marie nodded again, and a choked sob broke her tenuous composure. "I am dismissed, mademoiselle. As soon as I have finished with you here tonight, I must leave."

Zoë frowned. "Tonight? But it's dark. Where will you go? Do you have family nearby?"

Marie shook her head. "No family, mademoiselle. I am an orphan."

"So what will you do?"

Marie's eyes filled with tears again. She gave a hopeless shrug.

"Well, let's see to that nasty cut, first. I have some very good ointment that my sister made." Zoë fetched the little case filled with Clarissa's products and pulled out a small jar. "This will help." She soaked a clean cloth with the warm water Marie had brought and gently cleaned the girl's face, then smoothed the ointment carefully over the cut and the bruise.

"Oh, that feels nice," the girl said.

"My sister is very clever."

"Thank you, mademoiselle. You are very kind. Now, I must leave or the housekeeper will be angry."

"Nonsense! You can't go out into the night with nowhere to go! It's, it's inhumane. Anything could happen to you," Zoë said.

"But I must, mademoiselle. I was told to be gone as soon as I had completed my duties."

"But what would you do?"

Marie said in a hopeless voice, "Walk to the village, I suppose, and try to find another position."

Walk to the village?

Without a character reference, Marie would have no hope, Zoë thought. And walking that distance at night? It was not to be thought of.

"You're not going anywhere," Zoë told her. "Certainly not out into the night with nowhere to go! Would you work for me?"

"For you, mademoiselle, of course." Marie brightened. "You mean it?"

Zoë nodded. The maid's plan to walk to the village had given her an idea. She eyed the maid thoughtfully. "We're about the same size, aren't we?"

Marie looked puzzled. "*Oui*, mademoiselle," she said cautiously.

"Good. Take off your dress."

"My dress?" Marie didn't move.

Zoë laughed at her expression. "It's all right, we're going to swap clothes, that's all."

"Swap clothes? Mine for . . . yours?" Marie said incredulously.

"Yes. Here." Zoë tossed her the plainest of her dresses,

still much finer than anything Marie would own, and one of her fine lawn chemises.

Marie stared at the garments. "Such fine fabric . . . But mademoiselle, this chemise has lace on it."

"Has it? I suppose so." Most of her underclothes were trimmed with lace.

"Never have I ever worn real lace."

Zoë smiled. "Good. There's a first time for everything. Put these on, please, and pass me your clothes."

With a bemused expression, Marie took off her dress. When it came to her chemise, she hesitated and shook her head. "It's not fitting, mademoiselle."

Seeing the garment, Zoë understood. It was clean enough, but worn thin and so often mended it was almost entirely made of patches. It reminded Zoë of the underclothes she'd worn in the years before Clarissa Studley had found and claimed her as a sister. Zoë's life had changed dramatically as a result, but she would never forget the life she'd had before.

"It's perfect," she said briskly. "Exactly what I want. Now, help me off with this gown."

Marie unhooked Zoë's evening dress and folded it away, then the two young women exchanged clothes. Zoë examined herself in the cheval mirror and grinned. "I don't look like a fine lady now, do I?"

"No, mademoiselle, not at all," Marie agreed worriedly.

Zoë laughed. "Excellent." She glanced around the room. "Now, I'll need something to cover my head. My usual hats aren't at all suitable. Do you have one?"

"I usually wear a headscarf, mademoiselle. I have several downstairs with my things."

"Good. Run and fetch your things. You are not going out into the night! You can stay here with me, and we'll both leave early tomorrow morning."

"Both of us, mademoiselle?"

"Yes, both of us." She grinned. "I gave Monsieur Eti-

enne a taste of his own medicine earlier this evening." She
jerked her knee up in explanation.

Marie's eyes widened. "You didn't!"

"I did and I thoroughly enjoyed it. But I won't stay here
after that."

"No, of course not. Oh, mademoiselle, you are so brave."

Zoë sobered. "No, you are the brave one, Marie. The
despicable poltroon can't do anything to me, but you risked
everything by resisting his nasty ways. And I won't allow
you to be punished any further for it. Now, go and fetch
your belongings."

Marie smoothed down her dress. "I will make sure nobody sees me in these clothes, mademoiselle."

While Marie hurried off to fetch her things, Zoë sat
down and added a postscript to Madame DuPlessis's note,
adding that she was not to worry, that she was taking a
maid with her so it would all be quite *convenable*.

Then she wrote a longer letter, this one to Lucy and Gerald in Paris. In it she briefly explained Marie's predicament
and asked them to take care of the girl until she returned
from the house party.

Dreadful though poor Marie's situation was, it could
turn out providential for both of them.

They left the château at dawn the next morning. Zoë,
dressed in Marie's drab clothes and wearing a headscarf, carried the cloth bundle into which Marie had fitted
all her worldly belongings. It now contained everything
Zoë thought she would need for the next few days. The
maid's pathetically meager collection was now stored in
Zoë's smallest portmanteau, which Marie carried. In Zoë's
clothes and wearing a smart dark green velvet hat she
looked quite elegant—apart from the scab and the dark
bruise on her swollen face.

She had been almost wholly silent all morning, but as

they approached the village, she said, "Mademoiselle, what do we do here?"

"You will catch the *diligence* to Paris, and—"

"I? To Paris?" She stopped dead and put the portmanteau down in the dust. "But I have never been to Paris! I have never been anywhere! I went from the orphan house to the Château Treffier when I was twelve."

Zoë smiled. "Well, now you will go to Paris."

Marie didn't move. "And you will be with me?"

"No," Zoë said gently. The girl's reaction had surprised her, but she supposed so much had already happened to Marie that she wasn't ready for further adventures. "Now, don't worry, Marie, you will be perfectly all right. I gave you the letter for my friend Lady Thornton—remember?— and the address is written on the front. The *diligence* will take you to Paris—and here is some money to buy food and whatever else you might need on the way." She handed Marie a small leather purse. "Keep it safe. There are thieves and pickpockets everywhere."

Nodding, Marie clutched the purse tightly. For herself, Zoë had fashioned a simple money belt that she wore around her waist, next to her skin.

"When the coach reaches Paris, hire a hackney cab and show them the address." She repeated the address aloud several times to help Marie remember, for of course she could not read. "The driver will take you to Lady Thornton's home, you will give her the letter and she will look after you. I will join you there later."

Marie didn't move. She looked doubtful and unhappy.

"You don't have to go if you don't want to," Zoë said gently, "but since you said you had nowhere to go . . . I thought this would be best."

"You are very kind, mademoiselle, it's just that . . ."

"You are nervous?"

She nodded.

"I understand. Until I was sixteen I had never traveled

more than a few miles from where I was born. But I promise you, it will all work out. You will have a job and a home with me at Lady Thornton's. And nobody will treat you cruelly."

"But why do you not come with me?"

"I have other things to do first—things that are important to me." Things that she had not told anyone about.

"Dressed like that?" Marie jerked a chin at the clothes Zoë was wearing.

"Yes, because it will be easier for me if nobody thinks I am a lady. And it will be easier for you dressed in my clothes because people will assume you are a lady. And you will be seated inside the *diligence*, not outside or on the roof."

"Inside?" Marie's eyes widened. Poor people invariably rode on top of the *diligence* coach; it was more expensive to sit inside. "But will you not be frightened, mademoiselle? It is dangerous for a woman to be on her own, especially someone young and pretty like you."

"Don't worry, I know how to look after myself," Zoë said with more confidence than she felt. Really, it would be more sensible to give up the idea of visiting Maman's former home and return to Paris with Marie. But there had been some unrest in Paris, so once Lucy's morning sickness had passed, she and Gerald planned to return to London, taking Zoë with them. This would be Zoë's last chance. "I handled Monsieur Etienne, didn't I? And I will be careful."

Marie bit her lip doubtfully.

Zoë said, "Now, make up your mind—the *diligence* will depart soon. Do you go to Paris, or do we part ways in the village?"

Marie ran her palms down the fine cloth of her dress. "Can I still keep the clothes?"

Zoë's heart sank a little. "Yes, of course. And the money

I gave you. And the portmanteau. But I will want the letter back."

There was a short silence. Birds twittered noisily in the hedge that bordered the road. In the distance a rooster crowed. "Well?" Zoë asked after a minute.

Marie considered it for a few more moments, then said decisively, "I will go to Paris."

Zoë grinned. "Excellent." She produced a length of black lacy netting and a small paper of pins. "Now, let us pin this around the brim of your hat."

Marie frowned. *"Pourquoi?"*

"Because it will disguise that nasty bruise on your face and make you look mysterious and like a lady who does not wish to be drawn into conversation with curious busybodies. But please, one more thing—do not tell anyone I have gone off on my own. I will be perfectly all right, but I don't want anyone to worry. Do you promise?"

"I promise, mademoiselle," she said, but she didn't look happy about it.

They pinned the veil into place and walked into the village. Just in time, because after a few minutes the *diligence* bowled into town. A short time later it moved on, with Marie safely installed inside and waving a nervous goodbye to Zoë.

Zoë took a deep breath. So, that was that. Now to start on her own adventure.

She picked up Marie's bundle and headed northwest along a narrow road. She'd hoped that someone at the house party would drive her there, but that was before she knew what Etienne was like, and wild horses wouldn't get her into a carriage with him. Shanks's pony it would have to be.

She was completely free to do as she wanted. The thought cheered her. Ever since her mother had died, she'd been subject to the control of others—first the strict and repressive control of the orphanage, then Clarissa and Lady

Scattergood, and later Izzy, the half sister who looked exactly like her.

Oh, they'd been endlessly kind and benevolent, but their expectations and sincere desire for her to better herself had been, now that she was considering the matter, a little stifling.

And then there had been dear Lucy, who had taken her up as a challenge, to turn a street urchin into a lady, and was always correcting her grammar and English pronunciation so that no sign of her early life showed. Zoë was grateful to all of them—well, perhaps not Miss Glass at the orphanage—but certainly to her sisters and Lucy and Lady Scattergood, who had offered her not only security and a home but also unconditional acceptance and love.

But it did get a little wearing at times constantly striving to be perfect.

Now, dressed in the shabby clothes of a maidservant, in a place where nobody knew her, heading out on a pilgrimage that meant something only to her, it was as if a small weight had been lifted from her shoulders.

It had briefly rained in the night and the world smelled fresh and clean. She gave a small skip of delight. It would be like a little holiday.

There was very little traffic on the road. So far she'd passed two women and a youth heading in the opposite direction, the youth pulling a handcart laden with vegetables. They'd nodded and sent a cheery greeting and continued on their way.

A short time later a cart appeared, heading in the same direction she was going, but the driver had smiled ruefully and indicated by gestures that he was turning off the road shortly, and indeed she'd seen him do it.

Otherwise Zoë was wholly alone.

But it was a glorious sunny day, and she was young and

free and doing what she'd always wanted to do—seeing her mother's old home.

An hour later it was getting hot, and her feet were starting to get sore. *How much farther to Maman's home?* she wondered. Was it twenty miles or twenty kilometres? She wasn't used to walking in these boots.

Hoofbeats clopping along behind her made her turn. A cart with three men sitting on the driver's bench was approaching. She waited, wondering whether they would offer her a lift, but as they drew nearer, she decided she didn't much like the look of them. Their horse was bone-thin, dirty and unkempt, and anyone who treated an animal like that was not to be trusted.

"Hey, pretty girl, you look hot. Want to ride with us?" the driver, a man with a villainous-looking mustache, called to her as they drew near. He wasn't much cleaner than his horse. The thickset man next to him sent her a broken-toothed grin and waved her over. The third man said nothing, but the way he was staring at Zoë sent a shiver down her spine.

"No, thank you, I'm almost home." She crossed to the opposite side of the narrow road, hitched up her bundle and waited for them to drive on.

The driver shrugged and said something to his friends, who laughed. They drove on.

Zoë waited until they'd turned the corner and were out of sight, then she trudged on. *I know how to look after myself. I handled Monsieur Etienne, didn't I?*

She gave a small shiver. Talk about misplaced confidence. What would she have done if those men had insisted? Next time a cart or wagon passed her she would hide.

She turned the corner and froze. The cart was just ahead of her, the horse tied to a tree, and two of the three men were walking toward her. Two? Where was the third?

A rustle in the bushes opposite told her where he was

lurking. She whirled and saw him stepping forward, his thick arms reaching out to grab her. She flung her bundle at him and ran, diving into a thicket of scrub and pushing her way through it, heedless of the scratches caused by thorns and sharp twigs, fleeing for her life.

She did not know how far she ran or for how long, but she had a stitch in her side and was gasping for breath when she noticed a hole, a fox hole probably, half-hidden under a thicket of brambles. Without hesitating she wriggled in backward, dragging some weeds and a fallen branch after her to hide the entrance.

She hoped there was no creature inside. Even if there was, it would surely be less dangerous than the three animals that were searching the scrubby undergrowth for her, crashing about and swearing most foully.

She lay there, her heart pounding, trying to breathe silently. Footsteps came and went, passing so close all she could do was to hold her breath and close her eyes and pray.

Eventually the sounds faded. Had they given up? Or were they bluffing, pretending they'd left in order to lure her out?

What a fool she'd been, convincing herself she could manage alone. When she was a child roaming the back streets of London, she'd been wary of everyone, alert to the slightest hint of danger. But after years first in the orphanage, which was run like a prison, then living in luxury with Clarissa and Lady Scattergood and later Lucy and her husband, those finely honed instincts had been dulled.

She waited for a long time, huddled in the hole until her cramped limbs drove her to wriggle carefully out. She brushed dirt from her clothes, listening for any sound that might alert her to the men's presence. But all she heard was birdsong, untroubled and cheerful.

She cautiously crept back to where she had left the road. There was nothing very valuable in her bundle—just some of Marie's clothing, her sketchbook and pencils and some bread and cheese and sausage—but she needed them.

Thank goodness she'd made that money belt, still firm and tight around her waist.

It took a while to find her bundle. They'd torn it open and flung her things about. The women's clothes, shabby as they were, hadn't tempted them. The food was gone, and her sketchbook—oh no!—it had been tossed into the road and lay half in a muddy puddle.

She dived on it and did her best to wipe it clean of mud and damp. The paper would dry in the heat and the sketches, though stained with mud, were still mostly visible. At least they hadn't taken it or ripped it to shreds in their rage at being balked of their prey. And where were her pencils? She searched among the roadside weeds and found them broken in pieces. She collected them, regardless. A stub of a pencil was better than none.

Her arms stung, crisscrossed with fine lines of dried blood where they'd been scratched. She'd brought a little pot of Clarissa's healing salve, giving Marie the rest, but where was it? Had they smashed it? She searched through the long grass at the side of the road and eventually found it, undamaged. Applying it to her scratches, she felt instantly better.

She knotted up her bundle again and resumed her journey in a much more sober state of mind. She would be far more careful in future. At the first sound of horses or men, she would melt into the scrub at the side of the road.

Whether it was twenty kilometres or twenty miles, she would rather walk than take the risk of what had almost just happened.

Chapter Two

Five hours later she was starting to limp. The sun overhead beat down relentlessly. The road was dusty, the fields on one side were filled with serried rows of grapevines and on the other, open fields bordered by a thick hedge. There was no sign of the next village. Zoë was wearing her own leather half boots—Marie's feet were too large for an exchange of footwear—but they were new, and she'd never had to walk very far in them. She was hot and thirsty and a blister was starting.

Cursing herself for not planning this better, she brightened when she heard the sound of water nearby. Pushing through the long grass and weeds that lined the road, she came across a little stream, burbling clear and fast over a bed of smooth stones.

She scooped up a few mouthfuls of the water, then splashed some on her face and carefully washed her scratched arms. She pulled off her boots and stockings and plunged her aching feet into the blissfully cool water. She lay back, her eyes closed, enjoying the sunshine now that her thirst was quenched and her feet were cooling.

"Blisters, eh?" The deep voice startled her. She snatched up her boots and stockings, ready to run.

In careful French the man said, "Your feet, they are sore, mademoiselle, *n'est-ce pas?*"

He stood a dozen yards away, tall, lean and tanned, his jaw dark with several days' worth of whiskers. He wore no hat. His nose was bold, his hair dark brown, untidy and overlong. He was dressed simply in worn trousers and a faded blue shirt, open at the neck to reveal a strong column of tanned throat. His eyes were the color of his shirt—no, the color of the sea, the Mediterranean Sea.

Gerald had taken her and Lucy to the South of France one summer, and Zoë had been amazed and entranced by the color of the sea there. When she'd last seen it, the English Channel had been gray and sullen, like tarnished silver, but the Mediterranean had sparkled between green and turquoise.

She'd never seen eyes that color.

She was hard put to place him. He was English, she could tell by his accent, not to mention his initial comment, which she hadn't noticed at first was in English, and he carried himself with unconscious assurance, but he didn't look like a gentleman, or even a farmer. Romany, perhaps? Though he didn't look or sound like any of the Romany she'd seen. He was English, surely.

He smiled, a slash of brilliant white in his tanned face, and she swallowed. He was very good-looking. "Don't worry," he said in his accented French, "I did not intend to um, *disturber*? no, *déranger* you. I just came to fetch water for my horse and me." He held up a small blackened pot and a bucket. "I'm making tea."

Tea? She would kill for a cup of tea.

He swished the bucket and the pot through the clear water, and lifted them, dripping. He turned to leave, then said,

"Perhaps you'd care to join me for a cup of tea, mademoiselle?" And then he added to himself in English, "Probably not. You French don't much care for tea, do you?"

Zoë hesitated—he was an unshaven, shabbily dressed stranger and they were all alone in the middle of nowhere. And after what had happened earlier, she ought to avoid him, but he was just one man, and for some reason she didn't feel threatened by him. Perhaps it was his Englishness, or maybe that smile of his. Or his blue—sea-blue eyes. Or the offer of tea. It seemed somehow . . . civilized.

Nevertheless, she would not be foolish: caution must prevail. She would love a cup of tea, but she would keep her distance. And she would not confess her own Englishness— that might spark awkward questions. In French she said, "*Merci*, monsieur, it is very kind of you."

He smiled again, and again she swallowed. "Excellent. I will be over there"—he gestured—"with my horse and wagon."

Zoë dried her feet and put her stockings and boots back on. She picked up a large stone—it would be a weapon of sorts if she needed one—then went to find him. A thin column of smoke guided her to a shady overhang in a small clearing beside the road. She reached the edge of the clearing and halted at the sound of someone talking.

A rawboned old horse stood beside a covered wagon that had once been painted in bright colors, but which were now faded. She almost laughed aloud at the sight of his horse. An unprepossessing creature, it wore a battered straw hat decorated with faded old fabric flowers. Its ears poked through two holes in the hat. The animal was old and bony, but its coat was clean and seemed well groomed.

She couldn't see anyone else, and she quickly realized that the man was talking to his horse. He'd placed the bucket of water in front of it, but the animal showed no inclination to drink. "Not good enough for you, is it?" He addressed it in English. "Or are you demonstrating an adherence to that irritating proverb? But I didn't lead you to water, I brought the water to *you*! At great personal effort. And good sparkling, clear water it is, too, so why would you turn your nose up at it? Perverse and ungrateful, that's what you are, my lady."

The horse tossed its head then nudged his pocket.

"Oh-ho, like that, is it? You want more oats? Cupboard love, that's what it is." He scratched the horse's long nose. "And don't bat those preposterously long lashes at me, I'm impervious to your wiles. You know perfectly well that you've already had your oats for the day. It's grass for you now, my girl."

The horse nudged him again, and the man rubbed the animal's nose, saying, "You are aware, I suppose, that most women would kill for lashes like that, aren't you? You certainly make good use of them. But are you grateful? Not in the least. Shameless, that's what you are, as well as perverse and greedy."

Zoë stifled a giggle. It was quite charming, the one-sided conversation with the ancient, rawboned horse in the silly hat. But he spoke with no particular regional accent, which gave her no clue as to where in England he came from. Another reason to hide her Englishness from him.

The horse nudged him again, and he said severely, "Oh very well, you insatiable female." He pulled a handful of grain from his pocket and fed it to the horse.

Somehow the silly hat on the old horse and the way the man talked to it made her feel safer. And it was all in English, so presumably he didn't expect anyone overhearing it to understand, so he wasn't putting on a show.

He left the horse and checked the fire. The small pot he'd filled earlier hung from a metal tripod set up over the flames. Steam rose from it.

She moved closer, still keeping the stone hidden in the folds of her skirt, though she no longer expected to have need of it. Nevertheless, caution prevailed.

He turned his head, saw her and smiled. That smile again. It was irresistible: she found herself smiling back. He gestured to the steaming pot and said in French, "Not long now. Come and sit down." He patted the grass beside him.

She sat down opposite him, keeping the fire between them. She gestured to the wagon. "You are Romany?"

"No, I bought it from them, though. The horse, too. Paid too much for them both, but still, it gets me from place to place in comfort, if not in style. Ah, there we are, it's boiling." He carefully unhooked the little pot from the tripod, poured a little water into a battered enamel teapot and swished it around. Warming the pot. His hands were shapely but strong and deft.

Then he spooned three generous spoonfuls of tea into the pot.

Zoë blinked. Three heaped spoonfuls? Tea was expensive. He poured boiling water into the teapot. She caught a whiff of tea. It smelled wonderful.

While they waited for the tea to steep, he squatted on his heels and said, "So, have you come far?"

"Just from the last village."

"A hot day for walking."

"Yes, I was pleased to come across that stream."

The tea being sufficiently steeped, he produced two tin mugs and poured the tea. "Sugar?" He held up a small tin that rattled.

She nodded. "One lump, if you please. And do you have any milk?"

He grimaced. "Sorry. Don't take it myself, but if I see a cow . . ." He winked.

He approached her, mug in hand, then put out his free hand as if to touch her head. Zoë flinched, ducked and scuttled backward.

"I'm sorry. I didn't mean to startle you," he said mildly. "I was just going to remove the leaves from your hair."

"Leaves?" She ran her fingers through her hair and found several dead leaves. She brushed them free, then sat down again.

His eyes ran over her and she suddenly felt quite self-conscious. "You're a little sunburned, too." He passed her the mug. "You don't have a hat?"

"No, I was wearing a headscarf, but I lost it when— I lost it." She took the mug, and wrapped her fingers around it, inhaling the fragrance. She sipped the tea slowly. It was glorious even without the milk—hot and strong and sweet, just the way she liked it. French people did drink tea, of course, but not quite like this. They had a preference for coffee, and herbal teas and tisanes, which she enjoyed, but sometimes she just craved plain English-style tea.

He watched her curiously. "In my experience not many French people like tea—at least not the way I make it."

No doubt the people he met were poor and couldn't afford it. But all she said was "It's delicious. Thank you so much."

While she savored the tea, he produced a loaf of bread and proceeded to cut several slices, to which he added some cheese and a few slices of ham. Zoë's stomach rumbled. She hoped he hadn't heard it, but without asking, he passed her a thick slice of bread topped with cheese and ham, saying, "Here. I usually have a bit of something to eat with my tea. No biscuits, I'm afraid."

"This is wonderful, thank you." They ate in silence, gazing into the flames of the fire. She kept darting glances at him. He had an interesting face. She wouldn't mind drawing him. No, painting him. Those eyes . . .

When he'd finished, he lifted the teapot. "A top-up?"

She nodded and he shared the rest of the tea between them. Once they'd finished, he tossed the dregs onto the fire, which startled Zoë. Was he not going to reuse the tea leaves? Maman had always been very frugal with tea, and had reused the tea leaves at least once. But this vagabond was oddly extravagant. Wasteful. Generous.

Was it because he was a man and knew no better? Household thrift was usually the province of women. She watched as he used the rest of the water and what remained in the horse's bucket to put the fire out completely.

He swiftly packed everything away and said, "Now, can I offer you a lift?"

Zoë hesitated.

"Just to the next village if you like," he said. And then, when she still hesitated, he added, "You'll be perfectly safe, my word of honor on it."

That was all very well, but how could she know whether he had any honor to base his word on? A man might be handsome and charming and still be untrustworthy.

But her feet were still aching, the blister was stinging and now that the sun was high in the sky it was even hotter. Besides, he'd been nothing but kind so far. And she still had her stone.

"Thank you," she said. "It's very kind of you."

He smiled. "Then, since we will be fellow travelers, we'd better introduce ourselves." He gave a funny little bow. "I am Reynard."

Interesting. *Reynard* meant "fox." It was clearly a made-up name, perhaps a kind of warning. That he was cunning and without scruples?

Two could play at that game. "I am Vita," she told him.

"That means 'life,' does it not?"

She nodded. "From the Latin, I am told." *Zoë* also meant "life," only it was from the Greek.

"An interesting name." For a maidservant, he meant.

She lifted an indifferent shoulder. "My mother's employer named me."

"Well then, mademoiselle Vita-from-the-Latin, I will just harness Rocinante here and then we'll be on our way."

He led the horse to the wagon and backed her into the shafts.

"Rocinante?" She gave a choke of laughter. It was perfect. Except that the original Rocinante was male.

He raised an eyebrow. "You are familiar with *Don Quixote*?"

"Who? No." She shook her head. "Just that it's a funny name." A French country maidservant would be unlikely to know the Cervantes novel. She only knew it because Lady Scattergood had gotten her to read it aloud. "And I was thinking of her hat."

"Rocinante might be old, but she's an elegant lady. I would offer you her hat, only she would miss it," he said so seriously that she laughed again.

Recognizing the name had been a careless slip. They would be able to communicate much more easily in English—his French was confident, but fairly basic, and when he was stuck for a word, he had a tendency to Frenchify an English one, which she found quite entertaining. But as long as she maintained her role as a poor country girl, she couldn't admit to any knowledge of English, let alone familiarity with a classic of Spanish literature.

A maidservant traveling alone by foot would not engender much curiosity; a young English lady traveling alone through the French countryside would certainly be cause for speculation. And Zoë wished to remain anonymous.

Her pilgrimage was personal and private and nobody else's business. Besides, she might cry, and she didn't want anyone to witness that. She hadn't cried since Maman died.

He gave Zoë a thoughtful look, fed Rocinante an apple core and finished fastening the traces. Then he leaned inside the wagon and brought out a man's hat.

"You're getting sunburned," he explained as he held it out to her. "It's not as elegant as Rocinante's but it's all I have."

He was right. She could feel the sun tightening her skin.

She glanced inside the hat, but it seemed quite clean and unstained. His hair was also clean and glossy. She put it on, and then laughed as it slid down until it rested on her nose. "Thank you. It's a bit too big, but it will do for the moment." She twisted her hair into a knot and tucked it into the hat, which cooled her neck and helped position the hat so she could see.

He donned another hat, this one quite disreputable-looking, climbed up on the wagon and held out a hand first to take her bundle, then to help her up. She grasped it and felt a slight frisson at the skin-to-skin contact. His hand was warm and strong and he lifted her to the seat without apparent effort. Wiry strength, not meaty muscle.

They set off, Rocinante at a steady amble. Still feeling a little wary, she perched on the very edge of the seat, her bundle between them, close at hand.

"We don't go fast," he commented, "but we get there in the end. And the scenery is beautiful."

"Beautiful?" It was all just hedges—not exactly neat, at that—and beyond them fields and rows and rows of grapevines.

He glanced at her and gave a soft huff of laughter. "I don't suppose a country girl would see anything special in it, but I like to observe the birds and small creatures. Hear that?" He tilted his head. "Those are chaffinches, and if you look carefully, you'll see them—they're probably nesting in that hedge there." Then he pointed to the sky. "And there's a pair of hawks, looking for their next meal."

She looked and saw two birds high in the sky—just dots, really—gliding effortlessly. As she watched, one of them suddenly plummeted like a falling stone. She gasped, thinking it was going to crash into the ground, but at the very last minute it swooped back up and flew off, some small, doomed creature wriggling in its beak.

"Amazing, isn't it?" he murmured. "I could watch them for hours."

"Mm." She was wondering about the poor little wriggling thing.

He glanced at her and smiled. "Nature isn't softhearted, and neither are we."

She sighed. "I know. But I'd rather not watch." Which was a bit cowardly of her, she knew.

The wagon rumbled on. They rode in silence, and Zoë started to relax.

"So, Mademoiselle Vi— Oops!" The wagon hit a pothole and jolted so hard that Zoë was almost thrown from her seat. His arm shot out and wrapped around her waist, pulling her to safety.

"*M-merci*," she gasped.

"Sorry, I should have spotted that hole. Still, no damage done."

His arm was still around her waist, warm and strong, her bundle squashed between them. She moved a little uncomfortably, and he seemed to notice where his arm rested and withdrew it immediately. "You shouldn't sit so close to the edge. This road is full of potholes and I might not be so quick to catch you next time."

She nodded and moved a few inches closer to him. He glanced at her and chuckled. "I won't bite, you know." He gave her a droll look and added, "Not unless you want me to."

It was just harmless flirting, she knew, so, feeling a little foolish, she moved another few inches closer and placed her bundle on her lap. She was probably being overcautious, but her earlier experience with the three men had rattled her.

"Would you like to pop that in the back?" He indicated a small trapdoor behind him.

"No, thank you. It's fine where it is. What were you going to say before we hit that pothole?" she asked, striving for a little normality.

"Oh yes, I was wondering, Mademoiselle Vita-That-

Means-Life, how does a young woman like you come to be all on her own, walking along a lonely country lane?"

She was ready for the question. "I was dismissed from my post."

"Which was?"

"I am— I *was* a maidservant in a big house." Borrowing Marie's story as well as her clothes.

He gave her a searching sideways look, as if assessing her afresh.

Not wanting to be taken for a thief or anything, she added, "Because my mistress is stupid, and her son is a nasty lustful pig, and when he tried to . . . you know, I—I hit him. Hard. Where it hurts most. And of course they blamed me, so I was dismissed."

He gave a shout of laughter. "Good for you. So now, where are you headed? Home to your family?"

She shook her head. "No family." And then, realizing it might not be clever to admit that she was alone in the world, she added, "Just my grandmother. I'm going to stay with her."

"And where does she live?"

"Not far." She gestured vaguely ahead. It was one thing to obtain directions, but they'd turned out to be rather less precise than she'd realized.

"Good thing you're not wearing a red riding hood."

She glanced at him, puzzled for a moment, then caught the reference. "I have dealt with wolves before," she said crispy. "I'm sure I can deal with a fox. Or anything else."

He chuckled. "I'm sure you can."

"And you," she said, turning the subject, "where are you heading?"

"Oh, me, I'm just a vagabond. I go where I please, where the road takes me."

"A vagabond?" She gave him a sideways glance, taking in the strong, clean profile.

"It's a life that suits me well."

"But how do you make a living?" The question was out before she considered it. It was most uncivil of her to ask such an intrusive question, but he was a stranger and she was a maidservant. And she was curious. He didn't look or dress or act much like a homeless vagabond—though he did need a haircut and a good shave. And he was English, and they were in France.

"Oh, doing this and that."

Serve her right. They traveled on in silence.

A few hours later they approached a small stone bridge. Zoë tensed. This must be the bridge she was expecting. On most quiet country roads, small rivers and streams were crossed via a ford, not a bridge. The bridge would have been constructed by some rich person for their carriage's convenience. Her ancestors perhaps?

She leaned forward. Not far now to the entrance to her mother's childhood home, if her information was correct. More than thirty years since her grandparents and uncle had been sent to the guillotine. And her eleven-year-old mother smuggled out of the country by a loyal nurse.

Through the tangled weeds and vegetation that edged the road, she caught glimpses of a long, high stone wall, in poor repair now. The estate boundary? No doubt it had been partially pulled down during the riots. Years of neglect had done the rest.

Up ahead she could see two tall stone pillars, one of which bore a headless eagle, the other just a shapeless lump of stone that had once been a matching eagle. What gates there had once been were no longer in evidence. Ripped down, probably, and the iron reused.

"If you could stop up there, I'll be getting off, thank you," she told Reynard, pointing.

He gave her a curious sidelong glance. "Up there? That's barely a road. I doubt if it leads anywhere."

"It leads to Grand-mère's." It wasn't really a lie.

He shrugged, and the wagon slowed and then stopped.

He gave the weed-choked driveway a thoughtful look. "Are you sure she lives up there? Doesn't look as though anyone has been along there for a good long time."

She didn't answer, just passed him his borrowed hat, picked up her bundle and jumped down. "Thank you for all your help, Monsieur Reynard. The best of luck with your . . . enterprises."

"You can keep the hat. As you see, I have two."

She shook her head. "Thank you, but no. Goodbye."

He nodded, but frowning, made no move to continue on. Zoë hitched her bundle over her shoulder and set off up the drive. She wasn't expecting—or even hoping—to come across any long-lost relatives; it was clear that nobody came here any longer, but she wanted to see it for herself. Had to see it for herself. Where her mother had started life. Where her ancestors had come from.

She knew how Maman's life had ended, and it was grim: in sickness and poverty in the slums of London. But her childhood, Maman always maintained, had been a happy one. Up to the age of eleven, anyway.

Chapter Three

She trudged along the long, curving, tree-lined driveway, weaving through clumps of weeds and keeping an eye out for things that slithered.

The sun beat down. She stopped once or twice to wipe her brow, and hoped she would come across a stream or some source of water soon.

She turned a corner and stopped dead. There it was. Château de Chantonney, once home to the Comte de Chantonney and his family. And Maman. She put down her bundle and just stared up at the château.

Once a beautiful fairy-tale castle, with a round turret at each corner—she remembered Maman telling her about those turrets—now a ruined, crumbling, abandoned wreck, with a partially collapsed roof, smashed windows, and signs of a long-ago fire.

She looked cautiously around—there was nobody in sight—and approached the château. The remains of the front door, once a grand carved oak entrance, hung crookedly on warped hinges. They had smashed their way in, whoever they were, all those years ago.

She pushed it open and entered. The formerly elegant entry hall had chipped and smashed tile work on the floor, the walls were covered in delicate murals, now faded and ruined by violent gashes. The remains of what had been a chandelier hung crookedly from the ceiling, the crystals taken.

Carefully she mounted the stairs. Most of the delicate wrought iron banisters had been wrenched off and carried away. A few twisted bits stubbornly remained: a memory of past elegance. She peered in room after room, seeing ragged shreds of wallpaper, ruined statuary, smashed plasterwork and years' worth of dust and dirt and cobwebs. No paintings, no furniture, except those things too heavy to move, and they were either smashed or partially burned. And in many places there was the smell of damp. And mold. And decay.

It was heartbreaking, seeing so much beauty so wantonly destroyed. The echoes of past violence, the rage of the mob, too long denied the necessities of life, were almost tangible.

She climbed and climbed, recalling Maman's stories until she came to what she was sure had been the nursery. More delicate frescoes gouged and slashed at. Furniture and toys broken, the remains flung wantonly about.

A scrap of dirty lace caught her eye and she bent to pull it out from beneath a splintered piece of wood. And gasped. It was a doll, her once dainty blue silk dress in shreds, faded and dotted with mold. There was no head. Zoë searched and found it, cleanly severed from the little doll's body.

As if guillotined.

Maman had told her about this doll, how she'd wanted to take it with her, but she'd been hustled away in the night in a rush, and there had been no time to find it. Marianne, her favorite doll, the best friend of a lonely little girl. Maman had even painted her, years later, from memory.

Feeling ill, Zoë cradled Marianne against her chest, imagining the scene. Acid curdled in her throat. Such anger and hatred. Against *a doll*.

A drop of water fell on her hand, startling her. She glanced up at the ceiling, but it wasn't a leak—she was weeping. She hadn't realized it. She went to wipe her eyes and found her cheeks were wet with tears. She scrubbed them away.

Thank God for the intervention of Berthe, Maman's nursemaid, who, catching wind of the revolutionary unrest brewing in the surrounding villages, had bundled Maman into a cart and spirited her away before anyone realized the daughter of the comte was still here. The other servants had taken what they could and fled. Or joined the mob.

Maman's parents and her brother, Philippe, the heir, were already in Paris, but Maman had come down with measles and had remained behind, too ill to travel.

So she'd been alone, except for servants, many of whom secretly despised the aristocracy. Zoë swallowed, thinking of it. A little girl, helpless, unprotected, waiting to be torn apart by a screaming, raging mob.

Ironically, her illness had turned out to be fortuitous. Had Maman gone with her family to Paris she would have gone to the guillotine with the rest of them. And had it not been for Berthe, she would no doubt have been murdered here, like her doll.

Berthe had stuffed her bodice with what jewels Grandmère had left behind: a canny decision. She'd taken Maman to the coast and used some of the jewels to bribe a fisherman to smuggle the child out of France and take her to England. As she bade Maman farewell, she'd pressed a gold locket and bracelet into her hand. "You can sell these when you get to Angleterre," she'd said.

And if she'd kept the rest of the jewels herself, who could argue with that? She'd saved Maman's life, at considerable risk to her own.

Maman had described that journey to Zoë: eleven years old, sailing with strangers into the dark, all alone, in fear for her life, going to a strange country where she knew no one and didn't even speak the language.

Zoë had heard the story a hundred times, but now, standing in the ruined château, holding the viciously beheaded doll, she could imagine it as never before.

"Oh, Maman," she whispered. Tears rolled down her cheeks, unheeded.

By late afternoon, Zoë had had enough of exploring her mother's former home. Emotionally she was wrung out like a wet rag. She supposed she could spend the night there, gather up some dusty fabrics and make a nest on the floor—very little furniture remained intact—but it was too depressing, too evocative of tragedy and violence.

She'd hoped she might find some small thing to take with her as a memento, but the only thing she had found was the poor decapitated doll, and she didn't want that. So she left the way she'd arrived: empty-handed.

And perhaps that was better. No sad talismans, just memories.

She'd noticed a farmhouse on the way to her mother's house; she would ask there for a bed for the night. She would even sleep in the barn if there was no bed available. Country people were reputed to be hospitable, and besides, she had money to pay.

But when she knocked on the door and inquired, the reaction shocked her. She'd no sooner made her inquiry when "Begone with you! We don't want your kind here!" And the woman had slammed the door in her face.

Zoë blinked. *Your kind?* What kind was that? Did the

woman think she was a beggar? Admittedly her clothes had picked up a little dirt, first from the fox hole and then dust from the abandoned château. But she'd been very polite when she asked whether she could procure a bed for the night. And she was happy to pay. There was no call for such rude hostility.

Pondering that hostile reception, she walked back down the lane, heading for the intersection where she'd parted company with Reynard.

We don't want your kind here!

Your kind? Realization hit. No, the woman didn't think she was a beggar—quite the opposite, despite her dusty clothing. It was her aristocratic accent at fault. Zoë hadn't thought twice about it, having learned her French from Maman, but Lucy had drilled into her the importance of accents.

Lucy had been working to eradicate Zoë's English accent, which reeked of the slums of London. It wouldn't matter how elegantly she dressed and how ladylike she appeared, Lucy often said, Zoë's lowly upbringing had been obvious to all the minute she'd opened her mouth.

Lucy herself had personal experience of it, having developed her own elegant English accent in a series of exclusive private schools, and learning Viennese accented German from a well-born opera singer, as well as aristocratic French from a comtesse.

Accent prejudice worked both ways. The farm woman was probably a rabid revolutionary. Oh well, lesson learned. She would be more careful in future, not just wearing Marie's clothes, but imitating her soft country accent.

The sky was darkening. With any luck she was not too far from the next village, otherwise she'd have to find a place in the open to sleep. Under some bushes or beneath a bridge, perhaps.

It was a sobering thought. Her impulsive decision to go by herself to see her mother's former home was proving far riskier than she'd imagined. Still, although having to sleep in the open was a daunting prospect, she couldn't regret the decision. She was glad to have seen for herself where her mother came from. And seeing for herself that Maman's tales were true, and not fantasies or wishful thinking, as some people had thought—and said.

"You? Daughter of a count? Pull the other one." Émigrés often had stories like that, boasting of their grand former lives. Nobody believed them anymore.

But Maman's was true.

Ruined as the château was, it was better than knowing you sprang from a run-down slum in the back streets of London. Or a strictly run orphan asylum where you were nobody and a nuisance—and where they even changed your name because they said the name her mother had given her was "too foreign" for an orphan.

No, she had no regrets about coming here.

She reached the road and began to walk. She hadn't gone far when a voice called out, "Grand-mère not home, then?"

She whirled around and saw the painted wagon parked in a shady nook just off the road. Reynard strolled forward. "So was there nobody—?" He broke off with a look of concern. "But you've been crying."

She swallowed, tried to think of what to say and decided on the truth. Well, some of it. "My grandmother is dead. There's no one left."

"I'm so sorry," he said gently.

She gave a fatalistic little shrug, and picked up the bundle she'd dropped when he first spoke.

"What will you do now?"

She shook her head. "I'm not sure. Maybe catch the *diligence* to Paris and look for a job there."

His brows rose. "The *diligence*? It's not cheap."

"I have sufficient."

"And the *diligence* doesn't pass through this way. You'll need to get to a bigger town, a busier road."

"I know."

"It's quite a way even to the next village." He regarded her thoughtfully. "And in the meantime it's getting dark."

She shrugged. *"Ça se voit."*

"I know it's obvious," he said impatiently. "What I mean is, where are you going to sleep?"

"I will find somewhere."

"At this time? Don't be ridiculous. Come and have some dinner—I have stew simmering in the pot. You can sleep in the wagon."

She opened her mouth and he added, "And I will sleep *under* the wagon. I've done it often. It's quite pleasant when it's as warm and dry as it is now."

She hesitated, and he said, "You have no need to worry. My intentions are honorable, and even if they weren't, the wagon has a bolt on the inside of the door. You will be quite safe. Now come along, I don't want my stew to burn."

The man calling himself Reynard discreetly observed the girl while he stirred the stew. She intrigued him, and not just because she was beautiful, with those dazzling green eyes, pure complexion and curly dark hair. She'd pulled her hair back in a knot, but tiny dark curls clustered like feathers around her forehead and her dainty ears and at the creamy soft nape of her neck. Her mouth was a soft and satiny dark pink. She was temptation personified.

But she wasn't the kind of girl he could seduce: a virtuous maidservant who'd lost her position by refusing a gentleman's advances was hardly likely to succumb to the charms of a shabby vagabond.

Though it was a shame—apart from being lovely, she intrigued him in other ways. She was guarded—as nervous as a doe in hunting season. Understandable, he supposed, seeing she was traveling alone and he was a stranger. She was bright. Quick, too, with an answer for everything . . .

He tasted the stew and tossed in a little more salt.

That story about her grandmother . . . It didn't quite fit. Oh, he didn't doubt her grief—those tearstains were real— but he'd been up that lane before and had a poke around the ruined château. It was deserted and had been for decades, and the only house nearby housed a farmer and his wife, both around thirty and too young to be grandparents.

Her hands were very soft, too, and not the hands of a maid who did menial work. Although he supposed she could be a lady's maid, and her hands kept soft because she was handling silks and satins on a daily basis. Her mistress wouldn't want rough skin catching on those delicate fabrics. Still, there was something about her . . .

He stirred the stew and pondered.

"You're not from around here," she said.

"No, I'm English. But I like this part of the world and have traveled this way several times." And the pickings had been good enough that he thought it well worth another visit.

But her disingenuous question intrigued him. He was well aware his French accent wasn't particularly good and that she must already have realized he was English. So why ask?

"And yet you travel around France?"

"That's right. I like it here."

She gave him a thoughtful look, and it occurred to him that she thought there was something shady about his being here. As if he were wanted for some crime in England. He smiled to himself. He wasn't going to enlighten her. He produced a couple of bowls, dished up the stew and cut a few slices of bread to mop up the juices. It wasn't fancy, but it was filling and tasty.

She tasted it cautiously, then looked up in surprise. "This is very good."

He laughed. "You think men can't cook?"

"No, I mean, I've never eaten anything cooked in the open over a fire before."

He raised a brow. "Not even when you lived in the country with your grandmother?"

She shook her head. "I never lived with her. I was raised in an orphanage by nuns." She ate another spoonful. "What's in this?" A deft change of subject, he noted.

"Vegetables, beans, a rabbit and some herbs. And a splash of wine, which reminds me." He poured a little wine into the mugs that they'd used for tea earlier, and passed one to her, saying, "No glasses, I'm afraid."

She thanked him and continued her meal.

"So, when you went to find your grandmother," he prompted.

"Do you have a home?" she said, once more changing the subject.

"Several."

She blinked and looked up from her meal. "Several?"

"Yes."

"Oh." She dipped a corner of the bread into the stew. "And do you have a family? A wife? Children?"

She was a curious little cat, but he wasn't born yesterday. If she was angling for a husband, well, he had ways of dealing with that kind of thing.

"Yes. Three wives, and—"

Her spoon fell into her bowl with a clatter. "*Three* wives?" she exclaimed. "Three?"

"Yes," he said placidly. "And four—no, what date is it? Probably five children by now. One of the wives was due to give birth this week."

She stared at him. "But that's illegal."

"Giving birth? I don't think so."

"No, having three wives."

"Why shouldn't I have three? Or four if I want. What business is it of anyone else's, as long as the wives don't mind? And they don't—they each have a house, and I support them and the children well enough."

"How? By 'doing this and that'?"

He grinned at her indignation. "Exactly. Now, I'm afraid there's no dessert, only apples." He pulled two out of his pocket and tossed one to her.

She caught it deftly, then eyed it with suspicion. "These look like the apples that were growing a milc—a kilometre or so back."

"Do they?" he said innocently. "They're delicious." He bit into it.

She hesitated.

"If you don't like apples, you can give that one to Rocinante."

She eyed him disapprovingly, but bit into the apple.

"See, delicious, isn't it? There they were, lonely and unloved. A shame to have left them hanging over the roadway where anything could happen to them." She was delightfully easy to tease. Clearly she was, at heart, an honest little soul.

The meal finished with, she offered to clean the dishes, and he left her to it, saying he had a little local business to see to and that he would be back in an hour or so. "You won't be frightened, will you? If you're nervous, just get in the wagon and bolt the door. I'll knock to let you know I'm back. Or if I'm late, just go to bed and lock yourself in—here's the key to the outside door in case you're worried about being locked in from the outside—and I'll see you in the morning." On that thought he took a couple of blankets from the wagon, and the piece of canvas he used as a groundsheet.

She hesitated.

"You'd trust me with your belongings?"

He laughed. "I do—you have an honest face. Besides, there's nothing in there worth stealing." It wasn't true, but she didn't need to know that. His valuables were already securely locked away, and he wasn't offering her those keys. "So, I'll see you in the morning."

She nodded and accepted the key, though her expression remained doubtful. Reynard repressed a smile: no doubt she thought him off on more nefarious adventures, like stealing apples.

He had no doubt she would be there when he returned. She had nowhere else to go, it seemed.

He strolled away into the night.

The stream was not far away—Reynard had chosen a good spot to camp. Zoë went to check the horse had enough water, fed Rocinante her apple core and filled a bucket from the stream. She heated a fresh pot of water and used it to wash the dishes. When she'd finished, she heated some more water and washed herself and dressed in her spare clothes. She rinsed out her underclothes and sponged down her dress. Finding a leafless, but bushy fallen limb nearby, she dragged it close to the fire and draped her washing over it to dry.

Now what? she thought. She sat staring into the flames and pondered her options. She'd done what she'd come to do—see her mother's old home for herself—so in the morning she would make for the nearest town that the *diligence* passed through and head back to Lucy and Gerald in Paris.

Which was closer? The town where Marie had caught the *diligence*, or one farther ahead? To go back was to pass the place where those vile men had chased her. They might live close to the road. So she'd go forward to the next town that the *diligence* passed through.

And then what? Prepare for returning to London, where she'd make her come-out into society. She shivered. The whole idea made her nervous. So much depended on people not finding out she was yet another bastard daughter of Sir

Bartleby Studley. Her half sister Izzy had managed it—
despite the whispers—but that had more or less ended
when she'd married Leo, Lord Salcott, whose reputation
was that of a very high stickler. But when Zoë appeared,
she was sure her strong resemblance to Izzy would cause
tongues to wag again, even though she'd be presented as a
French cousin.

For herself, she didn't much care what people thought of
her, but she was utterly determined not to have the shame
of her irregular birth rebound on the sisters who'd given her
love and acceptance and so much more.

She added more wood to the fire and turned her clothes
around to speed the drying.

A hoarse scream in the distance startled her. What was
that? Some creature, or perhaps a woman in trouble? She
picked up a stick destined for the fire, and glanced fearfully
around, waiting and listening.

It was a mild night and the half-moon shone fitfully
through drifts of cloud, casting shadows that shifted and
darkened. She couldn't see much beyond the light thrown
by the fire. Anything could be out there. There were still
wolves and bears in France, she'd heard.

Something rustled in the bushes and she jumped. The
scream came again, closer this time. What on earth could
it be? She was a city girl, familiar only with the sights and
sounds of central London. And Paris.

The scream sounded a third time. That did it. She wasn't
going to sit here waiting to be eaten. She hurried to the
wagon. A candle stood on a shelf by the door. She lit it from
the fire, grabbed her damp clothes and climbed into the
wagon.

There was a bolt on the inside, as he'd said. She shot the
bolt and immediately felt much safer.

She held the candle high and looked around. Inside, the
wagon was neat and clean. Clothes hung on hooks, and a
line had been strung from one side of the wagon to the

other. For hanging washing, perhaps? She hung her damp clothes over it, hoping they'd be dry by morning.

At one end of the wagon there was a wide bed, the width of the wagon. To her surprise it was made up with sheets and blankets and a pillow: an unexpected luxury for a vagabond. She bent and sniffed. There was a very faint smell of Reynard, but otherwise it seemed clean. Across the opposite end of the wagon was a large cupboard. She tried it. It was locked, which seemed curious. A vagabond with locks? But she supposed if he had to leave the wagon unguarded, locks were necessary.

How on earth did he earn enough to support three wives and five children?

She also found an ironbound wooden chest. She tried it, but it was also locked. On a shelf above it she found several books in English. He could read, then, which made him an educated vagabond. Interesting.

Next to the door there was a small cupboard lined with zinc. In it she found few crumbs, the heel of a loaf of bread, a stub of sausage and some cheese wrapped in a cloth. A mouseproof food cupboard, she decided. Above it was another cupboard, in which were stored the enamel mugs they'd drunk tea from and a few bowls and spoons and knives. Really, this wagon was very well set up. It had everything but a bath. Almost.

Three years living the life of a lady and she'd forgotten how little you really needed to live. She and Maman had owned only a few bowls and spoons. And in the small room in which they'd lived, there was nowhere to cook. Not that Maman had ever learned to cook.

What was an educated Englishman doing here in rural France? How did he make a living, wandering from place to place—doing what? Was he in some kind of disgrace? Had he been exiled?

Were those three wives and five children a tease? They could be. But he was definitely living the life of a vagabond. She supposed she'd know more when he returned from doing whatever business he was off doing.

She hoped it was something honest, at least. Though what difference it would make to her, she had no idea. She'd be leaving as soon as they reached the next village.

She yawned. After the day she'd had, she was exhausted. She wouldn't wait up for him. And she certainly wasn't going to go outside to face whatever was making those horrid noises. She was so grateful to have a safe place to sleep. If it wasn't for Reynard, she could be sleeping out in the open, and then who knew what might have happened.

She undressed to her chemise, climbed into bed and lay awake thinking about Reynard.

He might be handsome and charming, but he clearly was someone to be cautious about. That smile of his would seduce anyone. And there was something about his expression, a lurking amusement in those blue, blue eyes as he told his stories that made her doubt their truth.

And yet he'd been nothing but kind.

He'd certainly stolen those apples, but that wasn't such a big thing—although how did he get the rabbit for the stew they'd eaten? Was poaching a crime in France these days? She didn't know. And anyway, tomorrow they would reach the next village and she would see about getting a ride to a town where the *diligence* stopped.

Outside, that ghastly hoarse scream sounded again. She shivered and snuggled down, pulling the bedclothes more tightly around her.

He would be sleeping outside. With whatever that creature was making that dreadful sound. She swallowed. If he knocked on the door, she would *have* to let him inside. She couldn't leave him outside, not with that frightful creature lurking out there in the dark.

And then what? There was only one bed.

She'd face that problem when it came, she decided. She closed her eyes and slept.

* * *

She awoke to bright sunlight filtering into the wagon. It took her a few moments to realize where she was, but once she did, she sat up, mortified. Had he come knocking on the door last night and she'd slept right through it? She quickly dressed, stepped out and found him by the fire, attending to a sizzling pan. The small black pot hung over the fire on a tripod.

"Ah, there you are. Sleep well?" he said, and without waiting for her response, added, "Ham and eggs all right for breakfast? And there's bread there." He gestured to a plate containing several slices of bread.

"Y-yes, thank you," she stammered. "And I slept very well, thank you"—too well—"what about you?"

"Oh, I always sleep well," he said carelessly. "One or two eggs?"

"One, please."

He cracked four eggs into the pan, and a few minutes later said, "Pass me a couple of plates, will you?"

He deftly scooped an egg and some ham onto her plate and scooped the rest onto his own. It looked and smelled heavenly, and despite eating well the previous night she found she was very hungry.

Silence fell as they ate. "This is delicious," she commented. "You cook very well." The ham was tender and her egg was perfect, with a firm white and a runny yolk.

"For a man, do you mean?" He grinned at her sheepish expression. "I like to eat, and thus I learned to cook." He used his bread to mop up some egg yolk. "I'll make some tea in a moment."

If he was going to do it, Zoë decided that she could also mop up her yolk with bread. It was not what a lady would do, but she wasn't a lady, was she? At least not yet.

"You really slept all right?" she asked him between mouthfuls.

He gave her a quizzical look. "Yes, as I said. I always do."

"But what about the . . . the wild animal?"

"What wild animal?"

"I heard it—or them—several times. A terrible kind of scream. At first I thought it was a woman in trouble, but then I realized it was some kind of beast."

He grinned. "A kind of scream? A fox, then."

"A *fox*? But it sounded . . . I thought . . ."

"You thought it was some dreadful beast?" He sounded amused.

"Yes," she muttered, feeling foolish.

"I thought you were a country girl."

"There were no foxes at the orphanage." Not in the heart of London, anyway.

"No, the nuns wouldn't allow them," he agreed solemnly. "And in the great house where you worked? No foxes on the estate?"

"I didn't go outside much. We were kept too busy."

"Yes, of course." He set his empty plate to one side and set about making tea. Three heaped spoonfuls, just like yesterday, she noted. So lavish—for a vagabond.

"Did your business prosper?" she asked, changing the subject.

"Yes, most excellently. I have a commission from a farmer. That's where I got the eggs and ham and also"—he held up a small ceramic jar sealed with a cork—"some fresh milk, just for mademoiselle."

"Lovely, thank you. So, what was this commission, if you don't mind me asking?"

"Not at all. He wants a painting of himself and his prize pig."

"A painting? You're an artist?" She was stunned.

"Of sorts." He poured the tea, added sugar and milk to her mug and passed it to her.

She drank it thoughtfully. He was a painter. It put a whole new light on things. She could see some sense now in his wandering lifestyle. Though how he could make a living from portraits of country farmers and livestock, she had no idea.

"It means I won't be moving on today. The farmer lives just over that hill, and I'll be working there."

"Yes, of course," she murmured. He was an artist! Like her.

"The next village is about three or four miles—no idea what that is in kilometres; I still don't have the hang of them yet—but it should only take an hour or two to walk there. Or"—he shot her a quick glance—"you could stay here until I've finished the painting. I'm quick; two days, three at the most, and then you could travel on to the village with me. You'd be most welcome."

"Thank you." She should move on, she knew, but her blisters were still sore. And though she'd been lucky in finding a safe ride with him, her previous nasty experience had eroded her confidence. Besides, Reynard, for all his mystery, was easy and pleasant company. And he was an artist, which had aroused her curiosity. Being one herself, she really wanted to see his work.

He climbed into the wagon and brought out a large rect-angular canvas holdall. His artist's equipment? "And while you're thinking about it, since the farmer—or rather, his good wife—has offered to provide us with all the food we'll need, you need not worry about that kind of thing."

She nodded. Did he actually *want* her to stay?

There was no real hurry. Marie would be in Paris by now and Lucy would have taken her in. And Lucy didn't know what Zoë was doing. She wouldn't be expecting Zoë until the house party ended the following week, and Zoë would be back in Paris before then.

"I'll stay," she told him. "At least until I've done the dishes."

He nodded. "And make sure Rocinante has water, please. And that she doesn't get tangled in her tether." He slung an ingenious device, which held his easel, onto his back, hesitated, then put down his holdall. "If you do decide to leave after all, thank you for your company, mademoiselle. It has been a pleasure knowing you." To her surprise, he took her hand and planted a light kiss on it. "*Au 'voir*, Mademoiselle Vita."

At the touch of his lips on the back of her hand, she felt a warm shiver go through her. She stood still, watching him stroll away.

Chapter Four

Zoë washed the breakfast dishes, checked on Rocinante, who was placidly cropping grass, and repacked her bundle. She glanced around the campsite and noticed the folded pile of blankets that Reynard had slept in. She placed them inside the wagon—the sky was clear, but it might rain—and took a final, wistful look around.

Wistful? She took herself to task over the thought. Really, she had no good reason to stay. Yes, she was quite enjoying the carefree life of a vagabond, and Reynard was attractive and good company, but there was no future for her here, no real reason to stay on.

She picked up her bundle and walked into the village. It took longer than she expected, and her feet were sore by the time she arrived, and the blister worse, despite the ointment she'd rubbed on it. There were perhaps twenty whitewashed cottages, built around a square, lined with well-swept cobblestones. A round stone well stood in the center of the square, with a wrought iron frame above holding the winding system. On the hill overlooking the village there stood a small, ancient-looking church.

On the far side of the square she spied a tavern with an iron sign hanging above the door, declaring it to be Le Poisson Rouge. Several tables and benches had been set outside, and a motherly-looking woman bustled about, scrubbing the tables down. Zoë approached her. She turned out to be the tavern keeper's wife and was full of local information.

"The *diligence*, mademoiselle? Oh, but you must go to Nantes, the next big town, to catch it. How far? Maybe seven or eight hours if you are walking. A ride?" She pursed her lips, thinking, then gave Zoë a searching look and shook her head. "To be sure, I know several people who will be traveling to Nantes, but I would not recommend them to a pretty young demoiselle traveling alone— you are alone, are you not?"

Zoë nodded.

Again the woman shook her head. "Then no, there is nobody I would recommend. But I will ask around. In any case, you have missed the *diligence* for this week—it only passes through Nantes on a Thursday around noon, so you have plenty of time to get there."

So, the decision was made for her, Zoë thought. There was no point moving on just yet. She was safe and comfortable and enjoying Reynard's company. She would stay another few days.

"You might try the miller's son," the woman added on an afterthought. "He takes a load to Nantes every Thursday morning. He's a good lad, a little simple and slow, but safe and a reliable ride. I'm sure he'd be happy to take you with him."

Zoë thanked the woman, and, once she'd learned where she could find the miller and his son, asked her advice on purchasing some supplies. If she was going to stay with Reynard for the best part of a week—and he'd stressed she was welcome to—it was only fair that she shared the costs, even if the farmer's wife was feeding them.

"Alas, mademoiselle, you have missed market day, but if you try that house, and that"—she pointed—"they will sell you good cheese, and that one makes very good sausages. And in the house with the blue half door, open at the top, you will find the baker. As for vegetables or eggs, those you must get from farms. Just ask. Most people here produce what they need to live, and what they don't produce, they buy at the weekly market, which is finished for this week."

Again Zoë thanked her, and in gratitude bought a couple of bottles of the local wine from her. Following her directions, she soon found the miller and learned that his son, Jean-Paul, would be happy to take her with him. He left around dawn every Thursday and would get her to Nantes in good time for the *diligence*.

She left the village feeling satisfied with her discoveries and laden with provisions: a round yellow cheese, several fat, spicy sausages—*saucissons secs*—a cheese, leek and egg tart and two long, thin loaves of fresh, crusty bread as well as the wine. The bread was still warm and smelled glorious. Unable to resist, she broke off a piece of the crust and ate it.

Truth to tell, she wasn't at all averse to spending more time with Reynard. He was very good company and he didn't make her at all uncomfortable. In fact, she found him fascinating, far more interesting and attractive than any of the gentlemen she'd met at the social occasions she'd attended in Paris.

In truth, she was enjoying herself more than she had in ages. Nobody had any expectations of her, and wasn't that a wonderfully freeing feeling?

She limped along, observing some of the things that Reynard had pointed out to her the day before.

By the time she reached the wagon, she'd eaten almost a quarter of the smaller loaf. There was no sign of Reynard, so after checking that the horse still had water and was not tangled in her tether, she tended her blister, which had burst. It would heal more quickly now.

Then she cut herself several slices of the spicy sausage and some cheese and bread and put the rest away in the wagon. It was a simple lunch but delicious.

What to do next? The fire had died, so she decided to make herself useful and went looking for fallen branches and twigs for fuel. She made a sizable pile, then settled down to read. Thinking of the horse, Rocinante, she selected *Don Quixote*, which she'd started reading several years before with Lady Scattergood but had never finished.

She found a cozy spot under a tree taking the book, as well as her sketchpad and pencils in case she felt like drawing something. She read for a while, but though her reading had improved hugely in the last few years, under first Lady Scattergood's mentorship then Lucy's, some books were still heavy going.

Zoë had come to reading late in life. Her mother read and spoke French, of course, but having arrived in England as an eleven-year-old refugee, alone and unsupported, her education had stopped in favor of scraping a living. And once Zoë came along, there was barely enough money to feed them both, let alone educate her. Maman had done her best to pass on what knowledge she had, but that was all.

Zoë had always adored her mother, but now, having seen where she came from, and thinking about the life Maman had lived once she came to England, she marveled anew at how she had survived, against all the odds. From the age of eleven.

She knew—Maman had told the stories often enough—how she'd first started drawing pictures in chalk on the footpath. Later, when she could afford paper and pencils, she'd drawn portraits. They weren't very good, Maman said, but people were generous toward a young girl, and eventually her activities drew the attention of a real artist, who hired her as a model. Which had become her main source of income.

Eventually that had led to her meeting and becoming the mistress of Sir Bartleby Studley, Zoë's father. Who'd abandoned her the minute her pregnancy started to show, the swine.

Then, when Zoë was twelve, Maman died, and Zoë was placed in an orphanage, where the education the girls received was wholly devoted to training them as obedient servants or wives. *Reading and writing is quite unnecessary for orphan gels*, the matron, Miss Glass, used to say. Silly old bag! It had been her sisters and old Lady Scattergood and now Lucy who had taught her to read and write with relative ease. And to read for enjoyment.

Lost in memories, Zoë found herself gazing blankly at the same page for ages. She set the book aside, reached for her sketchbook and pencil and began idly drawing, faces at first—they were her preference. She drew the tavern keeper's wife and the baker and then Marie sitting nervously in the *diligence* coach. Her pencil flew and she went into that dream state she so often did when she was working.

A rustle in the grass nearby startled her out of her reverie. She looked around anxiously—and saw a squirrel foraging for acorns. Smiling at her foolishness, she looked down at her page and found she'd drawn half a dozen sketches of Reynard.

Of *Reynard*? What on earth had she been thinking? Granted, he had an interesting face, with those high cheekbones, firm chin, the dark lock of hair that fell over his forehead and those flashing blue eyes—and that smile of his that caused her insides to . . . She thrust the thought away.

Six drawings of him? Really? It was ridiculous.

Hastily, she turned over the page and did a quick sketch of the squirrel, and then one of Rocinante. She hardly ever drew animals these days—Lucy and Gerald had no pets—but she'd enjoyed drawing them when she'd lived with Lady Scattergood and her herd of little dogs.

The sun was low in the sky when she heard him return at last. He was whistling, obviously in a good mood. Would his mood change when he saw her there? She'd long since returned his book to the shelf and hidden her sketchbook. She wasn't sure why she was being so secretive—he was just a vagabond. But he was an English vagabond and an artist, and somehow it felt wiser to conceal her true self from him.

There would be too many questions otherwise.

He appeared in the clearing, carrying the canvas bundle slung over his shoulder and a small iron pot in his hand. When he saw her standing uncertainly there, a wide white grin split his tanned face. "So, Mademoiselle Vita, you have elected to stay with Rocinante and me?"

"I hope you don't mind. I did go to the village, and I asked about the *diligence*, and the woman said I'd missed it for this week. It passes through Nantes every Thursday. So, if it's all right with you, I'll stay a little longer. Do you mind?" For some reason she didn't tell him about the miller's son. Why, she wasn't quite sure.

"Not at all, I'm delighted." He glanced at the pile of wood beside the fire and said, "I see you've been busy. I don't suppose you've cooked the dinner?"

"No, sorry." Guilt flooded her. Of course she should have cooked something. It wasn't as if she didn't know a bit about cooking—they'd been taught the basics at the orphanage, and she'd picked up some fancy techniques when she'd first come to Lady Scattergood's and spent time in the kitchen helping Cook. But cooking in the open over a campfire—she hadn't even thought about it. "But I did buy some provisions—cheese, sausage, bread and a cheese-and-vegetable tart. And some wine."

"Excellent. I hoped you might still be here. The farmer's wife offered to feed me, but when I said I had to get back, she gave me some cassoulet"—he gestured with the small pot—"which is still warm and smells very tasty. Fetch the dishes, bread and wine and we'll dine in style tonight. We can save the tart and sausage for tomorrow."

He built up the fire and hung the cassoulet to warm while he checked on his horse. Zoë fetched the dishes and spread a rug for them to sit on. Every meal was a picnic with Reynard.

"How is your commission going?" she asked as he dished up the cassoulet, which was some kind of bean stew studded with pork, sausage and chicken and fragrant with herbs and garlic. It smelled absolutely delicious.

"Well enough. The pig is enormous."

She almost dropped her spoon. "The *pig*? You're painting *a pig*?"

He said in a mock-outraged voice, "What? You question the right of a pig to have his portrait taken, Mademoiselle Vita? I'm shocked, utterly shocked by your shameful ignorance." His face was solemn but his eyes were dancing. "I'll have you know, this pig—by name Le Duc de Gaudet—is no ordinary porker. He's a champion pig, you understand, the finest pig in the district, sire of champion—and delicious—piglets by the dozen. Sows far and wide line up to be, um, introduced to him. And you question why such a noble creature should have his portrait painted?" He shook his head in deep, sorrowful reproach. She giggled.

In a more ordinary voice, he continued, "Gaudet, the farmer, is immensely proud of his pig, so much so that it was all I could do to persuade him to let me include his wife in the painting. He wanted the portrait to be just himself and his glorious pig." He gestured with his spoon to the cassoulet. "Madame Gaudet was very grateful for the inclusion. She knows she comes second in importance to her husband's pig."

Zoë chuckled. "And the painting is coming along all right?"

He leaned forward and poured some more wine into her mug. "Yes, I'm quite fast. The background is easy—just the house and some trees. And the pig is looking good, if I say so myself. I'm good with animals."

"And the farmer and his wife?"

He grimaced. "People are more difficult. But I'll get there. I'll fill in some more of the background this evening. It's not so detailed that I'll need much light."

After dinner, while Zoë washed the dishes and put everything away, Reynard set up his easel and began to paint. "Could I see what you're doing?" she asked diffidently.

Some people hated having their unfinished work observed, but he shrugged indifferently and said, "If you like. I have only the pig and the background at the moment. Gaudet and Madame Gaudet are just outlines at present. I'll do them tomorrow."

She walked around to look at the painting over his shoulder. The light was fading and he'd hung a lantern from a nearby tree. He was adding to the background, which, as he said, was not very detailed: a blur of greenery behind a whitewashed stone barn. As he'd said, he'd painted only the pig and the background so far—the farmer and his wife were just sketched in lightly.

The pig was good, quite lifelike, and huge, as he'd said. She smiled, recalling the creature's grand name—the Duke of Gaudet.

As she watched, Reynaud dabbled several shades of paint on parts of the greenery, which gave the previous plain green vegetation fresh depth and texture. Next he feathered faint gray and light brown lines and light daubs of paint on the barn. Under her gaze the plain white surface took on the dips and shadows and rough surface of whitewashed stonework.

"That'll do for tonight," he said, and began to clean his brushes and pack them away.

"You're good," Zoë said, and he turned his head and grinned at her, a flash of white in the dying light.

"At some things."

"What made you decide to become a painter?" she asked him later. He'd packed up his things, and they were sitting beside the fire, talking as they finished off the last of the wine.

The fire was burning low. Reynard leaned forward and poked the coals with a stick. Sparks flew, twirling and dancing up into the velvety dark sky.

"I've always wanted to paint," he said. "Ever since I was a boy. I don't really know why. My father, of course, was appalled."

"Why?"

He gave her a searching look. "You really want to know?"

"Yes, of course. I'm interested. So why was your father appalled?"

He made a careless gesture. "Oh, proper men don't waste time on effete and frivolous nonsense like painting—certainly not the men of our family. He tried to thrash it out of me when I was a boy, but the beatings didn't take. I'm quite stubborn, you see." He grimaced. "I was the second son, so my disgrace was not as dire as it would have been had I been his firstborn; nevertheless, it was bad enough. So he decided to enlist me in the army—make a proper man of me, you see."

"And did he?"

"Oh yes. On my sixteenth birthday. He would have sent me to war as a twelve-year-old drummer boy if he could have."

"Twelve?" She was shocked. "Surely not?"

"Yes, well, we were at war with—" He stopped, suddenly realizing they had been at war with her country. "With, um, Napoleon by then, you see—but my mother kicked up a terrible fuss. So he shoved me into a really strict school, where he hoped I'd have the painting nonsense beaten out of me—they tried, but didn't succeed—and then on my sixteenth birthday, he had me enlisted and shipped to the war on the Iberian Peninsula."

"And did that put an end to your artistic aspirations?"

He gave a short dry laugh. "Far from it. Contrary to Papa's expectations—and mine, for that matter—in between battles I learned to draw and paint. I also saw all kinds of wonderful paintings, far better than anything I'd seen at home—despite so many being looted by Napoleon's forces, only some of which were returned after the war. But it was an education in itself. And there were other fellows in the army who also painted. So, though I've never studied art—not properly—I managed to pick up a few techniques here and there."

"How fascinating. I would never have thought of painters in the army. I suppose we only ever think of soldiers fighting."

"Oh, we did our share of that, believe me. But there is a lot of waiting around in war, as well as fighting. And while a good deal of that time we spent foraging—"

"Foraging?" she said, startled.

"Oh yes, army rations were, apart from being endlessly dreary, often in short supply, so we learned to hunt and trap and forage—and cook." He grinned. "Which is why I was able to serve you that delicious rabbit stew the other evening. Compliments of my army experience."

"I see."

"After Waterloo, I decided I didn't want to settle down. I decided to become a vagabond artist, and so I began my travels."

She was silent a moment, thinking about those supposed three wives—each in their own house. There must have been some settling down, even for a short while.

"But then my brother, Ralph, died."

"I'm sorry—" she began, but he didn't appear to hear her.

"He was my older brother, and so"—he contemplated the glowing coals, and leaned forward and stirred them again, sending a spiral of dancing sparks into the night—"I had to go back to England. My father had a seizure—shock, I suppose—when he heard the news. And rage. I was the one who was supposed to be killed, you see, but instead I went through a dozen battles with only a few scratches here and there while Ralph died of a small cut that was left untended." He gave her an ironic look. "Real men don't fuss over little cuts, you see. But it turned septic and he died of it."

"I'm so sorry."

He sighed. "It was all so stupid and unnecessary. I'd always looked up to him—my big brother, you know—but to die for such a small, stupid thing." He shook his head. "He was the apple of everyone's eye—mine, too. He'd been trained from birth for the family business, you see. And then a few days after he heard the news, my father died. My mother had died years before—not long after I'd gone to war—and so everything was left in the hands of my maternal grandmother."

A long silence stretched, broken only by the gentle hiss and crack of the fire. He stared into the fire, and she gazed at his strong profile, limned by firelight, but otherwise cast in shadows. Even in silhouette, he was a beautiful man.

"So I had no choice but to go home and pick up the reins," he said eventually, his tone light.

Zoë was silent. He clearly wasn't home now, so what had he done? And what was the family business? He surely hadn't left his grandmother to run it. But something in his demeanor made her reluctant to ask.

"Ah well, I'm for bed," Reynard said, standing and stretching. He held out his hand to help her to rise, and when she placed her hand in his, she once again felt that unsettling frisson. He drew her lightly to her feet and paused, looking down at her, her hands still clasped in his. His thumbs caressed them gently. "I'm sorry. I didn't mean to get so maudlin. The wine must be stronger than I thought. You must have been bored to tears."

"I wasn't bored at all," she murmured. They were standing so close their bodies were almost touching, but somehow she couldn't make herself move. She couldn't see his expression: his face was in shadow. But she could feel his gaze on her, like a warm caress.

For a moment she thought he might be about to kiss her. She waited, unmoving, her face turned up to him, hoping the darkness hid her blush.

But he released her hands and stepped away, apparently unaffected by their brief contact. "I plan to make an early start in the morning. With luck, I'll get this painting finished by tomorrow evening."

"Tomorrow evening?" she exclaimed.

"Yes. I said I was quick." He picked up the painting. "If you don't mind, I'll leave this in the wagon to dry overnight, avoid the dew. It will smell a bit, I'm afraid."

The smell wouldn't bother her in the least—she was so used to the smell of oil paints, it was almost like perfume—but the idea that she was turning him out of his bed for a second night bothered her.

"If you like, I will sleep under the wagon tonight," she offered.

He gave her a shocked look. "But what about all those shrieking, man-eating wild animals?" His eyes gleamed in the firelight.

"Now that I know what that sound is, it won't bother me at all," she said with dignity. "Besides, you will be here, and if wild creatures come, I will expect you to help chase them off."

He laughed. "Brave words, *ma belle*. Nevertheless, I will continue to sleep under the wagon, and you will bolt the door and keep yourself safe from foxes—animal or human."

Animal or human? She gave him a narrow look. Did he mean she should protect herself from him? But she didn't like to ask and start what could prove to be an awkward and possibly embarrassing conversation.

She'd been very aware of the way he'd looked at her from time to time. She'd felt it and felt her body stirring in response. He was clearly attracted to her, and it was mutual, she knew. But it would be foolish to give in to a passing tendre for a vagabond. No matter how attractive she found him.

She thanked him, and once he'd put the painting inside and gathered his bedclothes for the night, she wished him good night and bolted the door.

Reynard arranged his bedding, wrapped himself in blankets and slipped under the wagon. The ground was perfectly dry, the faint scent of the crushed dry grass beneath him fragrant and pleasing. Lord help him if it rained, but farmer Gaudet had assured him the weather for the next few days would be clear.

The nights were getting chilly, though. They were well into autumn, and while the days were sunny and warm—almost hot on some days—the nip of oncoming winter was in the air. It would mark the end of his idyll here.

And it was an idyll. He knew it couldn't last.

He sighed, thinking about what awaited him. He wasn't looking forward to going home. But he'd made a promise and would honor it.

In the wagon overhead he could hear Vita moving around. He was glad she'd decided to stay a little longer. He was enjoying her company. Far too much, probably. He'd almost given in to his attraction and kissed her tonight. The way she'd looked up at him with those wide green eyes . . .

He'd been sorely tempted. But . . . no.

She was a virtuous girl who had lost her position and her home in defense of her maidenhead, and he was damned if he'd cheapen that by seducing her—much as he ached for her. And he was going back to England soon.

She was planning to go to Paris. No doubt like most young country folk, she had notions of a glamorous life there, the big city paved with gold, that sort of nonsense. He hoped that what awaited her there wasn't a position in a brothel, which he thought the most likely, especially if she didn't have a character reference, and given the way she'd left her previous employment, he doubted she had one.

He shifted uncomfortably. The ground was hard tonight.

Nearby a fox screamed. Reynard smiled. He knew how the poor frustrated devil felt.

He woke at dawn, rolled out from under the wagon, feeling a bit stiff—in more ways than one. He got the fire going and put the water on to boil. The first cup of tea of the day was always bliss. While he waited for it to boil, he fetched more water from the stream, had a quick wash, fed Rocinante a handful of oats and gave her coat a quick brush.

He ran a hand over his chin. The bristles were getting thicker: if he wasn't careful, he'd have a beard. Should he shave? Would she prefer him clean-shaven or scruffy, like now?

He put the question from his mind—no, he wasn't going there—and decided to stay scruffy.

As though his thoughts had conjured her, the wagon door opened. She stepped down, muttered something about going for a wash and disappeared into the bushes. She appeared a short time later, skin fresh and glowing, hair brushed, trying to conceal a small bundle of wet clothing.

"You can hang those up there," he said gesturing behind

the wagon to a line he'd strung between two trees. She nodded, flushing, and hurried away.

By the time she returned the kettle was boiling and he'd sliced up some bread ready to toast. "Eggs for breakfast?"

Her eyes narrowed. "More eggs? Where did you get these ones?"

From her expression she thought he'd stolen them. He smiled. "The farmer's wife."

"Oh. Then yes, please." She stretched her hands to the warmth of the fire. "What can I do?"

"Toast the bread." He passed her a toasting fork, really just a bit of bent wire he'd made himself. He liked the feeling of being self-sufficient, which was ridiculous because he knew he wasn't, not in the least.

She took the fork and threaded some bread on it and held it near the fire. He poured a little boiling water into the teapot, swished it around and emptied it, then added tea leaves.

She gave him a sidelong glance. "You're very prodigal with the tea leaves."

"*Prodigue?* Does that mean I'm wasteful?"

She said carefully, "You use a lot of tea for each pot. Tea is very expensive."

He carefully poured boiling water onto the tea leaves and flashed her a quick grin. "Perhaps, but I like my tea and I like it strong. I presume you want some." He set a pan over the fire and dropped in a lump of butter.

"Yes, please. I'm sorry, I shouldn't have said anything."

"You can say whatever you like, I don't mind. I'm used to being criticized. The wives never stop," he said with a wink. "That's why I like this life. I can live how I want, answering to nobody." He cracked four eggs into the sizzling butter and stirred them gently. "Is the toast ready?"

In answer, she held out two plates containing several pieces of toast. He scooped out a portion of the eggs onto one. "Say when."

"That's plenty, thank you," she responded. He scooped the rest onto his plate and poured out the tea, adding milk and sugar to hers.

They ate in silence. Finally she put her empty plate down, picked up the mug of tea and sipped. "Oh, that's lovely," she said, "a perfect breakfast. And those eggs were delicious, thank you. Will you be working again at the farm today?"

"Yes, would you like to come with me?" She must have been quite bored the day before, but she hadn't mentioned it. She wasn't a complainer, this girl.

She brightened. "Could I? You wouldn't mind?"

"Not at all. Now, get ready—I want to leave in ten minutes."

She grabbed the plates and used the last of the hot water to wash them. She played fair, too, he reflected. He cooked so she cleaned up. It was probably her training as a maid.

Though she didn't act like most of the maids he knew. She wasn't at all subservient or meek; in fact, she treated him quite like an equal. Nor did she flirt and play the co-quette toward him, which so many women did. He liked that. And she intrigued him. Most women were only too keen to share every single thought they had. She made him work to discover the most basic things.

What did he know about her, after all? She was French, an orphan with no family left. She was clean and neat in her habits—and modest, he thought, recalling her embarrass-ment at his noticing her washing. She'd been a maidservant, and a virtuous one at that, dismissed for resisting the ap-proaches of her master. And she'd bought food to share and made herself useful around the camp.

She hadn't complained once—not when he'd left her to her own devices for a whole day, nor at the discomforts of the life he was leading: fetching water from the stream, washing there, cooking simple food over an open fire. It made her a rarity among his female acquaintances.

And yet despite the little he knew of her—or perhaps because of it—he was far too attracted to her for his own peace of mind.

"I'd better introduce you as my cousin," he said as they set off for the farm.

She gave him a sideways glance. "Why?"

"Gaudet and his wife would be shocked at the idea of us traveling together and not being married. You and I know there is not the slightest impropriety in our arrangement, but country folk are not known for their broad-mindedness."

She gave him a long, thoughtful look, then nodded.

"Tell me about these three wives of yours," she said as they walked. "You said, I think, that they all lived in separate houses."

He laughed. "Lord yes. There would likely be bloodshed if they were all under the one roof. So, you want to know what they're like?"

He glanced at her, as if considering whether to answer her, then shrugged. "The first one is the oldest, naturally. How to describe her? Hmm." He thought for a minute then said, "Very bossy. She considers that she rules the roost—that goes for all of us, the other two wives and me. She tries to keep me at home and under her thumb."

"She's obviously succeeded there," she said dryly.

He laughed. "Yes, it's a constant battle, but she never gives up."

"You like her, though?"

"Oh yes, difficult as she is, I'm quite fond of her. And she takes charge of things while I'm away."

"Which makes it easier for you to go away?"

"Correct."

"What about the other wives?"

"Oh, they never mind if I'm away—they leave it all up to her. Oh, you mean what are they like? Well, wife number two"—he rolled his eyes—"makes endless demands on behalf of herself and her two daughters. Never-ending demands. She's never satisfied and she makes sure I—and the rest of the world—are fully informed of my deficiencies."

"I see." That fact that he referred to "her" daughters, not "our" daughters, was outrageous. Honestly, men were the limit, sometimes. But she was a stranger and in no position to criticize. The relationship between him and his wives was none of her business. Though she was very curious.

"And the third wife? Presumably she's the youngest."

"Yes, she's the one who's just had a baby—at least I suppose she's had it by now and that all went well. With two boys already, she was hoping for a girl."

Zoë gave him a searching sidelong look. It didn't seem to have occurred to him that things might not have gone to plan with the birth, and he seemed quite indifferent as to the sex of the new child. "You haven't written to find out?"

"No. I'll find out eventually."

The farm came into sight, and Zoë was left with her thoughts as Gaudet came to greet Reynard, and there was an exchange of masculine chat from which she was more or less excluded.

Those wives of his, what a strange and shocking arrangement it was. Presumably, if she acted on her attraction to him, he would carelessly add her to his collection of wives and treat any children she gave birth to with the same callous indifference he showed to the other five.

It was an absolute disgrace and she would never be part of that kind of arrangement. Never!

Chapter Five

When they arrived at the farm, Reynard introduced her as his cousin. Monsieur Gaudet nodded indifferently, but Madame Gaudet was a different kettle of fish. Arms akimbo, she took one long look at Zoë, then gave a loud, skeptical sniff.

She didn't even give Zoë a chance to visit Le Duc de Gaudet in his pen, just bustled her into the kitchen and set her to work, washing dishes, peeling potatoes, podding peas, peeling and slicing apples for a tart, kneading bread, sweeping the floor and doing all manner of household chores, all the while popping out for short breaks to pose for Reynard's painting. Each time she returned to the kitchen, she inspected Zoë's work and shot questions at her about Reynard, his family and their so-called relationship.

It was exhausting, but at least Zoë proved relatively competent at the various tasks, thanks to her training in the orphanage and the time she'd spent helping in the kitchen at Lady Scattergood's. She managed to evade a lot of questions about him by saying she'd grown up in a different part of the country, and hadn't known him well.

Finally, in desperation, she borrowed Marie's story about the lecherous son of the house and being dismissed, saying that upon finding Reynard in the district, she'd taken shelter with him and would be returning to the family in Paris as soon as they reached Nantes, where she would catch the *diligence*.

At that, madame's attitude changed—Vita was a good girl; it was a disgrace the way those aristos thought they were entitled to whatever took their fancy and thought nothing of ruining a decent girl for a moment's pleasure.

Zoë thought of the violence done to her family and to Maman's home and shivered. The resentment might be old, but it was still there.

But when Zoë told her what she'd done to discourage Monsieur Etienne, the woman laughed until tears ran down her cheeks. After that, though she kept Zoë working just as hard, the atmosphere in the kitchen was much more pleasant, and at the end of the day, she sent her home with an apple tart, a large container of soup and a loaf of fresh bread.

Zoë and Reynard walked back to the camp. "Well, that's done," he said. "The painting is finished."

"That was quick," she said in surprise. "I thought it would have taken much longer." Her own paintings certainly did.

"Yes, I told you I'm fast. But once it's dry, I'll frame it in Monsieur Gaudet's frame." His hands were full of the painting—still wet—and all his painting supplies, and Zoë's were full carrying food from Madame Gaudet. "He has an old painting he doesn't want, so I'll frame mine in that one. It's gold leaf and very ornate, and madame is very proud of it. And Gaudet will like a painting of him and his precious pig much more than the old painting—have you ever seen such an enormous porker?"

"No, never." In fact she hadn't often seen a living pig. They weren't common in the city. She was looking forward to seeing the finished painting. He was carrying it carefully with a protective cloth over it.

"And what did you get up to? I hardly even saw you," he added.

She described her day of nonstop labor and interrogation and he laughed and laughed. "But you finally convinced her that you weren't a scarlet woman traveling with a shiftless vagabond?"

"As you see." She indicated the pile of food she was laden with. "And I earned every pound."

"Gram," he corrected her. "It's all grams and kilograms in France now, don't forget."

When they got back to the camp, he took the painting into the wagon for it to dry away from the evening dew, and then set about lighting the fire, seeing to his horse and fetching water. Zoë put the soup from Madame Gaudet into the small pot, hung it over the fire to heat and sliced some of the bread and cheese.

It had only been a few days, but she was getting very used to the outdoor life. And, unexpectedly, she was enjoying every minute of it. In fact, she thought as she stirred the soup in the pot, she could happily live like this, traveling from place to place, painting for a living. Making meals together, sitting around the fire in the evening, talking and telling stories by firelight, while overhead the stars twinkled and the moon shone benignly down.

The faint evening breeze changed direction and suddenly her eyes and lungs were full of smoke. Coughing and rubbing her eyes, she moved to a different position. It wasn't this life that she was thinking of—she was romanticizing there. They'd been lucky with the weather, but in winter it would be cold and wet and unpleasant. And she was already tired of washing in the chilly water of the stream. Oh, for a hot bath, with some of Clarissa's bath oils.

She glanced at the tall man vigorously grooming the ancient horse, taking as much care as if Rocinante were a thoroughbred. It wasn't the carefree outdoor life she was dreaming of; it was life with Reynard.

But that was ridiculous. She hardly knew the man—not even his real name—and he didn't know hers. He was full of contradictions and mystery, and she would be a fool to throw in her lot with a man who claimed to have three wives and who knew how many children, no matter how charming and apparently chivalrous he seemed.

Besides, she had another life waiting for her in England, and people who loved her, who'd given her so much. She owed it to them to live the life they'd made possible for her. It was the life Maman would want for her, too.

"I'm off to the village," Reynard said the next morning after breakfast. They'd lingered over scrambled eggs and several cups of tea. "I might be gone awhile. I'm planning to walk into town and see if I can get any more commissions." He grinned. "Apparently Gaudet has been boasting about getting a portrait of his pig done. With any luck, more people will want one."

She laughed.

"Will you be all right here on your own?"

"Of course. Besides, I have Rocinante for company."

"Good. Just watch out for the man-eating foxes, then." He strolled away.

Zoë was dying to see the finished painting. It had been too dark in the wagon to see it the previous night, so after she'd cleaned up the breakfast things, she climbed into the wagon and brought the painting into the light. And stared, frowning.

The pig was certainly the star of the portrait—it was so vibrant and lifelike that one could almost imagine it stepping out of the picture. But the people . . .

They were . . . flat, not quite two-dimensional. Both Madame Gaudet and her husband would be quite disappointed, she was sure, though Gaudet might not care, because the pig was magnificent.

She set up the easel and examined the painting more closely.

What kind of painter could paint a brilliantly lifelike pig and yet fail with people? Oh, you could tell who they were—the features were accurate enough, and the clothing, but somehow, they just didn't look real.

Reynard had said it was finished.

But it wasn't.

She glanced at the road he'd disappeared down.

She could fix it. She poured herself some tea from the leftovers in the pot. It was lukewarm and bitter, but she didn't like to make herself a fresh pot.

She looked at the painting again. The basic appearance of the farmer and his wife, their poses and the shapes of their bodies were fine, but the eyes were . . . wrong. And so was Madame Gaudet's expression. And her husband's mouth. All it would take would be . . .

No, she couldn't. It wasn't right for one artist to interfere with another's work. Especially not without permission.

But Madame Gaudet had been, beneath her brisk bossiness, kind. And Zoë wanted her to look her best. If Gaudet had been boasting around the village about his portrait, how would madame feel when it looked as though she was of less importance than the pig?

Zoë nibbled a slice of the apple tart and decided. She would do it. And risk Reynard's wrath. He might not even notice. She would just fix the eyes.

She fetched his paint and brushes and started to paint. She'd only intended to make a couple of tiny adjustments, but one tiny brushstroke was followed by another, then another, and gradually, as Zoë's brushes flew, Madame Gaudet and her husband came to life: madame with the skeptical expression that seemed so much part of her, but also showing the kindness underneath. And the pride that Gaudet had in his pig shining from his eyes.

It was early afternoon when she finished and stood back to examine the painting. She nodded, satisfied. Yes, it all worked. Now the pig *and* the people were equally vividly portrayed. The Gaudets would be happy, she was sure.

She cleaned the brushes, put everything away and picked up the painting, ready to put it back in the wagon. She took one last, long look, and slowly the pleasure in her work died.

What had she done? How would Reynard react? Would he be furious? She would be if someone had interfered with one of her paintings unasked. What on earth had she been thinking? She'd been arrogant, thinking she could do better—and she had, but she should never have done it.

Guilt curdled in her stomach. But it was too late to undo what she had done. She would have to take the consequences. Reynard would be back soon.

She waited.

❧

It was late afternoon when Reynard strolled into the campsite, carrying several large, heavy paintings, wrapped carefully in a cloth. It had been a mixed day, and he was glad to be back in his camp.

Vita was waiting for him, standing beside the wagon, wringing her hands. As he approached, she suddenly stiffened, looking past him.

"What is that?" she said in a tense, low voice. "Behind you."

He glanced behind him and sighed. "It's a dog." He set down his burden carefully. It must have followed him. Serve him right for feeding the wretched beast.

"I can see that, but what does it want? It's huge, and it looks rather fierce."

"I found it chained up beside a deserted house."

"A deserted house?"

"Yes, I checked. There was nobody there and it was clear they'd been gone for some days. More. There was dust everywhere and it didn't look like they planned to return."

She frowned. "But they'd left the poor dog behind?"

"Yes, chained up, so he couldn't get away. The poor devil was half-mad with thirst and starvation when I found him—there wasn't even any water left." He clicked his fingers, and the dog took several wary steps closer. "You can see where he fought against the chain. I'm afraid I gave him the rabbit I'd intended for our dinner."

"Oh, I'm glad you did. And you gave him water, of course. And freed him from that horrid chain. I can see where the poor fellow rubbed himself raw. I can't believe anyone would do such a terrible thing to a poor defenseless creature. Some people don't deserve to have animals." She rose slowly and held out her hand to the dog. "Poor old fellow, you've had a bad time of it, haven't you? But you're with us now, and everything will be all right," she crooned.

Reynard eyed her, surprised. A few moments earlier she'd been nervous of the dog, who admittedly was a large intimidating-looking creature—a lurcher crossed with something big and menacing-looking, if he wasn't mistaken—and yet now she was crooning at it like a baby. And calling it a poor defenseless creature. And it was "with us" was it? He liked the sound of that "us."

He smiled to himself. So Miss Vita, who'd been frightened by the screaming of foxes mating, liked dogs, did she?

The dog gave a tiny, half-hearted wag of its ragged tail and took another few cautious steps toward them. He was big and gray and scruffy with liquid dark eyes. Clearly he wasn't the only one who wasn't able to resist the appeal of those eyes.

"I'm surprised he found me," he said. "After I removed the chain, I fed him the rabbit and gave him water—both of which he gulped down in record time—and he immediately bounded off and disappeared. I thought I'd seen the last of him, but here he is."

Vita continued her crooning, and he wasn't at all surprised when the dog came close enough for her to pat him, then flopped down and rolled over to have its stomach scratched.

If she used that seductive tone on him, he'd happily roll over as well, though not to have his stomach scratched.

"This animal is filthy," she declared. "And he's crawling with fleas. We can't keep him like that—we'll have to bathe him."

"Will we?" he said, amused.

"Yes, in the stream." She hesitated and bit her lip. "I only have a tiny piece of soap left. I don't suppose you have some we could use?"

"I do. I used it to wash the horse."

Her eyes widened. "You washed the horse?"

He shrugged. "She was filthy when I got her." And destined for the knackers if he wasn't mistaken. He had a weakness for lost causes. He went to fetch the soap, and the three of them headed for the stream.

He rolled up his trouser legs, and Vita hitched up her skirt, exposing a slender pair of shapely calves, which he tried not to ogle. Though it was difficult.

She entered the water first and coaxed the dog to come in after her, which he did with cautious reluctance. Reynard followed with the soap and a bucket and set to work. The dog made it clear he was here on sufferance, enduring the lathering with soap only because Miss Vita was crooning softly to him all the while. From time to time, he turned his great shaggy head to Reynard with an expression of deepest reproach, making it clear who he blamed for this latest indignity.

But when it came to rinsing, the dog decided he'd had enough. Shaking wet suds all over them, he broke free of

Reynard's grip and capered madly around in the water splashing and leaping and bouncing off them until they were both equally drenched. And laughing. And presumably free of fleas as well.

"What are you going to name him?" Vita asked as they sat by the fire while the dinner was heating. She'd applied some kind of ointment to the raw sores around the dog's neck, where the poor beast had fought a losing battle against the chain that had been killing him, and was now gently brushing out the tangles in the dog's fur.

"Name him? I'm keeping him, then?"

"Of course," she said, as if there was no question of it.

He considered the dog, who gave him a sleepy smug look, clearly lapping up the girl's attentions. Half his luck.

"Hamish," he said.

"Hamish?"

He nodded. "He reminds me of a fellow I went to school with who had just such a lugubrious expression. Hardly ever cracked a smile. Always looked gloomy."

"He's not at all gloomy," she objected. "He's perfectly sweet."

Perfectly sweet? The dog was huge, shaggy and grim-looking, the kind of dog you'd go down a dark alley to avoid. Anything less sweet you'd be hard-pressed to come across.

"At least he's clean."

"Yes, and I have some very good ointment that my sist— I mean a girl I know made, which will help heal those nasty sores where the chain rubbed him raw."

Reynard hadn't missed the slip of the tongue. So there was a sister, was there? And she'd said she was all alone in the world.

"So," he said, changing the subject, "what did you get up to today?"

She jumped, flinching at his words, and gave him a look that was a curious mix of horror and guilt. "Oh no. I quite forgot. In all the excitement of meeting Hamish, I forgot to tell you."

"Tell me what?"

She bit her lip, almost chewing on it. "I did something today. Something bad."

"Did you, now?" He hid a smile. No doubt she'd bathed naked in the stream or something of that sort. Nothing could dampen his good mood—actually, the thought of her naked in the stream only added to it, especially since their frolics there with the dog. The way her damp dress had clung to every curve . . .

Even before he'd rescued the dog, he'd been well pleased with his day's work. He'd run into Gaudet at the village tavern, where the man was telling anyone who'd listen that he was having his portrait—and that of his prize pig—painted by a famous artist.

Reynard had then explained to Gaudet's audience his "old for new" arrangement, where they would retain the ornate, gold-leafed frames—for many, the frames were the best part, he knew—and they would exchange their unwanted painting for a painting of whatever subject they desired. Two men had immediately hurried home to fetch their old paintings, and after a cursory glance—and careful not to show his excitement—he'd agreed to accept them.

This trip was proving to be very successful. Miss Vita-from-the-Latin had brought him luck.

His painting would need to be left for a day or two to dry thoroughly before he put it in the frame. He bent to check the soup that was heating and stirred it, saying, "So, are you going to tell me what you did that's so bad?"

"I did something to your painting." She swallowed convulsively. "I painted over it."

He jerked his head up, frowning. "You painted over my painting?"

She nodded.

He swore under his breath. "Where is it?"

"In the wagon." She was almost in tears, he could see, but dammit, so she should be. If she'd ruined his work . . .

He hurried to the wagon, grabbed the painting and stepped outside with it to examine the damage in the fading light.

And froze, staring. It most certainly wasn't the painting he'd left to dry the previous night. It was . . . amazing. The skin tones—he'd painted them pink, but now they were . . . flesh, with texture and depth. And how she'd done it, he had no idea, but somehow, the personality of each person was now there, on the canvas: Gaudet with his pride in his pig, and Madame Gaudet with her caution and her kindness. All kinds of tiny details had been added that made it look as though the people, as well as the pig, could step out of the frame and walk away.

"*You* did this?" he said eventually.

"Yes. I'm so very sorry." Her voice was husky. "I only meant to touch up a few small things, but then I . . . got a bit carried away."

He stared at her, his little maidservant traveling companion, then back at the painting, then back at her. "You painted over my people?"

Dumbly she nodded, the picture of remorse.

He carefully set the painting down, then swooped on her, picked her up and twirled her around. She clutched at his shoulders. The dog barked, but he took no notice. "It's brilliant! Utterly brilliant. And you did it?" He still could barely believe it.

When he finally put her down, letting her slide down his body, she gaped up at him. "You don't mind?"

"Mind? Does it look like I mind?" He stared down at her, amazed at the difference she had made to his painting. He'd always known that portraits of people were his weakness, and she'd just demonstrated why.

She didn't move, didn't push him away, just stood there, gazing up at him, flushed, a little doubtful, a little shy, her rosy lips parted. Soft, satiny, inviting lips. Without thought he kissed her. He'd meant it to be just an exuberant buss of a kiss, but after the first brief taste of her, he stopped, stared down at her for a long moment.

In the distance he heard the shriek of a fox. She didn't react. He bent and brushed his mouth lightly over hers. The barest brush of skin against skin. She didn't move. Her eyes were in shadow; he could not read her expression.

But she made no move to escape, so he did it again, grazing his mouth over her lips. He could feel her breath. A sweet tremor of heat. A wisp of sensation.

She shivered against him, but still she made no move to step away.

He was only human. So he kissed her again. Properly.

Her mouth softened under his, and her lips parted. She twined her arms around his neck, pulling him closer, returning his kiss with shy eagerness, loosing a ravening hunger deep within him. He pulled her hard against him, deepening the kiss, inflamed by the taste of her, the feeling of her in his arms.

Heat spiraled through him, and he drew her closer, feeling her softness pressing against him, against the hardness of his arousal.

He was brought to a realization of what he was doing when the dog thrust his damp nose in between them and shoved. Heart pounding, Reynard forced himself to release her and step back. Thank goodness for the dog's intervention. If he hadn't, they would have ended up taking things too far.

She was an innocent, he reminded himself, a girl who'd sacrificed her secure job in defense of her virtue. Who was he to seduce her on a whim?

Although, was it a whim, or something more? He didn't like to think about it. It simply wasn't possible.

Shaken by the strength of his reaction, he turned away and bent over the fire again, piling on twigs to get the flames burning—though there were enough flames burning inside him.

He busied himself tending to the soup, then feeling that he'd finally gained control of himself, he turned to her.

She hadn't moved, just stood there, her hand resting on the dog's head—she didn't even need to bend—gazing at him with an expression he couldn't read.

"I've never been able to paint people," he said, deciding to be matter-of-fact. "I normally travel with a partner, and he does the people and I do the animals and the backgrounds. But he got married last year, and his bride wasn't willing to take to a wagon, and he wasn't willing to leave her, so I thought I'd try to do it all myself. I know it wasn't very good, but for Gaudet the pig was the thing, and the pig turned out well. But what you did—"

"You really don't mind?"

"Not in the least." He grinned. "In fact, I think you should marry me. We'll make the perfect painting partnership."

She laughed. "And become your fourth wife? I don't think so."

"No, but seriously, I'm delighted with it. You can really see Gaudet and his wife now, and you've managed to make them really look like themselves—I mean their personalities show through, not just their appearance. How did you do that?"

"Oh, well . . ." Blushing, she made a self-deprecatory gesture.

"No, I mean it, there's not just talent in what you've achieved, there is skill and real technique. So how did a maidservant learn to paint like that?"

She wrinkled her nose, looking uncomfortable. He waited. "I'm curious." He really wanted to know. She'd been an enigma from the start, and now she was even more of a mystery.

The dog suddenly pricked up his ears. Then like a wraith

in the night, he disappeared into the scrub surrounding their campsite. She gazed after him, then turned to Reynard with a question in her eyes.

"Shouldn't we—?" she began.

He shook his head. "If he wants to leave, I won't make him stay." He squashed a sense of disappointment at the dog's abandonment. "Now, you were about to tell me how you learned to paint like that," he reminded her.

"Oh, yes." She squirmed a little under his gaze. "Well, I've always liked drawing, but of course, I never had a chance to practice it. And even if I could get pencils and paper—let alone paints—orphanages find that kind of thing frivolous, even sinful."

"So what changed?"

She frowned at him, then sighed and looked away. "In my first position the daughter of the house was getting lessons; the upper classes consider painting—mainly watercolors—a desirable ladylike accomplishment. I was sent to sit with her as a kind of chaperone, even though I was quite young—the artist engaged to teach her was a handsome young man. The young lady had little interest in painting and no skill, but she did like the young man—she was a terrible flirt—and she wanted to prolong the lessons as long as possible. So she got me to do her paintings while she flirted with the tutor. The artist said I was talented, and he taught me a great deal."

"Fortunate for you," he said dryly.

"Yes, wasn't it?"

He served up the soup in silence. He wasn't sure he believed her story, though it could explain her ability, at least some of it. But the techniques she'd demonstrated in bringing the Gaudets to life were the result of advanced study and skill with oil paints, not merely a few happenstance lessons in painting pretty scenes in watercolors.

The mystery of her deepened. He sipped his soup.

From the edge of the clearing came the sound of crunching bones. A few minutes later he heard splashing, then Hamish stepped into the firelight, his ragged, plumy tail swishing gently. His muzzle was wet and dripping, his expression content.

He went straight to Vita and nuzzled her shoulder with his damp muzzle. She laughed, exclaiming, "Ugh, you're all wet!" But she happily put aside her soup and scritched around his ears. "You clever boy, you didn't leave us after all, did you? I was so worried that I'd never see you again." The moment she stopped, the dog nudged her shoulder again then glanced at Reynard with a smug look.

"At least we know he can feed himself." At her quizzical look, he explained, "Unless I miss my guess, Hamish has just caught and eaten a rabbit. Didn't you hear all the crunching and munching earlier?"

"No, I didn't." She pulled back and regarded the dog with a severe expression. "I don't suppose I can blame you," she told him. "Just don't let me see you doing it, all right?"

The dog gave her an imperious nudge, and she sighed and resumed her attentions.

The following day was a Sunday, and Reynard had told her to sleep in. "Most people around here will be at church in the morning. I should have asked—do you want to go to church?"

She shook her head. Maman had been a regular churchgoer when she first came to England, and whenever she could, she lit candles for her parents and brother. But when she'd learned, some years later, that they'd been guillotined, she'd lost her faith, she told Zoë.

They'd still gone into a church from time to time to light a candle for their souls or to ask for intervention from one of the saints—Maman was bit vague about that—but though Zoë had been christened, she'd never been confirmed.

Later, after Maman died and Zoë was taken to the orphanage, church attendance had been compulsory, but the church was a different sort, with no friendly saints to turn to, and where, she was told by the matron of the orphanage, lighting a candle for the souls of the dead was a heathenish, popish practice and not to be thought of.

So Zoë had never had much faith to lose. And since Reynard said he'd never had any to lose in the first place, they spent the morning tidying the campsite and doing a bit of washing.

And trying not to think about that kiss.

Chapter Six

❧

In the early afternoon Reynard took the painting back to Gaudet's farm to show him and his wife the finished product and transfer it into the ornate gold-leafed frame. He took with him his painting supplies and easel, strapped to his back in case he was given another commission. He liked to be prepared.

"*C'est magnifique!*" Gaudet exclaimed when he lifted the painting out of its wrapping, and both he and his wife went into raptures—Gaudet about the portrait of the pig, Madame Gaudet about the portraits of herself and her husband.

Reynard was delighted. "Then if you're happy with the exchange, I'll just remove the old painting and put this one into your frame."

Gaudet snorted. "More than happy, monsieur. Who wants to have stiff-rumped aristos staring down their noses at honest people going about their business? But this"—he gestured proudly at the new painting—"this is about real people. And the only aristo in it is Le Duc de Gaudet, who well deserves his place." He guffawed loudly at his joke.

Reynaud then took the old painting and set about removing it from its frame, first the back cover, then the old canvas, which he set carefully aside.

Gaudet, who had been watching, asked, "What will you do with that? Sell it?"

Reynard shrugged. "Perhaps. I haven't decided." It was a lie. He knew exactly what he was going to do with it. He placed a protective cloth on either side of the old painting and rolled it up. He reached for his own painting, and added, "A lot of artists reuse old canvas and paint over old paintings."

Gaudet snorted. "And a good thing, too."

"Is that what you will do?" Madame Gaudet asked curiously.

Reynard carefully fitted the new painting into the old frame. He'd measured well: it fitted perfectly. "I'm not sure. All I know is 'waste not, want not.'" To which both Gaudets nodded in agreement.

The new painting framed, they all went into the house to choose a place to hang it. No question, really—it was to hang in pride of place on the wall opposite the entrance, where every visitor would be sure to see and admire it. Then they toasted it—and the artist—with homemade wine, which was surprisingly good.

His plan had been to go into the village to try to drum up another commission, but when he mentioned that, both Gaudet and his wife had suggestions for him. It seemed at church they had boasted widely of their special personal artist and what he was doing for them. They gave him several people to call on.

An hour later, he had three new commissions and the promise of two old paintings minus their heavy gold-leaf frames. That suited him perfectly: he had no interest in the frames. He started on the first commission then and there.

It was of a widow and her three children. And their small dog.

"I hate having that thing in the house," the widow told him, gesturing to the old painting. She'd produced it from a dark cupboard. "My father-in-law gave it to us as a wedding present, and my husband was very proud of it. But me"—she grimaced—"I don't like the reminder, and I want it out of my house."

Reynard, sketching busily, nodded understandingly. "I hope you will be happy with my painting, madame."

She snorted in amusement. "I will be happy just to have that one gone. I would have given it to you for nothing. I would have burned it, but I do like the gold frame. You're not taking that, are you?"

"No. I will use it to frame the new painting."

By late afternoon, Reynard had sketched in the widow and her children, aged twelve, ten and six, painted the dog and the background and took notes for Vita. The children were unable to stay still for long, and he could tell the widow was getting anxious about doing nothing for several hours. She ran both the farm and the household on her own, with the help of the children, so her work was really cut out for her. So after roughing in their poses on the canvas, he did a pencil sketch of each of them.

He didn't know why, but for some reason he could draw faces quite well, but when it came to painting them . . . He shook his head. He would watch Vita when she did them and hope to pick up some of her techniques.

When he had done as much as he could, Reynard returned to the camp carrying, along with his easel, paints and other supplies, the rolled-up old canvas from the Gaudets, another gold-framed painting from a neighbor, and a warm rabbit pie. It smelled divine—the widow was a good cook.

The neighbor had marched into the widow's yard, carrying the large painting and demanding Reynard paint him and his prize bull. He had just seen the portrait of Gaudet's pig.

Delighted to oblige—especially after seeing the painting the man was offering in exchange—Reynard accepted the commission. He wrapped both framed paintings in an old cloth given to him by the widow. She hadn't wanted her frame chipped or damaged.

When he walked into the camp laden with paintings, paint supplies, pie and more, the dog and Vita flew to meet him. "Good heavens, what have you got there?" she said, relieving him of the pie. "Is this from Madame Gaudet? Were they happy with the painting?"

"Ecstatic," he said. "And no, the pie is from another woman, our next client. Down, Hamish, this pie is not for dogs!" he added to the dog in English. Hamish far from being wary and lugubrious, was now frolicking around him like a puppy.

Vita laughed. "He's really coming out of his shell, isn't he? Yesterday he seemed quite an elderly dog, but now, with several good feeds, a wash and some love and care, I've decided he's much younger than we thought. Shall we eat this pie now while it's still warm?"

Reynard set down his burdens and, laughing, gave the dog a good scruff around the head and neck. Then he took the wrapped framed paintings and Gaudet's rolled-up canvas into the wagon, placed them carefully in the big cupboard and locked it.

She watched curiously, but didn't comment or ask.

He headed for the campfire, running his hands together. "I'm parched."

"Me, too. The water is boiling. I thought you'd want tea when you got back." She'd placed the pie by the fire to keep warm. The teapot, tea caddy and mugs were set out ready, but she hung back, apparently waiting to let him make the tea.

He warmed the teapot. "Why didn't you make some yourself?"

She made a self-deprecating sort of moue. "Tea is expensive. I didn't like to presume."

Shaking his head in wry amusement, Reynard made the tea. The girl was full of contradictions. She could paint over his painting without a by-your-leave, and yet she wouldn't presume to make herself a cup of tea.

"I have two more commissions," he told her as he poured the tea.

Her face lit up. "Oh, Reynard, that's wonderful."

He grinned. "You've brought me luck, Mademoiselle Vita-from-the-Latin. I started one painting today—it's of a widow and her three children. And dog. I've roughed out most of it, but I thought you could work your magic on the woman and children."

She beamed at him. "So you truly didn't mind my interference, then? You weren't just being polite? Of course, I'd be delighted to help."

He sipped his tea. "We could do this permanently, you know—collaborate, I mean. I do the background and animals and you do the people."

The sparkle in her eyes died. "It's very kind of you, but I'm only here for a short time."

He frowned. "You mean you're still planning to go to Paris?"

She nodded.

He pursed his lips. It was one thing for her to think about going to the city when she'd just been sacked and learned her grandmother was dead and she had nowhere to go, but for the last few days things had been going so well. He'd been sure she was enjoying this life of his. She was an innocent from the country and had no idea that in Paris, she'd be taking herself into a den of lions. Worse.

"But you know no one in Paris. You have nowhere to go and nobody to help you. You don't even have a job, and without a character reference you're not likely to get one." He shook his head and added, "No doubt you've formed some romantic image in your head of Paris, but it's not like that, I promise you. The city is a jungle and full of dangers, especially for young women on their own." Especially beautiful young women.

She lifted a shoulder. "Nevertheless, I am going." She didn't meet his eyes.

The strength of his desire to keep her with him shocked him a little. How could he persuade her? She was safe here with him. And they'd been happy, hadn't they?

Ah well, there was still time to change her mind. "I thought you could come to the widow's farm and paint her. You don't have to. I made a few sketches of her and the children, but I thought it would be easier for you to see them in the flesh."

She cut a large slice of the pie, slid it onto a plate and handed it to him. "You wouldn't mind her knowing that I do some of the painting?"

He shook his head. "People's opinions of me don't matter. What counts is the quality of the final painting, and we both know that if you paint the people, it will be better. We'll go to the farm after we've eaten."

She glanced at the dog, who'd been watching every mouthful they took with a mournful gaze. "What about Hamish?"

"What about him?"

"Do we take him with us or leave him here?" She hesitated. "It's just that this morning he was quite happy to stay here with me, but we don't know how he is with children. Or other dogs. Or chickens or any other creature. And we don't know whether the widow would mind us bringing him. But if we make him stay in camp, we'd probably have to tie him up, and after his experience of being chained— the sores around the poor fellow's neck are starting to heal, but—"

"We won't chain him or tie him up," he said decisively.

He glanced at the dog and said to it in English, "I don't suppose you've been trained to stay, have you? Otherwise those villains wouldn't have left you chained up." Hamish gave him a doggy smile and thumped his tail.

"Look, he knows you're talking to him," she exclaimed. "Even though you're talking in English. Who's a clever boy, then?"

The tail thumped faster, and she broke off a piece of piecrust and gave it to him. He took it from her gently and swallowed it in a gulp.

"You shouldn't feed him at the table."

She gave him a sardonic look, and gestured to her surroundings, which were conspicuously lacking in a table.

He ignored that. "We'll just have to see how it goes. I'll tell him to stay and guard the camp, and"—he made a helpless gesture—"hope for the best."

Zoë spent the rest of the day painting Madame LeBlanc and her three children. The lady had, at first, demurred about letting Zoë paint her. Whether it was a question of preferring a male painter or worries about Zoë's competence, she wasn't sure, but all objections vanished when Zoë did a quick pencil sketch of her little girl.

The minute Reynard had strolled off, heading for the property of their next client, the widow had bombarded her with questions: about Reynard, about herself and particularly about their relationship.

As agreed, Zoë said she was Reynard's cousin, who he was escorting to the next town.

"Cousin?" the woman said suspiciously. "But he is English, surely, and you are French, yes?"

"Yes, but I am half-English, too. The family is split between two countries."

Madame LeBlanc nodded understandingly. "The war?"

Zoë nodded. "His wife is French, too," she added recklessly, having no idea whether the wife—or the three he claimed—were real, let alone their nationality.

The widow's brow cleared at the mention of a wife and she quickly settled down to accept Zoë and let her paint her and the children.

A short time after she'd started painting, the children started smiling and nudging one another. She glanced around and tensed. Hamish stood a few yards away. The LeBlanc dog, a stubby, tough-looking creature, was walking toward him, growling and stiff-legged, his back bristles raised.

Hamish just stood there, looking unperturbed, his plumed tail gently swishing.

She was about to rush up and—do what? She didn't know, but she wasn't going to let them fight. But before she could move, the LeBlanc dog lowered its bristles, and the two dogs started sniffing each other's behinds. And two tails, one stumpy, one long and ragged, started wagging.

They weren't going to fight after all. She heaved a sigh of relief.

"Hamish!" she exclaimed. "I'm sorry, madame, we thought he would stay at the camp, but— No, don't touch him!" she added as the littlest child ran eagerly toward him. She lunged forward and grabbed Hamish by the scruff of fur at his neck just as the little girl reached him.

Hamish merely thumped his tail and licked the child's hand gently. Zoë breathed again as he endured the enthusiastic attentions of the little girl.

The widow laughed. "You cannot keep that child away from any dog. One day some dog will bite her and teach her to be more cautious, but it obviously won't be today," she added as Hamish rolled over to have his tummy scratched. One of the boys whistled, and the LeBlanc dog gave one last sniff and trotted back to his young master.

"It's all right, mademoiselle, I know this dog. It lives over there." The little girl waved a vague arm, pointing.

The widow snorted. "Those people . . ." She shook her head. "They left, and good riddance to them. So, you bought their dog, eh?"

Zoë nodded. There was no point telling the woman how Reynard had found the dog chained up and left to starve to death. She smiled at the sight of the gentle animal patiently enduring having his ears affectionately pulled by the little girl. "He's a beautiful animal."

"*Beautiful?*" The woman snorted with laughter. "They say it's in the eye of the beholder, but I wouldn't call that one anything like a beauty. And it's too big. It's going to cost you a lot to keep it fed."

Zoë also decided not to tell her how Hamish had already found and dispatched several rabbits. She hoped he was too full—and hopefully too well mannered—to be interested in the hens that peacefully scratched and clucked around their feet.

The afternoon flew.

"If only you and your cousin had come past three years ago." Madame LeBlanc sighed. "We would have had my husband in the painting, and we would have his face to look on."

"I'm sorry . . ." Zoë began.

"Take no notice of me, my chick," she said. "I don't need a painting to remember my Henri. All I have to do is look at that one." She gestured to her eldest boy. "Every day he grows more and more like his papa. And just now he looks exactly like Henri did at that age. We were neighbors, you see, my Henri and me, and knew each other all our lives."

She sighed and added, "No, I would have liked a painting of him so the children would remember their father."

"But we do remember him, Maman," the oldest boy said.

"Yes, we will never forget Papa," the middle one added.

The little girl looked up from where she was fondling Hamish. She opened her mouth as if to disagree, but her brother shook his head at her and she subsided.

Zoë painted on. The little girl would have been three when her father died and would have few memories.

"Did you always know you would marry?" she asked the widow.

The woman laughed. "Well, our parents planned our wedding almost from the day we were born. Our farms were next to each other, and so of course they wanted the extra land—I was my parents' only child. But Henri and I, we had different ideas." She chuckled reminiscently. "For many years we did not like each other one little bit."

"Because you felt you were being pushed into marriage?"

She nodded. "Partly, I suppose. But I thought him an arrogant fellow. He was the best-looking boy in the district"—she nudged her eldest—"just like this one, and didn't he know it?"

"Papa used to say you were the prettiest girl for miles," the oldest boy said, grinning.

The widow blushed. "And so I was." To Zoë she said, "It wasn't until I was nearly sixteen that my feelings about him changed. And his must have changed, too, for soon he came courting."

"He brought you your fur," the little girl prompted. It was obviously a well-loved family story.

Madame LeBlanc nodded. "He had trapped rabbits all through the winter, when their fur was thickest and softest— of course his mother cooked them up for their dinner—but my Henri, he cured the skins himself and stitched them together to make me a beautiful fur tippet. I still have it."

"I'll fetch it for you, Maman." The little girl ran into the house and a few moments later emerged with a long glossy tippet.

"*Merci, petite.*" The widow draped the tippet around

her neck, then pulled a handkerchief from her sleeve and dabbed at her eyes. "Sorry for the tears, mademoiselle, but these are happy memories, you understand, not sad ones."

Zoë nodded, working fast to capture that elusive faraway look in the woman's eyes.

This—this!—was why she preferred to paint people, rather than scenery or still life. Or even animals. People had such stories in them, and if she could get them talking, with luck, she could capture the moment, the fleeting yet telling expression.

Once she had the salient details down, she let the widow and her children go about their daily business. She had it all in her head. Now all she had to do was to get it down in paint. Zoë painted furiously.

By the time the sun was low in the sky and the shadows were starting to creep across the land, she'd made real progress on the painting. The faces had come up beautifully. She was quite happy with them. There were still a few details to touch up, but she could do that in the morning, back in the camp.

She was just packing up her things when Hamish scrambled to his feet and galloped off somewhere. A few minutes later Reynard strolled into view, the dog frisking about him. Her mouth dried as she watched his long, easy stride. Shabby as his clothes might be, he outshone every other man she'd ever met. His blue, blue eyes lit up as they met hers, and he smiled a small, intimate smile just for her. Her heart beat faster.

He greeted the LeBlancs and strolled over to look at her painting, but she stopped him, saying, "It's not finished." She quickly draped a cloth over it.

He gave her a lazy grin. "Precious, are we?"

"Yes." She knew she was a perfectionist and refused to apologize for it. As it was, she'd painted faster than she usually did. Or maybe she was just getting more confident.

They strolled back to camp, Zoë carrying the painting—

she didn't like to leave it where the children might knock it. Reynard carried a large canvas holdall, with his painting paraphernalia on his back. Madame had offered them food, but Zoë had refused, saying they had plenty that needed to be eaten back at their camp. "Besides," she added, "I'm still full from that delicious soup you fed me earlier."

"I didn't get any of that delicious soup," Reynard said plaintively once they were out of sight of the farm.

"We have plenty of food, and that woman is struggling to stay afloat, with a farm to run by herself and three children to support," Zoë began, then stopped when she saw from his expression he was teasing her. "I suppose you had an enormous meal at wherever you were."

"Enormous, and also delicious," he agreed.

"How did your painting go? A bull, wasn't it?"

"Yes, a big ugly brute of a thing, with evil little eyes. Oh, you meant the bull, did you? I assumed you meant the farmer, seeing as you prefer painting people. No, the bull was quite handsome."

She chuckled. The soft evening light slowly dimmed, wrapping around them as they walked. They talked about their day and about their paintings and the people. The dog zigzagged ahead, sniffing various fascinating scents and christening them, until he paused, ears pricked, and darted off into the scrub, presumably in search of his evening meal.

It felt like coming home. But she was supposed to be leaving soon.

She told Reynard about the widow LeBlanc and the stories she told. "It was sad, bittersweet, and yet so romantic. I couldn't paint her late husband in, of course, but I did include the tippet he made for her. It's not quite glossy enough. I'll fix that tomorrow."

"So it's finished, then?"

"No. I'll need another day at least." And then she would leave.

She glanced at the large canvas bag he was carrying. It looked heavy. "Is that more paintings?"

He nodded. "Yes, I'm collecting them before the owners change their mind." He gave her a quick grin. "Striking while the iron is hot. Besides, it will be easier if I frame them all in one go rather than bit by bit."

When they got into camp, Reynard went to lock the old paintings in the big cupboard in the wagon while Zoë busied herself getting the fire going. Reynard had shown her how to set a fire and where to find the best wood to gather to keep it going, and she was quite proud of her new skill.

She was really starting to enjoy this life. Oh, there were inconveniences, to be sure—washing in the cold stream, having to fetch and heat water and so on, but she had memories of her childhood in the slums of London, when she and Maman had had no means of heating water or cooking and no place to wash except with a basin in their one room with cold water fetched from the neighborhood pump. And everywhere—except their own room—it was dirty, whereas here, out in nature, there was dirt all around them, but somehow it was clean dirt.

Clean dirt. She smiled to herself at that little piece of nonsense.

Even at the orphanage, she'd washed in cold water in a basin. The first ever proper bath she'd had—almost fully immersed, with warm water and delicious-smelling soap— was at Lady Scattergood's home. The old lady loved her baths and wallowed in her large bathtub for an hour or more most days.

The first time Zoë had climbed into the bath, oh, it was heavenly. Betty, the maid, had even scrubbed her back for her, and afterward she felt so wonderfully clean from her head to her toes. Yes, she would miss baths, that was certain. But it was a small thing to miss.

She hung the small pot over the fire to heat, then fetched the rug and spread it out. The best part of the day was the evening, eating supper, drinking tea, or wine if they had it, and sitting by the fire with Reynard.

They talked—oh, of nothing special, really, but it was pleasant, and it flowed easily without her having to think up ways to make conversation, the way she so often did with strangers. He was no longer a stranger. Not quite a week they'd been together, but it felt almost as though she'd known him forever.

Which was foolish, because she still didn't know very much about him. Even so, when she was with him, it felt as though she had a small bubble of happiness inside her.

Sometimes he told a funny story, often about his time in the army. He never referred to the grim times, and listening to his tales, one would be forgiven for thinking the war had been nothing but a series of entertaining japes. Though having been enlisted at sixteen and staying in the army until after Waterloo, and having been in "a dozen or so battles" and receiving what he'd called "a few scratches," she knew full well that there must have been some utterly horrific times for a young boy.

And there were times during these quiet, companionable evening sessions when they hardly talked at all, and yet it wasn't the slightest bit awkward, as silences could be. She would sit, gazing into the dancing flames and the glowing coals, and all that she could hear was the wind soughing through the leaves and the fire crackling and, in the distance, the call of a bird or some wild creature. She'd feel no obligation to break the peace of that silence. And neither would he.

But the thought of those three wives and the children ate at her. One night she asked him again, straight out. "Did you really marry three different women?"

He turned his head and looked at her. "No, of course I didn't." There was no twinkle in his eyes. His voice was quiet and matter-of-fact and sincere.

She was inclined to believe him.

"Then why . . . ?"

He shrugged. "Strange as it sounds, there is an occasional woman who will go to extreme lengths to lure me into marriage. Saying I have three wives and a handful of children tends to discourage them."

"So you didn't marry three women?" She had to be sure.

"No." He glanced at her and added, "My word of honor on it. Not even one woman."

She blinked. "You're not married *at all*?"

"No, not at all. I'm entirely single and fancy-free." It was a flat statement of fact.

She believed him. He wasn't just saying it to allay her qualms. After all, he'd made no attempt to seduce her. His treatment of her had, from the very beginning, been that of a gentleman, letting her sleep in safety in his wagon while he slept on the ground outside. He'd even stepped back from that kiss, when she had been more than willing to continue. They weren't the actions of a seducer, or those of the kind of man who would deceive a woman into a bigamous marriage.

It was a weight off her mind. But now, knowing that he wasn't married at all, and that the three wives story was a bit of nonsense he'd initially used to keep her at a distance, it became even more difficult to resist him.

Sometimes she would find herself gazing at Reynard staring into the fire, lost in thought, and she'd watch the way the firelight gilded his face, the bold nose, the shadows beneath his cheekbones, the mobile, sensitive mouth, the strong throat. A man of light and shadow.

And sometimes he'd catch her watching him and give her a quick, intimate smile, a gleam of white in the darkness, and she'd swallow and look away, her throat suddenly thick and dry.

He was too handsome, too charming for her own good.

She was too strongly attracted to him, and to this life. The idea that she could join him, as he'd suggested, enticed her. They could travel leisurely through the countryside, painting together, sitting by the fire at night, talking and laughing and . . . dreaming.

But it was just that, she told herself firmly: a dream.

Had she been the Zoë Benoît who'd simply left the orphanage at the age of sixteen and never met Clarissa and Izzy Studley or Lucy or Lady Scattergood or Lady Tarrant—that Zoë might have been able to take up the wandering life of an artist with a handsome, laughing man. But she wasn't that girl anymore.

Clarissa and Izzy had taken her into their family and their hearts, even before they'd known for sure that they shared a father. Old Lady Scattergood, taking her on trust, had given her a home and had even made her—what had she called it?—oh yes, her "artist in residence." And Lucy and her husband, Gerald, had brought her to Paris, where for the last two and a bit years Lucy had taught Zoë to speak and act like a lady, and she and Zoë had studied painting together.

So many people who'd offered her so much, and all they wanted of her in return was for her to be able to enter their world as a lady. Maman would have wanted that, too, she knew. No doubt they also expected her to find a husband, someone rich and gentlemanly.

Not a kind, shabby, handsome, charming vagabond who lived in a wagon. No, even knowing he was single and free, for her, it was—*he* was—simply not possible.

Even if his kisses swept her away. And featured in her dreams on a nightly basis.

She'd been given so much in the last three years, and none of it was for their benefit. It was all for her, and she couldn't, she just couldn't let them down. She loved them.

She lay in bed at night, restless and torn, her thoughts swirling like leaves caught in a whirlpool. She wanted him—and she was sure he wanted her, too, so why didn't he act? Was he just being honorable?

* * *

The nights were getting chillier.

The following day Zoë returned to the LeBlanc farm and worked on the painting. Hamish accompanied her, and much to the disgust of the LeBlancs' dog, allowed himself to be pampered and spoiled by the LeBlanc children, and even their mother, who produced a bone for him to gnaw on.

The little girl had found a pink ribbon and used it to tie the straggly locks that half hid Hamish's face into a top-knot. He wore it with dignity all day . . . until they were on their way home and out of sight of the farm, when he sat and vigorously scratched, then walked on, leaving the ribbon in the dust. Zoë picked it up. She didn't want the little girl to see it lying in the road.

More and more she found herself wishing it were possible to live this life, traveling with Reynard, painting by day, sitting around the fire talking by night. She was enjoying every part of it: meeting the people, the subjects of their paintings, and listening to their stories. They were poor and lived hard lives, and yet they rarely complained. And they'd been so generous toward her and Reynard; they'd been fed—and fed well—almost every night. Since that first day, Zoë hadn't had to break into her small cache of money hidden in the pouch around her waist.

But it wasn't just the life she wanted: it was the man. Without Reynard, much of the magic would be gone. He fascinated her. He was intelligent and witty, and his conversation was always far ranging and interesting and often unexpected. It was probably how he managed to get so many commissions: people liked him.

She liked him, too. A little too much. A lot too much.

That kiss . . .

It had been just that once, and yet she hadn't been able to get it out of her mind. Afterward he'd acted as if it had never happened, and because of that she had decided it was safer to put the kiss right out of her mind. But it was not so easy. At night, lying in his bed, knowing he was lying beneath her outside on the ground, so near and yet so far, she relived it over and over.

It wasn't as though she'd never been kissed before. She had, a number of times by a number of different men. It was natural to be curious, after all. And though those kisses had mostly been quite pleasant, none of them had moved her the way that Reynard's had.

Nor had any man's touch affected her the way his did. Even the slightest brush of his skin against hers, accidental or not, sent a frisson of deep awareness shivering through her.

It was not to be . . . but the thought occurred to her that she could invite him into the wagon one night. And then . . .

It was risky. She was a virgin, but she wasn't innocent. Living where she had in the slums as a child, she'd picked up things. She'd heard how women could prevent a pregnancy. Something about a small sea-sponge soaked in vinegar. But what did you do with it? And where would she get a sea sponge? They were miles from the sea. She wished she'd taken more notice at the time.

One night for love. It was such a strong temptation. And then she'd return to London and enter society as her sisters' long-lost French cousin. And make an appropriate marriage.

An appropriate marriage. The thought did not appeal. They wouldn't make her marry, she knew. But she'd always wanted a family—her own family, with children to love. And since visiting Maman's château and thinking about what had been lost, she wanted a family of her own even more.

The birds outside cheeped and twittered excitedly, welcoming the dawn. Zoë lay in bed, pondering the future. She would finish the LeBlanc portrait today. Without false modesty, she knew it was good. They would be happy with it, and that pleased her.

She'd really grown to like them: Madame LeBlanc worked like fury to keep the farm going until her sons were able to take it over, and the two boys, still children in some ways, worked just as hard. Even the little girl worked.

Just a few little touches and the painting would be done. Reynard had lined up several more commissions and was expecting her to paint the people.

But it wasn't thoughts of the painting that had disturbed her sleep and woken her so early. The time had flown. On Thursday morning the miller's son would take his wagon to Nantes, and the *diligence* would leave at noon.

Would she go or would she stay?

She ought to go, she knew. The longer she stayed the harder it would be to leave him.

They hadn't made love. But the more she thought about it, the more she wanted to, and hang the consequences. She'd heard an old lady say once that at the end of her life, it wasn't the things she'd done that she most regretted, but the things she hadn't done.

Love was always a risk, was it not?

Besides, she'd only just finished her courses, and she knew from Lucy's long campaign to conceive that the middle time between her courses was the most likely. And if she did conceive, well, she would deal with that if it happened.

Did she *have* to leave on Thursday?

Once she left here she'd never see Reynard again, never see his smile, hear that deep voice and that irresistible chuckle. Or gaze into those eyes, those sparkling Mediterranean-blue eyes.

She'd be introduced to dozens of eligible young men and was expected to choose one for a husband. She owed it to everyone who'd helped her and who hoped for so much for her. And loved her.

But she couldn't imagine feeling for those polite, pleasant, well-dressed young gentlemen anything like what she felt for Reynard.

One night for love. It wasn't much to ask.

But would it be enough? What if she stayed for another week? She could. There was nothing urgent requiring her return.

She could write to Lucy and Gerald and tell them she was extending her stay. She could get a letter to the miller's son today and he could post it in Nantes tomorrow in time for delivery to Paris by the *diligence*. Then they wouldn't worry.

Yes, that's what she would do. She sat down immediately and wrote to Lucy, explaining that she was going to be away another week, but not to worry, that she was safe and having a wonderful time.

She folded and sealed the letter. She would take it to the miller's son before she went to the LeBlanc farm. And then she'd finish the painting.

And tonight she would invite Reynard into the wagon. A shiver of anticipation ran through her. She couldn't wait.

"There," Zoë said a couple of hours later. "It's finished. You can look now, but don't touch—the paint is still wet." Madame LeBlanc and the children clustered excitedly around.

"*Mon Dieu*, do I really look like that?" Madame LeBlanc exclaimed.

Zoë gave her a sharp look, but by her expression the woman was pleased.

"You make me look almost pretty. So flattering."

Zoë shook her head. "I paint what I see, madame. There is no flattery." It was true. She admired this woman, battling on, keeping the farm going on her own while raising three children, and if that admiration was reflected in her painting, it was her truth she portrayed.

"*Oui*, Maman," the little girl piped up. "*Tu es très jolie, et moi aussi.*" She jiggled happily up and down. The boys, too, seemed pleased with the portrait, but were much gruffer in their praise.

Madame LeBlanc laughed and hugged the little girl. She gazed at the painting for a long time, then wiped her eyes on her apron. "My Henri might be dead, but I can see him in my boys' faces, so I have them all here for me now, all my family. And my little one can see what her papa looked like as a boy. *Merci*, mademoiselle, a thousand times. I shall treasure this painting forever."

Zoë was touched by the woman's sincerity and was delighted by her pleasure in the painting. "I'll take it back to camp and when it's dry—which might take a day or two—Reynard will frame it."

Madame LeBlanc nodded. "Yes, he has my frame already. You will bring it, yes? I don't need to come?"

Zoë smiled at her eagerness. "Yes, I will." Because she was staying another week.

Later that afternoon, Reynard strolled into camp with his easel on his back and his large canvas holdall bulging, Hamish at his heels. "I've finished the LeBlanc painting," she told him.

"Excellent. May I look now?"

"Of course." She brought it out and gave it to him. He took it into the best light and examined it carefully, taking such a long time, she started to get quite nervous. Then he ran a hand through his thick, glossy hair and shook his head. "I don't know how you do it. This is marvelous, Vita. You are so talented."

She blushed, relieved and delighted by his praise.

He put it in the wagon. "I'll be able to frame it as soon as it's dry, along with the other paintings we've done. Tomorrow I'll string up a canvas to work under and remove the old paintings. I framed Gaudet's, but that was so he could show it to his friends, and thus drum up customers for us. But in general I prefer to frame them all in one go, rather than one at a time over a series of days. That's why I've collected the frames."

"You have?" She hadn't really taken much notice.

"Yes, I have half a dozen now, safely locked in the wagon, not to mention these." He patted the canvas holdall.

It seemed odd that so many people had old paintings they wished to have replaced, but Zoë didn't question it. Reynard obviously knew his market. He'd been doing this for quite some time, whereas until she'd met him, she had only ever painted people she knew, friends who could afford to have new frames specially made for their paintings. Poor people let nothing go to waste and reused everything.

In any case, her mind was not on work at the moment. Tonight she was going to invite Reynard to her bed. Earlier she'd bathed in the stream—she was almost down to the last of Clarissa's lovely soap—and washed her hair. The dinner was a chicken and vegetable stew, warming by the fire, and she'd opened a bottle of wine.

Her nerves were jumpy, skittering from one thought to another and back, but in a different part of her brain, deep down, she was calm. She'd made up her mind. Tonight she would invite Reynard into the wagon.

Soon she would have to return to London, leave this life and do her duty in England, but she would have this, another week with Reynard, a time to look back on and remember, something to keep her warm through cold English nights and possibly a cold English marriage. Something just for her, done without any feeling of obligation, just joy, her own private and personal joy.

She sat by the fire as he put the contents of the holdall in the large cupboard in the wagon and packed his painting things away. When he emerged, he stopped and gave her a long, thoughtful look.

"Is everything all right? You seem a little . . . *distraite*."

She felt herself blushing. "No, I'm fine. I, er, I bathed in the stream and washed my hair." She groaned to herself. Why did she have to tell him that?

He nodded and gave her a slow, intimate smile. "Then I suppose I should do the same." He reached into the wagon, pulled out soap, a towel and some fresh clothes. "Be back shortly. Keep an eye on that stew, will you?" A short time later she could hear splashing.

She closed her eyes and breathed deeply. Soon; it would be soon, she hoped.

Hamish, who hadn't followed him to the stream, sniffed hopefully at the pot with the stew in it. "No, Hamish, not for you, sweetheart," she told him, and placed the lid on the pot. He gave a lugubrious sigh and slumped dolefully to the ground. A moment later he sat up with his ears pricked and bounded away into the scrub. His dinner sorted.

Zoë moved the pot away from the fire. As if she could think of stew, knowing Reynard was a few yards away, naked in the stream. She sat, poking sticks into the fire, stirring sparks and wondering how she was going to say it.

"Dear Reynard, would you like to go to bed with me?" No, too blunt.

What about *"I've noticed that the nights have been getting colder"*? No, too much like farmer talk, discussing the weather.

What about *"Reynard, I like you very much and I think we should—"*

"Yeeeks!" she squeaked as two hands dropped lightly on her shoulders from behind, shattering her silent reverie.

"Sorry," he said, laughing. "I didn't mean to give you a fright."

"You startled me, that's all. I was miles away." The warmth from his hands soaked into her.

"So I see." He crouched down behind her, his hands still on her shoulders, and buried his nose in her hair. "Mm, your hair smells delicious. I did bathe, but I fear I won't be able to match that." He lifted her hair and feathered kisses along her nape, and she found herself arching back against him as tiny shivers of heat ran through her

"I did, however, manage a kind of shave, though without hot water, it's not very good."

She turned her head and looked back at him. "I don't mind," she said softly, and lightly rubbed her palm along his jawline, enjoying the faint texture of his bristles, the freshness of his skin. His hair smelled clean and damp. He rose, and she rose with him, turned in the circle of his arms and raised her face to his.

Chapter Seven

His eyes darkened, the flames of the fire reflected in them.

"Reynard," she whispered. He didn't move. Nervously she ran her tongue over her dry lips.

He made a sound, low in his throat, and cupped her cheek in his hand. His hand was strong, the skin firm and masculine, and she rubbed her cheek against his palm like a cat. His eyes were burning. She raised her face to him in mute invitation. He muttered something she didn't catch, but she forgot everything as he drew her close and claimed her mouth with his.

The kiss was sweet and tender at first, a quiet exploration. He pulled back slightly then and looked at her. "You know where this is going, don't you?"

She nodded, and pressed herself closer.

He resisted for a moment, then smoothed his thumb lightly in a gossamer caress over her lower lip. Her breath hitched. "Are you sure, Vita? Because if we go on like this, it won't stop at kissing." Her blood leapt at his words.

"Very sure." And she was. She'd been thinking about this for days, wanting it, dreaming of it. And now that one brief kiss had made her hungry for more, she didn't want to wait a minute longer. Her body was tingling, expectant. She stood on tiptoe, pulled his head down and kissed him.

He groaned and pulled her hard against him, then lavished her with tiny kisses: her face, her eyelids, down the line of her jaw. His fingers speared through her curls, tilting her head as, under his guidance, she parted her lips and he deepened the kiss.

Oh, the taste of him . . . She'd never imagined it could be like this. Hot. Darkly spicy. Dangerously addictive. It raced through her, flickering along her veins like fire. Every part of her was alive, responsive . . . even as she felt herself melting against him like thick, rich cream, like honey.

The moon drifted behind clouds, one moment basting the world in silver, and the next in darkness. The autumnal scent of drying leaves and damp earth was all around them, spiced with the faint acid tendrils of smoke from the dying fire. A time of change . . .

He looked down at her, stroking his thumbs along her jawline. She stood still, expectant, gazing back at him, her lovely eyes wide and dark in the dusky evening. And inviting. Her lips were full and moist. He swallowed, looking at them. His body tightened.

In the distance he heard a fox scream. She heard it too and smiled a little, acknowledging their shared understanding, inviting him to share it with her. Ah, but she was special, this woman. A gift.

Her skin was warm, moon-pale and silken to the touch. He lavished light, tender kisses on her at first, wanting to devour her but needing more to take his time, to savor every moment, every gesture. She was an innocent.

She smelled clean and sweet, like fresh-baked bread. Her mouth was warm and satin-soft like dark rose petals.

He brushed his mouth over hers and felt her breath hitch. Her lips parted slightly and he deepened the kiss.

She tasted like spiced, wine-dark honey, sweet, slightly sharp, addictive. She reached up and pulled him closer, returning his kisses eagerly, a little clumsily, driving him wild.

Slowly, unable to stop kissing, they moved together toward the caravan.

He opened the door. "After you, my lady." But before she could climb in, Hamish reappeared and shoved his cold nose in between them.

She laughed, saying, "Not inside, sweetheart," and for a second he thought she might be talking to him. But the dog flumped gloomily down in front of the steps and laid his head on his paws.

"He's keeping watch," she said, and turned back to him. Her eyes darkened and she ran her tongue over her lips. He swallowed. His body, already aroused, tightened. Silently she held out her hand to him and led him, stepping carefully over the sprawled dog, up the steps into the caravan. She'd made it ready, he saw, with everything tidy and the bed neatly turned back. Several candles were lit, throwing out small pools of golden light and dancing shadows.

He was glad she hadn't decided to do this in the dark. He ached to see her.

She was looking a little uncertain, so he kissed her again, and soon they were lying on the bed, kissing and kissing and kissing. He could never get enough of her, and she was all luscious heat and sweet, intoxicating acceptance. But he wasn't going to rush this, rush her. Her first time—their first time: it had to be special and it was up to him to make it so.

He pulled back and sat up on the edge of the bed. Her eyes were a little dazed, full of questions.

"Do you need help getting out of that dress?"

She blinked, and then gave a shaky laugh. "No, maids' dresses are not as complicated as ladies' ones. Just a drawstring here, and another one there." She pulled the ties at the neck and waist undone, and the neckline instantly drooped, revealing creamy skin and an enticing shadow of cleavage.

She wriggled off the bed, took a deep breath, pulled the dress off over her head and tossed it aside, leaving herself clad only in a worn, thin and many-patched chemise. The fabric was so thin he could see through it, see the dark V-shaped shadow at the apex of her thighs, and the rosy circles of her areolae. As he watched, her nipples lifted and tightened: small needy points of desire. He reached up and brushed his knuckles slowly across them. She shuddered and sat down suddenly on the bed. "Now you," she gasped. "Do you need help undressing?"

"No." He wouldn't have minded letting her undress him, but he was full and hard and didn't know how much longer he could wait.

He tossed his coat aside, pulled his shirt off over his head and tossed it aside too. His chest was bare—vagabond artists wore no undershirts—and he was very aware of her gaze running slowly and appreciatively over him. He sat on the edge of the bed, yanked off his boots and socks, then stood and reached for the buttons on the fall of his breeches.

They dropped to the floor. Her eyes widened. He was wearing cotton drawers—this vagabond artist did wear drawers—but they did nothing to disguise his very definite and insistent arousal.

She eyed it curiously. She didn't seem worried or anxious, which he might have expected from a virgin. But Vita was no ordinary girl.

He sat beside her on the bed, kissed her, slowly and leisurely, then bent and placed his mouth over her breast and, through the threadbare chemise, teased her nipple with his tongue. She gasped and arched and clutched his head to her. "Do that again."

Smiling, he obliged, until she was gasping and moving restlessly against his mouth. "Lift up," he said, and pulled off her chemise. He gazed at her for a long moment, devouring her with his eyes. She watched him watching her, her expression a little shy, a little uncertain.

"You are so beautiful," he murmured.

"Now you," she said, indicating his drawers.

He pulled them off and kicked them aside. It was her turn to gaze at him then, not at all shyly, but curious and fascinated.

"You are beautiful, too," she said.

He gave a huff of laughter. "Men aren't beautiful."

"You are to me." She put out a hand as if to touch him, then hesitated and glanced at him.

"Touch me however you like," he said, hoping his control would hold.

She ran a careful finger down the length of him, her eyes widening as his erection grew even more. He gritted his teeth as, with another glance at him for permission, she wrapped her fingers around the length of him and then squeezed very gently.

He moaned. She dropped him like a hot coal.

"It's all right," he assured her, his voice a little hoarse. "That was a pleasure moan."

Zoë gave him a doubtful glance. A pleasure moan? Was there such a thing? Or was he being tactful?

He must have seen her doubt, because the next minute he was pushing her gently back on the bed. "I'll show you."

He explored her then, thoroughly, with hands and mouth. He started with her breasts, licking and nibbling and teasing her nipples, which were already hard and aching, with his teeth. Shivers of heat, of indescribable sensations, shuddered through her, and she found herself writhing, at first pleasurably, but soon it was more than pleasure, almost pain, except it wasn't. She needed . . . she didn't know what, but she ached for it.

His hands were everywhere, caressing, arousing. He slipped his fingers between her thighs, and she stiffened. He soothed and stroked, and gradually she relaxed, but the more he stroked, alternately teasing and soothing, the tenser she became, writhing against his hand. The sensations built, first ripples washing through her body, then shudders racking her.

She heard a moan, and it wasn't from him, but she didn't care, she just wanted . . . needed . . . craved . . . she didn't know what.

He moved over her then, and her legs fell apart, trembling with anticipation. With need. She felt him, heavy and blunt at her entrance, and her body clenched with recognition and longing.

"Sorry about this," he murmured, and before she could collect her scattered wits to ask him what he meant, he entered her with a long, hard thrust.

A sharp pain shot though her and she gasped. He lay, buried within her for a moment. The pain faded to a tiny sting, and she felt her body stretching to accommodate him.

His fingers dropped to where they were joined and resumed their cunning dance, soothing and arousing, and before she knew it her body was closing around him, clenching, tightening.

He began to pull out of her. "No," she gasped and locked her legs around him, hauling him closer, taking him deeper.

Then he was moving inside her, plunging . . . thrusting . . . driving her . . . to frantic need. Desperation. And ecstasy.

Sensation built and built. She shuddered and thrashed around him. He gave a final, husky groan, and she felt a gush of warmth within her. She trembled on the pinnacle of . . . something . . . and then . . . and then . . .

* * *

She woke slowly, golden shards of sunlight piercing the interior of the caravan. She lay curled on her side, Reynard's body curved around her, skin against skin, one arm across her waist. Protective. Possessive.

She lay quietly, taking stock of how she felt. Alive, she felt gloriously alive, warm and safe and deliciously relaxed.

Parts of her body ached a little, but they were small aches, she decided, and they made her happy. She'd made love with Reynard, and it had been like nothing she had expected and yet everything she'd unknowingly craved. It had been exciting. A little bit shocking. The raw intimacy of it. And slightly . . . animal, the way she'd lost all control. As had he, she thought. But then, they were all animals, in a way, weren't they? And she felt wonderful. Freed in some fashion, she wasn't sure how.

She lay quietly, enjoying the feeling of the man breathing soft and steady beside her, reliving the night before. This was how she wanted to wake every morning for the rest of her life.

There wasn't just one bubble of happiness in her chest now, there were dozens. Like champagne, like soap bubbles filled with sunshine. She'd made up her mind: she was staying. She would live with this man, this funny, charming, twisty, kind man, with all his stories.

Her sisters would understand, she told herself. They'd be disappointed, but once they saw how happy he made her, they would understand.

She felt him stirring, and turned in his embrace and watched his eyes open and the light come into them. He smiled, slow, warm, intimate. "Good morning, Vita my sweet. How do you feel?"

"Wonderful." She kissed him, and would have done more, but he pulled back slightly.

"Not this morning, love. You're still too tender. Besides—" Her stomach rumbled and he laughed. "There, your stomach spoke for you. Stay there and relax. I'll make breakfast and bring it to you here." He kissed her again and then slid out of bed and pulled on his clothes.

She lay back in a dreamy haze of contentment, hearing him move around the camp, getting the fire going, talking to Hamish, feeding Rocinante.

Some time later the door opened and he entered, carrying a plate and a steaming mug. "Here you are, my lady, scrambled eggs on toast and a mug of tea."

She sat up, tucking the bedclothes around her, feeling a little self-conscious to be naked when he was fully dressed. He fetched his own breakfast and they ate it together, planning the day.

It was a little disconcerting to realize that while her world had changed completely, his seemed to be going on as usual. But she supposed that was what life was like. It couldn't all be lovemaking. Unfortunately. He had a living to earn. She understood that.

"I have one more old painting to collect," he said, "then this afternoon I'll set about removing them from their frames and replacing them with the new paintings. People will be anxious to see them displayed in all their golden glory." He collected the plates and set them on a narrow bench. "Do you want to come with me?"

She shook her head. "No, I think I'll stay and have a bath."

He smiled. "I wish I could provide you with a proper hot bath. Perhaps another time. Meanwhile, the stream is clean and bracing. Do you want me to stay while you bathe?"

"No, it's all right. Hamish will look after me."

His smile deepened. "I wasn't thinking of privacy, but you're right, it's too cold to spend time frolicking in a stream. In summer, now"—he bent and gave her a swift kiss—"it's a pleasure we can look forward to." He leapt lightly down from the van and disappeared.

She lay there for a while, dreaming in her warm nest of bedclothes, then finally gathered herself and her clothing together—and the sheet that showed a few spots of blood—and headed for the stream. He was right, it was very cold, so she bathed swiftly, using the last of her sister's lovely soap. Hamish watched, his expression mildly bemused at this unnatural fondness for soap and water.

She washed the sheet, scrubbing out the bloodstains—cold water was good for that, at least—then wrung it out and draped it over the line Reynard had strung behind the caravan, along with her underclothes. Then she waited for Reynard to return.

He returned late in the afternoon, walking into the camp, whistling, his large canvas bag slung over his shoulder. He greeted her with a smile and a kiss that left her shivering with desire. She couldn't wait for tonight.

First he set up a kind of trestle table, then collected some of the paintings he'd stored in the caravan, stacking them on their sides, large paintings in ornate gold-leafed frames.

Then, working methodically, he placed the largest painting face down on the trestle table and removed first the backing, then the painting from its frame. He carefully lifted out the canvas and laid it aside, face up.

Curiously Zoë wandered over to look at it—and gasped.

He glanced at her and gave a quick smile. "What do you think?"

She didn't answer. She wasn't sure what she thought. The painting was old, beautifully painted and undoubtedly valuable. It depicted a sumptuously dressed man with flowing dark locks and a pointed beard. He was reclining comfortably on a chair, partially wrapped in a red velvet cloak. You could almost feel the rich softness of the velvet. Scattered carelessly around him were several small statues, a bust, a globe and various tapestries and paintings—the possessions of a rich, cultured man.

She wasn't sure, but she thought it might be by Charles Le Brun. She'd seen several of his paintings in her studies with Lucy in the last few years.

How had a painting of this quality ended up in a farmer's house? And why on earth would a farmer be willing to swap it for a much less skillful painting? Reynard's work was quite good, but this was by the hand of a master.

Reynard straightened and saw her still staring. He gestured at the painting. "What do you think?"

"I'm not sure. Is this the painting you got from your bull farmer?"

"Yes. Isn't it a beauty?"

She frowned. "It's magnificent. But I don't understand. Where did he get it from?"

He shrugged carelessly. "No idea. I didn't ask. Not my business."

She said slowly, "I'm not sure, but I think it's quite valuable."

He gave her an enigmatic look. "You think so, eh?"

She nodded, gaining confidence in her judgment. "I'm sure of it. So if the farmer didn't want it, why didn't he sell it? For actual money?"

Again Reynard made a careless gesture. "Who knows how people's minds work? Maybe it was too much trouble—presumably he'd need to go to Paris to find a buyer, and that's a long way to travel. And even if he did, where would a simple country farmer start? The point is, he didn't want it—said he was sick of looking at some rich old dead aristo showing off his treasures and would rather have a good honest painting of what's important to him—himself and his bull. So he was happy to swap an old painting for a new one—as long as he kept the frame. Me, I don't look gift horses in the mouth."

She gave him a troubled look. "But doesn't he realize it might be worth a lot of money?"

Reynard shrugged. "It's not for me to tell him what to do. I offered to swap old paintings for new, and he liked the bargain."

"But . . ."

He turned away. "I'm not going to argue about this, Vita. He gave me this painting, and in return I will give him one he much prefers." He turned to the next ornately framed painting and set about removing the old painting that was in it.

Zoë watched, even more troubled. It was also valuable, she was sure. She didn't recognize the artist, but again, it portrayed people she was sure could have nothing to do with a rustic farmer: a family group this time, the woman in silks and embroidered satins, laden with jewels, her hair piled high and powdered. Her husband, too, wore satin and lace and an ornate powdered wig. Several beautifully dressed children were posed around them, children she was sure had never lived on a farm in their lives.

"But you can't do that! These are valuable paintings, I'm certain of it."

"Value is in the eye of the beholder." His voice was indifferent.

"That's nonsense and you know it. You're cheating them! These people are poor and unsophisticated, and you are taking advantage of their ignorance. They haven't the least idea of the value of what they're trading!" She'd seen how poor the local people were, having to work so hard— even the children—just to make ends meet. And yet they'd been so generous to her and Reynard, sharing food with them. And he was depriving them of money she was sure they needed. How could he?

He straightened and said in a harsh voice, "Use your brain, Vita! Where do you think these poor ignorant country folk got paintings like this in the first place?"

She stared at him dumbly. How would she know?

He picked up the next framed painting waiting to be swapped over and began to remove the backing. "This one came from your beloved widow, Madame LeBlanc. Do you know what she said the other day when we made our deal? She told me in no uncertain terms that she wanted it out of the house. It was a wedding gift from her husband's father, she said, and it had hung in her house until her husband died—apparently he was very proud of it. But she couldn't bear to look at it, and after the funeral she took it down and put it in the back of a dark cupboard. Do you know why?"

Zoë shook her head, puzzled.

"Because it made her feel guilty, that's why! Think about it, Vita. It was a gift from her father-in-law. Where would a man like that—a simple ignorant countryman—get a painting of such quality?" He made a wide furious gesture. "Think! What was happening here thirty-odd years ago?"

"Oh my God," she whispered, realizing. "The Revolution." Of course. She should have realized it earlier, especially having seen what had happened to her mother's château. But somehow she hadn't connected the living people she'd met with "the mob" who'd attacked the château.

"Yes, the Revolution. These poor ignorant country folk you're so worried about *looted* these paintings from the homes of aristocrats. Oh, maybe not all of them, but they would all know from whence these paintings came. That's why Madame LeBlanc wanted to be rid of it. She felt guilty just looking at it.

"She would have been a child at the time, but she knows what happened, and she has a conscience. So she traded a painting, a looted family portrait that she couldn't wait to get rid of, in exchange for the one you did of her and her children." He removed the old painting from its frame and brandished it. "This is the one she traded! A family portrait: mother, father and two children. She's a good woman, and she didn't want it in her house, not with those two little children looking out at her from the frame. Can you blame her?"

Zoë glanced at the painting and felt the blood drain from her face. She staggered, suddenly dizzy. Oh God. She knew those faces.

There was her mother as a child, sweet-faced, wide-eyed and a little bored from having to sit still for so long. Clutched in her arms was the doll, Marianne, in blue silk and lace, with her head still intact. And there was Maman's brother, Philippe, and her parents, Zoë's own grandparents, who had been guillotined during the revolution.

This, the painting he was brandishing so angrily, was of her family. She had no doubt of it. Maman had painted a similar painting from memory. It was back in London, in her room at Lady Scattergood's. Maman had talked about watching the painter working. It had inspired her, she'd said.

Feeling sick to her stomach, Zoë gazed at the painting. How stupid was she not to have realized? She'd seen for herself how Maman's home had been attacked and looted. And this painting was from there. And nice Madame Le-Blanc's father-in-law had been one of the looters. And probably farmer Gaudet. And who knew who else she'd met—and liked!—in this area had paintings stolen from Maman's home?

Old paintings for new. It had seemed so simple, she hadn't even questioned it.

Acid roiled in her throat. She stood, frozen, unable to think or speak. The dog must have sensed her distress, for she felt a cold nose nudging her hand and a warm body leaning against her. She fondled his ears, her mind miles away.

There was a long silence. Then Reynard said in a gentler voice, "I've shocked you, I see. It didn't occur to you that these paintings were looted?"

Unable to speak or drag her eyes off the painting, she just shook her head.

He turned the painting around and busied himself removing it from the frame.

"What will you do with them?" she asked when she was able to speak.

"Take them to Paris." He removed her mother and grandparents from the frame and draped it carefully with the other one he'd removed, a large square of protective fabric between them.

Yes, she saw now how it was that he could make a living. He would sell these in Paris for a great sum.

What he was doing was still wrong, she felt sure, but now that she knew the whole story, the issue was not so clear-cut. He was swindling these people, cheating them out of the money they could get for these valuable paintings.

And yet . . . they'd stolen—looted!—the paintings in the first place. Part of the mob that had caused a little girl to flee for her life. Committing arson and who knew what other crimes as well.

But that was in the past, more than thirty years ago. It was a war, a revolution; were people still to be held accountable for the horrors of that time? And yet, should they still profit from those horrors today? Should he, who had fought in the army against the forces of Napoleon? Did not these paintings belong to France? If not to the descendants of those who had owned them? Assuming they still lived.

Contradictory thoughts tumbled madly around in her head. She didn't know what to think, couldn't think at all. She felt sick to her stomach.

"I'm going to bed," she said weakly.

He nodded, his expression compassionate. "I'm sorry to have distressed you."

She waved his apology aside and opened the wagon door. He looked at her, a question in his eyes. She shook her head. No, she would not have him in her bed tonight. He nodded understandingly, his eyes sympathetic. "Life is not so simple, is it, Vita?"

He had no idea how shattered she felt.

"Put these inside, will you?" He handed her the rolled-up paintings and the canvas bag containing more paintings. "I'll lock them away tomorrow. I don't want them out in the night air."

Numbly she held out her hand and received them, including her family, all neatly rolled up ready to be sold to some Parisian dealer. She wanted to scream, she wanted to weep. She ached with it all.

She climbed inside the wagon and shut the door. Then, for the first time in days, she bolted it.

She curled up miserably on the bed, feeling sick, disheartened, bitter.

What a fool she'd been. Reynard was not the man she'd thought he was. Oh, he was charming and handsome and the rest, but more importantly he was a cheat, a swindler. Cheating people out of the true value of their paintings. And who knew what else? She'd believed him about those imaginary three wives, but now she wondered. Had she believed him because she *wanted* to?

And the local people she'd met here weren't the nice, friendly, generous people she'd thought they were. They, or their parents, had attacked her mother's home, sending her fleeing for her life as they destroyed it, looting it, smashing, burning—even guillotining her little doll, no doubt in frustration over not catching Maman.

It was all too distressing to contemplate.

Why had she not *see*? Not even guessed, or wondered?

Because she was a fool, letting herself be dazzled by a good-looking man with a—yes, a seductive line of chat and appealing, engaging ways. And she'd fallen for it.

Had he not decided to remove those paintings from their frames this evening, she might, even now, be in here with him, on this very bed, making love.

The thought made her feel quite sick.

She would not stay another day. She would meet up with the miller's son at dawn, and by the time Reynard was awake, she'd be on her way to Nantes and the *diligence*. She would never see Reynard again.

Reynard. Fox. Cunning. A warning she'd been too stupid, too dazzled to see.

She slept very little that night. For most of the evening, she lay on the bed, listening to Reynard move about the camp, talking nonsense in English to the dog. In the past that sort of thing would have made her smile or giggle, would have made her want him more.

Now it simply flayed her.

Aware that she would have to catch the miller's son at dawn, she barely slept, waking every hour or so, peering cautiously out at the night sky. It was hard to tell what time it was. She had to guess by the angle of the moon. Thank God it wasn't a cloudy night.

It was still dark when she rose and prepared to creep out of the camp. She'd packed her bundle earlier. She picked it up, then put it down again. Moving very slowly and carefully—he was asleep under the wagon—she removed the painting of her mother's family from the rolled-up canvases he'd passed her. Thank goodness he hadn't already locked them away.

She rerolled the other paintings, then rolled up her mother's painting, wrapped it in a protective cloth, then tied it in string.

Guilt pecked at her. It wasn't stealing, she told herself. This was her mother's painting. It was hers by right.

It wasn't stealing to take from thieves, she reminded herself.

But she still felt uncomfortable about it. Even though she *knew* she shouldn't.

She took the remaining sausage from the tin-lined cupboard and tucked it into a fold in the bundle, then opened the door and stepped cautiously down, her bundle in one hand, the rolled painting in the other. The moonlight was faint. The camp was all gray shadows.

Oh lord, Hamish! she thought despairingly as the dog scrambled to his feet and came toward her. She dropped her bundle and held up her hand, whispering, "Sit."

Blessedly, the dog sat.

Ever since they'd adopted him, he'd slept under the wagon, beside Reynard, lying along his back. She'd thought it was cute before: now it had the potential to be a disaster. If Reynard woke . . .

"Stay," she whispered. The dog watched her curiously, his tail gently thumping the dust, but thankfully, he didn't make a sound. She peered under the wagon to where Reynard slept. He hadn't moved. She breathed again.

"Stay, Hamish. Stay," she whispered, gesturing for him to stay—and praying he would, for once, obey.

The dog tilted his head in a silent question.

Zoë picked up her bundle and crept out of the campsite. Once out of sight of it—and hopefully out of hearing—she glanced back. And saw a large, scruffy, beautiful, loyal animal following her. "Oh, Hamish, no," she murmured, but she'd prepared for this to happen.

He trotted up to her, his tail waving gently like a plume. She gave him a last enthusiastic embrace, finishing with a good scritch around the ears, then bent and kissed him on the forehead. "I'm sorry, darling, but I can't take you, not on the *diligence*. I'm sorry. You be good for Reynard, won't you? He'll look after you, I know." It was one thing—the only thing—she now trusted about Reynard, that he would take care of his animals.

She took out the sausage. The dog's nose twitched. "Here, Hamish, fetch!" She hurled the sausage deep into a dense thicket of bushes. Hamish happily bounded off after it.

Zoë picked up her bundle, and half-blinded by tears, she ran toward the village.

Chapter Eight

Reynard woke later than usual: the sun was well up in the sky. It had taken him a long time to fall asleep; he'd been kept awake by thoughts that kept circling in his mind. He shouldn't have let her go off to bed like that. He should have explained his point of view better, should have trusted her.

Not let her stagger into the wagon early, looking so devastated.

She was an honest girl. He'd seen that from the first.

He'd already decided to come clean to her and explain everything. He'd planned to do it that evening, by the fire, which was always so conducive to good conversation.

If only he hadn't started removing the old paintings from their frames. It had totally disrupted his plan. She'd been shocked, deeply shocked, and terribly dismayed.

And he'd been so thrown, so disturbed by the strength of her reaction—and by her clear repudiation of him—that he'd just let her go to bed. Instead of which he should have sat her down by the fire, given her a glass of wine and explained.

He'd been a fool not to tell her everything in the first place. But he hadn't known her then, and previous experience with women had taught him not to trust first impressions.

But Vita was different.

He wanted her, wanted her to be part of his life. Oh, he knew there would be problems, serious ones, but he didn't care. She was what he wanted.

He lit the fire and put the water on to heat. Where was she, anyway? She was usually up by now. Though, come to think of it, she'd probably slept badly, too. The thing that had finally helped him to sleep was the warm weight of Hamish, lying against his spine.

He glanced around, suddenly aware that the dog was missing. No doubt off hunting for his breakfast. Reynard busied himself preparing breakfast.

The water boiled, but instead of making tea, he decided it was time to shave. If he was going to put the question to her, it would surely be better not to look like a shabby, unshaven vagabond.

He shaved, enjoying the feel of a clean, smooth jaw. He boiled a fresh pot of water but delayed making the tea. He didn't want it to stew, and she still hadn't emerged from the wagon. She wasn't usually such a late sleeper. Was she ill?

Or perhaps still upset after last night's quarrel?

He knocked on the door. "Vita?"

There was no answer. He knocked again, but . . . nothing. He tried the door. It swung open. But last night she'd bolted it against him; he'd heard the snick of the bolt—felt it—and was ashamed at his harsh words.

That wounded look in her eyes when she realized the paintings were looted, that people she'd known and liked had looted them from the homes of aristos. It had flicked him on the raw, and he'd been defensive and somehow angry. He'd spoken harshly, he realized, partly in anger at her expression of wounded innocence, of silent accusation. How could she not have known the history of her own country?

Though, of course, she was young. And most people preferred to sweep the ugliness of the past under the carpet, pretending it had never happened. And that none of them had been involved. They did, however, like the advances that had come with the revolution, the fairer laws, especially for poor people.

Of course he hadn't explained what he was doing, just that he swapped old paintings for new. But how had she not guessed?

That look in her eyes as she'd stared at Madame Le-Blanc's painting, it still haunted him.

Was she perhaps washing in the stream, as was her habit? Had he somehow missed her exit from the wagon?

He climbed into the wagon and looked around.

Everything was neat and clean. None of her things were hanging on their usual hooks. Nothing of hers was visible. She'd gone. But on the neatly made bed lay the half-rolled paintings. He picked them up. And swore.

There should have been three paintings, but there were only two. He could hardly believe his eyes. One of the valuable old paintings was missing—the one from the widow LeBlanc.

She'd *stolen* it! He checked again, and yes, it was true: his "honest" little artist had vanished, taking with her one of his more valuable paintings. Damn it all!

Thank goodness the others had been locked in the cupboard.

Though, why hadn't she taken the other two paintings? Did she think she was entitled to that one because she had painted its replacement? They never had come to any agreement. Why hadn't she talked to him about it?

He sat down heavily on the bunk, holding the roll of canvas in nerveless hands. How could she? He'd trusted her. Been sure they were fall— becoming closer.

He knew she had secrets, that one or two things in her tale didn't add up, but everyone had secrets. He did himself, but he'd been about to lay himself open to her, tell her everything, even to make her an offer he'd never in his life offered to any woman.

What a fool!

She'd accused him of cheating, of swindling the "poor ignorant peasants"—and he'd actually felt a twinge of guilt—but she was the one who'd turned out to be the cheat, the damned little thief!

He searched the wagon, but nothing else was missing. She hadn't even left him a note! She probably couldn't even write. But she could deceive and betray—almost as well as she could paint, he thought savagely.

She'd certainly made a fool of him. She'd probably planned this all along.

He thought of her face after he'd explained the true source of the paintings, the way she'd climbed into the wagon as if deep in shock. Hah! What an actress she was.

He stepped woodenly down from the wagon, baffled, betrayed and furious. But not heartbroken, he told himself. No, certainly not that. She was a deceitful baggage! He'd made a lucky escape—yes, that was it, he was relieved.

Heartbroken? How ridiculous.

Hamish appeared in his usual wraithlike manner, bounded across the clearing and leaned heavily against Reynard's thigh.

Reynard crouched down to pat him. "She's gone, did you know?" The dog gazed at him with a mournful expression, then licked his chin.

"Thank you. Yes, I shaved. Not much point, though. It was going to be an occasion." He huffed a dry, humorless laugh. "I suppose it was an occasion after all, just not the sort I'd planned on." The dog sighed.

Reynard stood. "Come on, she can't have gone far. Let's go after her."

When had she left? Before dawn? Probably. No doubt it

was when he'd finally gone to sleep after tossing and turning most of the night.

He hurried into the village, the dog trotting at his heels, but there was no sign of her.

The innkeeper's wife was sweeping the cobbles outside the inn. "Looking for your cousin?" she said. "She's long gone, monsieur. She left with the miller's son. I saw them leaving just after dawn."

"The miller's son?" He'd never heard a thing about this miller's son. Who was he and how did Vita know him?

"Yes, he was giving her a lift to Nantes. You have no need to worry, monsieur; he's a simple lad, but good and reliable. She wanted to catch the *diligence*. It passes through the town every Thursday around noon."

So that was it. He'd never catch her. Even if he hired a horse and rode *ventre à terre* after her, she'd be almost in Nantes by now, and it was maybe a half hour before noon. She was gone.

Even if he went to Paris to look for her, how would he find her? A maidservant in Paris? Needle in a haystack.

Besides, he had commitments here, paintings to paint and exchange. He didn't need to waste time wondering about the light-fingered baggage who'd made a fool of him.

She'd gone to Paris. Did she know anyone there, or was her so-called ignorance of Paris another lie? He hoped for her sake she did have somewhere safe to go.

Not that he was worried about her. Not at all.

It was just that the city was a dangerous place for a beautiful young woman. Any young woman. Even a scheming, untrustworthy baggage.

"There you are!" Lucy, Lady Thornton, pulled Zoë into a relieved, slightly tearful embrace. "We were getting so worried about you. Gerald was about to drive down to Château Treffier in search of you."

Zoë pulled back and stared at Lucy. "But didn't Marie tell you—"

Lucy snorted. "Marie is a good girl, and a terrible liar. She told us the story you told her to tell us, and gave us your letter, but I could see at once that you were off on one of your starts!"

Zoë tried not to smile. "One of my starts?"

"Oh, don't give me that butter-wouldn't-melt look," Lucy said severely, and hugged her again. "I know you. And if you were so desperate to visit your mother's birthplace, why on earth didn't you tell us? Gerald would have taken you there."

"I did ask you."

"No, you mentioned it *once*."

"And Gerald told me the Château de Chantonney was a ruin, and you said it would be too, too melancholy a place to visit and so far away it wasn't worth it." And besides, he was so busy these days, she didn't like to trouble him. Lucy and Gerald had already done so much for her.

"And was it? Melancholy, I mean," Lucy asked as she led Zoë upstairs. She stopped to give orders to the housekeeper and then continued, "I'm going to put you straight into a bath and have those dreadful clothes burned. You look a fright!"

Zoë grinned. "I think I look pretty good for someone who's had to wash in a cold stream the last week or so."

Lucy shuddered. "Serves you right. Had you just explained—but there, it's all water under the bridge now, and you're home safe, and I won't say another word. So, was it too, too melancholy?"

"It was, but I needed to go there and see for myself. I don't regret anything"—she glanced at Lucy's face—"except causing you anxiety."

"And Gerald," Lucy added. "You know how he takes his responsibilities so seriously."

"Yes, I'll apologize to him when he gets home. But I

honestly didn't think you'd worry. I did explain in my letter that I'd be fine."

"Yes, and when I questioned Marie, I could tell at once that you hadn't told us the full story. And when Gerald questioned her, she burst into tears and said you were planning to walk wherever you were going—she didn't know where—by yourself. By yourself!—dressed in her old clothes!"

"Gerald made her cry?" Zoë began indignantly.

"Don't be silly! You know what a gentleman he is. The truth is, the poor girl was worried sick about you, certain something dreadful would happen to you and that we'd hold her responsible and throw her out on her ear to sink or swim on her own in the big, bad city."

"But I told her you'd take good care of her."

"And of course we did. But she's a good, responsible, truthful girl."

Zoë sighed. "I suppose I owe her an apology, too. Where is she, by the way?"

"Out shopping with one of the kitchen maids. I'll send her up to you when she gets back. By then I hope you'll look more like yourself, although what we'll do about your complexion I have no idea."

Zoë put a hand to her cheek. "My complexion?"

"Frightfully brown, my dear. You've been out in the sun too much." She glanced at the cylinder that Zoë had just placed on the bed. "I suppose that contains paintings. You managed to get some work done, then?"

"Yes. I'll show you later." Zoë couldn't wait to show Lucy the painting of her mother as a child. But she needed to think about how to present it. She didn't want to mention Reynard or what he'd been doing. She wasn't sure why. Partly she didn't want anyone to know that she'd spent a week alone with a man, entirely unchaperoned. But more than anything, she didn't want to talk about how she'd felt about him. Lucy was far too perceptive and would have no inhibitions about asking awkward questions. And how she felt about Reynard, well, that was still too raw a wound.

A knock came on the door.

"Ah, here's the water for your bath," Lucy said. "Come down for luncheon when you're clean and dressed. And then, Miss Gadabout, I will want to hear everything, all your adventures."

A short time later Marie returned and had a tearful re union with Zoë. "Oh, mademoiselle, I'm so sorry I told, but I was so worried. And milor' and milady have been so kind."

Zoë reassured her, and while Marie helped her to dress in blessedly clean clothes, she gave an animated account of her journey to Paris, and all the amazing sights she had seen since she'd arrived. "Always I was told that people in the city were wicked and ungodly, mademoiselle, but it's not true! Some of them are, yes, to be sure, but everyone I have met, from the butcher to the greengrocer and the people at the market—and milor' and milady's servants—everyone has been so good and kind to an ignorant girl from the country."

Over luncheon, Zoë gave Lucy an edited account of her adventures, and then, when Gerald came home for dinner that evening, she repeated it all again.

Lucy listened, and at the end of her recitation, said shrewdly, "There's a man involved in this somewhere, I'm sure of it."

Zoë, fighting a blush, said, "Well, yes. I'm surprised Marie didn't tell you about the despicable Monsieur Etienne." She told them all about him, from his first surreptitious pinches to the final dramatic showdown. She made such a good story of it that by the end they were both laughing—though Gerald was heard to mutter that if that blasted Etienne ever showed his face in Paris, he'd make the swine regret he was ever born.

Then she showed them the painting of her mother as a child, with her grandparents and uncle. Inevitably, this time there were a few tears in the telling.

"But you see now why I had to go."

Gerald frowned. "You don't mean you found this just lying around at the Château de Chantonney?"

Zoë swallowed. "No, of course not, not after all this time. It was actually an amazing coincidence, a lucky accident. After I left the château, I met some of the people living in the area. There was a woman, a widow with three children, and she had this painting. I spent a few days with her. Her late father-in-law had given it to her as a wedding present, but she must have known where it came from and had never liked having it in her house. She kept it in a cupboard." It was the truth, sort of. Just not the whole truth.

She hurried on, trying to gloss over the holes in her story. "We made an exchange—I did a painting of her and her children, and she gave me this."

"Good heavens!" Gerald exclaimed. "You mean she just gave it to you?"

"Yes, we got talking and I said I was a painter. I showed her some drawings in my sketchbook, and then she fetched this one and showed it to me. I recognized it at once. Maman had painted something similar from memory, and I knew that was her beloved doll, Marianne." She pointed to the doll in the painting, but didn't tell them what had happened to the doll.

"So then we made a bargain—my painting of the widow and her children in exchange for this one that she didn't want. She told me, in fact, that she was glad to be rid of it." Madame LeBlanc had actually said that to Reynard, but that was a moot point.

"What an amazing story," Lucy said. "And what incredible luck for you."

Zoë smiled. The way she'd told it, finding that particular

painting was an incredible coincidence, but it wasn't when one considered that Reynard's whole strategy was to gather as many paintings as he could that had been looted from the Château de Chantonney and any other grand houses in the area. As one painting out of a dozen or more that he'd retrieved so far, it was not nearly so coincidental.

She'd worked out his plan, his strategy, on the long journey by *diligence* back to Paris. It was clever, but she still felt it was dishonest. Though, was it really dishonest to cheat people out of profiting from paintings that had been stolen—looted—in the first place? Even though it had happened several decades ago?

Her thoughts and feelings about him were still a great tangle of contradictions. Painful ones. Had he been furious when she left? Or hurt?

If only he'd been the man she'd imagined he was. But he wasn't. He was a cheat and a swindler.

Though, what did that make her? It wasn't the same, she told herself. This painting was of her family. She, more than anyone, had the right to it. And Madame LeBlanc was satisfied, so it was just Reynard who would be angry.

And she didn't care about him. Or his feelings. Not a bit.

She was going to forget all about Reynard. In fact, she'd quite forgotten him already. Reynard? Who was that? Nobody, that's who.

The unprincipled rat.

After two hours of trying to be coolheaded and businesslike and refusing to think about a certain beautiful, deceitful, light-fingered baggage, Reynard packed up his paints, hitched Rocinante to the wagon and drove to the widow LaBlanc's farm, where he asked her and her children, in exchange for a handsome sum, to look after his horse and his dog until he returned. He had urgent business in Paris, he told her.

The widow nodded sympathetically. "Yes, monsieur, I heard she had run off to Paris."

"Run off? Nothing of the sort. She lives there. With my uncle and aunt," he added, recalling that he'd claimed Vita as a cousin. "But I'm not concerned about her. My trip to Paris is purely for business purposes."

"Yes, of course, monsieur," the woman said, clearly humoring him. "I hope you find her. Paris is no place for a young girl."

"My going to Paris has nothing to do with Vita. Nothing at all."

"No, monsieur, of course not," she said in an annoyingly soothing voice. "You will find her, I'm sure of it."

In the village he hired a horse and rode to Nantes, where, the *diligence* being not expected for another week, he hired an elderly chaise for an exorbitant sum and drove in stages to Paris. It took forever.

He hoped to hell that she did have someone to go to in Paris.

He needed her to be safe. And when he was sure she was, then he would . . . what? Strangle her. Probably.

He actually did have business in Paris, though he could have taken care of it at any time; there was no urgency. Not wanting to leave them behind, he'd brought the paintings, a thick, heavy roll of valuable canvases.

He made his way first to a small gallery. A bell jangled as he entered. A small elderly man with a neat, pointed beard came forward, smiling. "Reynard, my friend, I'm delighted to see you."

Reynard gave a wry laugh. "You're delighted to see what I've brought you, Gaston, you rogue."

The little man spread his hands in a very Gallic gesture. "But of course. You bring me such delights, so why not?" He locked the door, saying, "Come through to the back room and show me what you have."

An hour later, Gaston having almost exhausted his repertoire of extravagant compliments, they returned to the main part of the gallery. "Are you sure you won't—" Gaston began.

Reynard laughed. "Absolutely not. You know my conditions."

Gaston's narrow shoulders drooped. "I know, but it is so wasteful. What do you do now?" the Frenchman asked as the two men shook hands. "Back to the hunt?"

Reynard shook his head. "Not just yet. I have business in the city first."

"Then *bon chance*, my friend."

Good luck? Reynard thought as he walked away. It was an impossible task, finding one lone female in a city of thousands. But he had to try.

He'd taken one of his drawings of her—he was surprised how many he had—and then used watercolors to color it in—especially her midnight hair and beautiful green eyes. Getting the right shade for those eyes had been more difficult than he'd thought. But they were unforgettable—she was unforgettable. He was sure people would remember seeing her.

He went to the *diligence* office, showed several people her picture and asked whether they'd seen her. The sixth person he spoke to recognized her. "Yes, monsieur, the young lady did arrive on the *diligence*. When? I do not recall exactly which day—we are very busy here, monsieur, with coaches arriving day and night from all corners of the country—but certainly it was in the last week. I remember the so-pretty young lady. Where did she go? Oh, that I could not say, monsieur. I think she hired a cab, but which one and where it was going, I could not say. But she seemed to know her way around."

That should have reassured him. If she'd hired a cab with confidence, she must have had somewhere safe to go to, but strangely it made him angrier. More lies, and he'd thought her so honest.

With the reluctant assistance of Gaston, the gallery owner, he'd made a list of all the galleries and dealers where someone might try to sell a valuable old painting. He'd had to work to assure Gaston that he wasn't in search of an alternative source to take the paintings, that he was trying to track down a particular painting that had been stolen from him.

He still couldn't understand why she hadn't taken the other paintings as well, but that didn't matter now.

He tramped from one end of the city to the other, visiting gallery after gallery and dealers who dealt privately, starting with the less reputable ones. If a young woman arrived with a loose but valuable canvas, the more respectable ones would instantly smell a rat and send her packing. Assuming that she knew how to sell a painting in the first place.

She probably would, he thought. She'd recognized the Charles Le Brun portrait at a glance, after all. She knew a lot more about painting and artists than she'd let on.

But none of the people he questioned admitted to recognizing the girl in the picture, and every single one of them claimed not to have seen the painting he described to them—though if he recovered it, they would be very interested in discussing a price.

It was all very frustrating. He couldn't tell if they were telling him the truth or were lying to cover up a disreputable transaction.

By the end of the day, he was utterly fed up. He knew searching for her in Paris would be like searching for a needle in a haystack, so why had he bothered? But he wasn't prepared to give up yet.

He returned to his hotel, ate a good meal and had an early night.

The next morning he rose early, made a hearty breakfast and then set out to continue his search for Vita. He started with employment agencies. She'd claimed to be a lady's maid, and though he suspected that was a lie, too, it was worth checking.

But again, he had no luck. It seemed that employment agencies, or at least the dozen or so he visited, were universally run by hatchet-faced gorgons, who eyed him suspiciously— some through a lorgnette, some merely down a long, disdainful nose—sniffed at the picture he showed them of Vita and informed him in freezing tones that they ran "a *respectable* agency, monsieur, providing employment for deserving, decent, virtuous and hard-working females, not *that* sort of girl at all!" Several ended their blistering dismissal with variations on "You are clearly in search of *quite* another sort of establishment, so I will thank you to begone, monsieur!"

That inspired him to visit those other sorts of establishments, but the madams in charge were just as unhelpful and equally irritating. They questioned him closely—some with ill-concealed amusement—as to how he had lost his young woman in the first place—and such a pretty one, too—which made him stiffen outwardly while squirming inside.

They looked at the picture of Vita and offered him girls that they assured him would be just as good, if not better. "We have blondes, brunettes or redheads—even girls with green eyes—all just as pretty as that one, and all extremely amenable to whatever monsieur desires of them. You can take your pick, monsieur."

In vain he tried to explain that he didn't want a girl who *looked like* Vita, he wanted *her*. Upon which the various madams shrugged indifferently and dismissed him.

He walked along the riverbank, accosting complete strangers, showing them the picture, to no avail.

He tried the main markets, visited the more popular parks, the streets where there were the kinds of shops that might attract a young woman who had come into money recently, but to no avail.

But despite his lack of success—or perhaps because of it—he kept seeing her everywhere. There she was, just ahead of him in a crowded street. But when he reached her and touched her arm and she turned around in surprise, it wasn't Vita at all, just some other slender young woman with dark curly hair. It happened several times—this one walked like Vita, that one tilted her head just like Vita often did.

One time he even thought he caught a glimpse of her in a very smart carriage that bowled smartly along the street. She was sitting with a very fashionable lady, and at the sight of her profile he caught his breath. But the carriage turned, and by the time he reached the corner, it was gone.

It couldn't have been her, he decided. She was too richly and fashionably dressed, and that very elegant carriage was pulled by a magnificent pair of matched bays, with a liveried driver in front and footman on behind.

He was hallucinating, he decided, imagining he was seeing her everywhere. With a heavy heart he collected his baggage and returned to where he'd left his hired carriage. His search had failed. It was time to return to his wagon and his dog and finish the commissions he'd agreed to.

For Zoë the days passed quickly in a frenzy of shopping and dress fittings in the finest Parisian establishments. She thought she already owned more dresses than any girl would need, but apparently she knew nothing of what it took for a London Season. She spent hours standing patiently, being fitted for walking dresses, morning dresses and ball gowns and the various underclothes that went with each style, as well as pelisses and spencers. Then there were shoes and hats and gloves and fans and all kinds of things to purchase, though Gerald pointed out that many of these could be acquired in London.

The quantity of baggage they would be taking with them

was overwhelming. Gerald said he would have to hire a carriage just for the baggage. Zoë couldn't help but marvel at all that was considered necessary for a young lady making her come-out, and to tell the truth, the expense worried her. Most of her life, as a child with Maman and in the orphanage, she'd been lucky to have one spare dress, and her recent time with Reynard had reminded her of how little you really needed to be perfectly happy.

Still, Lucy had made the journey from an obscure scoundrel's daughter to a titled lady, and she knew exactly what was required. And she stressed that Clarissa and her husband, Race, had told Lucy to spare no expense in preparing Zoë for her come-out.

"Clarissa and Izzy would be the first to complain at anything less than perfection," Lucy told her more than once when Zoë had demurred at some extravagant purchase. "They want you to make a splash, for you to dazzle London society wearing the very latest French fashions."

Zoë knew it was true. Her two sisters and Lady Scattergood had written weekly, ever since she'd first come to France with Lucy and Gerald, and the most recent letters had been filled with excitement and fashion advice and anticipation of Zoë's return to London.

But though she was looking forward to being reunited with her sisters and Lady Scattergood, Zoë wasn't at all eager to make a splash in society. She preferred, in fact, to remain in the background. Oh, Lucy had trained her thoroughly, and she'd had plenty of experience in Paris with balls and routs and dances and other social events, and she'd always managed quite well. She'd learned all the various dance steps, never lacked for a partner and had received many compliments.

She grimaced, thinking about it. Compliments often made her uncomfortable. The French gentlemen she'd met had lavished compliments on her, but she'd always felt that somehow they were practiced compliments, flowery, well-rehearsed and applied almost indiscriminately. She rarely felt they applied just to her. It was the nature of "polite society," and it helped grease the wheels of social interaction, but though she saw the value in everyone being pleasant—at least to your face—she still didn't feel comfortable with it.

She knew it was all a kind of game, but what about when you wanted to stop playing the game and be real?

Reynard had never given her flowery compliments. His compliments were more in the nature of a softening in his eyes when he looked at her, a warm glow of approval at something she'd said or done or a delighted laugh when she'd said something funny or witty. As for the way he showed open respect for her painting skills—even being willing to learn from her—in her experience, that made him a rarity among men. She'd valued that much more than any flowery compliment.

And so often he'd exchanged a glance with her, a silent invitation, sharing their reaction to the same thing, such as Monsieur Gaudet's enthusiasm for his pig. Or he'd raised a sardonic eyebrow in her direction, and she'd just known what he was thinking and sometimes struggled not to laugh aloud. It was rare that she met people with the same sense of humor, and that instant sense of connection with Reynard had been part of why she'd fallen for him so hard and so quickly.

But it wasn't possible to fall in love in just a week, she told herself a dozen times a day. It just wasn't, no matter how she felt.

Besides, there were plenty of reasons why he shouldn't—didn't!—appeal to her at all. Probably he'd been playing a game all along and she was the silly girl who'd thought it was real. Well, she knew now that it was not to be. She would be in England soon, and her new life—her real life—would start.

And she'd be so busy she wouldn't even think about a man called Reynard.

She was taking Marie with her, much to Marie's surprise. "Me, mademoiselle? Go to England with you? But I speak no English."

"You'll pick it up," Zoë told her. "I'll help you, and we'll speak in French all the time anyway."

Marie wasn't sure. "The other servants will look down on me," she said unhappily.

"Oh no they won't," Zoë told her firmly. "If anyone is unkind, I'll deal with them. But I expect they'll look up to you. In fact, I wouldn't be surprised if some of the ladies tried to steal you."

Marie looked horrified. "Steal me? But why?"

Zoë grinned. "A real French maid is something of a status symbol in England. But don't worry, I wouldn't let anyone take you."

Marie's brow remained furrowed. "I am not sure, mademoiselle."

"You don't have to go if you don't want to. If you want to stay in Paris, Lady Thornton and I will find you a good position with someone we know and trust, and—"

"Leave me alone in Paris, mademoiselle? No, no and no! After you and milady have been so kind? No!" She took a deep breath. "Very well, I will go to this England. It will be another adventure, yes?"

"Yes. For both of us."

Chapter Nine

Zoë leaned on the rail of the ship, gazing through the mist, breathing deeply of the cool, moist salty air.

There they were at last, the White Cliffs of Dover.

Last time, when she'd left England for the first time, on her way to a new life in Paris with Gerald and Lucy, she'd never really looked at them. She'd been looking forward, not gazing back.

Now, as England loomed ever closer, her feelings were very mixed. Living in Paris, she'd never really been homesick, perhaps because she'd never really had a home. With Maman she'd moved from one rented room to another, all in the same general area. Then, after her death, there was the orphanage, and that had certainly never felt anything like a home. Even in these last few years with Lucy and Gerald, she'd known that she was their guest, though they treated her more like family.

And though Clarissa and old Lady Scattergood had welcomed her—embraced her, really—she'd never considered Lady Scattergood's house her home. Despite their warmth and generosity toward her, she'd always felt, deep down, that she was there on sufferance—that any day she might have to leave.

Now, gazing through the faint mist at those white cliffs, she felt quite apprehensive. What would this new life bring? Would anyone recognize her as Izzy's half sister? Reveal her—reveal both of them—as Sir Bartleby Studley's bastards. She shivered. It was a daunting prospect.

She really didn't want to be a society lady, would much rather live the life of a vagabond artist traveling in a painted wagon with a charming rogue by her side, but that wasn't possible now that she knew the truth about him.

Though, if she'd never been found by Clarissa, would she have joined Reynard? No, of course not, if only because she'd never have had the opportunity to go to France and meet him. But if she had . . . She just might have thrown in her lot with him. No, not might, *would*.

But that was not to be thought of. Fate—and Lucy—had trained her to become a lady, and they all—her sisters, Lucy and Lady Scattergood—were so excited by the prospect, they couldn't wait to launch her. And Lucy had spent nearly three years training her until she looked, sounded and acted like the perfect aristocratic lady. She just hoped she didn't let them down.

"Ah, the first sight of home," said Gerald, coming up to join her on the rail. "The sight of those white cliffs never fails to move me."

"How is Lucy?" Lucy had felt queasy the moment she set foot on the ship. Luckily Gerald had booked a stateroom and she'd managed to sleep for most of the voyage.

He smiled. "She'll be all right the moment she sets foot on dry land. She's never been a good sailor. I'll go and tell her now. She'll be glad to see the cliffs and know we're almost home."

Zoë took a deep breath. Yes. Home.

Marie came up beside her at the rail and eyed the misty

outline of the cliffs. "They are more gray than white." As she spoke, a light drizzly rain began. She eyed it disparagingly. "I have heard this England is always wet and cold, and now I see it is true. Come inside, mademoiselle, out of the rain."

The closer they came to London the more excited Lucy was, and the more tense Zoë became. Would her sisters be pleased with how she had turned out? Had she done well enough in her lady lessons?

And the big question was where and with whom would she live?

Both her sisters had invited her to live with them, but they were both married now, and would their noble husbands want a bastard half sister living with them? Cramping their style? She would hate to cause difficulties for either of her sisters. And though she'd lived in Lady Scattergood's house before, the old lady was no relative of hers—she was her half-brother-in-law's great-aunt, or something, and she'd originally stayed there as a guest, invited by Clarissa.

"There it is, London at last."

Their carriage had crested a hill, and there was the dome of St. Paul's just visible on the horizon rising above the tall buildings, along with several church spires wreathed in a faint veil of yellow-gray mist. In minutes they were in the city, the carriage slowed by carts and hawkers, horses, dogs and people of all kinds cluttering the streets.

Zoë, leaning out the window, breathed in—and there it was, London, the smell she didn't realize she knew so well, the smell of home. Not a pretty smell, but home, all the same.

The home of her childhood, not where she was going to live now, wherever that would be.

Finally the carriage pulled up outside Lord and Lady Tarrant's house in Bellaire Gardens. Lady Tarrant was Lucy's godmother and Gerald's aunt, and their plan was to stay with her and her husband. Gerald would have to return to France, but Lucy intended to remain with Lady Tarrant until her baby was born. She was the closest that Lucy had to a mother, and she, her husband and his three little daughters had become Lucy's only family.

But although Zoë knew and liked the various members of the Tarrant family—they lived across the garden from Lady Scattergood—she wasn't part of their family.

The front door was flung open before the groom had even let the carriage steps down, and three little girls hurtled from the house to greet them, followed in a more stately fashion by the butler and several footmen. Alice, Lady Tarrant, the girls' stepmother, waited in the doorway, beaming with pleasure.

She was increasing again, Zoë saw.

Gerald helped Lucy and Zoë to alight, then, since they were surrounded by the excited little girls, he ran up the stairs and kissed his aunt. It was a joyous, noisy and chaotic welcome, and Zoë couldn't help but laugh and feel touched as she was drawn warmly into the group.

"Come inside, out of the cold," Alice said, laughing. "Girls, let Lucy and Zoë catch their breath. You can ask them everything after they've gone upstairs to freshen themselves and have come down for tea."

Was she to stay here, then? Zoë wondered, following Alice and Lucy upstairs. But when she came downstairs a few minutes later, there, waiting at the foot of the stairs were her two half sisters, Clarissa and Izzy. They hurried forward and embraced her warmly.

"Lady Tarrant sent a footman over with the news the moment you arrived," Clarissa explained, hugging Zoë for the third time. "Oh, I'm so excited. And look at you, all grown up and so elegant and lovely. My little sister."

"And mine," Izzy said, hugging Zoë again. "Welcome home, Zoë darling. We've missed you."

The exuberant affection of their welcome deprived Zoë

of words: she was deeply moved. Any doubts she might have had about her welcome vanished in an instant.

"Oh, I'm so, so happy you're finally with us again." Clarissa wiped tears away. "Don't mind my tears, Zoë dear, I'm increasing. Apparently it turns people into watering pots, even when they're happy."

"You're increasing, Clarissa?" Zoë exclaimed in delight. She knew from Clarissa's letters that she had been hoping to conceive, and it seemed she'd finally succeeded. "Congratulations. When is the baby due?"

"Oh, sometime early next year," Clarissa said vaguely.

Izzy said, "You'll have to come over and see my beautiful babies later." In the last three years Izzy had given birth to a boy and a girl.

Gerald appeared. "Sorry to interrupt," he said after greeting Izzy and Clarissa, "but where shall I have Zoë's luggage taken? I have to warn you, there's mounds of it. My wife went mad, shopping in Paris for Zoë's come-out."

"How exciting! I'm so glad she did." Clarissa clapped her hands in delight. "I'm looking forward to Zoë making a real splash when she comes out in society. I can't wait to see all her lovely French clothes."

A real splash? Zoë didn't want anything of the sort.

"Yes, I want to be there for the unpacking, too," Izzy said. "And who is that?"

Zoë followed her glance and saw Marie hovering uncertainly in the background. She'd been traveling in the second carriage with the baggage. "Oh, poor Marie. She's my maid," she told her sisters, "but she doesn't speak any English yet." In French she explained to Marie that these were her relatives and that she didn't yet know where they were to live. She turned back to her sisters. "Where will I be living?"

Izzy and Clarissa exchanged glances. "It hasn't been decided yet," Clarissa confessed, and Zoë's heart sank a little. She didn't want to cause any problems.

"Now, don't look like that, silly," Izzy said briskly. "We both want you, of course."

"But so does Lady Scattergood," Clarissa said. "In fact, she insisted we bring you straight over to her the minute—"

"The *very* minute!" Izzy said with a wry grin.

"Yes, the very minute you arrived," Clarissa finished. "She was absolutely adamant." She paused and said, "I'd better warn you, she's looking rather poorly at the moment. She had a nasty bout of influenza a couple of weeks ago, and though she's recovered, she's still quite pale and wan, and has lost weight and still tires very easily."

"Oh, I didn't realize," Zoë said. It explained why she hadn't received any letters from Lady Scattergood in the last few weeks.

"She's still very much herself, though," Izzy assured her. "Now, shall we go?"

Zoë glanced at Marie and hesitated.

"Bring her with you," Clarissa said. "My maid, Betty, will look after her."

"Does Betty speak French, then?" Zoë knew she didn't. Betty had been an orphan, like her, and had been in service since she was twelve.

"Ah. No."

Lucy, coming down the stairs with Lady Tarrant, overheard the discussion. "I will look after Marie for the moment," she said. "We know each other well, don't we, Marie?" she said in French, smiling kindly at Marie, who nodded shyly.

"Lovely. So that's all settled," Izzy said. "Now come along or the old lady might just explode from impatience." She and Clarissa linked arms with Zoë and headed out the back gate, entering Bellaire Gardens, the large garden that was entirely enclosed by a square of houses.

All of them—Lady Tarrant, Izzy and Leo, Clarissa and Race and Lady Scattergood—had houses that backed onto the garden, so they could visit one another whenever they liked. Clarissa's husband, Race, had bought their home especially so Clarissa could still have her beloved garden and be close to her sister.

Late in the season though it was, the garden was looking beautiful. A few late roses were still in bloom, though most were finished. The leaves of the trees were turning russet and gold and the last of the Michaelmas daisies were blooming in vibrant clumps of pink and lilac and white. In another bed, white and dark red penstemons were nodding their dainty heads, interspersed with spikes of blue and white salvia. Lastly there were shaggy-headed chrysanthemums in gold and pink and bronze. Clarissa pointed them out as they passed, reminding Zoë of the names. Clarissa adored the garden and knew the names of everything.

"I'd forgotten how lovely this garden was," Zoë said. She'd spent a lot of time out here when she first came to live with Clarissa at Lady Scattergood's.

"And we'll soon—Oy, you, Jimmy!" Clarissa broke off, and hurried over to where one of the gardeners was about to prune a rosebush. "Please don't prune them yet," she told the man. "I want to harvest the rose hips first. I promise I'll get them all picked in the next day or two."

The man doffed his cap and moved away.

"Did you say you wanted the rose hips?" Zoë asked Clarissa when she rejoined them.

"Yes, they make a wonderful syrup that's very good for winter colds. And a very nice tea, too. And I use them in some of my creams." Clarissa's hobby was making all kinds of cosmetic and medicinal creams and potions. They were very good, too. Zoë had used one of Clarissa's medicinal creams on the cut on Marie's face and had also applied it to poor Hamish's rubbed-raw neck.

How was he getting on? she wondered. Would Reynard keep him? He would, she hoped. He was clearly very fond of animals. If only he wasn't such a . . . such a . . .

Catching herself—she was *not* thinking of Reynard at

all!—she turned to her sister. "If you like, I'll help you pick them," Zoë offered. She'd always enjoyed helping Clarissa with her herbs and flower potions and creams.

Clarissa beamed. "That would be wonderful, thank you, Zoë darling. Meet me out here first thing tomorrow morning and bring an old pair of gloves—preferably kid—to protect your hands." Zoë nodded and glanced at Izzy.

"Don't look at me," Izzy said. "I wouldn't know a rose hip from a dandelion."

Clarissa laughed. "You would, too, it's perfectly obvious, and besides, dandelions are very useful, too. But I want to pick the rose hips first thing in the morning, while the dew is still on them, and I know you're not an early bird, so I forgive you."

They walked on, passing the summerhouse, which had been their own special gathering place. The small, pretty glassed-in structure belonged to all the residents, but not many of the other residents used it, apart from Milly Harrington, a nosy girl who often poked her nose in to annoy them. But Milly would be married and gone by now, Zoë reflected. Thank goodness.

They entered Lady Scattergood's house and were greeted by a pack of excited little dogs, leaping and barking and wriggling with delight. Lady Scattergood collected abandoned and mistreated little dogs—females.

"You're late!" Lady Scattergood said, presenting a wrinkled, rouged and powdered cheek for Zoë to kiss. "I've been waiting here for ages. I thought you'd forgotten me." She did look even thinner than usual, but the pallor Clarissa had warned her about was well hidden by a thick layer of cosmetics and a lavish application of rouge. She was sitting in her favorite peacock chair, draped with her usual half dozen vibrantly colored and patterned silk shawls.

"Of course I haven't," Zoë said, gazing around her, appreciating anew the exuberantly cluttered collection of images and statuettes from far-flung corners of the world that the old lady surrounded herself with. It was like visiting some grand potentate from another world. "How are you, dear Lady Scattergood?"

"Oh, struggling along. I'm all alone here now, you know," the old lady said in a tragic voice. "Nobody cares about an old lady these days." She heaved a sigh and drooped feebly back in her chair.

Zoë frowned. The pathetic tone sounded quite unlike the Lady Scattergood she remembered, who'd been feisty and assertive. Was it a result of her recent illness?

"What about Mrs. Price-Jones?" An old friend of Lady Scattergood's, she'd acted as her companion and as chaperone to Clarissa when Zoë had lived there.

"Althea? Gone. Left. Abandoned me," Lady Scattergood said in a die-away voice. Concerned at the gloomy way the old lady was speaking, Zoë glanced at Izzy, who winked.

"Mrs. Price-Jones got married," Clarissa explained.

"Yes, she left me, and now I'm all alone, rattling around this big old house with nobody to care for me. I might as well be a ghost." She sighed again and shot Zoë a swift glance from under her heavy eyelids.

Izzy said, "Yes, all alone, you poor dear, apart from your butler, the cook, your dresser, several maids and a footman—and your six little dogs."

The old lady snorted. "Servants don't count. The dogs do, of course, but otherwise, I'm all alone."

"Except for the visitors who call on you almost every day," Clarissa said.

"Which include Clarissa and me," Izzy added. "And then there are the friends who come to play cards with you most evenings."

The old lady glared at them, sat up and stamped her cane. "Enough of your impudence, gels! It is quite clear to me that the only place for young Zoë to live is here, in her old room—which I have had especially redecorated for her. Almost three years ago I appointed her my official Artist in

Residence, and that position has not changed. No, don't argue—I have spoken!" She banged her cane on the floor again and sat back in her chair, having delivered her decree.

Zoë couldn't help but smile. There was no sign now of the bereft, lonely old lady—here was the Lady Scattergood she knew and loved: autocratic and imperious. She might never leave her house, but within it she ruled like the empress she appeared.

She glanced at her sisters, who, smiling, both nodded their silent agreement. They'd obviously known what the old lady was going to say, and though they had both invited her to live with them, they'd all be living so close—just across the garden—that Zoë could see them whenever she wanted.

She came forward and hugged the old lady. "Lady Scattergood, I would *love* to live here with you. Thank you so much."

"Oh pish-tush! Lot of fuss about nothing. Of course you'll live here with me! Never any question about it," the old lady said gruffly, deeply pleased.

Clarissa said, "And since we're all just a few steps across the garden, we can pop in and out as much as we want. And meet in the summerhouse as we always used to."

"And, of course, Clarissa and I and our husbands will be on hand to escort you to all the various social events," Izzy added, "so we won't need to hire a chaperone."

It was the perfect resolution, Zoë decided. She wouldn't be underfoot in her sisters' marriages, but would be able to see them whenever she wanted. Best of all, Lady Scattergood would *expec*t her to paint, whereas for her sisters, social occasions and the search for a husband would come before what they probably regarded as her hobby.

They didn't yet understand how her time away and her lessons in painting from some of the best French painters—not to mention that magical week working with Reynard—

had cemented in her the desire to become a professional artist.

With a heavy heart, Reynard gave up the search for Vita and returned to the village where they'd been working. It was the last thing he felt like doing, but he'd made commitments and needed to honor them. Besides, he'd left Hamish and his horse in the care of Madame Le-Blanc's son.

"So you didn't find Mademoiselle Vita, then," the inn-keeper's wife greeted him on his return.

"No."

"You forgot the address of your uncle and aunt, then?" she added ironically.

"Of course I didn't. She wasn't there," Reynard said crisply, and strode off to where he'd left his wagon, horse and dog. As he approached the LeBlanc farm a large crea-ture burst from the bushes, almost knocking him over. Laughing, he scruffled his dog's ruff and suffered some exuberant, sloppy licks in return.

The LeBlancs had taken good care of him; Hamish was in excellent condition, and not only had someone—he sus-pected the little girl—brushed his scruffy coat, but they'd carefully tied his fringe back with two pink ribbons. "Very fetching," he told the dog, who snorted and shook his head vigorously. The ribbons failed to be dislodged.

Feeling better than he had in days—you could trust dogs at least—Reynard continued on to the farm, where he found Rocinante in excellent condition as well. Her hat had even been refreshed with some new flowers.

He thanked madame and her children for their care, and when madame refused the money he offered, he quietly tucked some notes under a pot of honey on the kitchen table and gave a few coins to each of the children.

But the questions didn't stop. Like the innkeeper's wife, Madame LeBlanc wanted to know where Vita was and why she'd run off without so much as a goodbye. She wasn't subtle about it, either.

And later, as he reconnected with people who'd commissioned paintings from him, it seemed nobody had believed the "cousin" story, and they almost universally assumed that her abrupt disappearance was because of something he'd done. The implication was that he'd made unwelcome advances, and, being a good and virtuous girl, Vita had taken herself off to safety out of his lecherous reach.

Of course, he denied it, reiterating that she was his cousin, but the skeptical expressions told him how little that story was believed. And he couldn't explain that she'd stolen one of the valuable old paintings, because he didn't want them to start speculating about the true value of the paintings they so willingly exchanged.

Refusing to dwell on it, he got on with painting the replacements, and though it was clear that Vita was by far the better painter of people, he'd picked up a few techniques from watching her work, and the result, if not as good, was adequate enough. At least nobody complained. Not to his face.

It was lonely, working on his own again. It was ridiculous that he missed her so much when she had spent only a week with him, but somehow he did. He missed her in the morning, returning from her wash in the stream, her complexion bright and dewy, her gorgeous green eyes sparkling with life, then sipping her morning cup of tea with a blissful expression. She didn't have a lot to say in the morning, which he liked. It was companionable and peaceful.

Most of all, he missed her in the evening, sitting by the fire, talking about their day, the firelight gilding her dark curls and turning her pure, pale skin peach and gold. She'd made him laugh, too, with her stories and her pithy observations about the people she'd met. But now, thinking about it, though he'd told her a little of his own story, she'd told him almost nothing about herself.

He'd kept quite a bit back himself—things that were significant but, when he thought about it, not really important. Admittedly he'd bent the truth quite a bit. But then, so had she.

So he painted on alone. Of course, the dog kept him company, but there were times when Hamish's eyes rested on him with what Reynard would swear was reproach. And no matter how many times he reminded himself that all dogs learned to do "reproach" as puppies, Hamish's lugubrious expression and heavy sighs quite clearly conveyed that he was missing Vita and that he knew who was to blame.

Dogs! What did they know? The sooner he finished his paintings, passed on to Gaston the rest of the old ones he'd collected and returned to England, the happier he'd be.

As evening grew nigh, Lady Scattergood declared she was too tired to stay up late and sent them off to dine elsewhere. Izzy and Clarissa, having anticipated this—the old lady was still sadly pulled by her recent bout of influenza—had arranged to dine at Izzy and Leo's home. Their Neapolitan cook, Alfonso, had been working all afternoon, preparing all their favorite dishes.

But first there was a visit to the nursery, where Zoë was introduced to her niece and nephew. Little Louisa, aged two and a half, was an adorably lively toddler with her mother's green eyes and a mop of dark curls. Seeing Clarissa, she ran toward her, shrieking, "Aunt Rissa, Aunt Rissa, up up up!" Laughing, Clarissa picked the little girl up and kissed her.

Baby Joey had just a bare fuzz of dark hair covering his

little head. His eyes were more hazel than green, but he smiled readily, giving everyone a drooling, toothless, happy grin.

"He's really Josiah Leonard Thorne," Izzy said, jiggling him on her hip. "It's Leo's family tradition to name the firstborn son Josiah Leonard Thorne, and each generation takes it in turns which name they use. Leo's father was called Joe, but Joey suits my baby boy better, I think."

Zoë agreed. Little Joey seemed a serene, chubby baby, who gazed out at the world with an air of benevolence.

It was fascinating to see her sisters as mothers. Clearly they both adored the children, and it was obvious that they spent a good deal of time with them, which many young, fashionable society mothers didn't.

But the big surprise of the day was when Leo, the children's father, arrived home early and came straight up to the nursery. "PapaPapaPapa!" little Louisa screeched, and wriggling out of Clarissa's arms, she hurled herself at her father.

Zoë had always been a little intimidated by Leo, Lord Salcott, who, though invariably polite, had always seemed rather cold, a bit stern and stiffly correct. But with a laugh, Leo scooped up his daughter and tossed her, screaming with delight, in the air and caught her again. Winding one arm tightly around his neck, she scruffed up his neatly arranged hair and gleefully ruined his intricately arranged neckcloth.

To Zoë's astonishment, Leo simply chuckled. And with his daughter in his arms, he kissed his wife—in front of them all—then bent to greet his son, who drooled and grinned and waved his chubby fists at his father.

Zoë marveled at the change in him. He clearly doted on his wife and children and wasn't afraid to show it. It was the last thing she would have expected of him. Izzy had always said Leo was a wonderful husband, and now Zoë could see it was true.

* * *

Dinner that evening was a most convivial gathering with Leo and Izzy, Race and Clarissa, Lucy and Gerald and Alice and her husband, James. Leo's chef had cooked a magnificent meal, with English favorites like roast beef and steak and kidney pie, along with Neapolitan dishes like lamb ragù, a kind of stew served with noodles with meat that melted in your mouth, and a delicate but delicious dish of fish cooked in butter and herbs, as well as several vegetable dishes.

To follow he gave them a delicious English-style steamed lemon pudding, a big wobbly red jelly studded with berries and cream, a bowl of flummery and a special Neapolitan cake made with some Italian soft cheese and deliciously flavored with candied citrus peel and rosewater.

Matteo, Leo's general factotum, who presented the meal with flamboyant Neapolitan flair, explained that the cake was usually only served at Christmas and Easter. "But this is special family celebration, no? So Alfonso, he make something special to celebrate you coming back to us, Miss Zoë."

Zoë was deeply moved by the welcome she'd received and was still receiving. Why on earth had she been worried about it?

Everyone had gone to so much trouble on her behalf.

When the meal had been eaten, the ladies retired to the sitting room, leaving the men to their port and brandy.

"Leo and I are going to hold a reception to introduce you to society," Izzy told Zoë as she poured tea and passed around cups.

"A reception?" Zoë's heart sank. Starting so soon? She'd thought she would have several months at least before she needed to face society. At this time of year most people would be at their country estates. They'd return, like swallows, in spring when the Season would start.

"Yes, there aren't enough people in London for a full-scale ball—we'll hold that once the Season begins—but in the meantime we want you to make a small splash."

"Why?" Zoë didn't want to make any sort of splash.

"Yes," Clarissa said eagerly. "We have a plan."

"But first you need a dress," Izzy said.

"A dress? But I have dozens of dresses, all never worn."

"Yes, we saw them when you were unpacking, and I must say, Lucy, you did very well. If I don't miss my guess, Zoë's going to set a fashion when she steps out in her elegant French gowns. But Zoë, this is a special dress we need, so Clarissa and I will take you to Daisy Chance's establishment and get you measured up for it."

"Why? Are you planning a costume party?"

Izzy and Clarissa laughed. "No," Clarissa said. "But that's a good idea, don't you think, Izzy? Race and I could hold one later in the Season when it gets warmer. Maybe even in the garden."

"So if it isn't a costume party, why would I need a new dress?"

"Wait and see. It's a surprise," Izzy said, her green eyes, so uncannily like Zoë's own, dancing with what Zoë could swear was mischief.

The conversation then turned to other matters. Lucy shared stories about their time in Paris, Alice talked about her beloved children and how quickly they seemed to grow. They told Zoë and Lucy about Mrs. Price-Jones, Clarissa's erstwhile chaperone, and who she'd married—not one of the "silver suitors," the two gentlemen who'd been assiduously courting her when Zoë had left the country, but Sir Alfred Nicolas, a younger man who was rich and vigorous and who apparently thought the world of her. Then the talk turned more general and touched on various people they knew in society, few of whom Zoë had met.

"When do you plan to hold this reception?" she blurted out in the middle of a conversation about some neighbor. Then she blushed at her rudeness.

But Izzy didn't turn a hair. "After Christmas, close to the New Year. New year, new you!"

Zoë breathed again. So, almost a month before she needed to grit her teeth and make her entrance into English society.

She hadn't yet told her sisters that she wasn't at all keen to enter society. They were both so enthusiastic and had gone to so much trouble to ensure she was fit to enter the ton; she couldn't bring herself to tell them.

She'd attended dozens of French society events, and though she'd been quite popular and hadn't blotted her copybook—apart from the incident with Monsieur Etienne— somehow, doing it in England was different. For a start, she was nervous that she'd revert back to her old accent.

Everyone here had been delighted with the improvement in her speech, and when she wanted to, she could even insert a faint flavor of French into it, as a real French cousin would.

But driving through London, she'd heard a cacophony of accents out in the streets, and she was a natural mimic. It had helped enormously when Lucy was teaching her to sound like an English lady—she had a good ear—but Zoë also had a tendency to reflect someone's manner of speech back at them, which was not so good. She'd discovered that when she'd met a Scottish lady in Paris and found herself, after fifteen minutes' conversation, responding to the lady with a soft Scottish burr. Lucy had been horrified; Zoë hadn't even realized she was doing it.

And even though she'd met dozens of charming Frenchmen, several of whom had even proposed marriage to her, none of them had given her the slightest desire to even consider marriage. It wasn't because they were French, either— she just couldn't see herself as a wife, living the life of a society lady. She just wasn't made like that.

It was telling that the only man she'd ever been able to envisage herself marrying was a footloose vagabond English artist. Who was a charming, untrustworthy rogue.

* * *

The following morning after a delicious breakfast—
Cook's way of welcoming her back—Zoë joined Clarissa in the garden to pick rose hips. First Clarissa showed her how to pick them—she used scissors to snip them off—and for the first little while they worked side by side.

"Did you enjoy your time in France?" Clarissa asked as she snipped and dropped rose hips into her basket.

"Yes, very much. Lucy has been simply wonderful. I learned so much."

"I'm glad." Clarissa gave her a sidelong glance. "I was worried that you'd fall in love with a Frenchman and never want to come back to England. You didn't, did you?"

Zoë laughed. "No, not at all. I met some very charming Frenchmen and some who were terribly handsome, but none of them caused my heart to beat the least bit faster." She'd fallen instead for an English scoundrel, and what a mistake that had been. She added quietly, "I'm not sure I even want to get married."

Clarissa turned to her in dismay. "Oh, but married life is so wonderful. I'm sure it's just that you haven't met the right man yet. Look at me—I was sure I was going to have to make a practical marriage, and certainly not to anyone who had a reputation with women, you know what I mean." She sighed happily. "But Race wore me down and convinced me that he'd make a good husband, and I've never been happier."

Zoë smiled. She'd seen at dinner the previous night how very well suited Clarissa and Race were. In fact, both her sisters had made very happy marriages, as had Lucy and Gerald. And Lord and Lady Tarrant.

"Perhaps there's something wrong with me," she said lightly. She couldn't tell Clarissa—and certainly not in the face of her sister's happiness—that the idea of being a society wife didn't appeal in the least. Bearing children, being endlessly decorative and presiding over teapots, dinners and balls—it was simply not enough.

"Oh no, don't say that. I'm sure you'll meet the right man one day. Izzy and I will help you. Being married to the right man is blissful. Really, it is. Besides, don't you want children?"

Zoë considered that. Yes, she did want children—as long as they were born in wedlock. It was bad enough being illegitimate herself, but to deliberately bring an illegitimate child into the world would be unforgivable.

On the other hand, she was an aunt now. She could love her sisters' children. Perhaps that would be enough. Hoping to distract Clarissa from the issue of Zoë's marriage prospects, she asked Clarissa about Izzy's children and the one she was expecting, and from then on, the talk was all about babies.

As each rosebush was stripped of its hips, they moved farther and farther apart until they couldn't even see each other, and talk was no longer possible.

Working in the garden was very peaceful, with the birds twittering and chattering in the trees and the scent of damp earth and flowers all around. Zoë snipped rose hips, her hands busy and her mind far away, in a small French village where people would be exchanging old paintings for new . . .

How could he, in all conscience, justify it? Those people were poor. The price he would get for those old paintings would make a big difference to their lives. Did it really matter that they had been stolen in the first place? It was thirty years ago, after all. But then she thought of the painting she'd taken and how much it meant to her. She sighed. There was no easy answer. She just wished—

"Izzy?" Milly Harrington, their annoying neighbor, stood there. She blinked when Zoë turned. "Oh, it's you."

"Yes," Zoë agreed.

"So you're back, are you, Zoë whoever-you-are?"

"Apparently. And it's Zoë Benoît."

She lifted a disdainful shoulder. "Zoë Ben-whahhhh, then, if you insist."

"I do. And I see you're still here as well."

There was a short silence, then Milly said, "What are you doing cutting those knobbly things off my roses?"

"They're rose hips."

"So? You're not allowed to cut flowers and things from the garden."

"They're for Clarissa. And the gardeners know she's doing it. Besides, it's not your garden; it belongs to all the residents."

"Yes, but you're not one of us."

"Residents means people who live in these houses"— Zoë gestured—"and since I'm now living here with Lady Scattergood, I am, therefore, a resident."

Nettled, Milly just glared at her. Zoë went on snipping rose hips. "I see you're happy to talk English now. And not the sort of English you did however many years ago. You sound almost like a lady." She smirked. "Almost."

"Would you prefer me to speak to you in French?"

Milly snorted. "It's not very patriotic, so no, I don't."

Zoë hid a smile. Milly's French was almost nonexistent. She glanced at Milly's ringless hands. "And you, Miss Harrington—it is still Miss, isn't it?—what has it been, three seasons, and yet you still don't have a husband? My commiserations."

Milly stiffened. "I'll have you know, Zoë Ben-whahhhh, that I've had *several* offers of marriage from eligible gentlemen."

"What happened? Cried off once they got to know you better, did they?"

Milly's color heightened. "Not at all. They were each devastated when I had to refuse them. Dev-a-stat-ed."

"Had to refuse them because?"

"Because Mama did not consider them sufficiently . . ." She paused, groping for the right word.

"Sufficiently handsome? Sufficiently rich? Or were they lacking a title?"

"Not all of them." Milly tossed her head. "I refused a baron *and* a baronet, actually."

"So what was wrong with them?"

"Mama has her position to consider. She is second cousin to a duke, you know."

"I should think anyone who has ever met her must know that. I'm surprised she doesn't hand out cards announcing it. So Mama wants you to marry a duke, does she? You're not getting anxious about being left on the shelf, are you?"

Milly shrugged airily. "Mama knows what she's doing. Anyway, I don't see any rings on your finger."

"Perhaps because I'm wearing gloves. But you're right, rings would get in the way of my work."

"Work? What work?" She glanced at the basket of hips. "Is that it? Are you a servant now?"

"No."

"Then why are you picking those things?"

"They're very good for the complexion. You know how perfect Clarissa's skin is. Well . . ."

"You mean you *eat* them?" Milly screwed up her nose.

Zoë was getting fed up with all the questions. "Well, what else?" It wasn't true—not raw, anyway. Clarissa made syrup and rose-hip jelly and tea from them.

Milly watched her busily picking, and when Zoë moved away to another rosebush she followed. Milly watched in silence for a few moments, then reached out and, with her nose screwed up, cautiously plucked several rose hips.

She wiped them on a handkerchief, stared at them a moment, then shrugged and popped them in her mouth.

She chewed, clearly finding the taste and texture disgusting. Then she spat them out. "Eurgh!" she exclaimed, spitting again. "They taste horrid." She scrubbed at her mouth with a handkerchief.

Zoë kept a straight face. "You probably ate a spider."

"Urgh!" Milly spat again. "Why didn't you warn me?"

Zoë shrugged. "It's your garden, I thought you would have known. There are loads of spiders in the garden. There are webs all over the place, so pretty with the morning dew on them, like strings of crystals."

Milly pulled a face. "You are so strange! Everything about spiders is disgusting—everyone knows that."

Ignoring her, Zoë kept picking while Milly watched, glowering, her mouth puckered. Then she said, "People really eat these things to improve their complexion?"

"You have to suffer for your beauty." A crow cawed from the rooftops, and Zoë cocked her head. "Isn't that your mama calling you?"

Milly scowled. "I didn't hear anything. You're just trying to get rid of me."

"Am I? Your mama won't mind if you don't come, then, will she?"

"Oh, you!" Milly hesitated, grabbed a couple more rose hips and flounced off.

Zoë grinned to herself and kept picking rose hips.

Chapter Ten

That afternoon, Izzy and Clarissa went out to make morning calls. They explained that they'd rather Zoë not go out into society until she'd been presented—not to the Queen; illegitimate girls, even pretend French cousins, didn't do that. They were terribly apologetic, but they wanted her to meet all their friends and acquaintances at the reception Leo and Izzy were organizing for after Christmas, and since Lucy and Gerald had brought her back to England earlier than expected, it had caught them out.

Especially since it was winter and the Season wouldn't really start until spring.

Zoë assured them that far from being disheartened at the delay, it suited her down to the ground. It was, after all, what she'd done when she'd first come to live with Clarissa and Lady Scattergood.

Her sisters put her reluctance to move in society down to shyness, or perhaps anxiety about the masquerade as a

French cousin. But Zoë wasn't shy, and she knew she could handle society events with ease—Lucy had trained her well. She simply wasn't interested in society life. And far from being disappointed, she was secretly delighted because the delay would give her more time to paint.

She was keen to start establishing a reputation as a portraitist, and she knew she'd have Lady Scattergood's approval.

She started by painting another portrait of the old lady. The one she'd painted of her three years ago was promising, for a beginner, and Lady Scattergood liked it very much, but Zoë knew she was much better now and was keen to paint something that showed off her new skills.

Lady Scattergood was, of course, delighted. Zoë painted her seated like some kind of Eastern potentate in her peacock chair, wearing one of the large, flamboyant turbans she'd taken to wearing to disguise the thinning of her hair, and draped in multicolored shawls, with her beloved dogs around her. In the background were some of the fascinating and unusual objects her late husband had sent her from his travels to the far-flung corners of the world.

Her time painting people with Reynard had given Zoë experience in painting people who moved and talked and came and went, and so she told Lady Scattergood that she would be quite happy for her to receive visitors while she painted. Which, of course, she did.

It brought an unexpected bonus. The old lady's visitors were fascinated by the painting process and returned again and again to watch the portrait emerge. Before it was even finished, she had several more commissions. All were of old ladies, but Zoë didn't mind that at all. She wasn't the kind of portraitist who wanted to paint only beautiful people. She preferred evidence of character and personality in a subject, and she found old people endlessly absorbing and frequently beautiful.

* * *

"We've made an appointment with Daisy Chance for you to be fitted for your new dress," Izzy told Zoë at dinner one night at the home of Clarissa and Race. "It's for quite early in the morning, so nobody will see you."

Zoë was bemused by the secrecy. "You do know that dozens of Lady Scattergood's visitors have already seen me, don't you?"

"Yes, but they don't count."

"Izzy is talking about the leaders of the ton seeing you," Clarissa explained. "Will you try some more of this berry ice? It's delicious, don't you think?"

Zoë agreed and allowed the butler to fill her a tiny crystal cup with the frozen berry confection.

"You see, we want to make a splash with you at our reception," Izzy said.

"Yes. Which is why you need this dress," Clarissa said.

Zoë had no idea what it was all about—her sisters were being so mysterious, but all she said was "Very well. What time do you want me to be ready?"

The House of Chance was a small, elegant establishment, just off Piccadilly. It was clear to Zoë that her sisters were well acquainted with the proprietor, Miss Daisy Chance, a short, elegantly dressed woman who, to her surprise, had a bad limp and spoke with an unashamed Cockney accent.

After the greetings and introductions, the small elegant woman scanned Zoë from top to toe. "So this is your French cousin, eh? Yep, you and her are two peas in a pod, just like you said, Lady Salcott." She gave a brisk nod. "Perfect."

She then sent an assistant to bring her sisters tea and

biscuits and some fashion magazines to peruse and whisked Zoë behind a velvet curtain to where some of the working aspects of the business took place. She took out her measuring tape, chatting in a friendly way as she measured every aspect of Zoë's body while another assistant wrote everything down.

She soon understood not only why her sisters and Lady Alice liked Miss Chance but also why they patronized her business almost exclusively. Daisy Chance was an original, both in personality and in designs, several of which were displayed in the shop, and several more were draped, awaiting their final fitting, in the back section.

And she'd made no attempt to improve her accent. "Nah," she said when Zoë tentatively asked her whether or not she felt pressure to change how she spoke. "Most of the other dressmakers in London give themselves French names like Estelle or Amélie and put on fake French accents to hide the fact that they were born as common as me. And because so many people think French mantua makers are the best." She chuckled. "Me, I can't be bothered with all that. Me designs are what people come for, and if people think an accent is more important than one of me special designs, then more fool them."

Zoë liked that.

The measurements taken, to Zoë's surprise, she was then ushered back to join her sisters. The appointment, it seemed, was over.

"But what about the design?" Zoë asked.

"Oh, that's all settled," Izzy said, her eyes twinkling. "We worked it out before you got here. Miss Chance has done us proud."

Us? she wondered, but clearly they weren't going to explain. "And the fabric?"

"That, too. It's green silk. Don't worry, it will be perfect on you," Clarissa said with a laughing glance at Izzy. "You're going to make a real splash."

Miss Chance, who was obviously in on whatever plan her sisters had hatched, grinned and said, "Yeah, you'll look a treat, miss. Mind you, you'll need to come back for at least one more fitting, but I'll let you know when that is."

It was an odd way to do business, but Zoë didn't really mind. She'd already spent hours and hours with Lucy in Paris, poring over designs and standing endlessly, having things fitted and pinned and draped and repinned and redraped until everyone was satisfied. She liked fashion and had decided ideas about what she liked and disliked, but the long process of getting there was frequently tiring and very boring.

Who knew what this dress would look like in the end? But in the meantime it gave her more time to paint.

Lady Scattergood had been so delighted with her new portrait that she insisted on hanging it in pride of place above the mantelpiece in her drawing room, where everyone who visited could admire it. Naturally, they commented on it, and such was their interest that the old lady set up a workroom for Zoë to paint in, on the ground floor so it would be easy for her visitors—most of whom were elderly—to pop in and observe Zoë at work.

She also directed her butler, Treadwell, to set up a number of chairs there so ladies could sit and watch Zoë at work, painting the portraits that had already been commissioned. Treadwell then instructed the young footman, Jeremiah, to fetch them. Butlers did not carry furniture around.

Zoë, not bothered by an audience, was entertained by the fuss Lady Scattergood made of her and her paintings and was delighted by the commissions. She was even acting as a kind of agent for Zoë, urging her friends to get their portraits painted before Zoë got so busy and well known that they could not afford her, and taking charge of the payments. She charged far more for Zoë's paintings than Zoë would ever have dreamed of asking, and even opened a bank account in Zoë's name.

"Now, Zoë, my dear," she said, "you must *promise* me that you will *never* divulge the existence of this bank account to *any* man, especially if you are ever foolish enough to marry."

Bemused, Zoë agreed. "But—"

"A woman should always have control over her own money," the old lady continued. "It is iniquitous, positively iniquitous, that according to the law, all of a woman's property becomes property of the man upon marriage. All of it! An heiress becomes a veritable pauper overnight, totally dependent on the goodwill and honesty of her husband— and you know as well as I do how many men are to be trusted!" She snorted. "I've written several times to the prime minister about the matter, but of course, he's a man, so he does nothing. So keep this bank account hidden, do you hear?"

Chuckling, Zoë agreed. She had no plans to get married anyway. And it was very good of Lady Scattergood to take such an interest in her career.

So she painted and painted, morning and afternoon, unless Clarissa and Izzy had some plans for her. And the visitors kept coming.

"What is it, Treadwell?" Lady Scattergood said one morning as she and two of her friends were sitting, watching Zoë work and chatting.

"A caller, m'lady." The butler bowed and presented a silver salver, on which rested a card.

Lady Scattergood picked it up, snorted and tossed the card toward the fire. "That woman again! What did you tell her?"

"I took the liberty of telling Lady Bagshott—again— that you were not at home."

"Quite right!" The old lady turned to her friends. "Do you know her? No? An *arriviste*, my dears, and quite pushy.

She's called I don't know how many times, and each time, Treadwell sends her off saying I am not at home. But the wretched woman cannot and will not take a hint!"

"What does she want?" one of the old ladies asked.

"What any *arriviste* wants, of course: *entrée* to my home and access to my friends. And a portrait by Zoë. The creature has had the temerity to write to me—several times—requesting one."

"You're a snob, Lady Scattergood," Zoë told her. "She can't help her birth. None of us can." She was particularly sensitive to that sort of thing, having herself been born in the back streets of London, not to mention illegitimate.

The old lady sniffed. "Perhaps not, but apart from her background in trade, the woman is aggressively forward and I cannot abide her." She added smugly, "And every time she writes to request a portrait, I increase the price and tell her she cannot afford it. Which, of course, makes her want it even more. She always did want the best of everything."

"You knew her before now, Olive?" one of the ladies asked.

"Vaguely. Back when I was a child," Lady Scattergood said dismissively. "Our families did not 'know' each other, of course—my mother would not have dreamed of receiving hers, for instance—but we attended the same church and I could not help but become acquainted with her. Even then she was trying to push herself into my world."

The visitors tsk-tsked and the conversation continued on the problem of mushrooms and *arrivistes*. Zoë went back to her painting. The conversation was sobering. Lady Scattergood and her friends might be treating Zoë like a favored pet at the moment, but not everyone would see her in the same way. There would be people in society who would be as ruthlessly exclusive toward her, just as they were toward Lady Bagshott.

A few minutes later the ladies left to take tea in the

drawing room, and as soon as they'd gone, Zoë retrieved Lady Bagshott's card from where it lay against the grate. She felt sorry for her and wanted no part of Lady Scattergood's unreasonable exclusivity.

Zoë put the finishing touches on her most recent portrait, then set it aside to dry. Two other completed paintings were sitting on a ledge, waiting to be framed before going to their new owners. She'd painted so many since returning to London that she'd lost count.

She cleaned her brushes, tidied her work area and washed her hands. Lady Scattergood had several more commissions awaiting her. Which one to do next? Her gaze drifted to the card left by—what was her name again?—oh yes, Lady Bagshott.

Lady Scattergood's exclusivity and hostility toward the woman just because of her background in trade bothered her. Art was for everyone. And if this lady was so keen to have Zoë paint her portrait, why shouldn't she?

She wrapped up the completed paintings and rang to have the carriage brought around.

"Where are you off to?" Lady Scattergood asked when she came downstairs.

Zoë indicated the wrapped bundle. "To the framers."

"Take your maid and Jeremiah with you." Lady Scattergood was always nervous when people went outside and insisted on Zoë being accompanied.

After meeting with the framers and deciding on the best frame style for each painting—and subject—she returned to the carriage and showed the card to the coachman. "Take me to this address, please."

He gave her a narrow look. "Are you sure, miss?" Clearly she was not the only one who knew about Lady Bagshott's unsuccessful attempts to storm Lady Scattergood's bastion.

"Quite sure."

A few minutes later the carriage drew up outside an imposing white three-story house. The doorbell was answered by a very correct butler.

"Miss Zoë Benoît to see Lady Bagshott," she said.

He hesitated, and seeing she was about to be refused, she added, "Lady Bagshott left this card. I am returning her call."

He took it, scrutinized it with a skeptical air, then said in a dampening manner, "I will inquire as to whether m'lady is at home." He left Zoë cooling her heels in the hall. She looked around her. The furnishings and decorations were too ornate for her taste, but the lady clearly did not lack money.

Fifteen minutes later, the butler returned. "M'lady will see you now."

She was ushered into rather a grand drawing room. Lady Bagshott received her seated in an ornately carved chair. She did not rise, nor did she invite Zoë to sit.

Instead of greeting Zoë, she held up the card Zoë had given to the butler. "Where did you get this card?"

"You left it with Lady Scattergood's butler last week."

The old lady sniffed. "And who might you be? Some maidservant, I suppose."

Zoë said composedly, "I am Zoë Benoît, and I am Lady Scattergood's artist in residence."

Lady Bagshott snorted. "A likely story. You're far too young and pretty to do the portraits I've seen."

Tired of standing, Zoë sat down on a hard chair next to a small rosewood table. "Nevertheless, I painted them." She took out a small sketch pad and pencil, and while Lady Bagshott shot questions at her, trying to ascertain whether she was indeed the correct painter, her pencil flew over the page.

"In the portrait of the Dowager Countess of Fenchurch, what was at her feet?"

Zoë frowned. "Was that the one with the little dog, or the one with the cat on her lap?" Having watched Reynard work, she was a lot more skilled at painting animals, but she'd been working so fast, on so many portraits in quick succession, she'd forgotten the various ladies' names.

"It was a dog, but anyone could guess that. I suppose you were dusting the room and saw it." The old lady raised her lorgnette and peered at her. "What are you doing, gel, scribbling away while I'm talking to you? It's very rude."

"Drawing." Zoë turned the page and started another quick sketch.

"I haven't agreed to allow you to do any such thing! Stop it at once! And I never gave you permission to be seated in my presence!"

Zoë ignored her. "I believe Lady Scattergood informed you of my fee." Before she'd met Lady Bagshott she'd been more than half-inclined to give her a substantial discount, but having met the arrogant old battle-ax, she'd changed her mind.

"Hah! And I suppose you want me to pay you up front and then you'll take my money and disappear."

Zoë put the finishing touches to the second sketch and said in a bored voice, "My clients pay Lady Scattergood, not me. I would expect you to do the same."

Lady Bagshott regarded her sourly. "If you are that artist—and I don't for a minute believe you are—why would you paint so many raddled old women? Why not beautiful young ladies or handsome men?"

"I paint all sorts of people. And while you might call some of my subjects 'raddled' and 'old,' I see faces that are full of character. And that's what I paint. In any case, beauty is in the eye of the beholder."

"Hmph! Trotting out rubbishy old clichés, are you now?"

Zoë ripped two pages from her sketch pad and rose from her seat. "As the painter, I'm the beholder, and beauty comes in all sorts of guises. So I could portray you like this." She passed her the first sketch, which was quite a flattering portrait.

The old lady peered at it through her lorgnette, and from her expression Zoë could see she was both surprised and pleased.

"Or I might portray you like this." She passed her the second sketch, which was more of a caricature—a cruel but accurate portrayal.

The old lady gasped. "This is outrageous!"

Zoë glanced from her drawing to the old lady and back again. "No, it's quite accurate. They both are."

"How dare you! I've never met such an insolent chit!" She kept looking from one sketch to the other.

Zoë said indifferently, "Not surprising. I hear you don't get out much."

Lady Bagshott stamped her foot. "You brass-faced hussy!"

Zoë shrugged. "I just thought I'd give you an idea of your choices if I decided to paint you."

Lady Bagshott lurched from her chair and in two steps flung the sketches into the fire. Unmoved, Zoë watched them blacken, curl and burst into flame.

"Hah! See?" The old woman gloated. "I choose no portrait at all—not from you, you impudent baggage!"

"Very well, but I think I'll paint you anyway. You have an interesting face."

"Nonsense! I won't sit for you, no matter how much you beg! I absolutely refuse!"

"Oh, I don't need you to sit for me. I have it all up here." She tapped her head.

She glared at Zoë. "I won't pay you a penny!"

Zoë shrugged. "I don't need your money. Apart from a waiting list of commissions, I have a private income. I'll put the portrait in an exhibition. Someone might buy it. We'll see."

The old lady's voice rose in outrage. "Put *my face*? In

an *exhibition*? Have every Tom, Dick and Harry staring at me?"

"Yes, it'll be fun, won't it?"

"It's not fun at all! It's an outrage. An appalling liberty! I refuse to allow it."

"It's not up to you, though, is it?" Zoë said pleasantly. "You've refused the commission, so I'll paint you how I wish, and it'll be mine to do whatever I want with it."

The old woman huffed and puffed in frustration and outrage and muttered under her breath. Zoë slipped her sketchbook and pencil back into her reticule and turned to leave. She had almost reached the door when Lady Bagshott ground out, "Very well, then, you dreadful gel, I agree."

"Agree to what, Lady Bagshott?" Zoë said innocently.

The old woman narrowed her eyes. "You know perfectly well what. I'll commission the dratted portrait and I'll even pay your exorbitant price. But I tell you this, young woman, it won't leave this house, not while you're painting it, and not once it's done—is that understood?"

"It will need to go to the framer."

Lady Bagshott's lips tightened. "Very well, but it must come straight back, or I will want to know the reason why!"

"Agreed. Now, I will need to inspect the room I am to work in. It will need good light."

Lady Bagshott tugged on the bellpull. "My maid, Sutton, will show you."

The butler appeared. "This insolent creature will be painting my portrait," she told him. "Fetch Sutton to conduct her to a suitable room."

"One with good light," Zoë said.

"Very good, m'lady."

The maid, Sutton, was surprisingly friendly for someone who worked for a dragon. "Oh, miss, you're ever so brave," she told Zoë as they climbed the stairs. "I never saw anyone get the better of Lady Bagshott like that. Only her grandson."

"Chip off the old block, is he?"

"Oh no, miss, he's a real gentleman. He just doesn't visit very often."

Zoë grinned. "I can't imagine why."

When Zoë told Lady Scattergood that she'd agreed to paint Lady Bagshott's portrait, her reaction was everything she'd expected.

"*What?* You're painting That Woman?"

"Yes."

"But why? She's a ghastly creature."

Zoë just smiled. Lady Bagshott was indeed ghastly, but it was too late now to change her mind. She'd made a commitment. "She interests me."

"She'll treat you abominably," Lady Scattergood warned her.

"She may try," Zoë said calmly. "I'm not easily bullied."

Lady Scattergood rolled her eyes. "I don't suppose you got any money out of her, either. I will send her an invoice immediately. I hope you charged her the full price."

"I told her it will cost whatever you told her in your last letter. I didn't know how much it was."

"At least you got that right. It's going to be a *very* expensive portrait. But, oh dear, she's going to be unbearable now, having an original Z-B portrait of her own." *Z-B* was how Zoë signed her work.

During the next week, Zoë went every day to Lady Bagshott's home to paint. She took Marie with her at Lady Scattergood's insistence. Poor Marie, it would have been so boring for her had she sat in the same room as Zoë, not understanding a word that was said, but luckily Sutton invited Marie to the servants' area, where she was more comfortable, and made herself useful while they taught her English.

It didn't get off to an easy start. First Zoë had to negotiate the pose in which Lady Bagshott wanted to be painted. She'd had practically half the contents of her drawing room—chairs, paintings, statues, even a large gold clock—carried up to the room where Zoë had set up her painting equipment. They argued until Zoë said, "What do you want, a portrait of you or of your possessions?"

It became clear that she wanted both, with as many of her most valuable possessions as possible, but Zoë stood firm, and they finally agreed on an elegant chair draped with a beautiful tapestry, an ornate pedestal with an imitation Greek statue on it, a carved screen and a vase of flowers. Wooden-faced, the footmen who'd lugged all the extra things up to the third floor carried them down again.

Lady Bagshott was wearing a mid-blue velvet dress trimmed with lace, of which Zoë approved. Another argument resulted in the lady wearing only one necklace instead of several: a handsome sapphire-and-diamond one, with matching diamonds in her ears and several large glittering rings on her fingers. Draped across her lap was a white fur stole, and in one hand she clutched a Bible, open as if she were reading it, while the other hand rested on an ebony cane with a gold knob.

"I don't want the cane in the portrait. It will make me look like a cripple!"

"It will make you look like a ruler," Zoë told her. "And as well as balancing the composition, it displays those magnificent rings perfectly."

"Hmph!" The cane stayed.

With the setting and pose finally agreed on, Zoë got started on the painting.

Despite the arguments—or maybe because of them—she was enjoying herself in an odd kind of way. As Lady Scattergood had predicted, Lady Bagshott did try to bully her, but Zoë soon learned that the less she reacted, the harder Lady Bagshott tried.

It was quite entertaining.

"I have been told you are French, but that cannot be true."

"Mm?" Zoë responded vaguely, dabbing paint onto canvas. "Please tilt your head a little to the right."

"Hmph!" The old lady tilted. "Where were you born?"

"I don't remember. I was quite young at the time. And you, Lady Bagshott, where were you born?"

"What impudence! As if I'd share intimate knowledge with one such as you."

"Oh," Zoë said innocently, "I assumed we were making what the English call 'polite conversation.'"

The old lady gave her a sour look.

Zoë said, "I see you have your lips pressed into a thin line—almost invisible—is that how you wish me to paint them?"

A forced smile appeared on the old lady's face. If she'd been painting a crocodile, it would have been perfect.

"It would help if you told me a little about how and where you grew up," Zoë said.

She stiffened. "Why? What business is it of yours?"

"It will help me to know what kind of things to include in the background of the painting."

The old lady gestured to her surrounds with her cane— since Zoë had called it the sign of a ruler, she'd taken to using it more frequently. "This is all you need. No one needs to know where I came from—it's what I have achieved that matters."

Zoë agreed with her, to a point. Sometimes knowing where someone started made what they achieved more admirable. But Lady Bagshott would never admit that.

"Perhaps not," Zoë said. "Some people are born with a silver spoon in their mouth, others must work to achieve wealth and position. I know which of the two I admire more."

The old lady narrowed her eyes and stared at Zoë, as if

she thought Zoë was making fun of her. But she wasn't. She just kept painting.

From time to time, the old lady rose a little stiffly from her chair to walk around the room and stretch her legs. Naturally, with each circumnavigation, she would stop to inspect the portrait. And offer advice.

"My nose is not that pointy."

"It is, I'm afraid."

The old lady's hand flew to her nose and briefly explored its contours. "I know my nose, and it is *not* pointy."

"I am the artist and I've painted your nose exactly as I see it. Do you want people to recognize it as a portrait of you or not?"

"Don't be insolent. I'm paying you, remember."

"You've already paid Lady Scattergood, remember?"

She huffed bad-temperedly. "I don't care. Change it at once."

Zoë pretended to consider it. "You mean make it pointier? Or fatter? I could give you a Roman nose if you like. Or one with more of a hook. It does have a slight hook, now that I come to look at it again."

Nettled, Lady Bagshott snorted and resumed her seat. Until the next time she needed to stretch her legs and inspect the portrait. And criticize.

And so it went, every day until the portrait was finished. The final result was, she grudgingly admitted after a long examination, acceptable. Just.

Zoë thought it was one of her better efforts: in fact, she was quite proud of it. The portrait wasn't just a very good physical likeness, it also gave an insight into Lady Bagshott's character: her need to dominate, but underneath, a hint of vulnerability; her will to succeed, balanced by a wish to be esteemed—a wish Zoë feared would never be fulfilled unless the old lady softened her attitude to others.

Gazing at the portrait, Zoë realized something else: despite all the difficulties, she had come to rather like the old harridan.

There was a brief but spirited tussle when Zoë needed to take the finished painting away to have it framed, but it was more of a token effort: Lady Bagshott simply didn't like not having the last word on any matter. But as Zoë pointed out, the framers didn't make home visits, and unless she preferred the painting unframed, she had to trust that Zoë would return it and not, as she feared, put it up for public exhibition.

"I'll be glad to see the back of you," were Lady Bagshott's parting words.

"And I you," said Zoë sweetly.

Zoë and her maid, Marie, were seated in Lady Scattergood's carriage on their way for the final fitting of the dress she was to wear at the reception Leo and Izzy were holding for her on New Year's Eve.

The streets were crowded and the traffic had stopped. Something up ahead—an accident perhaps—had brought them to a standstill.

Zoë gazed out the window at the people in the street, envying them their freedom to go where they wished, when they wished. She'd been feeling rather cooped up lately; the plan was for her not to venture out until she'd been introduced to society—well, all those in society who were still in London at this time of year.

So no walks in the park, no shopping expeditions, no wandering around a marketplace just to look . . . And the cold and rainy weather didn't help.

It wasn't as if she hadn't lived in virtual seclusion before—last time she'd lived in London it had been her choice to stay out of sight for fear of causing difficulties to her half sisters. That hadn't been too hard. She'd come from the orphanage, where she'd never had a moment to herself and every minute of the day was strictly supervised.

Now she had memories of wandering the countryside with a handsome vagabond, and she couldn't help but think that her time with Reynard would probably be the last truly free time she would have. Young unmarried society women were strictly chaperoned at all times, and the whole world watched out for them to slip. Even if she married— which she was not at all sure she wanted—a husband would command her obedience and expect her to be present whenever he wished it.

She was jerked out of her reverie by the sight of a female in a dark pink pelisse, her face hidden by a veil, hurrying along the footpath, weaving through the crowds, with a maid scurrying to keep up with her.

There was something both familiar and furtive about the lady in pink. It was Milly Harrington, she realized, out in public—without her mother. What on earth was she up to?

As she watched, Milly dived into Hatchard's Bookshop. Her maid, interestingly, waited outside, her gaze roving back and forth over the street. A lookout. How very interesting.

Zoë could see Milly through the window. A moment later a man approached her. She reached out her hands to him, and he took them and kissed her knuckles. Reverently.

So, Milly Harrington had a beau, one that Mama didn't know about.

Good for her, Zoë thought as her carriage moved on.

The following morning, Zoë was in the summerhouse, drawing the intricate patterns left on the glass by the frost in the night. She had to be quick, as they were melting quickly, but they'd given her an idea for a painting.

"What are you doing?"

She looked up. "Knitting socks, Milly. What are you doing up so early?"

Milly tossed her head. "I'm allowed to." She entered the summerhouse, sat down and looked around. "Where are the socks, then?"

Zoë sighed. The ice patterns were almost gone anyway. "Read any good books lately?"

Milly wrinkled her brow. "Books? What books?"

"Didn't you go shopping for books the other day?"

Milly looked away. "No." She didn't look happy, and Zoë decided to stop teasing her. Feeling a bit constrained herself, she had some sympathy for the girl who never went anywhere without her mother. Their shared garden was the only place where she wasn't clamped by her mother's side. Which made that brief sighting of her at Hatchard's all the more intriguing.

She finished off the drawing of the ice. Milly sat and fidgeted.

Finally she said, "I suppose you think you're clever, having a party just for you before the season has even started."

Zoë shaded in some of the lines. "No, not particularly. It was Izzy and Leo's idea."

After another long pause, Milly said, "I expect to be betrothed in the new year."

"Really? Who to?" She wasn't the slightest bit interested, but if Milly wanted to talk, she could hardly stop her.

"I'm not sure. Mama is still negotiating."

Zoë looked up at that. "You don't know the name of the man you're going to marry?"

Milly made a careless gesture, but Zoë noticed her hands were trembling. "Mama knows what she's doing. She's second cousin to a duke, you know."

Zoë put aside her pencil and pad and gave Milly her full attention. "She's planning to marry you to some stranger you've never met?"

"Oh, I've met him. He's seen me and likes me very

much. I just don't yet know which of the gentlemen I've met he is." Her voice wobbled as she said it.

Zoë could hardly believe her ears. "And you've agreed to this?"

Milly gave an awkward half shrug. "Mama knows what's best for me." But her voice lacked conviction, and it was clear to Zoë she was simply parroting her mother.

"Well, I wouldn't do it. I think it's outrageous."

Milly stared at her for a long moment, then burst out, "I hate you, Zoë Ben-whahhhh," and rushed off.

Zoë stared after her. She knew Milly's mother was ambitious, but this was appalling.

Chapter Eleven

Julian Fox, the seventh Earl of Foxton, sent his curricle and groom around to the mews, then ran lightly up the steps of Foxton House in Mayfair and rang the bell. The door opened immediately.

The butler, Purvis, ushered him in with restrained butlerish delight. "Welcome home, my lord. We weren't expecting you so early. Home for Christmas, is it?" The smile slid from his face as he saw what was standing beside Julian, panting slightly and waving a ragged tail. His gaze tracked from the large and scruffy animal to the lead in Julian's hand, then he said with faint disbelief, "Is that *your* animal, my lord?"

"It is. His name is Hamish," Julian said, offering him the lead. "Give him a drink of water in the kitchen, will you, Purvis?"

"In *the kitchen*, m'lord? I don't think Cook will—"

"Or the scullery or even outside. Hamish isn't fussy and it's only for a short while. We're not staying."

Relieved, Purvis accepted the lead gingerly, saying,

"Very well, m'lord. I will consign the animal to the care of the second footman, who has an affinity with such creatures. You will find your grandmother in the green drawing room."

Julian frowned. "I don't recall a green drawing room."

Purvis tsked and shook his head. "I'm sorry, m'lord, I forgot. M'lady had it redecorated several months ago. It used to be the pink drawing room. Shall I announce you?"

"No need. I know the way. You take care of Hamish." Julian headed to the erstwhile pink drawing room, gave a perfunctory knock on the door and entered.

His grandmother looked up from the magazine she was perusing. "Foxton, finally, you have deigned to return."

"As you see, Grandmama." He bowed over her hand.

"And what have you been up to in the last few months? Gadding about with who knows whom, I suppose, and getting up to who knows what!"

He inclined his head. "That's it, my life in a nutshell."

She glared at him. "Frittering your life away when you have responsibilities here! Leaving the estate to go to rack and ruin!"

"Is Cartwright dead, then?" he said mildly. Cartwright was his very efficient and capable estate manager.

"No, of course not!"

"Has he left my employ?"

"Not to my knowledge."

"Become a drunkard?"

"Don't be ridiculous! You know very well the man is a teetotaler."

"Then I fail to see the problem. Cartwright is doing the job he is employed to do, and doing it well, as I discovered when I called in on my man of business yesterday. He delivered an excellent report on the state of my various properties and businesses."

She drew herself up in outrage. "You called on your man of business before coming to see *me*?"

"Yes, Grandmama," he said mildly. "As you have told me for time out of mind, the business of the estate should be my first priority. I knew you'd want to know how everything is faring."

She compressed her lips and glared at him. "Family should *always* come first."

"You being its sole representative in London?"

"Exactly," she said, slightly mollified. "I don't know what would happen to this family if it weren't for my vigilance and care. But," she said, rallying, "I wouldn't be the sole representative if you would only do your duty and take a wife!"

Julian smiled. "I thought we'd come to that, and there it is, only"—he glanced at the ormolu clock on the mantelpiece—"four minutes since I arrived. That might well be a record."

"Don't be frivolous, Foxton. Taking a wife is a serious business."

Julian picked an invisible bit of fluff off the immaculate sleeve of his coat.

"Well?" she prompted after a minute. "Have you done anything about it in the months since I last saw you?"

He toyed with the idea of telling her he'd found the only woman he'd ever wanted to marry—a beautiful French maidservant he'd known for just over a week who painted like a dream and was full of life. And who had stolen from him.

But as entertaining as the notion was, if he did, she'd probably explode, and he'd never hear the end of it. Besides, Vita's betrayal and disappearance were still rather . . . painful.

In his saner moments, he told himself he'd had a lucky escape. The rest of the time, he missed her. Ached for her.

"No, Grandmama, no prospective brides on the horizon. But I'm in no hurry. I'm not yet thirty."

"Your father married your mother when he was just four-and-twenty."

"I know." The estate being in a mess, and with crushing debts, his father had been forced to marry Mama, who was an heiress. And thus Grandmama had come into their lives, since she was the one who held and controlled the majority of the wealth Mama was heiress to. Ambitious and autocratic, she held it still and didn't hesitate to wield her power. Or try to. She hadn't yet found the way to rule Julian. Money didn't motivate him.

"And your brother married at five-and-twenty."

"Yes, he fell madly in love with Celia." His sister-in-law had soon revealed herself as nothing more than a pretty face with a rapacious nature beneath. She was the bane of Julian's existence—well, one of them.

"Love! Pah! What nonsense! Your brother was a fool. He fell out of love with her fast enough, and then he was off frittering money on opera dancers and the like!"

"Grandmama, I'm shocked to hear you speak of such things," he said, amused.

She snorted. "I didn't come down in the last shower. I know what's what! But my point is, your brother did the right thing in marrying young. He did his best to secure the succession. It was that feckless wife of his who failed in her duty and only gave him girls. So now that duty is yours— you must marry soon and get yourself a son."

Julian smoothed a wrinkle from his breeches. He'd heard this refrain a hundred times, but he had no intention of dancing to his grandmother's tune.

It was funny—she'd come from a mercantile background herself. Both her father and her late husband had been wealthy millowners, and she'd poured all her efforts into first securing a knighthood for her husband and then moving heaven and earth to get her only daughter married into the nobility.

Now, with husband and daughter dead, she considered the Foxton earldom and all it entailed to be her business, and she was relentless in her effort to rule Julian as well, attempting to mold him into what she considered to be a proper lord.

But he was fond of the old despot, so he didn't quarrel with her. He simply let her ring a peal over his head from time to time and then quietly went his own way, doing his duty as *he* considered it to be and pleasing himself as well.

No one had expected Julian to become the earl—least of all himself. His brother, the heir, had died of an infection from what he'd considered to be a trifling cut. Shortly afterward his father had died of a rage-induced apoplexy at the realization that his despised second son, having survived numerous battles and taken a number of wounds that failed to fester, was now the heir.

His grandmother eyed him beadily, the unsatisfactory second son who, through some huge cosmic error—he had no doubt she'd had words with the Almighty about that—had become the seventh Earl of Foxton. She was determined to lick him into shape. "I've put you in the Chinese room. Purvis will have taken your bags up."

"No, he won't. I left my bags in my lodgings in St. James's."

She swelled up. "*Lodgings?* The Earl of Foxton in *lodgings!*"

"Your hearing is excellent."

"But your place is here! This is Foxton House, the town house of the Earls of Foxton."

"I know. Nevertheless, I have taken bachelor lodgings in St. James's."

"Apart from what you owe your name and position, it's a waste of money!"

"It's my money, Grandmama," he reminded her gently. "In any case, you're here to wave the family flag, aren't you? Now, I must be off. I have an appointment with my barber."

"Barber, indeed! Dandy!" She snorted, and as he bowed over her hand, she muttered something about the younger generation and young men who had no respect. But Julian didn't wait to hear the end of the tirade: he was inured to them.

Live under the same roof as his grandmother? Be on hand for her to watch and constantly criticize? She could rule the roost to her heart's content, but she wasn't going to rule him.

He sent for his curricle to be brought around from the mews and called for his dog who, going by his smug expression and the gravy-stained fringe of fur around his muzzle, had enjoyed the fruits of the kitchen. Cook was clearly more of a dog lover than Purvis.

Then, with Hamish sitting up in lordly fashion on the passenger seat, Julian drove away, heading to his barber.

Julian was driving his curricle through the streets of London when he spotted an elegant dark-haired lady approaching Hatchard's Bookshop with another female. He caught a glimpse of her profile and blinked. It was Vita!

But it couldn't be. She was in France.

The footpath was quite crowded, but he saw the woman turn to her companion, and say something that made them both laugh.

Dammit, it was Vita, he was sure of it! Calling to his groom to hold the horses, he jumped down and plunged into the crowd after her.

He reached them just as they were about to enter the bookshop. "Vita!" He grabbed her by the arm and swung her around to face him.

And stared, dumbfounded.

"I beg your pardon," the woman said in freezing accents.

He just stared, stunned.

Her gaze dropped pointedly to where he gripped her arm. He hurriedly released her and stepped back. "I'm so sorry, madam. I thought—I was sure you were—the resemblance is uncanny." Dammit, he was practically stammering.

She arched a skeptical dark brow in exactly the same way Vita used to. Her green eyes—the same color as Vita's—gleamed with humor. Or was it malice? He wasn't sure. She wasn't Vita, he could see that now. This woman was a few years older, more polished and sophisticated. And far better dressed.

Still, her resemblance to Vita was striking.

She gave him an amused look, smoothed her gloves and said to her companion, "I've had men try to scrape an acquaintance with me before, but never in a public street. It lacks finesse, don't you agree, Clarissa?"

Her companion murmured something he didn't catch and tried to draw her away.

"I do most sincerely apologize," he said firmly. "The fact is I mistook you for someone else."

"Indeed? I would never have guessed."

He felt so stupid. "Yes. Someone who looks remarkably like you."

"Really?" she said in amused disbelief. "And here I've always considered myself an original."

Dammit, he was digging himself in deeper. He took a deep breath. "Again, I must apologize, madam, for approaching you so intemperately, and for, er, touching your arm. I was clearly mistaken."

"I should think so." She said it severely, but her eyes were dancing. She linked her arm through her companion's. "Come, Clarissa, we shall leave this gentleman to his delusions." And the two women disappeared into the shop.

Julian returned to his curricle, which was now surrounded by carters and traders and other drivers, not to mention interested onlookers, all loudly objecting to the way his curricle was blocking the street and holding up the traffic.

Issuing curt apologies in all directions, he climbed back into his curricle, gathered the reins and drove off, cursing his foolish mistake. He *knew* Vita was in Paris, so why on earth had he imagined she was about to enter a London bookshop? She probably couldn't even read. Certainly not in English.

He was obviously doing the same as he'd done in Paris—imagining things, seeing Vita everywhere.

The sooner he left London and headed down to his country home, the better for his sanity.

"Well, you're a dark horse, aren't you?" Izzy said to Zoë later that day. The three sisters were gathered in the summerhouse with a pot of tea and a plate of delicious almond and orange biscuits that Izzy's cook, Alfonso, had baked.

"Me?" Zoë said. "What do you mean?" Her two sisters were smiling at her in a very knowing way.

"I was accosted in the street this morning," Izzy said.

"Accosted? Who b— I mean, by whom?"

"By a very handsome gentleman."

"Yes," Clarissa added. "Very smartly dressed he was, too."

Bewildered, Zoë looked from one to the other. "What has that to do with me?" She didn't know any gentlemen in London, apart from her two brothers-in-law and Gerald and Lord Tarrant, Alice's husband. And she couldn't imagine her sisters being mysterious about any of them.

"He mistook me for someone else," Izzy said and bit into a biscuit.

"Oh?" Zoë felt a small pang of misgiving.

"Oh, indeed. Very certain he was that I was someone else, until he got a proper look at me."

"Really?" Zoë tried to look uninterested.

"He called Izzy Vita," Clarissa said.

"Which we know, from our generally inadequate schooling, is Latin for 'life,'" Izzy said. "Interesting, isn't it, that your name also means 'life,' only it's from the Greek?"

Oh lord, it had to be Reynard. "Quite a coincidence," she said weakly.

Izzy chuckled. "Come clean, little sister, you've met a man, haven't you?"

"A man?" she attempted. "In London, no, not at all."

"In France, then. Look, Clarissa, she's blushing. Isn't that adorable?"

"Don't tease her, Izzy." Clarissa leaned across and put a comforting hand on Zoë's arm. "Don't worry, you don't have to tell us anything if you don't want to."

"Yes, she does," Izzy said. "Sisters tell each other everything." Clarissa gave her a look and Izzy said, "Oh very well, you don't have to tell us if it's a secret. Is it a secret?"

Zoë thought for a moment and then gave in. "It's not really a secret, but I don't want anyone else to know."

"We won't tell a soul," Clarissa assured her. "Not even our husbands."

Zoë looked at Izzy. "Promise?"

"I promise."

Zoë took a long sip of her tea. "I did meet a man in France—an Englishman."

"Hah, I knew it!"

"Hush, Izzy. Let Zoë tell her story," Clarissa said.

Zoë continued. "You said the man who accosted you was a gentleman, but the man I knew wasn't a gentleman at all. He was unshaven, shabbily dressed and lived in a Romany caravan, though he said he wasn't Romany. He was— or at least he told me he was—a vagabond artist, who traveled from place to place, painting pictures."

Izzy and Clarissa exchanged glances. "How curious," Izzy said. "The man I met was definitely a gentleman, very fashionably and elegantly dressed."

"Yes, and afterward I saw him climb into a very smart curricle and drive away," Clarissa said.

"What did he look like?" Zoë asked.

Izzy thought for a moment. "Tall, well built, with lovely broad shoulders. Stylish boots and doeskin breeches that fitted very nicely over—"

"He had dark hair, slightly overlong, and very blue eyes," Clarissa added hastily.

Oh lord, it did sound like Reynard. But she had to be sure. "Wait a minute. I might have a drawing of the man I met. I'll run upstairs and fetch my sketchbook."

A few minutes later she was back. Flipping the pages until she came to one of the sketches she'd done of Reynard, she showed it to her sisters. "Was this the man?"

Clarissa took it from her, and she and Izzy looked closely at it. "Our man was clean-shaven and tidier, but this is definitely him."

Izzy took the sketchbook and started turning pages. "Oh, here he is again. And here." She kept turning pages. "You really are very talented, aren't you, little sister? These are brilliant." She turned a few more pages and gave a small chuckle. "You *might* have a drawing of him, eh? I've spotted several here."

"I counted at least six," Clarissa said and gave Zoë a complicit smile.

Zoë felt her cheeks heat.

Izzy closed the sketchbook and set it aside. "So, what happened?"

They sent for a fresh pot of tea and more biscuits and Zoë told them the story, from the time she left the Château Treffier—and why—to how she'd traded places with Marie because she wanted to visit the place where her mother spent her childhood. And about her decision to travel with Reynard.

"He was a painter, you see, and it was such fun working with him, painting together. But I slept in the wagon—which locked from the inside—and he slept outside." Except for the one night he hadn't, but she wasn't going to tell them about that. It was still too tender, too painful to recall how she'd given herself to him wholly, believing him to be the honorable man she'd imagined he was. Believing it to be an act of love. And that he felt the same.

Instead he was just a cheating opportunist. And she'd been a fool.

"Pity," Izzy said, and winked at Zoë.

"Izzy!" Clarissa said, shocked and at the same time amused.

"But you liked him, this Reynard, didn't you?" Izzy said to Zoë.

Zoë nodded. "Too much," she said in a low voice. "But it was impossible, so I had to leave." She had no intention of telling her sisters or anyone that she'd discovered he was cheating the villagers. Or that she'd stolen a valuable painting from him, but that it wasn't really stealing because it had originally been stolen from her family.

She'd already shown them the painting of her family, now in a handsome gold frame, saying simply that she'd come across it in France and had acquired it.

"Impossible, why?" Clarissa asked. "Because he was a vagabond and an artist?"

"Partly. I know you all want me to make a grand marriage and so—"

"No! We want you to make a *happy* marriage," Clarissa corrected her firmly.

Izzy nodded. "In any case, it's clear that he's not a shiftless vagabond at all but an English gentleman playing at being a vagabond artist."

"And if he looked after you and slept outside on the ground, giving up his bed to you, he sounds truly gentlemanlike," Clarissa said, her eyes shining.

"So he's not impossible at all," Izzy concluded.

Zoë nibbled on a biscuit. She had to find some way to

discourage them. He was still impossible. She would never marry a man who cheated poor people for a living.

And if he was in pursuit of her, it was probably only to retrieve the painting she stole.

She brushed crumbs off her fingers. "Well, whether he's impossible or not, it's of no consequence because we have no idea who he is. So let's forget about him. I already have."

Izzy picked up the sketchbook and passed it back to Zoe. "Don't worry, we'll find him."

"No, I don't want you to."

Izzy just smiled. "The English aristocracy is rather like a village. Everybody knows everybody else, and eventually we'll find someone who knows him."

"Yes," Clarissa agreed. "Even if we don't go looking for him, he's bound to turn up somewhere."

Zoë hoped they were wrong. If he did turn up, lord, what a scandal there would be.

"So now that's settled," Izzy said. "What do you know about this 'special Christmas surprise' Gerald and Lucy are putting on at Alice's house on Christmas Eve? I confess I'm very curious."

Zoë shook her head. She knew what it was, but if Lucy wanted it to be a surprise, she wasn't going to spoil it. "All I know is that we're all invited to dinner on Christmas Eve at Lord and Lady Tarrant's home."

"Yes, but it's a very early dinner—six o'clock, isn't it?"

"Yes, because they want the little girls to be there."

"How intriguing," Clarissa said. "I'm looking forward to it."

"And only a few days after that is our reception to introduce Zoë to the world—well, our small corner of it," Izzy said. "And that will be fun."

Zoë smiled, but she wasn't looking forward to that party at all. She was still in the dark about her sisters' plans for it. She'd had her dress fitted—green silk with dark red piping, very elegant and stylish, and it suited her beautifully, so why all the mystery about it? But both her sisters were being very closemouthed and secretive, and so there was nothing to be done except wait for it to happen.

As Julian drove between the stone pillars that guarded the long driveway to his childhood home, he felt the tension between his shoulder blades ease. Foxton Place, home of the Earls of Foxton. He'd spent his first seven years living here in blissful innocence.

Then at the age of seven he'd been shipped off to school. His brother had been sent two years earlier and claimed he loved it. Julian had hated it. His brother had called it tough; Julian thought it brutal.

Then some master had called him "dreamy" on his school report and pointed out that he spent more time drawing than studying, so his father had sent him to an even more brutal school.

Being enlisted in the army—even if he was pitched into a war at the age of sixteen—had been a relief.

Now, every time he drove down the long, curving driveway lined with ancient lime trees, he felt a sense of release. And homecoming.

He spent the first few days going over the estate books with Cartwright, his manager, and visiting tenants and following up on the various matters that had arisen in his absence.

Hamish went everywhere with him and soon became a welcome sight, loping along beside Julian's horse or sitting up on the bench of his curricle, observing his surrounds with a dignified air. The children of his tenants ran out to greet him—not Julian, the dog—who endured all kinds of attentions with remarkable patience until he wearied of them and took himself off to somewhere inaccessible.

"That dog's your ambassador," Cartwright commented

one afternoon. "I reckon he's made you a lot of friends here." Julian agreed.

On the fourth day home, his butler, Crowther, approached him with a small problem. "One of the maids has reported a leak in her quarters, m'lord. A small matter, but I thought you should know."

Normally Julian would have simply sent one of the estate workmen to fix it, but it occurred to him that it had been some time—years, in fact—since anyone had inspected the roofs, so he decided to look for himself.

Foxton Place was ancient. It had begun as a sixteenth-century Tudor manor house constructed on the remains of a medieval hall. Various additions had been made over the centuries, depending on the state of the family coffers and the artistic leanings of the current earl, and it was now a mishmash of architectural styles. Constructed initially in a U shape, a final wing, called the Long Gallery, had been added some few hundred years later, creating a central courtyard.

Many called it an architectural monstrosity, and several of Julian's friends had urged him to demolish it and build something new and elegant—and convenient. But Julian loved it as it was, every twisty, crooked, ridiculous inch of it. All he'd done to the old place was have several bathrooms and a new kitchen range installed, which earned him the undying gratitude of Cook, and a handful of other innovations made mostly for comfort and convenience.

"Take me to this leak," Julian said. "And then I'll want to inspect the roof."

Crowther led the way, taking a shortcut through the Long Gallery, which had been turned into a portrait gallery by the fourth earl. Julian knew every painting by heart. All his ancestors were there, lined up in grim solemnity. His ancestral gallery of rogues, he'd always thought of it. But as he passed, something caught his eye. He stopped. "What the devil is that?"

"It's a portrait of her ladyship, m'lord."

"I can see that! But what the devil is it doing here?" The portrait gallery was for portraits of his family, the Fox family. His grandmother was not, never had been and never would be a member of the Fox family. She was only his father's mother-in-law.

"Her ladyship had it sent down here several weeks ago, m'lord, with instructions that it be hung in the portrait gallery."

"I bet she did," Julian muttered. She'd been trying to take control of his family ever since he could remember.

"I thought it a very good likeness, m'lord," Crowther ventured tentatively.

"Yes, I'm not arguing the quality, just the placement. Why the devil didn't she hang it in the town house?"

The butler simply looked at him. Of course he would have no idea.

"Take it down."

"Yes, m'lord. Er, what shall I do with it?"

"Hold on," Julian said as the butler moved to take it down. Something about the painting nagged at him, something he couldn't quite put his finger on. Who was the artist? He moved up close and peered at the signature in the bottom right-hand corner. *Z-B*. Who the devil was Z-B?

He scrutinized the painting carefully, and things fell into place. Whoever this Z-B fellow was, he'd clearly studied art in the same place as Vita. There were several distinct similarities in technique and style. Dammit, the portrait could even have been painted by Vita herself.

He stepped back and eyed the painting broodingly. Was he imagining things again? It simply wasn't possible that Vita had painted his grandmother's portrait. She was in Paris somewhere.

Crowther coughed discreetly. "Shall I have it removed, m'lord?"

"No. You might as well leave it there." His grandmother's

attempts to control him and act as the matriarch of the family were irritating, but although she wasn't a blood relation, he supposed she'd earned her place in the gallery of ancestral rogues. She, or rather her money, had pulled his father out of debt, and her interfering ways had ensured he stayed out of debt. Had she not married her daughter into the Fox family and started throwing her weight around, keeping his father and brother under her thumb, he supposed the estate would still be in a dire financial state. Or worse.

He kept staring at the portrait. Who the devil was Z-B? Did he know Vita? And if he did, how well did he know her?

The butler cleared his throat. "The leak, your lordship?"

"The leak. Right. Lead me to it."

That night Julian dreamed of Vita for the third night in a row. He woke up thrashing around in the bed, hot and bothered. And aroused. Cursing himself silently, he got up and fetched himself a glass of water. It was a cold night, but he hadn't bothered having the fire in his room lit.

He padded to the window and drank his water, gazing out over the scene below, etched in shades of gray and silver and darkness. The sky was clear and the moon was almost full. No doubt that was the cause of these wretched dreams. Moon madness.

Vita. What did he want with her? He didn't know. He just needed to see her, that was all. See her properly—in the flesh. To touch her. And to stop imagining her everywhere.

A cold damp nose nudged his hand. He looked down. "I know, boy, it's ridiculous. But I can't forget her."

Hamish gave him a soulful look and sighed.

"You, too? We're a sorry pair, aren't we? Come on, back to bed." Julian climbed into bed and Hamish flopped down at the foot of it, on the special bed of blankets one of the maidservants had made for him. He had a way with women, did Hamish.

Julian lay in bed, trying to go back to sleep. He could hear Hamish snoring gently. How did dogs do it, drop to sleep instantly? No worries, he supposed.

His head was full of things, plans, possibilities—and Vita. He refused to think of her anymore. Christmas was coming.

No doubt his grandmother expected him to drive back up to London and attend the service at St. George's Hanover Square with her on his arm. So everyone would see.

But no. He would stay here for Christmas, he decided. He'd dodged his Christmas obligations last year and for several years before that by being abroad. This year, having come home earlier than planned, he would be here to do his duty. The warm welcome home he'd received from the tenants, servants and villagers had shamed him much more successfully than his grandmother's lectures did.

So he would swallow his distaste for all the fuss and read the lesson in church, invite the vicar and others back for Christmas dinner and give out the Christmas boxes on Boxing Day. Cartwright had done it last year, but Julian and Hamish would do the honors this year.

And after Christmas he'd drive back to London and ask Grandmama about that blasted portrait. And find out who the devil this Z-B was.

Chapter Twelve

❧

It was Christmas Eve, and in Bellaire Gardens it was cold, with the moon and stars invisible behind a heavy layer of cloud. It was just before six and had been fully dark for several hours, but the street was lit by gas lamps that glowed golden against the dark.

"Might snow later." Leo glanced at the sky as he and Izzy strolled along. They'd decided to walk around to the Tarrant residence and enter by the front door instead of taking their usual shortcut through the gardens. It was, after all, an event, albeit not a particularly formal one. "We will be *en famille*," Lady Tarrant had told them.

"I hope it does snow. I love snow at Christmas. It's so pretty and feels somehow magical. And symbolic, although of what I have no idea." Izzy wore her warmest pelisse, which was dark red wool trimmed with fur, and a fur hat. One of her hands was thrust into a fur muff; the other was tucked into the crook of Leo's arm.

"As long as we don't have to travel in it" was Leo's pragmatic comment.

Usually at this time of year Izzy and Leo and Race and Clarissa would be at their respective country homes, but the severity of Lady Scattergood's illness and her slow recovery had convinced them to stay in town until after the New Year.

They turned the corner, saw Clarissa and Race walking toward them and waved. Clarissa was swathed in a dark amber velvet cloak, the hood of which was trimmed with swansdown. It almost hid her face. Race was his usual elegant self, in breeches and boots and a many-caped greatcoat. It being a casual occasion, formal wear was not required.

They were followed by Zoë, walking beside an elegant sedan chair carried by four strong men. She was talking to the occupant through its firmly shut curtains.

Leo raised a brow. "They even got the old lady to venture out of the house. I'm impressed."

"Yes, she's been dying to know what it's all about and couldn't bear to miss it. Besides, ever since Matteo suggested she use a sedan chair with the curtains closed, she's been leaving the house more often. Apparently, as long as she doesn't see the outside world, she can cope with passing through it in her chair."

Lady Tarrant's butler, Tweed, had obviously been waiting for them, for before Leo could run up the steps to ring the bell, he'd opened the door.

"Welcome, m'lords, m'ladies, Miss Zoë," Tweed said, taking their coats, cloaks and hats and passing them to a footman. "Lord and Lady Tarrant, Lord and Lady Thornton and the young people await you in the second sitting room." He turned to assist Lady Scattergood from her sedan chair, which had been brought right into the hall.

Izzy and Clarissa exchanged glances. "The second sitting room?" Izzy queried. "Not the front drawing room?" Which was the usual place to entertain guests.

"No, Lady Salcott, the second sitting room." Tweed was

clearly enjoying himself. "This way, please." They followed him down the hall, passing the closed double doors of the drawing room.

They entered the room to a burst of excitement. The adults rose to greet the new arrivals while the three small Tarrant girls simply rushed to hug the ladies.

"I'm sorry," Lady Tarrant said, laughing, "but they're beside themselves with anticipation and impatience."

"Yes, because we want to see what it is!" Judy, the oldest, said.

Finally they were all seated again and the children set to play half-heartedly with a puzzle. Sherry was passed around and small crisp almond biscuits. The adults made polite conversation, but truth to tell, they were as impatient as the children, only better behaved.

A few minutes later Gerald and Lord Tarrant exchanged glances, Lucy nodded and the men rose and quietly left the room.

The remaining adults sipped sherry and made small talk, which nobody actually listened to, while the children openly watched the door with avid expressions.

Then Lord Tarrant stepped in again. "I'm turning off the lights," he warned them. There was an excited murmur, then a hush as one by one he shut off the gas lights, leaving only the fire to light the room. The flames danced, throwing shadows and gilding their faces.

Lucy appeared in the doorway. "Now, I want you to hold hands—children hold hands with an adult—and come out into the hall." They obeyed. Lina, the middle child, clutched Lady Tarrant's hand while Debo, the youngest girl, held on to Clarissa's and Judy clasped Zoë's. Race held out his arm to escort old Lady Scattergood.

The hall was in relative darkness, too. Lucy gathered them to stand outside the double doors of the drawing room. "Now, everyone, close your eyes, and you must not open them until I say so or it will spoil the surprise."

There were a few excited giggles from the children, but they scrunched their eyes firmly closed. Finally, the doors opened.

The scent hit Zoë first. A pine forest, fresh and sharp and clean. She breathed it in. Pine and beeswax. Perfect.

"You can look now," Lucy said.

"Ohhhhhh." It was a universal gasp of awe and surprise and pleasure, and for a moment nobody spoke.

"Oh my, that's beautiful," Clarissa breathed. "Look, Race, isn't it lovely?"

"It's magic," Lina exclaimed.

"It's a Christmas tree," Lucy said, delighted with their reactions. "You know how when Gerald and I were first married, he was posted to Vienna? We spent several years there, and the Viennese—all the Austrians and Germans, actually—have this beautiful Christmas tradition, and we loved it so much, didn't we, Gerald, that we decided to adopt it ourselves."

They all gathered around to examine it.

A small fir tree had been placed in a solid red pot. The only light in the room came from dozens of slender candles clasped in tin holders that were wired to the branches. The tree glittered with shapes cut out in gold and silver paper that twirled gently on invisible threads, along with tiny parcels in bright colors, small painted wooden toys, gold-painted nuts, delicate crystal figurines, round glass baubles and small brown biscuits in various shapes tied on with narrow red ribbons.

"Those paper shapes are exquisite," Clarissa commented, examining them closely. "Look, there's a deer and that's a wolf and a swan—"

"And a sailing ship and a drum and a basket—"

"And cats," Debo said happily. "Lots of cats."

"Zoë made them. She's very clever, isn't she?" Lucy said. The children and several adults turned accusing gazes on her. "You knew about this, Zoë? And you didn't say a word!"

She laughed. "And spoil the surprise? Of course not."

"We bought the crystal ornaments, the glass baubles and the little wooden toys in Vienna. We put them on the tree every year," Lucy explained. "But the biscuits are freshly baked—they're ginger. And those brightly wrapped lumps with twisty ends are sweets. And the gold-painted nuts are real. You children can each take a nut, a sweet, and a biscuit every day for the twelve days of Christmas, starting tonight. Just tell Gerald or me which ones you choose and we'll get it for you."

"It looks a bit dangerous," Leo said. "Won't it catch alight?"

"That's my Leo!" Izzy said, laughing. "Always so practical."

"It's quite safe," Gerald said. "We trimmed the needles so the candle flame won't come into contact with them. And I have a bucket of water here, behind it, just in case."

"And we won't leave it unattended," Lord Tarrant added.

"It's gorgeous," Lady Tarrant said, "and it smells so beautiful and fresh."

"Yes, that fresh-cut pine smell is part of the magic, I think," Lucy said. "James and Gerald went out yesterday to one of James's properties and found us the perfect tree. They smuggled it into the house at dead of night so no little eyes would see them."

A hush fell then as they simply sat and gazed at the beautiful little tree. And then, out of the silence, a quavering old voice began singing "Joy to the World," and immediately they all joined in. By the end, most of the women in the room had tears in their eyes, Zoë too.

It was her first real experience of a family Christmas, surrounded by people she loved, who loved her, and with the added magic of children and their open delight. And then dear Lady Scattergood, who reminded them what Christmas was all about.

After a while, Lord and Lady Tarrant organized their children to select their nut, sweet and gingerbread biscuit and get ready for bed.

"One more thing," Lucy said. "Gerald?"

Gerald produced three small parcels. "A little Christmas gift for each of you." The girls immediately sat down on the floor and opened their little parcels. Each one contained some more sweets and a crystal Christmas bauble—a horse for Judy, a rose for Lina and a cat for Debo. "Take good care of them. Next year you can hang your bauble on the tree," Lucy said, "and by the time you're grown up enough to have your own tree, you will have a collection of your own."

Then the children said their good nights, with kisses and hugs and curtsies, and went off upstairs to bed, after which the men snuffed all the candles.

Later, they were still talking about the tree over dinner, and Lady Tarrant said, "You know, now that I think about it, our dear late Queen, Queen Charlotte, did something similar at Windsor one year. It was a party for children, I think. I didn't see it myself, but I heard talk of it. Did none of you hear of it? No, I suppose it was before your time. I was a new bride myself."

"I know several other people who do this sort of thing, but I've never seen it myself," said Lady Scattergood. Which was not surprising, seeing as she rarely left her house, but nobody pointed that out.

"It's a charming tradition, and I, for one, am going to adopt it," Alice said. "Thank you, Lucy and Gerald. And Zoë." They all raised their glasses in a toast.

"And James, for the tree," Gerald added, "even though he hadn't a clue what we planned for it." They all laughed and toasted Lord Tarrant.

After dinner, they escorted Lady Scattergood and her

sedan chair home, and then the rest of them went off in a group to attend the midnight service.

As they stepped out of the church, with bells across the city joyfully ringing out the birth of the Christ child, fat flakes of white began to drift down from the darkness overhead.

"Oh, snow! That makes this the most perfect of all Christmas days," Clarissa exclaimed. And the others all agreed.

Foxton Place, East Anglia
Christmas Eve

Christmas Eve dawned chilly and overcast, but Julian was up early and feeling energetic. He had a lot to do if he was to get through his Christmas duties. He planned to leave for London as soon as he possibly could.

It was several years since he'd spent Christmas at Foxton Place. He'd generally been abroad, which the locals had taken as a reasonable excuse, but now that he was here and Christmas almost upon them, the locals had been loud in their enthusiastic celebration of the fact that the earl was at home, where he belonged.

He'd completed his examination of the estate books and found everything in good condition. He and Cartwright had discussed some agricultural innovations he'd read about, and Cartwright had agreed to try them. So he could leave with a clear conscience once Christmas was over.

He'd already ordered the preparation of a Christmas feast and invited the vicar and most of the foremost citizens of the estate. With Cartwright's assistance, he'd arranged the Christmas boxes that would be given out on Boxing Day and also made a list of the poorer families in the neighborhood, who would be given an additional basket of food this morning so they could celebrate Christmas. He'd even glanced through the lesson that he would read in church.

Best of all, he'd written polite refusals to the many invitations to dinners, balls and other gatherings that had arrived from some of the foremost families of the county, many of whom, he suspected, had unmarried daughters. He explained that commitments in Town—unnamed and imaginary, though he didn't mention that—required him to be in London by the New Year.

Acting as Lord of the Manor had never come easy to him. His father and brother had relished their positions and given orders without hesitation or reflection, but Julian wasn't at all comfortable with that. He disliked having other people's fates in his hands, but he'd learned in the army that there was no avoiding responsibility. During the war he'd taken good care of the men under his command, and now he was conscientious in carrying out his duty as the earl. It didn't mean he enjoyed it.

But he refused to let the title and its attendant responsibilities dominate his life, so he'd made the compromise that made his life bearable.

It was late on the morning of Christmas Eve when a large traveling coach laden with luggage bowled down the drive and came to a halt in front of the house. Julian glanced out the window and groaned. What the devil was she doing here? When he'd seen her in London recently, she'd made no mention of coming to Foxton Place for Christmas.

Accepting the inevitable, he pasted a pleasant expression on his face and went out to greet his grandmother. Hamish followed and was instantly shooed away.

"I knew you would need my guidance in performing your duties as the earl during this season, seeing as you've generally managed to avoid it," she said in response to his greeting.

"I am very well aware of what's expected, Grandmama," he said, managing not to grit his teeth.

She snorted. "I will freshen up in my room. We will speak at noon in the front drawing room, Foxton. I presume a fire has been lit in there." It hadn't, as Julian never used that room, which he thought overly ornate and pretentious, but he glanced at the butler who subtly inclined his head. By the time her ladyship came downstairs the fire would be burning merrily.

Julian was tempted to take himself off and go for a long ride around the estate, but he knew he would only be putting off the inevitable. Grandmama had come with the intention of reading him a lecture about Duty and the Earl, and the sooner he let her deliver it, the sooner he could get on with his life.

She arrived downstairs with a list in her hand, seated herself in the chair nearest the fire and said, "Now, I suppose you haven't even thought about sending baskets of food—"

"To the poorest in the neighborhood. Yes, and it has been done." He'd done it first thing in the morning, and delivered most of them himself. He wasn't very comfortable playing Lord Bountiful, but he'd also had quite a lot of experience mingling with poor people, and didn't look down on them as his father and brother had. He knew better. *There but for the grace of God go I.* Besides, he liked some of them. And taking Hamish with him always helped to break the ice.

"Oh." She ticked something off on her list. "And the Christmas boxes?"

"Done and ready to be given out on Boxing Day. I consulted Cartwright as to the various needs."

She sniffed. "Well then, on Christmas morning, you will need to read the lesson in church. I suggest—"

"The vicar and I have already chosen the lesson."

"Oh. I see. And I don't suppose you remembered to invite—"

"The vicar for Christmas dinner? Of course I didn't forget. He gladly accepted, as did all the others I invited." He named the people he'd invited.

She stiffened. "Do you expect me to sit down to dinner with your agent and members of the hoi polloi?"

"I don't expect anything. You don't have to dine with us if you don't want to. I can have your dinner sent up on a tray if you prefer."

"Don't be ridiculous!"

"No, Grandmama," he said hiding a smile. She loved to play hostess, particularly to those she considered her inferiors. "And, of course, I've finalized the menu with Cook."

His grandmother's lips thinned. "I could have done that."

"Yes, but I didn't know you were coming, did I?" he said sweetly.

With a sour look she consulted her list again. "I don't suppose I'll need to remind you to take part in the Boxing Day hunt?"

"No, there is no need to remind me. I won't be joining the hunt."

Her voice rose. "Won't be hunting on Boxing Day? But the Earls of Foxton *always* take part in the hunt."

"Not this one."

"Your father and brother joined in the hunt every year. Led it as often as not."

"I know."

"And your grandfather before him."

"Yes, that's true."

"And his father before him, and—"

"And no doubt every Earl of Foxton since the year dot hunted, but I don't hunt."

"What do you mean, you don't hunt?"

"Would you eat a fox if it was cooked?"

Her face screwed up. "Of course not, you ridiculous boy. Who eats foxes? Nobody. Whatever gave you such an insane idea?"

"I only hunt for food, and then only when I need it." When he was in the army, there'd been times when food was short, and then he'd happily hunted in order to fill the pot—rabbits and hares mostly and the occasional bird. And when he was traveling in France, it was the same thing.

She stared at him a moment. "But you can't possibly be short of food."

"I'm not, and so I don't hunt." He could see she was prepared to argue the point, so he continued, "I particularly don't hunt for sport. I fail to see the sport in dozens of men and dogs chasing one small fox, making a great hullabaloo and careering all over the countryside, trampling crops and lord knows what else, all in the name of sport. So I won't do it. Now, is that everything on your list?"

She glanced at her list and gave a grudging nod.

"Good, because I have a question for you."

"A question for *me*?" She drew herself up, preparing to do battle again.

"Yes, that portrait you sent down here, the one you asked to be hung in the portrait gallery."

"I know you don't like it, but—"

"It's a very good portrait."

"Oh. Well, I thought it should be in the portrait gallery because—"

"I don't give a hang where you choose to display it. It can stay there for all I care. You've contributed as much and a good deal more to the Foxton family than some of the wastrel ancestors whose portraits hang there in pride of place."

Her jaw dropped open.

"What I want to know is the fellow's name."

"What fellow?"

"The chap who painted it."

"It wasn't a man, it was a chit of a girl."

Julian stiffened. "A *girl*? What girl?"

"An insolent baggage. You would not believe the cheek she gave me, always answering back and rarely with a civil response. I had to take a very firm line with her."

"*What girl?*" he repeated. A girl? It had to be Vita, it had to be. "Was she French?"

"Of course she wasn't French! Would I have my portrait painted by a Frenchwoman? I hope I'm more patriotic than that! What business is it of yours, anyway?"

"So she spoke to you in English?"

"Naturally."

"Without any kind of accent?" he persisted.

She said impatiently, "She was *English*, Foxton. Do you think I can't tell an English girl from a foreigner? And she spoke like a lady—though her manners were not those of a properly bred gel." She narrowed her eyes. "Why do you want to know?"

He ignored that. "What was her name?"

"Her name?" She made a pettish gesture. "How would I know her name? I don't bother with the names of such as she."

There were times when he could happily strangle his grandmother. "But the signature, Z-B, you must know what it stands for."

"Well, I don't. All I know is that she was a brazen-faced hussy with no respect for her elders. But despite her attitude and her youth, she was a competent enough painter, I admit, although she charged me an arm and a leg for a perfectly ordinary painting. *And* she got my nose wrong, and so I told her at the time, but would she listen?" She snorted.

The nose was perfect, and the portrait as a whole was superb, Julian thought, but he harnessed his impatience and forced himself to say in a calmer voice, "How did you find her, Grandmama?"

She gave him a long narrow look, then made a vague gesture. "Oh, she's some kind of protégée of Olive Barrington."

"Who is Olive Barrington? One of your friends?"

She snorted. "Hardly."

"Then how do you know her?"

"I knew her when I was a gel. Before my marriage."

"I see, so she lives in Manchester?"

She snorted again. "No, she's far too hoity-toity for that. She lives in London, of course."

"But you don't know where."

She gave him a surprised look. "Of course I know where."

Julian's patience was by now wafer thin. "Then could you please furnish me with her address?"

"There's no point. I doubt she'll speak to you. She hates men and is ridiculously reclusive. She won't even let *me* through the front door, so there's no point in going there. Now, I've had enough of this. I've had a long trip and I want to rest before dinner." She rose, tossed her list into the fire, said, "It's wasteful having a fire in such a big room when you use it so rarely," and sailed out.

Julian clenched his fists and muttered a few frustrated words to the ceiling. He was sure the painting had been done by Vita, which meant she was in England, in London. But according to his grandmother, her portraitist spoke English like a native. And like a lady. And Vita was—supposedly—French and a maidservant.

But he'd revealed his interest in her too soon, and his grandmother was being deliberately vague and annoying. She approached every one of their interactions as a battle and was determined to win. She was the stubbornest woman he'd ever known, so if she didn't want to tell him where this Olive Barrington lived, wild horses wouldn't drag it out of her. He was sure she knew exactly where he could find Vita, assuming it was Vita who'd painted her portrait. But he knew now he'd never get it out of her.

It was all quite a puzzle, and his grandmother was infuriating, but he was determined to solve the mystery. The minute his duties were done on Boxing Day, he was off to London.

He was going hunting after all: for Vita.

* * *

The first thing Julian did when he reached London was to take Hamish for a nice long run on Hampstead Heath. He then left him at his lodgings with a bone to gnaw on. After that he called on the only other relative he had in London, a second cousin who was about the same age as his mother would have been had she lived.

He'd decided to ask about the woman his mother said was Vita's sponsor, because asking about a young woman simply called Vita would get him nowhere, he was sure. He cursed himself for never asking her surname—though he hadn't exactly shared his own name or surname with her.

"Miss or Mrs. Olive Barrington?" the cousin repeated, shaking her head. "I'm sorry, Julian, I've never heard of her."

"Do you know anyone I could ask? The woman I'm seeking would be about the same age as my maternal grandmother, Lady Bagshott. They knew each other in their youth, I believe."

The cousin gave him a sheepish look. "I'm sorry, Julian, but I don't know anyone who would willingly associate with Lady Bagshott."

He sighed. "I understand. She's a difficult woman."

He called on several other ladies with whom he had even the slightest acquaintance. Doing their best to hide their amazement at receiving a visit from a man most of them barely remembered, they nevertheless showed great interest in his search for the mysterious Olive Barrington—until they discovered she was the same age as his grandmother.

"See, this is the result of your avoiding society events for all these years," one matron told him with ill-concealed satisfaction. She'd attempted to get him interested in her daughter, he recalled vaguely. He opened his mouth to inquire after the daughter, then closed it when he realized he had no idea of the girl's name. And if she hadn't married in the meantime, she would take it as interest in the girl—woman, lady, whatever.

Finally, with reluctance he rode out to Richmond and called on Celia, his widowed sister-in-law. She showed no surprise at his calling on her; she was simply furious that it had taken him this long. As expected, he had to sit through a long list of complaints and demands before he had a chance to slip his question in.

"No, Celia, I won't pay for new dresses for my nieces. You have a very generous allowance, and part of that, as you know very well, is for the maintenance of your daughters and yourself." His sister-in-law was a notorious pinch-penny, and every conversation he'd had with her ended up being a battle to get him to pay for things she could easily afford.

"No, I won't buy them horses. Apart from costing a fortune, neither of the girls enjoys riding—at least I've never seen them on horseback, not even when they've spent weeks at Foxton Place, where there are several suitable horses.

"And no, of course I won't pay for new riding habits. What would they want with—"

"Oh, I see, they want to go riding *with their friends*." The sudden interest in riding was to impress some man, he was sure. "Very well, I'll pay for the riding habits if—and I mean if—they take riding lessons for, let me see, six weeks. Then, if they still want to go riding, we'll speak of the matter again."

And so it went. Sukey needed new shoes. Ella needed a fur mantle. Both girls needed some proper jewelry, not the trumpery things they'd received when their poor papa died.

As he knew very well that the "trumpery things" they'd inherited included several fine pearl necklaces with matching bracelets and earrings, a ruby and an emerald pendant, dozens of bracelets and brooches and several other pretty necklaces—not counting the very valuable jewelry Celia herself had inherited as the earl's widow—he remained unmoved.

He briefly toyed with the idea of reminding her that many of the jewels she considered her own were, in fact, tied to the title, and when he married, they would have to be passed to his wife. But that was a battle for another day.

Finally he was able to ask his pouting sister-in-law whether she knew a Miss or Mrs. Olive Barrington. Her answer was short and snappy. "No, I do not. And no, I will not demean myself by asking my friends about some female I neither know nor wish to know."

On that note, he took his leave.

Dispirited, he was heading back to his lodgings when he saw two men walking along in conversation—familiar faces. He pulled over, and as they came abreast of his curricle, greeted them. "Colonel Tarrant. Paton."

There was a brief exchange of greetings and rapid updating of their current situations. All three of them were now out of the army, which was how he'd known them. Colonel Tarrant was now Lord Tarrant, and Gerald Paton was now Viscount Thornton. And they were both married.

"And I'm now the Earl of Foxton since my father and older brother died," he told them.

"I'm delighted to see you," Lord Tarrant said. "Gerald and I are heading to the Apocalypse Club, where we're meeting a couple of friends for dinner. Our wives are planning a party to be held on New Year's Eve, so we're taking refuge in an all-male bastion," he added. "You'd be most welcome to join us."

After the day he'd had, the idea of convivial male company was appealing, so Julian accepted. He sent the curricle away with his groom, and as they walked the few blocks to the Apocalypse Club they caught up on recent news.

"As for what I'm doing in town today," Julian finished, "I suspect I'm on a wild-goose chase." He told them about his fruitless search for Olive Barrington and wasn't surprised when neither of them had heard of her.

They entered the club, and he met the friends they were there to dine with, Lord Salcott and Lord Randall. "We're all neighbors," Tarrant explained, "and it's the wives of these gentlemen that are leading the party planning."

"Want to come?" Lord Salcott said instantly. "My wife is always on the lookout for eligible single men to invite to parties."

Julian laughed.

"He means it," Lord Randall said. "You'd be very welcome."

Julian hesitated, but before he could refuse, a waiter arrived to usher them to their table.

"You could ask people at the party about the mysterious lady you're searching for," Tarrant suggested as they were seated.

"Mysterious lady?" Lord Randall said.

"Yes, a *very* mysterious lady," Gerald said in a dramatically hushed voice. "No doubt very beautiful and very—"

"Grandmotherly," Julian said.

They all laughed, and he explained to Lords Salcott and Randall that he was looking for a lady who was an old acquaintance of his grandmother's. "I've been asking everyone I know, but nobody has ever heard of Olive Barrington."

"I have." Lord Salcott shook out his linen napkin. "She's my aunt."

Julian's jaw dropped. "Your *aunt*?"

"Yes, only she hasn't been Olive Barrington for fifty years or so. Barrington was her maiden name. She's Lady Scattergood now."

Of course, Julian thought as the waiter took their orders. His grandmother often referred to her youthful acquaintances by their maiden names. Why hadn't he thought of that?

"What did you want with her?" Lord Salcott asked, then when Julian hesitated, he added, "No, no need to explain now. Come to our party on New Year's Eve. My aunt will probably attend. The party is to introduce my wife's"—he indicated Lord Randall—"our wives' young cousin to our friends in the ton. My aunt is very fond of her. It's not a big formal occasion—we'll hold a proper ball at the start of the season. This is just a reception to introduce her to our friends, so when she does make her come-out she won't feel as if she's wholly among strangers."

"But there will probably be some dancing," Lord Randall added. "At least that seems to be the most recent decision. My wife is also involved in the planning."

"Yes," Lord Salcott said with amusement. "It did start off as a small reception, but it's been steadily growing. By New Year's Eve who knows what it will have become? So, Foxton, would you like to come to our party? I promise you our wives will be delighted to have another eligible young man added to the list."

Why not? Julian thought. The idea of being an eligible young man—in other words, marriage bait—didn't delight him, but at least he'd meet the old lady who knew Vita. "Thank you, I'd be delighted," he told Lord Salcott.

Chapter Thirteen

ॐ

It was New Year's Eve, and Zoë, Clarissa and Izzy were at Izzy's house getting dressed for the party with their maids in attendance. As Clarissa had said, "It's silly to come in a carriage when we're only a few steps across the garden, but the ground is damp, and we don't want our hems to get stained or dirty. Or our lovely silk slippers."

Zoë's nerves were strung tight, and they were not helped by what felt like a flock of swallows swooping around in her stomach. She probably should have eaten something, but she hadn't been able to force a morsel past her lips for fear it would come straight back up again.

She took slow, deep breaths. It was ridiculous to be nervous, she told herself. This was for her sisters, not her. For herself, she didn't care if people did learn she was an English bastard half sister, but she did care—very much—if that damaged the reputations of her sisters. So long-lost French cousin she was to be. Leo had even suggested she could add de Chantonney to her surname.

De Chantonney had actually been Maman's surname,

but in her fearful flight the nurse had changed her surname to Benoît, which did not signal "aristo" the way that de Chantonney did. The terror must have stayed with Maman, because she'd never changed it back.

And while de Chantonney did sound vastly more aristocratic than Benoît, she was still Maman's daughter, and she would respect her decision, even if the reasons for it no longer existed.

Taking on the de Chantonney name would also mean she was associating herself with a family and place she felt no connection with. The Château de Chantonney was an abandoned ruin, and the grand family who had once lived there was gone. It was all in the past, and she was stepping into the future.

Behind her Marie put the final touches to her hair and stepped back. "Oh, mademoiselle, *vous êtes très belle*."

Zoë stood and walked to the full-length looking glass.

Her green silk dress was gorgeous, there was no other word for it. The silk was the exact color of her eyes. It was simply but stylishly cut, with a low neckline—but not too low—and trimmed with dark red piping.

"Knock, knock," a familiar voice called, and Clarissa entered, dressed in peach silk. "Oh, but you look lovely," she exclaimed, and Zoë was about to return the compliment when she looked at who was behind Clarissa and froze. Her jaw dropped. "Izzy!"

Izzy, who had been posing in the doorway, laughed and stepped inside. She linked arms with Zoë in front of the looking glass. "Don't we look perfect?"

Zoë's breath finally came back. "But your dress is exactly the same as my dress! And our hair, too." Izzy had instructed Marie to put Zoë's curly dark hair up into a high knot, with a few loose tendrils about her face and one long ringlet falling to her left shoulder. Izzy's hair was identically arranged, only her ringlet touched her right shoulder. They were mirror images of each other.

Izzy laughed and pirouetted. "I know. Isn't it perfect?"

"Yes, but we can't wear the same dress and have our hair arranged the same. We'll look like twins. Everyone will talk."

"Yes, that's the idea," Izzy said, laughing. "Everyone is going to be commenting on how alike we are anyway, and so rather than trying to minimize it, we're going to *flaunt* it."

"But then they'll think . . . They'll all *know* I'm your bastard half sister." And, by implication, Clarissa's. The whole point of her masquerade as a French cousin was to prevent that very thing.

"No, they can only guess," Clarissa explained. "They will wonder about it anyway—your resemblance is too strong for them not to—but if we tried to hide your resemblance to Izzy everyone would *know* there was something to hide."

"But if we flaunt it, it will show everyone that we are proud of you and are delighted at how much we look alike," Izzy finished. "Which I, for one, am. And so we'll flaunt it, glory in it, celebrate it! It's going to be such fun."

"I don't know," Zoë began. "What will your husband think?" Izzy's husband had always seemed to her to be a stickler for correct behavior.

"Leo? When I told him of our plan, he laughed and said he was looking forward to seeing it."

"Really?"

"Yes, now don't look so anxious. We love you and we want you to enjoy yourself."

Clarissa slipped an arm around Zoë's waist and squeezed. "Truly, there's nothing to worry about, my love. Most of the people here are our friends and are looking forward to meeting our long-lost French cousin. And you look absolutely beautiful."

"Yes, you'll dazzle—no, *we'll* dazzle the lot of them," Izzy said.

There was a soft knock on the door, and it opened to

reveal Leo and Race, both looking magnificent in their evening clothes. "Ready?" Leo said. He gave Zoë and Izzy a
long look, raking them from head to toe, then nodded
briskly. "Perfect."

"By which he means you all look dazzlingly lovely,"
Race said.

Clarissa stepped forward and linked her arms with her
husband and Leo. "You and Izzy are to follow behind," she
said, and they stepped out into the hall. Zoë blinked. This
was not how she'd expected the night to start, but then neither had she expected to be dressed identically to her sister.

Izzy linked her arm through Zoë's. "Ready, little sister?" Zoë swallowed and nodded. She wasn't, but there was
no choice. She couldn't run away now. "Then let's go.
They're all waiting for us."

The guests were assembled at the foot of the stairs, all
waiting to meet Zoë. Clarissa, with Leo on one arm
and Race on the other, went first. Halfway down the stairs
they stopped. A hush fell. Then Leo said in a loud voice,
"Ladies and gentlemen, my wife and I and Lord and Lady
Randall are delighted to present our beloved French cousin,
Miss Zoë Benoît." They stepped aside to reveal Zoë and
Izzy standing arm in arm in identical dresses. Izzy raised
an arm in a kind of flourish, as if presenting Zoë to the
world. Which Zoë supposed she was.

A gasp rose from the audience, then a murmur of excla-
mations.

"And now we curtsy," Izzy murmured, and, beaming,
she gave a graceful curtsy. Zoë did the same. Izzy reminded
her of a ringmaster presenting an act to the circus—with
Zoë as the star—and they began a slow descent, with Clarissa and Lords Salcott and Randall acting as a kind of
escort on either side.

Below Zoë was a sea of faces, a few she recognized—
Lucy and Gerald, Lord and Lady Tarrant, Milly Harrington
and her mother, and several of the old ladies whose portraits she'd painted—but most were complete strang— Oh
no! A very familiar pair of Mediterranean-blue eyes were
glaring at her across the room.

She stumbled, missed a step and might have fallen, except that Izzy was still holding on to her and Race caught
her other arm. "Steady there," he murmured.

Zoë swallowed. Her heart was racing. What was Reynard
doing here, of all places? He was a vagabond, a rootless
artist.

Yes, and she was an unfairly dismissed French maidservant. Oh God.

She continued down the stairs, presenting what she
hoped was a serene visage. Izzy was talking in a hurried
undertone, pointing out various people, but Zoë didn't take
it in. She'd forgotten about the multitude of eyes watching
her. She was only aware of one pair of Mediterranean-blue
eyes, only this time his expression was as cold as the
North Sea.

Oh lord, what was she going to do? More to the point,
what was *he* going to do? Would he make a scene? And how
did he get invited? Everyone here was supposed to be a
friend. Was he invited? By whom? And why?

The swallows in her stomach had turned into crows.

Had he found out who she was, or was he here by coincidence and as surprised to see her as she was to see him?

Three more steps to go.

How on earth was she going to handle this? The only
thing she could think of was to feign illness, and she did
feel slightly ill, but only since she'd spotted Reynard. She
couldn't do that to Izzy and Clarissa and their husbands.
This party had been arranged especially for her. She
couldn't let them down.

But if there was a scandal . . . that would be worse.

She prayed silently for Reynard to be an illusion. Or to disappear. Spontaneously combust. Anything.

He disappeared from sight as she reached the floor, and people crowded forward to be introduced to her and to exclaim over her and Izzy's extraordinary resemblance.

Izzy was loving every moment of it, telling everyone the story they'd agreed on. "Yes, isn't it amazing? Of course, we always knew there was some sort of cousin in France—one of Papa's cousins married a Frenchman—but so many people simply disappeared during the Terror, we had no idea whether any of our relations had survived. And of course, Papa was never one for keeping contact with family. But by some miracle, one relative escaped Madame Guillotine and later gave birth to our beloved Zoë. Lord and Lady Thornton found her for us in France, and looking at her, you can see why we had no doubt that she was related. She could easily be my little sister, couldn't she? Even my twin."

She and Clarissa took Zoë from group to group, endlessly repeating variations of the story. Luckily Zoë's shock at seeing Reynard was taken to be shyness by most people. A few wondered whether she spoke English, and tried some French on her. She responded, of course, in English, which caused relief and congratulations on her pretty accent.

Several times she told the story of how her mother was smuggled to safety during the Terror. She didn't say how or to where and allowed people to assume it was to somewhere in France. And any halting in her recitation of the tale was ascribed to emotion—which it was; she was fretting about Reynard.

Where was he? What was he doing?

Finally it happened. She looked up and saw him plowing through the crowd toward her with a grim expression on his face.

She took a deep breath and braced herself.

"Ah, there you are, Foxton," Leo said as Reynard reached them. "You wished to meet my aunt, didn't you? Allow me to take you to her. She doesn't like crowds, so she's settled in the library. Come along."

"Oh, but—"

"You'll have plenty of time to meet Miss Benoît, but my aunt keeps early hours, so if you wish to meet her, now is the time."

Zoë breathed again as, with ill-concealed reluctance, Reynard allowed Leo to take him off to meet Lady Scattergood. There was really nothing else he could do without being rude to his host. She would have laughed if she weren't so nervous.

"Aunt Olive," said Lord Salcott, "I'd like to present Lord Foxton, who has been scouring London in the hope of meeting you. Foxton, my aunt, Lady Scattergood." He bowed and withdrew, no doubt to see to the rest of his guests.

Julian mentally groaned. It wasn't untrue, but saying it so bluntly gave entirely the wrong impression. Julian bowed over the old lady's hand, murmuring a greeting.

She was thin, almost scrawny, but was draped with a multitude of large multicolored silk scarves, several of which threatened to drip off her narrow shoulders. Seated in a large bamboo chair shaped rather like a peacock's tail, she was holding court with a collection of other old ladies seated in a semicircle facing her.

She lifted a lorgnette and trained it on him for an uncomfortably long time. "Scouring London for me, were you, sirrah? And why was that, pray tell?"

Julian didn't want to say that he was actually searching for Vita—Zoë—so he said the first thing that came into his head. "I believe you are a friend of my grandmother."

"Indeed? And who is your grandmother?"

"Lady Bagshott." Several of the other ladies tittered as if they knew something that he didn't.

"Bagshott?" She snorted. "She's no friend of mine."

"Oh? I understood you were friends when you were young."

The old lady snorted again. "Friends? What rot! I disliked her when she was a pushy young gel and dislike her just as much—possibly even more—now that she's a pushy old– ."

"Olive," one of the old ladies said warningly.

Lady Scattergood gave a pettish shrug. "Well, she is." She turned back to Julian. "Is that all you wished to say? Because if it is . . ."

"I am an admirer of the paintings done by your protégée, Miss Benoît. I saw the one she did of my grandmother. I wished to speak with her, possibly engage her services." And possibly wring her thieving little neck.

The lorgnette was trained on him again. "An admirer of the paintings or of Miss Benoît?"

"Both."

The old lady made a hissing sound. "I might have known it. You stay away from my protégée and keep your lustful thoughts to yourself, you rake!"

Julian blinked. *Rake?*

"My Zoë has her career to think of, and she doesn't need some wretched man dragging her down into domesticity and forcing obedience on her, not to mention other unspeakable acts."

Julian raised a brow. He couldn't see any man forcing obedience onto Vit— Zoë. And unspeakable acts? Was the old lady demented?

"Although"—she peered beadily at him through the lorgnette—"do you have any plans to travel abroad anytime soon?"

"Not in the immediate future, no. But I generally do travel abroad most years."

"Hah! But you come back, don't you, you blackguard?"

"Yes." By now Julian was quite bewildered.

"Ah, Foxton, there you are," Lord Randall said from the doorway. "Good evening, Lady Scattergood, ladies. Could I borrow you a moment, Foxton? There's someone I want you to meet." He gestured to Julian, who was only too glad to escape.

"Phew, I'm glad you came when you did," he said when they'd left the room. "That old lady is—"

"A terror?" Randall said and chuckled. "She's not so bad once she gets to know you, but she's somewhat hostile toward men."

"I did pick up a hint of that," Julian said dryly, and Randall laughed again.

"It took me months before I could even get past her front door when I was courting my wife. Clarissa was living with her at the time, so you can imagine how it rather inhibited us. The thing is, the old lady had what we suspect to be an unhappy marriage—it lasted a couple of weeks and then her husband sailed off to the Far East, where he remained for the rest of his life. He sent her back an endless flow of gifts, all kinds of statues and ornaments and—you saw the scarves. If you ever get inside her house, which you probably won't, you'll see it's crammed with an enormous clutter of priceless oriental art."

"So she resents being left alone all that time. I understand."

"No, you don't. As far as she's concerned, that was the best part of her marriage. Did she ask you if you planned to travel?"

"Yes, and I told her I did, regularly."

"And then I suppose made the mistake of telling her that you also regularly returned."

"Yes."

"Ah well, that's you done for," Randall said cheerfully. "I hope you got what you came for."

"I did," Julian said, though he could have done without meeting the old lady and skipped straight to Vita. Zoë. "By the way, who was it you wished me to meet?"

"Oh, no one. I just thought you probably needed rescuing."

"I did. And I'm very grateful." The band had finished one dance and was about to start another. "But if you could introduce me to Miss Benoît, I'd be even more grateful."

Zoë had started to relax a little. Everyone had been very kind and welcoming, nobody seemed to have any suspicion that the story they'd been told was only partially true, and now that the dancing had started, she didn't have to talk, just dance. Best of all, Reynard seemed to have disappeared. Leo had taken him away to introduce him to Lady Scattergood for some reason. She didn't care why, she just hoped he'd left.

The dance that had just finished was a country dance, and her partner had gone to fetch her a drink. She was good at dancing. She'd had plenty of practice in Paris with Lucy and Gerald. The next one was a waltz. She loved the waltz, and it had been bespoken by a pale young man whose name she couldn't recall. She remembered what he looked like, though. And there he was—oh no. There was Reynard with Race, threading his way through the crowd toward her.

Her mind went blank. She stood numb, helpless, silently panicking as Race introduced him. She barely took in a word, just stared, trying to think how to escape.

He bowed over her resistless hand, and said "Ah, they're about to begin the waltz, Miss Benoît. Our dance, I believe."

"Oh, but I say—" the pale young man began.

"Sorry, but Miss Benoît and I are old friends, and we arranged this earlier," Reynard said firmly, ignoring the fact that they'd just been introduced in front of the pale young man. "Better luck next time." He took her arm and turned her toward the dance floor.

"No," Zoë said. "It's . . . No, it's a waltz." She snatched the excuse out of thin air. "I can't dance with you. I don't have permission to dance the waltz." She wrenched her arm out of his grasp.

"No, my dear," a nearby matronly lady told her kindly. "This is a private family occasion. It's only at Almack's that a young lady needs to seek the permission of one of the patronesses in order to waltz. So go ahead, dance with your young man." She beamed.

"Yes, dance with your young man," Reynard said grimly, and led her on to the dance floor.

She glanced up at him as they prepared to take their positions, and the smug expression on his face turned her numb panic into anger. He thought he'd won, did he, manipulating her into this dance? What was he planning to do—expose her? Well two could play at that game.

"What are you doing here?" she hissed.

"Looking for you, of course."

"How could you? You had no idea who I was."

"Obviously I did."

"How?"

The orchestra played an opening chord, and he took one of her hands in his, and set the other lightly on her waist. They weren't wearing gloves—it was an informal dance— and instantly she was taken back to that moment when they'd been traveling and a pothole had almost caused her to fall off the wagon. His arm had shot out around her waist and pulled her to safety. And had remained there for several minutes until she'd forced herself to move slightly away.

In that moment, all that time ago, she'd begun to fall under his spell.

Well, it wouldn't happen again. Why hadn't he asked her for a country dance where he wouldn't loom over her so much and she wouldn't have to be so aware of him, dammit?

She placed her other hand lightly on his shoulder, refusing to meet his gaze. But from the corner of her eye she observed the changes in him.

His hair was no longer shaggy and overlong, but was cut short in a stylish masculine crop. She told herself she preferred it long, but it wasn't true. The new cut emphasized his fine bone structure, the sculpted planes of his cheekbones. They were dancing so close under the glittering chandeliers that she could see the fine-grained texture of his skin now that he'd taken to shaving off his habitual stubble. He was tanned, as few others in the room were. She'd lost her own tan through the dedicated application of a number of lotions.

He smelled wonderful—no, his *cologne* did. *He* smelled like a swindler and a cheat.

"So," he murmured as they moved into the dance, "Vita from the Latin turns out to be Zoë from the Greek."

"*En français*," she flashed, refusing to meet his eyes, those blue, blue eyes, now so cold and hard, as if the Mediterranean had frozen. She didn't want anyone overhearing their conversation. In French she continued, "At least it was my real name—or close to it. And what about the vagabond calling himself Reynard? Who does he turn out to be?" She added in a bored voice, "I wasn't listening when my cousin's husband introduced us."

"Julian Fox, Earl of Foxton, at your service." He tightened his grip on her waist, pulling her closer.

She stared up at him, almost forgetting to dance. "You're *an earl*? That makes it even more despicable." Suddenly becoming aware of how close his body was to hers, she pushed him back.

"What's despicable?" he asked. As if he didn't know, the rat.

She glared up at him, but the warmth of his hand on her waist and the way he clasped her other hand was very distracting. She tried not to let her body sway closer to him. It was surprisingly difficult. "The way you fleeced those poor peasants. I suppose you have gambling debts or something and try to justify it that way. Well, no matter the cause, I still think it's quite despicable."

"Yes, you made that clear in France. And as I said at the time, those 'poor peasants' had looted the paintings in the first place, and in any case, nobody forced them to make the trade. They were all quite happy with the replacements, which were paintings of them, not some stiff-faced aristos."

"Only because they didn't know the true value of the ones they traded."

"Ah, but you did, didn't you, my little *voleur*?"

"I am not a thief!" she flashed.

"So, one of my valuable paintings just happened to vanish mysteriously the very same day you disappeared? *Incroyable*." He squeezed her waist as he swept her in a circle.

She felt herself flushing. "Think what you like. That painting belongs to me."

"Because you painted its replacement for Madame Le-Blanc?" He snorted.

"No." She was silent for several rounds of the dance floor. She didn't want to tell him the truth about the painting, but she also hated the idea that he thought her a thief. When really he was the dishonest one.

"Do you remember which painting I took?"

"Yes, it was a family portrait, mother, father and two children."

She gazed past his shoulder, not meeting his eyes, and said, in a hard little voice—she was determined not to let her voice tremble—"The adults in that painting were my grandparents, the Comte and Comtesse de Chantonney." She waited but he didn't react. "The little girl in that painting was my mother, Lady Chantal de Chantonney. The boy was—would have been—my uncle, Lord Philippe Charles Rupert de Chantonney. They were murdered during the Terror, went to the guillotine. Only my mother escaped."

He said nothing. They twirled around. The warmth of his body soaked into her. Did he believe her or not? She could feel his gaze on her and itched to look up and see his reaction to her revelation, but those eyes: she had a tendency to drown in those eyes, and she wouldn't allow it.

She was still angry with him. And disappointed. He still couldn't see that what he had done was very much worse than what she had done. If he couldn't see why she had every right to the painting she'd taken, she wasn't going to argue. It was clear that for him, it was all about the money he'd lost being unable to sell it.

After a long silence, he said, "Why pretend to be a maidservant?"

She blinked. That was his first question? "For safety, why else? A poor maidservant draws less attention than an elegantly dressed lady would." Not that her disguise had guaranteed safety, but she didn't regret it. "Why did you pretend to be a poor vagabond artist?"

"For fun, why else?" His voice was dry, mocking. She wanted to smack him.

"For fun *and profit*," she corrected him. "Swindling the poor." She glanced up at him and found him staring down at her with an unreadable expression.

"If you say so." He spun her in such a rapid circle the room blurred and she almost lost her balance, but managed to retain it—just. She was never going to let him unbalance her again, not in any way.

Julian didn't know which he wanted more—to throttle her or to kiss her senseless. She twirled like thistledown in his arms, but she was warm and lovely and . . . furious.

He didn't understand it. *He* was the one who'd been betrayed. After a night of making love—glorious love, the likes of which he'd never experienced—she'd vanished into the night without a word, taking the painting with her.

How much of her tale did he believe? When he'd first arrived at the reception, he'd heard the buzz of anticipation and speculation. A surprise cousin from France? He wasn't sure he believed that. She could just as easily be an imposter, trading on her remarkable likeness to Lady Salcott.

But then there was her visit to the ruined Château de Chantonney. And her tears when she'd told him her grandmother was dead. They'd seemed genuine, and heartfelt—and she'd had no way of knowing he'd waited for her.

Though her grandmother had died decades before, if the tale about the guillotine was true. And those tears were fresh. He didn't know whether to believe her or not. It could just be a convenient tale she'd made up. She was good at that.

He glanced at the people watching the dancers and intercepted a hard look from Lord Salcott. He was no fool, Lord Salcott, and he wouldn't be giving a reception for Vit— Zoë if he wasn't convinced she was the genuine article.

But why would a gently born young lady—a beautiful one, at that—choose to travel alone, pretending to be a dismissed maidservant? Alone and unprotected. Anyone he'd met in France who had any connection to the aristocracy boasted of it—now that the danger of meeting Madame Guillotine was long in the past.

Was she penniless? If so, that would be a reason to contact her rich English relatives, he supposed. And they'd certainly done her proud with this reception and that dress she was wearing. Though the fact that she and Lady Salcott wore identical dresses was a surprise. Why had they chosen to do that? It couldn't have been an accident.

He twirled her in his arms, every fiber of his body aware of her. She continued avoiding his gaze. A guilty conscience? Or mixed feelings? He could appreciate that. He was equal parts angry and aroused, himself.

Her English was perfect. Too perfect. One would almost

imagine it was her native language—except that her French had seemed perfect to him, too. Not that he was an expert French speaker. But she'd *known* he was English, and yet all that time they'd been together she had feigned ignorance of the English language. Why, unless she had something to hide?

But what?

She couldn't possibly have planned to meet up with him on that dusty country road. It was a coincidence too impossible to believe.

If she'd told him her story back then—that she was a descendant of the Comte de Chantonney, down on her luck—he would have believed her, wouldn't he?

Maybe not. Too many people these days pretended to be other than who they were. He might even have thought her a maid pretending to be a lady. And why would she have confided in a stranger?

Except that they'd gone far beyond that, especially after that last glorious night they'd spent together. Surely by then she could have trusted him enough to confide in him?

And why *had* she slept with him? He'd assumed she felt as deeply as he had—and her virginity proved she hadn't taken the act lightly. As least that's what he'd thought at the time. Now he had no idea what to think. Surely it wasn't just to get hold of that blasted painting. She could have stolen that without giving herself to him.

It was all too puzzling.

He'd thought—no, he'd *imagined*—she'd felt something for him that night, as he'd felt for her.

But it was clear she'd had no expectation of meeting up with him in London. He'd seen her face when she'd first noticed him in the crowd. Her shock was unmistakable. He'd been just as shocked to see her here and, what's more, as the guest of honor they'd all been invited to meet.

And now he had her in his arms, but she was freezing him out. And still angry with him.

They were coming to the final movements of the dance. "We need to talk," he told her in a low voice.

"No, we don't."

"I think you owe me the courtesy of an explanation."

"I owe you nothing," she responded, but he thought he saw a flash of guilt in her expression.

"Did it mean nothing to you, then? That night we spent together?" He hated the way it came out, sounding faintly needy when he'd intended to sound angry and accusing.

She shook her head. "Nothing at all."

It was a lie, he was sure. And it sparked his anger.

She froze him out for a moment, then looked up at him. "What did you do with Rocinante?"

Ah, that was his Vita, more concerned with animals than people. Than him. But he was still furious with her. "Sent her to the knackers," he said indifferently.

She gasped. "You didn't!"

He said carelessly, "It was where she was headed when I found her."

She bit her lip. "And Hamish?"

"Can you imagine a dog like that in an English gentleman's home?" He achieved a scornful snort. "I had him drowned."

She stared at him in horror. The last chords of the dance sounded, and omitting the usual curtsy at the end, she wrenched herself out of his arms, saying, "You are more than despicable!" She kicked him on the shin and swept from the dance floor, leaving him standing.

"I think it's time you left, isn't it, Foxton?" Lord Salcott appeared on one side of him, Lord Randall on the other, their expressions implacable. "I don't know what you said to my young cousin, but I could see she was upset."

"Yes, come along, there's a good chap," Randall said in a pleasant tone, but the look in his eyes was icy. He took Julian by the arm, seemingly companionable, but quietly insistent.

There was no point in trying to argue with them, Julian could see. Besides, a crowded party was no place for the discussion he needed to have with Vita—Zoë. Holding her in his arms for the period of one waltz was enough to show him his feelings for her were unchanged, though his thoughts remained angry and confused. He was sure she felt something for him—apart from her current misplaced fury—and until he knew what it was and the reason why she had stolen off into the night without so much as a good-bye, he wasn't yet willing to let her go.

He bowed slightly. "Of course, gentlemen. Thank you for a very pleasant evening. I will call on Miss Benoît at a more convenient time."

"You are welcome to try," Lord Salcott said enigmatically. "Good evening."

Chapter Fourteen

"You were a splendid success at the reception last night," Izzy told Zoë.

"Yes, everyone I spoke to found you quite, quite charming," Clarissa added.

"Mm." Zoë nodded. She'd had very little sleep. He couldn't have drowned Hamish, surely? And sent Rocinante to the knackers? He was a beast, of course, but surely not that much of one. Or was he?

Oh, why had he come to her party? And how had he come? Who had invited him?

The three sisters had gathered in the summerhouse for a very late breakfast and to discuss the events of the night before. Outside it was cold with a light, misty drizzle, but inside the summerhouse it was surprisingly warm, thanks to Matteo, who had provided each of them with a metal-lined foot warmer, into which hot coals had been shoveled. As well, he had laid out a delectable array of treats for them: a large pot of thick, delicious hot chocolate, along with slices of Christmas cake, mince tarts, sweet rolls, almond biscuits and gingernuts, which Clarissa had recently taken to craving.

"And I had so many comments about our identical dresses." Izzy chuckled. "Some even said they thought we could pass for twins, apart from the fact that I'm a few years older and have given birth to two adorable children. You, however, still have the girlish slenderness I used to have."

"Izzy! You're still slender," Clarissa objected.

Izzy laughed. "Perhaps, but my figure is now more womanly than girlish. The point is, nobody seemed to suspect you weren't our cousin."

Matteo came in with a fresh pot of hot chocolate and to inquire whether the ladies were warm enough. He found their desire to sit in the summerhouse bizarre when they had warm houses to go to. But the summerhouse was their special place, and they assured him they were all quite warm enough.

"But please take those plates of cakes and things away," Clarissa said. "I've eaten far too many of them as it is."

"You're eating for two, remember," her sister reminded her.

"Yes, but when things like that are sitting there, under my nose, looking so luscious and delicious, I'm tempted to eat for four," Clarissa said gloomily, "so please take them away, Matteo." She resolutely picked up the pomander she'd been making, and started poking cloves into an orange.

After Matteo left, taking the remnants of the feast with him, Izzy turned to Zoë and said, "You've said precious little about last night, little sister. It was your night, after all."

"It was wonderful," Zoë said. "Everyone was so kind. Thank you again for giving me such a delightful party."

Izzy and Clarissa exchanged glances. "We're going to have to drag it out of her," Clarissa said.

"Drag what out of me?"

"The handsome young man with whom you quarreled—"

"—in French—"

"—in the middle of the dance floor—"

"—while waltzing—"

"—and then kicked," finished Izzy.

"Oh, him."

"Yes, him. Not that you would have done much damage with your dancing slippers, but it was a very definite statement in a very public situation. He was the man who accosted me in front of Hatchard's that time, calling me Vita, remember?" Izzy said. "We discussed him at the time, if you will recall."

Zoë remembered, all right. She'd hoped they hadn't.

"Race says he's Lord Foxton," Clarissa said. "You didn't tell us that before."

"I didn't know it until last night," Zoë admitted.

"He called at our house this morning," Izzy said. "Asking for you. Matteo told him you were not at home. And when Lord Foxton asked when you would be at home, Matteo shrugged and said since you were not a resident of the house, he had no idea." She chuckled.

"And then he called at our house," Clarissa said, reaching for more cloves, "and Hobbs told him that nobody of that name lived there and advised him to try elsewhere."

Zoë sighed. "He also called at Lady Scattergood's, and Treadwell said—in that way he has, like squashing a beetle—'Lady Scattergood and any guests she may have are not at home to gentlemen callers. Ever.'" She mimicked his ponderous tone, and the others laughed.

"Now stop feeling guilty about this, Zoë," Izzy said. "You don't have to talk to him if you don't want to."

"But clearly there is more between you than you suggested," Clarissa said. "At least he seems to think so. Not to mention that kick."

Yes, that kick. Zoë wished now she hadn't done it. Of course people would be talking about it. Only she'd been so furious at what he'd said about Rocinante and Hamish. She couldn't believe he'd done it—he was such a liar—but she wasn't sure.

But if he wanted to talk to her, why had he told her something he must know would upset her? The man was infuriating.

"Perhaps it would help to talk about it," Clarissa finished.

Zoë wasn't sure. She'd almost managed to put him out of her mind—for some of the time, at least—but his reappearance had thrown her thoughts and emotions into turmoil. As for that waltz . . . it had awakened all the wonderful sensations she'd experienced in his arms that night when they'd made love. She knew he was an unprincipled rat, cheating poor farmers to benefit himself, but it seemed her body didn't care about that. It had no conscience. It just wanted him.

But her sisters were right. And they were more experienced than she was in this sort of thing. "All right. I didn't tell you the whole truth when I told you about our time together."

Izzy leaned forward in her chair. Clarissa put her half-completed pomander aside. Zoë began, "When I first met him—oh!" she broke off as the door flew open with a crash. Milly, their irritating neighbor, stood in the doorway, panting, damp and disheveled.

"Good afternoon, Milly," Izzy said tersely. "I suppose you have a good reason for bursting in on us like this?"

Milly didn't answer. She just stared at each one of them in turn. Zoë watched her, a slight frown on her face.

After a few moments, in which Milly had neither moved nor spoken, Clarissa said gently, "Is everything all right, Milly?"

"I'm betrothed." The words burst from her.

"Finally," Izzy muttered. She and Clarissa offered routine congratulations, but Zoë wasn't sure congratulations were in order. "Who to, Milly?" she asked.

Milly swallowed. "To a m-m-marquess." Which was the kind of grand title her mother had been aiming for all along. So why did Milly look so . . . appalled? Overwhelmed? And not in a good way.

"Which marquess, Milly?" Zoë asked.

"The M-Marquess of Blenkinsop."

Izzy and Clarissa exchanged horrified glances. "Blenkinsop?" Clarissa said carefully. "You mean—?"

"That ghastly old man who looks like a desiccated spider and talks to everyone's bosoms!" Izzy said, and Milly nodded.

"But he must be eighty, at least," Clarissa said.

"No. Only seventy-eight," Milly said, and burst into tears.

They pulled out handkerchiefs and let her cry it out. When finally the sobs slowed and she was encouraged to wipe her eyes, blow her nose and have some still-warm hot chocolate, they tried to talk to her.

"Nobody can make you marry him," Izzy said briskly. "So just say no."

Milly shook her head. "Mama will make me. You don't know her."

Izzy said firmly, "You just need to explain to her how you feel. She can tell the marquess, you wouldn't even have to speak to him."

Milly's tears started again. "She won't. She's completely thrilled by this."

"She can't be, not to a man who's nearly four times your age," Zoë said.

But Milly was completely fatalistic. "Mama is delighted. She said his age is an advantage."

"Why, because he'll die soon and you'll be a rich widow?" Zoë said bluntly.

Milly started to nod, then shook her head, but the others were not deceived.

"Is he hoping for an heir?" Clarissa asked. "Didn't his wife die last year after years of being married?"

Milly nodded. "Yes, and he's going to try again . . . with me." She shuddered. Tears rolled down her cheek.

"He could live to a hundred," Zoë said with brutal honesty, "and that's twenty years of having a spidery old man groping and slobbering over you in his bed."

Milly shuddered. "Oh, please don't. I can't bear to think of it."

"If you can't even bear to think of it, you can't possibly want to marry this appalling marquess," Zoë said firmly. "So tell your mama you refuse."

"I t-t-tried," Milly wailed. "But she took no notice. She's thrilled to bits. He is everything she's ever wanted for me. He's obscenely rich—"

"He's obscene," Zoë muttered.

"—with several huge properties scattered around the country. And he's a marquess, which is almost as good as a duke."

There was a short silence, broken only by Milly's snuffles.

"If your mama loves him so much, she should marry him," Zoë said.

"Oh, don't be ridiculous!" Milly snapped.

"Actually, it's not so ridiculous," Izzy said thoughtfully. "I bet the marquess enjoys leering at your mama's bosom quite as much as he does yours. In fact, her bosom is even bigger. He could marry her, and then everyone would be happy."

"Marry Mama?" Milly said, shocked. "But he wants *an heir.*"

"Leaving it a bit late, isn't he?" Izzy said sardonically.

"You don't understand. Mama told me his late wife was unable to bring a child to term." Milly added in a whisper, "She had several miscarriages."

Clarissa leaned forward. "Your mother is still young enough to have a baby."

Milly stared at her. "She is not!"

"She is," Izzy agreed. "Didn't she give birth to you when she was seventeen?"

Milly nodded.

"And you're twenty now, which means she's only thirty-seven."

"And with proven fertility," Clarissa added. "Lady Tarrant was almost forty when she gave birth to little Ross, Lord Tarrant's heir. And she's expecting another baby soon."

Milly stared at them for a few minutes, as if considering it, and then dolefully shook her head. "No, Mama would never agree to it."

Exasperated at the girl's fatalism, Zoë said, "How do you know if you don't try?"

Milly just looked at her. "You don't know Mama. The marquess is everything she ever dreamed of for me, and besides—"

"Forget your mama's dreams—he's going to be *your* nightmare," Zoë said brutally. She sat back, watching as Clarissa and Izzy tried to encourage Milly to stand up to her mother. She never would, Zoë thought. Not without a good reason. Which, Zoë thought, she had—if she could only be forced to admit it.

"What does your gentleman friend say about all this?" she threw casually into the conversation.

Milly blanched, then blustered, "What gentleman friend? I don't have a gentleman friend."

"Yes, you do." Zoë grinned. "I've seen you with him in Hatchard's."

"You haven't. I mean, I don't have a gentleman friend, so you can't possibly have seen—"

"I have," Zoë insisted. "And also in that little park at the end of the street, the one where Jeremiah walks Lady Scattergood's dogs. You were holding hands."

"Holding hands with a footman! I would *never*—"

"Not Jeremiah, your gentleman friend."

There was a short, defeated silence.

"Not up to Mama's standards, is he?" Zoë said gently.

"He's a cit," Milly said in despair.

Zoë wrinkled her brow. "A what?"

"Not one of the ton," Clarissa explained. "No title, and he works for a living."

"He's actually quite well off," Milly said defensively. "He owns a very nice house and he has several prosperous businesses. And his father is a wealthy manufacturer. But Mama said he was impossible."

"But you like him."

"Oh yes," Milly said.

"And he likes you?"

Blushing, she nodded. "He asked Mama for my hand—twice—but she was furious and said it was impossible, that she would not contemplate such a frightful mésalliance. She sent him away and told me I must put him out of my mind. And she brought me to London."

"How old is this cit?" Izzy asked.

"Twenty-eight. His name is Thaddeus."

"Has he married anyone else since you came to London?"

"No."

"How do you know?"

She blushed and pulled from her reticule a crumpled letter, damp and blotched with tearstains. "He—he writes to me. At the address of my maid's mother."

Zoë clapped her hands. "You sneaky thing! Well done, Milly! And do you write back?"

Milly bit her lip. "I know I shouldn't have, but . . ."

"Of course you should have, and now he's come to London, which couldn't be more perfect," Zoë said. "The solution is obvious. You must marry Thaddeus."

"Oh, but I couldn't."

"It's a very simple choice," Izzy said firmly. "You can marry the horrid old spider, making your mother delirious with delight and yourself utterly miserable, or marry the man you care for and make yourself—and him—happy."

"He's quite good-looking, too," Zoë said.

"Oh, do you think so?" Milly began eagerly, and then caught herself up. "But there's no point in even thinking about it. It would never work."

"It could if you wanted it to," Zoë told her.

"No, Mama wouldn't even consider it. She'd be utterly furious with me."

"There are worse things than making your mama angry," Zoë pointed out.

Milly just shook her head. She'd never stood up to her mother in her life.

"Sometimes you have to *make* things happen," Clarissa said gently. "You can't just sit around wishing and hoping."

"And being miserable," Zoë added.

Milly sighed, her whole body drooping in defeat.

"Twenty years of having an ancient, spidery, toothless old man slobbering over your nubile naked body every night," Zoë said meditatively. "Think about that. And all because of the want of a little courage."

Milly stared at her. Her face crumpled. "I hate you, Zoë Ben-whahhhh," she wailed, and rushed away.

The three of them sat, looking at one another. It was a ghastly situation, they were united on that, but Clarissa put it best: "If she's not prepared to help herself, what can any of us do?"

It was a depressing thought. None of them were particularly fond of Milly: she'd been a thorn in their side for more than three years. But as irritating as she often was, she didn't deserve this.

Later that afternoon, when Matteo came to collect the used dishes from the summerhouse, he brought with him a note. "Lord Foxton, he come back and give me this. Is for the young signorina." He looked at Izzy. "Milor', he say not to admit the gentleman to the house, but he say nothing about notes. Is all right if I give?"

"Yes, it's fine," Izzy told him. "Give it to her."

Zoë took the note cautiously. It was sealed and addressed to Miss Zoë Benoît. She thanked Matteo and hovered impatiently while he packed up the dishes and cups. She wanted to rip the note open and read it straightaway, but the eyes of her sisters were bright, expectant and curious, and she didn't want to read it with an interested audience watching, even a loving audience. "I'll take this inside to read. It's, um, it's getting a bit cold in here anyway. I'll see you both later."

She hurried across the garden and entered Lady Scattergood's house via the back door, as usual, then swiftly ran up the stairs to her bedchamber.

She broke the seal and opened the note.

My dear Miss Benoît,

I am writing to apologize for embarrassing you on the dance floor last night. You were right in refusing to discuss our past together in such surroundings. It was discourteous of me to insist. There are, however, matters—important matters—that you and I need to discuss in private. Last night's brief conversation revealed several misunderstandings that I would dearly like to have cleared up.

*I would be most grateful if we could please meet—at
a time and place of your choosing. You may
communicate with me at the address below.*

Yours very sincerely,
Julian Fox, Earl of Foxton

Below that was an address, and below that, in a hastily
added, bolder, much less tidy script was:

Please, Vita, I beg of you, meet me.

She read it through swiftly the first time, then again,
pondering the phrasing and the intent behind each word.

It started quite formally. The apology was acceptable,
but as for the rest . . . What were these important matters?
She wasn't going to give her precious painting back, and
she'd made that clear. And she certainly wasn't going to
compensate him for taking it.

In any case, now that she was in London, there was almost nowhere she could go to be private. Lady Scattergood
wouldn't let him in the house, and from the sound of things,
neither would Leo or Race.

Was there any point at all in talking to him? It would
just stir up her emotions again. Though who was she trying
to fool? Her emotions had boiled up and threatened to
swamp her the moment she'd paused on the stairs and spotted him staring up at her.

And now that her sisters were involved . . . They seemed
to know, somehow, that she had feelings for him, feelings
she didn't want to have. She could tell they were eager for
her to continue her acquaintanceship with Reynard. Lord
Foxton. They thought him handsome and charming—and
he was, but that wasn't all he was.

They didn't know, and she didn't want to tell them, that

he was a cheat and a swindler. And she really didn't want them to know she had spent the night with him.

Or what a magical night it had been.

Before she woke the next day and the scales had fallen from her eyes.

Breaking her heart.

She glanced at the note again and sighed. For two pins she'd toss it in the fire. But if she did that, he would only keep trying to find ways of speaking to her. And the more he did, the more likely it was to start gossip.

No, she would have to meet him and hear him explain those so-called misunderstandings.

But where could she talk to him in private? She ran her mind through some possibilities, but almost all of them involved her being with someone who'd chaperone her. Unless . . .

She fetched a pen and ink and wrote a note, suggesting he meet her in Hyde Park at five that afternoon, driving an open carriage. He could take her up in the carriage and drive around the park without causing scandal, just a little gossip. They would be under everybody's eye but could still speak in private: it was perfectly *comme il faut*.

She sealed the note. How to deliver it? Jeremiah, Lady Scattergood's young footman, might do it, but she didn't want to get him into trouble. No, his note had come via Matteo, so the reply could go the same way.

She ran lightly down the stairs and hurried out the back door, cutting through the garden to Leo and Izzy's house. As she passed the summerhouse, a movement caught her eye and she glanced inside. And saw a hunched figure sobbing.

She entered. "Milly, what is the matter?"

Milly looked up, utterly woebegone. Her eyes were red and puffy with tears, and her left cheek was red and swollen.

"Milly," Zoë exclaimed. "Did someone hit you?"

Milly nodded, gulping back tears. "Mama."

"Your mother *hit* you?" Zoë could hardly believe it. Milly's mother had always been such a doting parent. She sat down and took Milly's hand. "What happened?"

Between sobs, Milly explained. "The marquess came calling, you know, to make the betrothal formal. And he— he *kissed* me. And it was awful, Zoë. He has terrible breath and he put his tongue . . . his tongue . . ."

"I understand."

"And then he put his hand down inside my dress and . . . squeezed my breasts and . . ."

"I understand," Zoë said soothingly. She could just imagine it, the horrid, creepy old spider.

"And so I remembered what you said, and when he left I—I told Mama I couldn't bear it and that I didn't want to marry him, and—and—and that's when Mama slapped me. Hard—it really hurt."

Seeing her swollen face, Zoë could believe it.

"Mama has never hit me before, never. So it just goes to show."

Zoë wasn't sure what it showed, except that Mama was ruthlessly ambitious.

"And when I stopped crying, Mama explained all that she had lost when she'd been forced to marry Papa. Mama said that though he was not precisely a cit, Papa was no aristocrat. And she, second cousin to a duke!" Milly wiped her eyes and blew soggily into the handkerchief.

"So then I understood. Mama had married beneath her and regretted it all her life. She said that she would marry me into the circle to which she belonged if it killed her!"

More like if it killed Milly, Zoë thought.

"I'd never before heard her talking like that about Papa. I loved my papa. He was kind and gentle, and he always had time to listen to me. And he tried to give Mama everything she wanted, but it was never enough. When he died, Mama sold everything so she could afford the house in Bellaire

Gardens and everything she and I needed for my Season. But it's taken three Seasons to get a suitable offer for me. Three Seasons! It's all so terribly expensive, but I didn't realize. So this is my last chance because most of the money is gone. She said if I didn't marry the marquess, we would both be h-h-homeless! And destitute!"

"Not homeless, surely?" Zoë said. "You will still have your house."

"It's rented," Milly wailed.

It was a ghastly situation, but Zoë couldn't help but think there must be a way out for Milly. Recalling her note to Reynard, she told Milly to wait there while she ran across to Izzy's house. "There is a note I must send. But I'll be back in a few minutes."

"Oh, I have one, too. Could you send this one for me please?" Milly drew out a crumpled, tear-blotched note and passed it to Zoë.

She glanced at the address. "Thaddeus Henshaw. Is that the fellow you've been meeting?"

Milly nodded. "It's to tell Thaddeus I'm going to marry the marquess." And she burst into sobs again.

"Wait here," Zoë said, taking the damp missive, "I'll be back in a few minutes."

"You won't tell Mama?"

"Don't be ridiculous, of course I won't."

Zoë returned in about ten minutes with Izzy and Clarissa. She'd filled them in about Milly's situation. Clarissa had come armed with some soothing cream for Milly's bruised cheek.

"Did you send my letter to Thaddeus?" Milly asked.

"Not yet."

"But I must tell him to give up all hope of me."

"No, you must not!" Zoë said impatiently. "Why should you sacrifice your life for your mother's stupid pretensions?"

Milly shook her head dolefully. "I must. Mama has

given everything to me, spent all her money so that I might marry well."

"No, she has spent *her* money so that you could fulfill *her* own vain ambitions," Zoë declared. "She doesn't give a fig for your happiness, Milly. If she had, you could have been married long since, but no, even your suitors with titles weren't good enough for her. And now she has dredged up this ghastly old spider and expects you to marry him and allow him to maul you all he wants."

Milly blinked at her, her eyes full of tears.

Zoë softened her voice. "You should see to your own happiness, Milly. Marry this Thaddeus of yours and leave your mama to deal with the marquess."

"I couldn't."

"You could if you cared about Thaddeus."

"I do. I love him. And he loves me. He has said so, often."

"Well then, what is it that woman in Shakespeare said? 'Screw your courage to the sticking point and you'll not fail'?"

"Kill Mama?" Milly said, horrified. "I couldn't possibly do such a wicked thing."

"Who said anything about killing her?" Zoë said, bewildered.

"You did! That's what that speech by Lady Macbeth is about—murder. Mama and I saw the play."

Zoë shook her head. "I don't know about that—it was just part of a speech that Lady Scattergood made me read to her one day—she's taken to having improving pieces read to her. I just meant you should be brave and do what you really want to do—run off with your Thaddeus."

"You mean to Gretna Green? Oh, I couldn't. It would be a terrible scandal, and Mama would be—"

"Foaming at the mouth and trying to find a way to make the best of it. While you'll be far away, blissfully married to your Thaddeus." She could see the image appealed to Milly.

"Besides, it doesn't have to be Gretna," Izzy added, seeing Milly's doubt. "Thaddeus could get a special license and marry you in a church, right here in London."

Clarissa frowned. "But she won't be old enough to marry without her mama's permission, will she?"

Izzy turned back to Milly. "When do you turn one-and-twenty?"

"In three weeks."

"That's it, then. All you have to do is to wait three weeks and then you can marry whoever you want."

Milly shook her head. "No, Mama wants me married quickly. She knows I don't want to do it, so she's making arrangements for the marquess to marry me in ten days' time. The notice will be in the newspapers tomorrow."

"Then you must elope," Zoë said. "Tell this Thaddeus of yours to arrange it."

Milly's eyes widened in horror. "To Gretna Green? I won't! I couldn't! It would be too, too shameful."

Zoë rolled her eyes, but Clarissa leaned forward excitedly. "No, no, of course you won't need to flee to the border. We'll hide you for the next three weeks, then, when you're one-and-twenty, you can marry your Thaddeus."

Milly blinked. "*Hide* me?"

Clarissa nodded. "That's how Izzy and I defeated our horrid father when we were children. He didn't want Izzy to live with me, but I hid her for, oh, weeks, until he eventually gave up."

Izzy nodded. "It's a good idea."

Milly looked doubtfully around the summerhouse. "But where would I hide? Here? She'd find me for sure."

"Not here. In one of our houses," Izzy said, then grew thoughtful. "Leo would allow it, I'm sure, but he wouldn't like it, and I wouldn't ask him to compromise his principles."

"She could stay with Race and me," Clarissa said.

"No, her mother's house is only a couple of doors away.

It's too risky," Izzy said. "But you could stay with Zoë at Lady Scattergood's. I'm sure she'd allow it."

"With that crazy old lady?" Milly exclaimed.

"She's not crazy, just slightly eccentric," Zoë said crossly. "And she's probably going to save you from marriage to the creepy old spider, so you'd better develop a little respect. And show some gratitude."

"Yes, as soon as she finds out that you're being forced into an unwilling marriage, she's sure to agree," Clarissa said.

"And your mother would never think of looking for you there," Zoë said on a rallying note.

"So that's settled," Clarissa said brightly. "We'll go and ask Lady Scattergood now."

As predicted, when they asked Lady Scattergood whether they could hide Milly from her mother, who was trying to make her marry a man she didn't like, she was initially delighted. "No gel should be forced into marriage," she declared, but when she learned Milly had plans to marry a different man—a cit—she hesitated.

She raised her lorgnette. "Wealthy, is he?"

"Yes."

"Good, that's good. And he'll be going abroad soon, won't he?"

Milly looked puzzled. "N-no, not that I know of."

Lady Scattergood frowned at that. "Then where is he going?"

Milly threw a helpless glance at Zoë. "Sheffield?"

The old lady pondered that a moment, swinging her lorgnette back and forth on its string while she considered it. "Oh well, abroad would be better, but I suppose Sheffield is far enough."

Confused, Milly looked at Zoë, who could see she was about to ask "far enough for what," and jumped in, saying,

"Milly's mother has arranged for her to marry the elderly Marquess of Blenkinsop."

Lady Scattergood stiffened, outraged. "You mean to say That Woman is planning to wed a young gel like you to a terrible old lecher like Arthur Blenkinsop? Why, he's practically old enough to be *my* father, and I'm no spring chicken."

It turned out she'd known the marquess in her youth, when he was still the Blenkinsop heir. "Tell me, my dears, does he still talk to ladies' bosoms? I was more abundantly endowed when I was a gel, and I often had to rap him hard with my fan on the knuckles—and on the nose several times when it threatened to delve right into my neckline—and point out to him that I was up here." She pointed to her face. They all laughed, and Milly confirmed that he did indeed talk to her bosom and to Mama's.

And thus Lady Scattergood gave her enthusiastic approval for the plan to hide Milly in her house. She sent the girls off to help Milly settle in and rang for her butler to give him the appropriate instructions.

Ensconced in a cozy upstairs sitting room, they then decided she should write a short note to her mother, explaining that she was very upset by her mother's response, reiterating that she refused to marry the Marquess of Blenkinsop and that she was staying with a friend and Mama was not to worry. Izzy added, "And tell her not to make a fuss or tell anyone, as she wouldn't want to make a scandal, would she?"

When the note was finally finished, with many pauses and worried hesitations and scratchings out and more tears, Izzy rose and plucked it out of Milly's hand, saying, "I'll have this anonymously delivered to your mother, Milly, which should at least minimize the fuss she is bound to make. Now I have some calls to make, so we will leave you to get settled in." She glanced at her sisters. "Meet back here later this evening?"

"But I can't just stay here," Milly said worriedly. "I don't have anything, no nightdress or—or anything. And Mama will be worried."

"That's the point," Zoë said.

"And don't worry about clothes—we'll provide you with whatever you need," Clarissa assured her. With Milly being on the plump side, Clarissa would be the best source of clothing.

Izzy glanced at the clock on the overmantel. "Zoë, didn't you say you wanted to walk in the park at five? It's almost that now."

"Oh good heavens, yes." She'd told Reynard she would meet him there at five. She jumped to her feet. "I have to leave now. Izzy, could you send the carriage around to the front and pick me up, please? I'll need to put on my warm pelisse and hat."

"But what about me?" Milly wailed.

"Don't worry, we're not abandoning you," Clarissa said soothingly. "I'll stay here and help you get settled in. We need to make a list of what you might need. And think about writing a longer letter to your mama. Oh, this is going to be so exciting."

"I suppose so," Milly said dolefully.

Chapter Fifteen

The drizzle had eased earlier, and weak winter sunshine had brought a surprising number of people out promenading in Hyde Park when Zoë and Izzy arrived. They had Izzy's driver drop them off at the gate so they could join the walkers. Zoë had told her sister about having asked Lord Foxton to take her up in an open carriage because he wanted to talk. "But I didn't mean you to have to stand about waiting for me," she said.

"Don't worry about me," Izzy said. "I won't lack for company. There are plenty of people here that I know, and they'll all be eager to discuss the events of last night."

"Oh. Of course. The kick." Zoë felt herself blushing. Perhaps it hadn't been the cleverest idea to meet him in the park.

Izzy gave a peal of laughter. "Goose. The whole point of last night was to introduce you to all our friends, and really, your little contretemps with Lord Foxton is all to the good. People will be so intrigued by that, it won't even occur to them to wonder whether you really are our cousin."

"Glad to provide further fuel for gossip," Zoë said dryly, and Izzy laughed again.

"Come on, let's promenade." Izzy linked arms with her, and they joined the crush of smartly dressed people moving slowly along.

Izzy did seem to know a lot of people, including quite a few strangers who she introduced to Zoë. Those who'd been at the reception the previous night were full of praise for the evening. Not a soul mentioned Zoë's little brangle with Lord Foxton, but she was aware of their sidelong, speculative glances from time to time.

Oh, where was the wretched man? Had he given up on her? They'd arrived well after five, which was late, but not that late. So she nodded and smiled and chatted and made polite small talk and was just about to give up on him when there was an outbreak of screeches and screams up ahead.

"Good grief, what on earth can that be about?" Izzy exclaimed. They couldn't see anything—the crowd at that point was too dense. But then the knot of people scattered in panic as a large, scruffy dog bounded through them. It hurtled up to Zoë and leapt at her. More ladies screamed as he raised himself on two rear paws, placed his front ones on Zoë's shoulders and gave her a joyous swipe on the chin with his tongue.

"Oh, Hamish," she exclaimed, laughing and pushing his paws off her. "You muddy, adorable, ridiculous creature." She crouched down and embraced him delightedly, scruffling him around the neck and ears and trying without success to avoid further enthusiastic doggy kisses.

Izzy stood by, chuckling and assuring the appalled onlookers that it was quite all right, the animal wasn't savage.

"I knew he couldn't have drowned you," Zoë crooned to the dog.

"No? You seemed to believe it at the time," a deep voice above her said.

She stiffened and rose, keeping a hand on Hamish's head. "I should have known better, but why did you tell me such a horrid thing in the first place?"

"I was angry."

"Well that makes two of us." They stood glaring at each other.

Izzy, trying hard to keep a straight face, interjected. "As I understand it, you arranged this meeting in order to have a private talk. May I just point out that you couldn't actually have ensured a more public one? Causing a minor riot with your dog was not exactly a master strategy, Lord Foxton."

He said stiffly, "I didn't plan it this way. I had him perfectly under control, but then he must have seen or smelled Vita—Miss Benoît, I mean—and before I knew it, he leapt out of the curricle and took off."

"Well, perhaps you'd better get back to your horses," Izzy suggested. "I presume you didn't leave them unattended."

"Of course I didn't," he said, irritated. "I got a fellow to hold them for me. But yes, I'd better get back to them. Shall we, Miss Benoît?" He held out his arm.

"I'll mind the dog, shall I?" Izzy said brightly. "You wouldn't want him climbing all over you and Zoë while you're trying to talk, would you?"

"I brought him so she would see he was alive," Lord Foxton admitted. "But yes, if you could mind him, Lady Salcott, I'd be most grateful."

"Does he have a lead?" Izzy asked.

"No," Zoë exclaimed, but at the same time, Reynard said, "Yes," and drew a leather lead from his pocket. He glanced at Zoë and said, "It's all right, he doesn't mind it now. I've been training him." He clipped the lead to Hamish's collar, handed the end to Izzy and said, "Stay."

"Yes, I intend to," Izzy said affably. She was enjoying this, Zoë could tell.

"I meant the dog," he said stiffly. "Miss Benoît?" He offered his arm again, and this time she took it.

They didn't speak until Julian had thanked the young man who'd held his horses for him, helped her into the curricle and driven a sufficient distance to ensure nobody would overhear them.

"Rocinante?" Zoë said when he slowed the horses to a walk.

"With the LeBlancs," he said gruffly. "She's boarding with them. I'm paying for her food and for the eldest boy to care for her. The family is very grateful—they were unable to drive anywhere before."

She turned and thumped him. Hard. "It was *horrid* of you to tell me they were both dead."

"I know, and I'm sorry about that. But I was angry at the time." He glanced at her. "And hurt."

"Hurt?" She stared at him. "Why were *you* hurt?" Suggesting she was the one who'd been hurt. A trickle of hope ran through him.

He stared back at her. "You left me without a word. And after the night we spent together . . ."

She shifted uncomfortably. "I didn't think it would matter to you."

"Not matter?" He shook his head. How could she think it didn't matter to him? "I thought you didn't care," he told her.

She snorted. "I didn't care? Why do you think I invited you into the caravan in the first place?"

"I thought I knew that night. But then, when you left without a word, taking a valuable painting with you . . ."

She rolled her eyes. "That again. I explained that when you called me a thief last night." She bared her teeth at him. "When *you* were the real thief."

"That nonsense again!" He swiveled in his seat so he could see her face to face. "Tell me, to whom do you think those old paintings rightfully belong?"

"Not you!"

"Agreed." His response was immediate.

Her brow wrinkled. "Agreed? But you took them."

"I did. But not to keep."

"No, to sell."

"Not that, either." She stared doubtfully at him, so he explained. "I have no need of extra funds, no gambling debts, in fact no debts at all—not even a mortgage on my estate. That was all paid off years ago."

The doubt remained on her face.

"My income supports me very well, and even without the income from the estates, I have a private income of my own from investments I made when I was young and which have grown since then. Which all goes to explain that I have no need to go abroad and cheat rural farmers."

She eyed him doubtfully, those glorious green eyes still unconvinced. "I don't understand. If you have no need of the money, why do you go to so much trouble to get those old paintings from people?"

"Apart from enjoying painting the replacements, you mean? And make no doubt about it, I do enjoy that, even though I'm better at pigs and horses and dogs than people, as you know. As for those old paintings, I take them to a gallery in Paris, the Galerie du Temps, where Gaston, who runs it—" He broke off as large drops of rain started to fall. "Oh, damn this blasted climate," he muttered. "Here, I have an umbrella somewhere." He pulled it out and got it open just in time to protect her—mostly—as it turned into a sudden downpour. He held it over her, but in the meantime he and the horses and the curricle were getting drenched. And the rain was setting in.

"I'll take you back to your cousin." He turned the curricle around and headed back to where they'd left Lady Salcott. But she was nowhere in sight. Nor was Hamish. Most people had scattered when the rain started, and only a few were left, all sheltering under umbrellas.

He looked around. Where had she gone?

"Over there." Zoë pointed. "In the carriage."

A smart carriage sat stationary not far away with a coachman hunched gloomily at the front, an oilskin cape pulled over him. A slim gloved hand waved at them from a window, and a hairy face pushed past it to observe the view.

It took a moment to transfer Hamish from the carriage—or rather, let him leap ungratefully out to gambol and frolic in the mud and the rain—while Zoë climbed down from the curricle, handed Julian back his umbrella and joined her cousin in the dry, comfortable carriage.

"We barely began our talk," he told her. "Could we meet again?"

She nodded. "Yes. You can't call on me—Lady Scattergood won't allow it—but I'll think of something and let you know."

Her carriage drove off, leaving him wet, frustrated and torn. The whole meeting had been a debacle, but at least he'd made a start. Besides, when he'd first arrived in England he'd never expected to see her again. So just seeing her and knowing where she was had to be an improvement. And at least she was still speaking to him. It was the barest shred of hope, but he clung to it.

Now, Milly, this letter," Zoë said, "needs to make everything very clear to your mother."

The fuss had already begun. Clarissa's maid, Betty, had reported that Milly's mother's servants had been combing the gardens, shouting and calling and beating the bushes in case she was lying beneath them, murdered.

She'd also sent them to inquire at every house surrounding the garden whether her daughter, Millicent Harrington, happened to be visiting. Without success.

Treadwell had been magnificently crushing in his denial of any Young Person of that name being Within.

Betty, relaying gossip from the Harrington servants, said that despite the note Milly had sent saying that she was safe and staying with a friend, Milly's mother, Mrs. Harrington, was inside, lying distraught on the sofa, alternately swooning and throwing hysterical fits, shrieking and weeping and claiming her daughter had been kidnapped or gone mad and was an ungrateful snake in the bosom.

"And it's quite a bosom, as I recall," Izzy said when Betty had finished reporting. She'd arrived with a bundle of Clarissa's clothing for Milly. "Which is something we should keep in mind for this letter."

"You can't discuss Mama's bosom in the letter," Milly said. "It's indelicate."

"We won't, not in so many words," Clarissa assured her. "But it won't hurt to drop a hint. If we're to turn the spider's attention from you to your mother, her lush bosom will be a factor."

"I suppose so," Milly said. "But I don't see how."

"Leave it to us," Zoë said briskly. She had other things to worry about, and while she was sympathetic to Milly's situation, the way Milly was whining and dragging her feet was irritating. If understandable.

The three sisters sat down and put their heads together to compose the letter. There was much rewriting and rephrasing and many tearful objections from Milly at the bluntness of the missive. But as Zoë pointed out, "Your mama does not understand subtlety, Milly."

And when her objections became too much, Zoë turned to her in frustration, saying, "So you want to marry the spider now, do you? Fine. We'll throw this letter into the fire and you can write to your Thaddeus and tell him to go back to Sheffield, forget about you and find some braver girl to marry."

Which stopped the objections, if not the tears, in mid-flow. The final letter read:

Dear Mama

I am sorry to Distress you, but I cannot and will not marry the Marquess of Blenkinsop. I am very Grateful for all you have done on my behalf, but I cannot be happy with that man.

I have met Another, and he has offered me Marriage. He is a most respectable young man, with a Handsome Fortune, but no Title. Most importantly, he Loves me and I love him. When you see me next I will be married. I am sorry that you will miss my wedding, but you have given me No Choice.

Mama, whenever we have met with the marquess, he has talked more to you than to me. I believe he Likes you Very Much. And, Mama, you are still a Young and very Attractive woman.

Lady Tarrant was almost Forty when she gave birth to Lord Tarrant's dear little son and heir, and she's now expecting a second child. You are several years younger than she. You could give the marquess the child he wants. And you would be a Marchioness, which surely is Better than being the Mother of one.

Don't bother to look for me. I am safe, staying with sympathetic friends.

I am sorry to part like this. I love you, Mama, but forcing me to marry the marquess against my will has driven me to this Desperate and Unhappy Course.

> *Your loving daughter,*
> *Milly*

They all heaved a sigh of relief when Milly copied the final version out in a fair hand—albeit with numerous tearstained blotches—but as Clarissa pointed out, "Her mother should know she hasn't made this decision easily."

Once sealed and addressed, Izzy took it to hand to Matteo, who would arrange to have it delivered to Mrs. Harrington by some anonymous and untraceable person.

Once that was done, Zoë's thoughts returned to the question of Reynard. Or, as she supposed she should learn to call him, Lord Foxton.

"You'd better invite the poor man to call on you at my place," Izzy told Zoë later that evening.

"What do you mean, 'poor man'?" Zoë began, but Izzy just laughed.

"I think half drowning him will give him enough pause for thought. Whatever he did, I suspect you've punished him enough. He clearly wants to talk with you, and is obviously anxious to make amends. And if you don't mind me saying so, little sister, you don't seem exactly indifferent to him, either, so hadn't you better get it over and done with?"

Zoë sighed. She was right. She'd been thinking about what Reynard—Lord Foxton—had told her about the paintings so far. She still had doubts, but she should at least let him finish. "Very well. What about tomorrow at two?"

"Perfect. Now write him a note—no, *I* shall write him a note inviting him to call at two tomorrow. I shan't mention your name at all. If he can't work it out, he doesn't deserve you."

"Deserve me?" Zoë was inclined to be indignant. "What makes you think this is anything to do with . . . with whatever it is you think it is?" She couldn't bring herself to name it. Her sisters were making too many assumptions as it was. They practically had her walking down the aisle already, and she hadn't yet made up her mind whether she believed a word he said, let alone any feelings she might have for him. Or not.

Izzy just smiled and patted her cheek. "We shall see, won't we?"

* * *

I started doing it after I left the army," Reynard told her. He'd arrived at Izzy and Leo's house promptly at two and was shown into the smaller of the sitting rooms, where a fire was crackling cozily. Zoë had awaited his arrival, pacing back and forth until she heard the front doorbell ring, upon which she threw herself into an armchair, snatched up a magazine and was languidly turning pages when he entered.

"A friend of mine had the idea of trying to retrieve the collection of a family he knew, one of the grand families whose home was destroyed in the Revolution. They'd escaped with their lives, but not much else, and many years later when they found one of their paintings for sale in a French gallery, it occurred to my friend that there might be more remaining. The looting was mostly done by the local peasantry. So he suggested the plan to me.

"I thought it a worthy pursuit. I had planned to just wander through Italy, going where the breeze took me, painting whatever I felt like—Italy is a glorious source of artistic inspiration—but he talked me into joining him in France. He's the fellow I mentioned who got married recently, whose bride wasn't interested in becoming a vagabond with him."

She nodded.

"And it worked. We were able to retrieve several of the paintings that the family of my friend had owned. They were delighted. And the people who owned them were only too pleased to have their own portraits instead. And since then, we've done it in several places and retrieved a number of valuable paintings."

She nodded slowly. It made sense. And she knew how she'd felt seeing that painting with her mother and uncle and grandparents. It wasn't just about money; it was about feelings.

He continued. "So for several years I lived the life of a

vagabond artist, doing something I enjoyed and felt was worthwhile. Nothing suited me better. Then, when I inherited my father's title and responsibilities, I was most disheartened."

"Well, of course, grief is natural."

"I'm not talking about grief—I meant the position, the expectations and responsibilities. I wanted none of that."

"Not even the income?" she said cynically.

He snorted. "I told you I have private means, enough for my needs anyway. No, it was the loss of my freedom that upset me most. Inheriting the title and estates tied me down."

"But surely you could do what you want anyway?"

He shook his head. "No, I've known enough fellows who shrugged off their responsibilities and lived a life of ease and pleasure—at the expense of their tenants and those who depended on them. I couldn't do that. When I was living as a vagabond painter I could do as I pleased and hurt nobody, but when I became the earl, it all changed."

"I see." It all sounded very noble, and yet when she'd met him he'd been exactly that—a carefree vagabond artist. She pointed that out, and he gave a rueful chuckle.

"And there my grandmother comes into the story." He settled back in his chair, crossing one long leg over the other. "Grandmama has been ruling the Foxton roost ever since her only daughter married my father. He was deep in debt, you see, and Mama brought a fortune with her. But Grandmama holds the real moneybags and soon had my father, and later my brother, firmly under her thumb. And dancing to her tune—and for that mangling of metaphors, I apologize."

"But she doesn't hold you under her thumb?"

"No, as I said, I have a private income." He looked at her as if to gauge her interest, then continued. "It started with a bequest from a spinster great-aunt on my father's side. She loved to paint and wished to encourage me in my ambitions. A school friend with whom I used to stay during school holidays came from a business background—which meant our schoolfellows gave him hell. His father, appreciative of our friendship and quite appalled that no provision had been made for me as a younger son, heard about my small legacy and taught me how to invest my money. It was a whole new world to me, and that modest sum has grown and grown. I've been investing in various endeavors ever since. He still advises me occasionally, and it's given me the independence I never would have had otherwise." He broke off, frowning. "How did we get onto this? I'm sorry for rambling on, Vita. You're too good a listener. Now, where were we?"

These snippets about his life were fascinating. He was supposed to be explaining about the paintings, but she wanted to know more about him. "You were explaining that your title and responsibilities oppressed you."

"Oh yes. Well, Grandmama, having ruled the roost all those years, is determined to rule me as well. She's quite a forceful lady. And despite coming from a mercantile background herself, she has very firm ideas on how members of the aristocracy should behave. Very firm ideas." He shot her a grin. "And traveling from place to place in a Romany caravan, painting portraits of the lower orders is *not* her idea of proper earlish behavior."

She laughed. "I can imagine."

"But though she drives me to distraction at times, I am fond of the old tartar, so I made a deal with her. For nine months of the year I'd be a proper earl, and for the other three months I'd do what I want. I didn't explain exactly what I was doing. If she knew, she'd probably have a fit. But as long as whatever it is I am doing is done abroad, she can turn a blind eye."

Zoë pondered his tale. "I can see why you'd prefer to escape your responsibilities for part of the year, but where does the trading of valuable old paintings come into it? You haven't explained that, just that you don't need the money from that."

"Oh yes, we were interrupted by the rain, weren't we? Well, simply told, I retrieve paintings that were looted from grand houses and châteaux during the Revolution and take them to a gallery in Paris. Gaston, who runs the gallery, keeps a ledger into which he lists the artworks retrieved and also the artworks that various families have reported missing. When he finds a match, he gets in touch with the family concerned—or the closest surviving relatives he can find. They can then purchase the paintings at a reasonable cost—sometimes merely a nominal cost, depending on their situation. Gaston takes a small commission, and the rest goes to support a charitable orphanage."

He chuckled. "Poor Gaston, it breaks his heart contemplating what some of those paintings could fetch if sold on the open market."

Zoë was stunned. "Is that really what you do?"

"Yes."

She thought about it. It made sense. "You mean all those paintings I saw, they would have belonged to my family, the de Chantonney family?"

"Undoubtedly. Every year we target the villages closest to some great house or château that was attacked and looted during the Troubles. It is surprising how many of the paintings—statues, too—remain in the district, even so many years afterward. As I told you back then, farmers don't have any idea how to sell them. And knowing they were stolen in the first place, they're probably reluctant to take them to Paris, where they might be brought to the attention of the authorities. But swapping them with a vagabond painter who lives in an old caravan? There's no danger in that."

She was silent a long time. It fitted with everything she knew about him. All those people she'd met—and liked. The paintings they'd traded had been looted from her family home, if not by the actual people she knew, probably by their parents or grandparents. It was a hard truth to swallow.

She recalled how Madame LeBlanc had said that her father-in-law had given her the painting as a wedding gift, and how she didn't want it in her house and was glad to get rid of it. She obviously knew where the painting had come from in the first place and felt guilty about it.

"If you contact Gaston, I'm sure he'll send you a list of the paintings that are rightfully yours. And the price for you would be very nominal," he said gently.

She shook her head. "No, they won't be considered rightfully mine. My mother's, yes, but not mine."

He gave her a puzzled look. "I don't understand."

She took a deep breath. "Can I rely on your discretion?"

"Of course."

Not that it would make much difference. He had it in his power to ruin her anyway—all he needed to do was reveal that she'd spent more than a week in his company, day and night, unchaperoned. But this also affected her sisters.

"Your word of honor?"

He looked slightly offended, but said, "My word of honor."

"My mother was a true de Chantonney, the legitimate daughter of the Comte and Comtesse de Chantonney." She took another deep breath. "But I am her illegitimate daughter. And as such I would never be considered the rightful heir of anything of the de Chantonneys." She lifted her chin and looked him right in the eye. "So in that sense, I suppose you were right: I did steal that painting. But I'm not giving it back."

"I see." He gave her a thoughtful look. "Do your cousins know you are illegitimate?"

She didn't answer, just shrugged and looked away. Let him think what he wanted. She'd probably said too much as it was.

"You've explained the painting swaps," she said, "and I suppose I must accept it." And thinking back over all he'd told her in the past, he hadn't actually lied to her, just hadn't told her the whole story. She'd even accused him of profiting from them, and he hadn't denied it. Still, they weren't outright lies, and they'd both been keeping secrets from each other.

"Gracious of you," he said dryly.

"There's just one more thing I want to kn—" she began.

"In here, ladies." The door opened, and Izzy breezed in, followed by Clarissa and her husband's cousin, Lady Frobisher. She stopped in well-staged surprise. "Oh. You still here, Lord Foxton? I suppose you've forgotten the time." She sent a pointed glance at the clock in the corner and turned back to Clarissa and Lady Frobisher. "Come in, come in, Lord Foxton was just leaving. He obviously forgot that morning calls generally only last twenty minutes." She gave a trilling laugh. "And here I've been a shocking chaperone leaving these two alone together for such a time. I beg of you not to tell a soul. It would be so awkward otherwise."

She winked at Zoë, then turned a bright, expectant look on Lord Foxton. "Matteo will show you out. So nice to see you again."

Lord Foxton rose to his feet. From his expression he knew exactly what Izzy was up to, but with two other ladies looking on, he had no choice but to take his leave with as much grace as he could.

"I did forget the time, for which I apologize." He bowed over Zoë's hand. "Perhaps we can continue this conversation another time, Miss Benoît."

"Oh, perhaps, perhaps," Izzy trilled, waving him toward the door. "You never can tell what the future will bring. Ah, there is Matteo. See this gentleman out, Matteo, please."

Lord Foxton left. As the door closed behind him, Izzy fell, laughing, into a chair. "Oh, that was fun. The poor man. He would have liked to wring my neck, did you see?" She turned to Zoë. "You were in with him for a long time. I told you to ring for tea if you needed rescuing."

"But I didn't need rescuing." Truth to tell, Zoë was a bit

annoyed at the interruption. They'd really been getting somewhere, and she still had questions for him. He was such a twisty person, but he'd claimed he hadn't lied to her. So what did that mean?

Izzy laughed. "No, I gathered that, but I thought he'd had long enough."

"But we didn't." There was more, so much more that she needed to know.

"No, my love, but a gentleman who's courting needs to be deprived of his intended's company from time to time. It keeps them keen."

"It keeps them cross," Zoë said, and all three ladies laughed. "And he's not courting me," she added. Especially now that he knew she was illegitimate, she was sure.

"We'll see," Izzy said blithely. "Now we need to set up another meeting. Perhaps at your house this time, Clarissa?"

"Yes, of course," Clarissa said. "But don't expect me to come barging in on them like you did. I wouldn't have the audacity. You were quite brazen, Izzy."

Izzy waved her hand airily. "It pays to keep men on their toes and guessing."

"I've never seen you treat Leo that way," Clarissa said.

Izzy's face softened. "Well, no, but my Leo is special. Now, shall I ring for tea?"

Over tea and cakes, they discussed Zoë's next appointment with Lord Foxton. "Not tomorrow," Izzy declared. "Make it the following day. Keep him waiting a little, sharpen his appetite."

For what? Zoë wondered. She was the one eager to see him, to know what exactly was the truth. And where she stood.

In France she and Reynard had been able to talk as much and whenever they wanted. But now, when she really needed to talk to him, they were back in London where decorum ruled.

Chapter Sixteen

It had to be admitted that Milly was not the easiest of houseguests. Used to going out and about with her mother at all hours of the day and night, she found her confinement in Lady Scattergood's house difficult.

She didn't enjoy reading, and even when Clarissa brought her some popular romances, she just glanced through them desultorily. And when Lady Scattergood asked her to read aloud to her to save her old eyes, Milly did it reluctantly and in a bored, flat monotone.

The only thing she did with any enthusiasm was write long letters to Thaddeus, which she did several times a day. Probably full of complaints, Zoë thought.

Clarissa was the most patient with her. Being in the late stages of pregnancy, Clarissa didn't go out much; mostly she just walked around the gardens a little. She brought over a pile of her clothes for Milly, saying she couldn't fit into them now, and if she ever did get her figure back, fashions would have changed. She, her maid, Betty, and Zoë's maid, Marie, had been adjusting them to fit Milly.

"But of course you won't want to wear one of my dresses for your wedding," Clarissa said. "We've made an appointment for you with Miss Chance of the House of Chance."

"The House of Chance?" Milly exclaimed. "No! That little woman is frightfully common!" She saw their expressions. "Mama says so."

There was a cold little silence. Izzy opened her mouth, but Clarissa held up her hand. "That 'little woman' is frightfully brilliant," she said. "Izzy and I have all our clothes made by her."

"Except for riding habits," Izzy said, "which are always made by a tailor. But Miss Chance makes everything else, even our nightgowns." She and Clarissa exchanged secretive smiles.

Milly sniffed. "That nightgown you lent me last night is nothing special."

"No, that one was a gift from my old nurse," Clarissa said. "The ones Miss Chance makes are more for married ladies."

"And for wedding nights," Izzy added.

Milly pouted. "But she's so common. A horrid Cockney accent, and the way she talks to people, as if she's their equal. Mama says—"

Zoë was getting fed up with Milly's constant sighing and complaining and bleating never-ending nonsense beginning "Mama says." "You know, Milly, isn't it time you stopped parroting your mother's words? Given what she thinks is important, you might want to start thinking and deciding things for yourself."

Milly blinked. "But—"

"Oh, let her get married in one of your old dresses, Clarissa," Izzy said. "If she doesn't want to meet Miss Chance—"

"No, no. I'll go. I do want a new dress. It's just, couldn't we go to—"

"It's Miss Chance or no one," Izzy said firmly.

Milly sighed. "Oh, very well."

So, time being of the essence, they bundled her into the coach, veiled and muffled to the eyebrows, and took her to the House of Chance.

Miss Chance greeted them in her usual friendly fashion and whipped Milly into a private room, where she was measured up. When she finished, she stepped back, scanned Milly thoughtfully and said, "You know, I reckon I've got something that'd suit you proper, Miss Harrington."

She sent an assistant off, and in a few minutes the girl returned with a cream wool dress. "This is almost finished, but the lady who ordered it is now in the family way and it won't fit her. Try it on. The wool is very fine, so it falls nicely, and it's lined with silk so it will feel lovely and also keep you nice and warm." Milly tried it on, and the others were invited in to look.

"It's perfect," Clarissa declared.

"It's very plain," Milly said doubtfully, having been raised in multitudes of frills, but she was overruled.

"I can get it to you by tomorrow morning," Miss Chance said. "There's only a couple of small adjustments to make and the hem to sew up. It mighta been made for you, miss."

Returning home in the carriage, Zoë said, "Well? What did you think?"

"Well, she is very common—that accent! But she was all right, I suppose. That dress is awfully plain, though. It has not a single frill or flounce."

"For which you should be grateful," Izzy said acidly. "The clothes your mother commissioned for you, all frills and fussery, made you look like a pig bursting out of a cushion!"

Zoë stifled a giggle. Clarissa stared fixedly out the coach window, her lips pressed firmly together.

Milly huffed. "You are horrid, Izzy Salcott."

"But truthful. Wait until Thaddeus sees you in that dress."

"And the nightgown on your wedding night," Clarissa said.

Milly's eyes widened. "You ordered me a nightgown as well?"

"Yes, it's a wedding present."

The rest of the journey passed in silence. From the faint, reminiscent smile on Clarissa's face, Zoë guessed she was recalling her own wedding night. Or maybe not. She was holding her swollen belly, stroking it as if the baby inside could feel it. Her sister Izzy was smiling fondly at her.

Zoë felt suddenly emotional. These were her sisters, her family. Their loving bonds were visible—and she was now part of them. It was such a gift for a girl who, from the age of twelve, had thought herself alone in the world. And their generosity wasn't only reserved for family. Despite Milly's constant irritation and ingratitude, they had stepped forward without hesitation and were helping her. She was so proud of them.

They arrived back at Lady Scattergood's to the news that Milly's maid, Lizzie, had been dismissed. "But why?" Milly asked.

Betty, the source of the news, explained, "Your ma blamed poor Lizzie for your disappearance, miss. She said Lizzie shoulda kept a better eye on you, and that she oughter've known what you was up to and where you were. She sent her packing then and there, miss. Dismissed without a character."

All eyes turned to Milly.

"Well, what can I do?" she said.

"You owe that girl," Zoë told her. "She's been a loyal friend to you, and you cannot let her be punished this way."

"How can I stop it? You think Mama will listen—not that I'm going to speak to her—but when Mama makes up her mind she won't listen to anyone. Besides, I have no money—you know that—so what could I do? I . . . I'll do something for her once Thaddeus and I are married. Write her a character or something."

On that note she sat down to write to Thaddeus about the dress she was getting for the wedding.

Julian stood on the front steps of Lord and Lady Randall's house and pulled out his pocket watch. Not quite ten thirty. He'd been invited to call on Miss Benoît at eleven. Impolite to arrive early, but he'd been on tenterhooks all morning.

Two days since he'd last spoken to Vita. *Zoë.* He must remember to call her that. No, it would have to be Miss Benoît now. Oh, hang it all, he wasn't going to loiter in the street any longer. He pulled the doorbell, and a moment later, the door opened.

"Lord Foxton to see Lady Randall," he told the butler. "She is expecting me." If not quite so early. The invitation to call had come from her, not Zoë, but he knew Zoë would be there, and he knew better than to ask for an unmarried girl.

The butler showed him to an elegant sitting room where a fire was burning brightly. He offered Julian refreshments, which he refused. "Lady Randall will be with you directly," the butler said, and left.

Julian paced around, ostensibly looking at the paintings on the walls, the ornaments displayed, but really, he took in very little. Eventually he forced himself to stand in front of the fire and wait, giving an illusion, at least, of patience. Where was she?

Ten or fifteen minutes later Lady Randall hurried in, looking a little flustered. "I'm so sorry to keep you waiting, Lord Foxton. I was in the middle of a tricky process with some ointment and couldn't leave it." She waved him to a seat, saying, "My cousin will join us directly. In the meantime, did Hobbs offer you any refreshment?"

He assured her he had, but that he'd declined. He apologized for arriving early, for which he was not sorry at all. She gave him a warm smile and assured him he was very welcome. She didn't have the beauty of her sister Lady Salcott, but she had a sweetness of expression that more than made up for it.

"Ointment?" It sparked a thought.

"Yes, I make herbal lotions and suchlike. It is an interest of mine."

"I believe Miss Benoît used one of your ointments on an injury my dog sustained."

"Very likely." She glanced again at the door. "She shouldn't be long."

"It was most efficacious."

She beamed at him. "I'm so glad. Ah, here is my cousin now."

Zoë entered, wearing a bronze dress with a paisley shawl in greens and cream that brought out the color of those glorious eyes. Her hair was loose, as it had been in France. She saw the way he looked at it and put a self-conscious hand to it. "I thought we were meeting at eleven. I didn't have time for my maid to finish doing my hair," she said with a look that skewered him and made it clear she did not approve of men who arrived early.

Ah, that was his Vita, outspoken and direct, unlike the smoothly polite Miss Benoît.

After greetings had been exchanged and Julian had made another insincere apology for arriving early, Lady Randall rose and said to Julian, "I, er, just need to pop out to see to something, Lord Foxton." To Zoë she said, "I'll send in some refreshments in fifteen minutes, but if you'd like them earlier, just ring for Hobbs." She gave her "cousin" a meaningful look and hurried out. Julian repressed a smile.

"Lady Randall is very sweet, but a very poor schemer," he commented when she had gone.

Zoë stiffened. "What do you mean?"

"It was your sister's ointment you used on Hamish's neck, wasn't it?"

"Y— No. What do you mean 'my sister'? Clarissa is my cousin."

"I should have said 'half sister.' As is Lady Salcott, I assume. Oh, don't bother to deny it. Apart from your uncanny resemblance to Lady Salcott, I remember when you first produced that ointment you said, 'I have some very good ointment that my sist— I mean a girl I know made.'"

There was a short silence. "You remember that?"

"I remember everything you've ever said to me, Vita."

Faint color stole into her cheeks, but she said firmly, "My name is Zoë."

"'That which we call a rose, by any other name smells as sweet,'" he quoted softly.

"Stop it. I don't want that kind of thing from you."

"What do you want, then?"

She was silent for a minute, then folded her arms and said, "The truth, for a start."

"I've never lied to you, Vita."

She snorted. "Really? What about telling me you'd had Hamish drowned and sent Rocinante to the knackers?"

He spread his hands. "For that I apologize—again. As I said, I was angry at the time."

He smiled and sat back in his chair, crossing one long leg over the other. He'd worn buckskin breeches and gleaming high boots—not at all the usual sort of attire for a morning call. Not that this was a morning call, exactly: he'd been invited.

He saw her eyeing his boots. "Do my boots offend you? I went riding this morning and came straight here afterward. There's a boy holding my horse outside."

She made an insouciant "don't care" sort of gesture.

"Do you ride? Perhaps we could go riding together? I gather your sisters are fine horsewomen."

"My *cousins* are, yes. I, however, do not ride at all." Because orphans on the parish are not, of course, routinely given riding lessons.

"Pity. I think you'd enjoy it."

"Don't change the subject. I'm not finished discussing the lies you told me."

He frowned. "But I apologized for that."

"And what about the lies you told about those three wives?"

"But those wives are real."

Her jaw dropped. "*What?* But you promised me, on your word of honor—"

"That I wasn't married and never had been. Yes. And that's the truth."

"But you just said—"

"That the wives were real, and so they are."

She shook her head, frustrated. "I don't understand."

"Then I shall explain." He sat back, relaxed, not seeming the slightest bit discomfited. "As I think I told you before, the oldest wife is the bossiest. She thinks she has all of us—the other wives as well—under her thumb."

"But not you?"

"No, not me."

She eyed him thoughtfully. This was sounding familiar. "Go on."

"In her youth she was never what you might call a beauty, but as she aged she has become . . . you might say handsome. A face full of character, not necessarily appealing, but strong and very definite. She does not tolerate fools lightly, and she considers most people fools."

"I gather you dislike her."

"Oh no, I might be very aware of her faults, but I'm very fond of the old tartar."

She frowned. "But you said that of—"

"My grandmother, yes. Oh that's right, you know her, don't you? You painted that brilliant portrait of her after all.

So, do you think I've described her sufficiently well?" He gave her an innocent look.

Zoë clenched her fists. How dare he play such games with her? His grandmother indeed! "She can hardly be your wife, though, can she?"

He placed a finger on his cheek and pretended to ponder the question.

She itched to smack him.

"I don't think I ever said I was married to her."

"You did. You said you had three wives!"

"And I do. Please be patient while I explain."

Oh, he was infuriating. "Very well, what of the other two?"

"The second wife is my brother's widow."

"Widow?"

"Yes, I told you that my brother died. Do try to keep up, Vita."

She glared at him and he chuckled. "You look very sweet when you're cross."

"How can your brother's widow be classed as a wife?"

"Oh, Celia's definitely a wife—or was. Or are you suggesting my two nieces are illegitimate? I assure you, there was definitely a wedding at least a year before Sukey, the first one, was born. Or was Ella the firstborn? I get them mixed up. Very dreary girls, just like their mother. Celia's now the dowager Lady Foxton, a title that doesn't please her at all. Dowager, such an aging word, don't you think?"

Zoë gritted her teeth. "And the third?"

"Ah yes, the youngest one—my sister, Dorothea, who just gave birth to a beautiful baby girl, which delighted not only her but also my brother-in-law, who already had two sons to carry on the family name."

Zoë took several deep, long breaths, then said in as calm a voice as she could manage, "So the truth is, you have no wives at all."

He gave her a mock-puzzled look. "But no, Vita my

dear, as I just explained, I have three." He gave her a faintly triumphant smile.

"Ooh, you! You're impossible!" She shook a fist at him.

He laughed and held up his hands in surrender. "No, no, don't hit me, I'll explain."

"You'd better."

"I think, if you think back, I told you I had three wives. I did not say that I was married. I let you jump to that conclusion. And quite entertaining it was, too, as well as convenient."

"You thought I was fishing for information?"

His brow rose in amused challenge. "Weren't you?"

"I was making conversation," she said with dignity.

"Yes, so was I," he said affably. "But before you burst into flames, I will explain. Grandmama, Celia and Dorothea are wives, the responsibility for whom I have somehow inherited. You know about Grandmama, but what I didn't explain, and what she doesn't realize, is that her fortune has dwindled to a bare competence. She lives in my houses—my town house in Mayfair and my country seat, though I am having the dower house renovated and she will move into it when I marry. I'm sure that will please you. It won't please her, of course, but we'll deal with that when it happens."

"Why should I be interested?" she said airily.

"I hope very much that you will," he said in a tone of voice that wasn't anything like his earlier lighthearted banter. His eyes darkened as he spoke. She swallowed and looked away. Her cheeks warmed under his gaze.

He returned to his matter-of-fact explanation. "Wife number two, my widowed sister-in-law, Celia, is a constant drain on my patience and my pocket. She was left a very generous jointure—part of the marriage settlements—which should easily support her and the girls, but the woman is the biggest pinchpenny I have ever met and resents spending a groat, especially if by nagging she can get two out of me. She refused to live in the dower house and won't share the Mayfair house with Grandmama—to say they don't get on is an understatement—so I offered her a house in Richmond, which she decided was just acceptable."

"I see. And your sister? How can she possibly be called a wife?"

"Ah yes, Dorothea." He smiled, as you would for a fond memory. "Her case is quite different. She fell madly in love with Sir Frederick Strangham. She adores him and he adores her back—but though he comes of good family, he's as poor as a church mouse. Everybody opposed their marriage— Papa, Grandmama, even my late brother, Ralph—but Dot stood firm, refusing to look at anyone else."

She was intrigued despite herself. "So what happened?"

He chuckled. "My sister, Dot, bids fair to becoming as indomitable as Grandmama, only a lot nicer. She took matters into her own hands and told Papa and Grandmama that she had lain with Fred and that she was to bear his child. Swore it was true—it wasn't—but they weren't going to risk it. They washed their hands of her, and she married Fred by special license. And gave birth to their first child more than a year later. They scraped by for a few years on Fred's pittance, but when Papa died and I inherited, I handed one of my estates over to Fred and Dot. He's now learning to become a farmer, the estate is starting to turn a profit and they're as happy as grigs."

There was a long silence. He rose, stirred the coals in the fire and shoveled in some more coal. He turned to face Zoë. "So, there you are, Vita my love, my three wives and their three houses explained. To your satisfaction, I hope?"

Vita my love?

She put up her hand as if to hold him off, or to block his words. "Don't call me that."

"Why not? It's the truth."

She looked up at him, at his tall, spare figure limned by firelight, just as it had been so often in France. But they'd been two different people then. Living a fantasy.

"Your truths are very . . . twisty," she said finally.

"Perhaps, but this one isn't. I love you, Vita."

"My name is Zoë."

"I love you, Zoë."

She shook her head in denial.

He took two steps toward her and took her hands in his. Hers were cold, his were warm. So much for "cold hands warm heart," she thought irrelevantly.

"It's marriage I'm offering you, Vita—Zoë, whoever you are."

She pulled her hands away, rose and moved behind her chair. She gripped it tightly, as if she needed it to support her. "I can't, you know I can't."

"Why not?"

She shook her head again. "I'm illegitimate, you know that."

"So?"

She sighed at his obtuseness. "You are an earl."

"Heavens!" He looked down at himself. "So I am."

"Don't! Don't make fun of me."

"I'm not, love," he said apologetically. "But you're being very foolish."

"I'm not." She gave him a desperate look. She'd have to tell him everything. "You guessed it earlier, I'm not the French cousin—I'm Clarissa and Izzy's illegitimate half sister, but it must never get out, or the scandal will affect them, and they've been so kind to me. I could never hurt them that way."

"Very well, we won't tell anyone."

"Oh, stop it! It's not so easy. Or so simple. I'm not French at all—I was born in the back streets of London. In a slum."

He eyed her solemnly, his blue, blue eyes no longer dancing.

"It's true that my mother was French—and the legitimate daughter of the Comte and Comtesse de Chantonney. And that she escaped the guillotine when the rest of her family were executed. She was eleven when she came to London, all on her own, and scraped a living as best she could, drawing pictures in chalk on the pavement. My father was an English baronet, Sir Bartleby Studley. He seduced her. She thought she was safe with my father because he was a titled gentleman. She wasn't. When she fell with child—me—he abandoned her."

"I see."

"When she died, some years later, I was taken to an orphanage. I was sixteen when Clarissa and her maid, Betty, came to the orphanage to hire a maidservant. They found me. Only they decided I wasn't to be a maid but a lady. But I'm not, not really."

"You're a lady to your fingertips," he said softly.

The soft sincerity of his voice brought tears to her eyes. She blinked them away. "Oh, stop it. I'm not. You know I'm not." She thought of the way she'd dealt with Etienne. No lady would even know to threaten what she had, let alone to be willing to do it. And no lady would ever kick a gentleman in public, on the dance floor, as she had.

"I don't know anything of the sort," he said. "And although I'm deeply honored that you've shared your story with me, I still don't see why you can't marry me."

She made a frustrated gesture. "Have you not heard a word I said?"

"I told you before, I remember everything you've ever said to me." He smiled. "I was even planning to marry you when I thought you were an illiterate French maidservant, unjustly dismissed from her post."

Shocked, she stared at him. "You weren't."

"I was. Though I was a little worried that you'd find the change to living in England and having a maid of your own difficult. But you won't, will you?"

"I have a maid," she said irrelevantly, her mind still spinning from what he'd just told her. "Marie. She was unjustly dismissed in the way I told you. They were her clothes I was wearing when I met you. She's here with me now, learning English and trying to adjust."

"Good. I'm glad she has a happy ending. Now, what about mine?"

She gazed at him, trying to think of what to say. He'd turned her world upside down with just a few words.

"What about your grandmother? We battled the whole time I was painting her."

He shrugged. "Grandmama enjoys a good battle. It keeps her young. But I don't care what she thinks. I go my own way, remember? In any case, she's desperate for me to marry and get myself an heir. So what about my answer? Will you marry me?"

"Tea." The door swung open, and Hobbs, the butler, stood with a footman bearing a tray with a pot of tea, cups, saucers and a plate of cakes.

"Tea?" He rolled his eyes, then gave a rueful chuckle. "It was how we met, after all. But honestly, those sisters of yours have the worst timing."

It was the best timing, Zoë thought, relieved at the interruption. Clarissa followed the tea tray in. "Have you had a nice chat?" she asked brightly, with a meaningful look at Zoë.

"We were until we were interrupted," Lord Foxton said bluntly. "I just asked your sister to marry me. She seems to think it impossible."

"Sister? But I thought . . ."

"He knows everything," Zoë told her miserably.

"Really?" Clarissa lowered herself awkwardly onto the sofa. "That's wonderful. Tea, Lord Foxton?"

Zoë stared at her. Did Clarissa not understand? She'd become a little vague since her pregnancy. And why was she beaming at Lord Foxton like that? He was smiling back at her, as smug as the cat that had swallowed the cream. She couldn't bear it. "I—I have to go," Zoë muttered, and ran from the room.

Julian rose to go after her, but Lady Randall waved him back to his seat. "No, no, let her go. She's a little mixed-up at the moment. Now, tell me what the problem is. And do you take milk or sugar?"

"Just one lump of sugar, thank you," he said, bemused by her composure.

"Will you have a slice of seed cake?"

"Thank you."

She cut a slice and passed it to him on a little plate and cut herself a slice. She must have noticed him eyeing her bulk, for she patted it, saying, "Only a few weeks to go. I can't wait."

She sipped her tea, broke off a piece of cake and chewed it thoughtfully. "She's a dear, sweet girl, Zoë, and very protective of those she loves. Meaning me and my sister Izzy, in particular. I gather she told you that we are sisters through our disreputable father."

He nodded.

"I was his only legitimate child, and when I found Izzy—we were eight, and Papa was about to throw her into an orphanage, horrid man—I made sure I kept her. And when we found Zoë, also in an orphanage, we kept her, too." She ate another piece of cake. "But darling Zoë was sure she would bring shame and scandal to us if anyone found out."

She glanced at him. "Our husbands knew, of course, and if they didn't care, why would we? But Zoë cared. It was her idea, not ours, that she pose as our cousin from France, you know. Her French is exquisite, thanks to her mother. But her English"—she grimaced—"straight out of the London back streets."

She sipped her tea. "So she hatched a plan with Lucy, the goddaughter of our friend who lives over there." She gestured across the garden. "She was going to France with her husband, Gerald, who is a diplomat."

"I know Paton—Lord Thornton as he is now—and Tarrant, too, from the war."

"Oh good. Then you'll understand. So Gerald and Lucy took Zoë with them to Paris, where for the last three years Lucy has been teaching Zoë how to be a lady."

"She needs no teaching. She's a lady to her fingertips, back-streets accent or no."

Lady Randall beamed at him. "Exactly, you dear man. But Zoë had to believe it, too, otherwise she did not feel worthy to be our sister. Or even our cousin. Foolish child. We loved her from the start." She polished off the last of her cake and dusted her fingers. "So now, Lord Foxton, you want to marry our darling girl, but she is being foolishly stubborn, right?"

He shook his head. "I don't know what she's thinking. She seems to think she will bring shame on me or something. Which is ridiculous."

"It certainly is, though it would matter to some people very much. Not you, apparently." She gave him another brilliant smile. "And not at all to my brother-in-law, Lord Salcott, who, despite his reputation as a high stickler, married my sister Izzy with all the pomp and ceremony any bride could want, in full knowledge of her irregular birth."

Julian sat back, slightly dazed. This lady, so sweet and apparently shy. He'd even thought her a little simple at first—her sister had done most of the talking before—but she'd stunned him with her warm acceptance and matter-of-fact approach to the problems Zoë thought so overwhelming.

"So, what should I do?"

She gave him that sweet smile again. "If you know her

objections—and I assume you do—and you love her enough—and I suspect you do—"

"I do."

"Good. Then deal with the objections and convince her you love her."

He laughed. "As easy as that?"

She smiled serenely. "The path to love is rarely easy. More tea?"

Chapter Seventeen

Zoë hardly slept that night. She tossed and turned, hearing his words over and over again.

I remember everything you've ever said to me, Vita.

That which we call a rose, by any other name smells as sweet.

Vita my love.

I love you, Vita.

You're a lady to your fingertips.

I was even planning to marry you when I thought you were an illiterate French maidservant, unjustly dismissed from her post.

Will you marry me?

Will you marry me?

Will you marry me?

The doorbell rang quite early in the morning, and she sat up in bed. It couldn't be him. Not at such a time. Surely?

She'd heard the birds singing in the trees outside for quite a while. In France she and Reynard were usually up by this hour. He'd have the fire going, and the water would be almost boiling, ready to make the tea.

Nobody in London would call at this hour.

Nevertheless . . . She slipped out of bed and, barefoot, hurried to the stairs, peering down between the banisters. She could hear voices, Treadwell's and one other. Indistinct. Treadwell didn't sound happy. Was he ever? She heard the front door close, and a moment later a bell ringing faintly.

A few minutes later, Marie came up the stairs, carrying a large, flattish square box with a gold logo. Zoë recognized it. It was from the House of Chance.

"Mademoiselle Milly's wedding dress," Marie told her. "Monsieur Treadwell, he very not happy. Parcel not supposed to come by front door."

Zoë nodded, feeling ridiculously disappointed. Of course Reynard would not call at such an hour. And in any case, he knew he would not be admitted: Lady Scattergood had given strict instructions.

She followed Marie into Milly's bedchamber. Milly opened the box and drew out the dress. "Oh, it's perfect," she murmured. "A bit plain, but very nice. And what's this?" A second garment wrapped in tissue lay under the dress. She drew it out, held it up and gasped.

It was a flimsy silk garment: a nightdress, Zoë gathered, only so fine that it was almost transparent. Milly's eyes were popping. "This—this can't be what I think it is."

"It's a nightdress," Zoë said.

"But it's so . . . so improper. Mama would never allow me to wear something so . . . so revealing."

The mother who'd dressed her in necklines so low-cut that Milly was almost popping out of them. Resulting in a proposal from a lustful old spider.

"Perhaps not, but I expect Thaddeus will love it. And,

Milly, remember what I said about parroting your mother's opinions all the time? I very much doubt your Thaddeus will appreciate it, given your mother's attitude toward him."

She left Milly then, feeling stupidly wistful. Milly would be marrying the man she loved and would wear that beautiful flimsy silk nightdress for him, whereas she . . . She was in an impossible position.

She loved Reynard, and if he'd really been Reynard the vagabond artist, she could have married him. Only her sisters and Lucy would have been so disappointed after all the trouble they'd gone to on her behalf.

They wanted her to marry Julian, the Earl of Foxton, but how could he marry an illegitimate girl who was born in the slums of London? A girl who was only masquerading as a well-born French cousin. What if she were found out? It had been nerve-racking enough making her entrance first in French society and now in English. The French had been so much easier, perhaps because she didn't care so much, and because she knew her French, at least, was flawless. But in England, with the eyes of the ton upon her, it felt as though she were walking on ice. Thin ice, at that.

If she married Julian the earl, he would be made to look a fool. His family would hate it. His grandmother already disliked Zoë intensely. She was a woman who set great store by people's position in society. She would be appalled—furious—to learn he was thinking of marrying her. And that, even before she knew about Zoë's shameful background.

Did she want to be a countess, anyway? Always having to be on her best behavior? Being a grand hostess, running his various homes, being gracious Lady of the Manor to his tenants, knowing they would look down on her if they knew the truth. Aristocrats were not the only snobs in the world.

And what about her painting? Would there ever be time for that? She knew from her sisters' experience that there was work involved in being the wife of an earl, just as there was work for an earl. So even if she did continue to paint, would it be regarded indulgently as "the countess's little hobby," fitted in between her more worldly obligations? And no doubt any praise for her painting would be because she was a member of the aristocracy, not because it was any good.

Good or bad, she wanted her painting to be taken seriously. She wanted it to be her profession.

Julian returned to his lodgings that evening only to discover that his grandmother had followed him to London. A note from her awaited him, demanding he call on her at the earliest opportunity. He sighed, but decided to get it over with. He had other plans for tomorrow.

His grandmother got straight to the point. "I have been informed that you attended a reception at the home of Lord and Lady Salcott."

"Indeed? Who told you?"

She brushed his question aside with an impatient gesture. "Well? Well?"

"Well what?"

"Did you meet any eligible young ladies there?"

"Dozens," he said wearily. He was fed up with her constant nagging.

"Well then?" She looked at him expectantly. "Did any of them look suitable?"

He was tempted to say "Suitable for what?" but he wanted to end this conversation and go home. "I didn't tell you before, Grandmama, but when I was in France, I met a young lady who I've decided is the very one for me."

"French?" She wrinkled her nose. "Still, better a French bride than no bride at all, I suppose. Tell me about this young lady. She is well born, I take it?"

He pretended to consider it. "She's possibly not the kind of well-born you're thinking of, but I think she's perfect."

Her eyes narrowed. "Explain."

He said in a confiding voice, "She's an orphan and very sweet. She's a former maidservant who was unjustly dismissed from her position." His grandmother started to swell up, and he continued before she could interrupt. "She's illiterate, but very clever, and I think she'll learn to read quite quickly. And of course, she's very beautiful."

His grandmother was turning a beautiful shade of puce. He added fuel to the fire. "The only small—really very tiny difficulty—is that she has a tendency to steal, but I'm sure—"

"*Steal?* You're considering *an illiterate maidservant who steals*?" Her voice rose to a screech.

"Oh, not all the time," he said reassuringly. "And I have every hope of curing her of her larcenous habits. I'm sure she wouldn't steal from you, Grandmama." He smiled.

His grandmother clutched her pearls and glared at him. She seemed lost for words, which he thought was a nice change. Her mouth opened and closed, rather like a goldfish's, but no words came out.

It didn't last. Her bosom swelled and she said in a voice of doom, "Are you telling me you brought this—this *creature* to London with you?"

He said with dignity, "She's not a creature, Grandmama. Please recall, you are speaking of My Intended. But alas, I was unable to bring her to London. She ran off with some of my valuables."

His grandmother heaved a sigh of relief, so he added, "But I have every hope of finding her."

Her eyes bulged. "Are you mad? An illiterate French maidservant, to be the next Countess of Foxton? You cannot be serious!" He wasn't sure, but he thought there might be steam coming out of her ears.

"Oh, but I am, Grandmama. Very serious." He gave her a beatific smile. "So you don't need to be fretting about me and the succession anymore. As soon as I find her, I'll be married and working on getting an heir. Just as you've always wanted." He rose. "I must be off now. I have a busy day planned tomorrow. Good evening, Grandmama. Sleep well and dream of my nuptials."

After breakfast Milly and Zoë were getting ready to go out for an early morning drive with Izzy and Clarissa. The plan was to take Milly someplace where she could walk in the fresh air, get some exercise and not feel so constricted. The garden, of course, was impossible; though her mother never usually ventured out there, she just might this one time.

It was not the season for flowers, but though it was cold outside, the skies were clear and Zoë was looking forward to the outing. Milly was not the only one who'd been feeling confined: everywhere Zoë went, Milly went, too, and it was driving her mad.

The carriage waited outside, the horses restless to be off. Zoë, Clarissa and Izzy had gathered downstairs in the front sitting room, talking with Lady Scattergood while they waited for Milly to join them. She always took ages to dress, dithering over what to wear, but also, today, how to make sure her mama wouldn't see her.

The front doorbell jangled. They exchanged glances. It was rather early for a caller.

"I'm here for Miss Harrington," they heard a deep voice say to the butler.

They stiffened. Had Mrs. Harrington discovered where her daughter was hiding?

Lady Scattergood made a dismissive gesture. "Treadwell will take care of it."

"I'm sorry, sir, but Miss Harrington does not reside here," they heard Treadwell say in his usual pompous voice.

"Nonsense. I know she's here, so fetch her at once."

"Good day to you, sir," Treadwell said in his most freezing dismissive tones. Then they heard, "Sir, I must protes—*Squawk!*" It was a most un-Treadwell-like sound.

They hurried to the entry hall. A man stood just inside, brown-haired, with regular features, of medium height, stockily built and quite stylishly dressed. He was a complete stranger.

Behind him, Treadwell stood outside, on the front steps, looking like an extremely ruffled owl.

The man bowed to Lady Scattergood. "Good morning, ma'am, ladies, I'm sorry to barge in like this—"

From behind him Treadwell bleated, "He did, I tried to stop him, but—"

The man dismissed him with a snap of the fingers. Treadwell stopped, swelling with wordless outrage. No one ever snapped fingers at him like that. He did the finger snapping in this house.

The man continued. "Your butler did try to stop me, but my case is urgent. I am here for Miss Harrington. My name is—"

"Thaddeus!" Milly screeched from the landing. Snatching off her veil and tossing it aside, she flew down the stairs, hurtled across the floor and threw herself into his arms, babbling, "I knew you would come. Mama didn't see you, did she? Oh, Thaddeus, I'm so unhappy and I don't know what to do. I can't bear being cooped up like this. And Mama will be furious when she finds me. Oh, Thaddeus, you're here, you're here."

He held her close and murmured soothing things into her ear, and eventually, when she had calmed, she said, "But why are you here? I won't turn one-and-twenty for ages yet. Weeks."

"I'm taking you away," Thaddeus said. "Today. Now, in fact. So run upstairs and pack your things. My carriage awaits you."

Zoë glanced at her sisters. This was excellent news.

Milly blinked up at him. "Your carriage? You mean we're eloping? Oh, Thaddeus, I don't think—"

"Of course we're not eloping," Thaddeus said calmly. "Would I ask you to do something so scandalous? No, I'm taking you to my mother."

"Your mother?"

"Yes, you will stay with her and my father until your twenty-first birthday. And on that day, my sweet, we will marry with all the ceremony your heart desires in the largest church in Sheffield. It's all arranged. Now, run and pack your bags."

"I don't have much to pack. Only some old things of Clarissa's."

"You will, of course, purchase an entire trousseau in Sheffield, with my mother's assistance, but in the meantime you will need enough clothes for several days on the road. Taking into account possible delays caused by bad weather, you should allow for at least a week."

"A week? In a carriage with you? Alone? Oh, Thaddeus, I don't think—"

"Of course you won't be alone with me, little goose. I wouldn't compromise you for the world. Your maid, Lizzie, is waiting in the carriage. Shall I fetch her to help you pack?"

"Lizzie? But Mama dismissed her. However did you find her?"

"I've been writing to you at her mother's address for the last three years, remember? She told me what happened, and she now works for me. Now, will I send for her to help you pack?"

Clarissa stepped forward. "No need for that, Mr. Henshaw, Zoë and I and Zoë's maid will help Milly. We are most familiar with her current wardrobe. Come along, Milly." She linked arms with Milly and gave Zoë a silent signal to do the same, and between them they towed a dazed and bemused Milly upstairs, where they immediately went into a frenzy of packing.

They soon stopped asking Milly what she wanted to take with her—she dithered uselessly, so they decided everything for her. Finally they laid her lovely wedding dress, carefully wrapped in tissue, on the top of the valise. "And now this," Clarissa said, draping the beautiful silk nightdress over it.

Milly frowned and snatched it up. "No, I don't want that. It's immodest and I won't wear it."

"But it's lovely," Clarissa said. "And on your wedding night—"

"No, I don't want it." She tossed it aside.

Zoë and Clarissa exchanged glances, shrugged and closed the valise. Clarissa reached for the handle. "No, you don't," Zoë said. "No weights for you. You're already carrying a baby, remember?"

She went to take the valise, but Marie brushed past her, saying, "No, no. I carry, mademoiselle. You take these ones." She passed the two bandboxes to Zoë and took the valise.

"Are we ready, then?" Milly asked impatiently. "Thaddeus doesn't like to be kept waiting." She opened the door and led the procession down the stairs, carrying her reticule.

Thaddeus, who had been taking tea with Izzy and Lady Scattergood, met them at the foot of the stairs. He took the valise from Marie, snapped his fingers at the footman, Jeremiah, passed it to him and indicated to Treadwell that he should take the bandboxes out to the carriage. Which he did with a sour expression, carrying the bandboxes in two fingers as if they were entirely odious.

Thaddeus tucked Milly's hand into the crook of his arm,

thanked Lady Scattergood and Zoë and her sisters for taking such good care of Milly, prompted Milly to do the same, and left.

Zoë and her sisters stood on the front step and watched the very smart traveling carriage bowl away down the street and turn the corner.

They went back inside, where Lady Scattergood called for more tea.

"Well," she said. "Well."

There was no answer to that. Clarissa sipped her tea. "Thaddeus was not at all what I expected."

Izzy nodded. "I liked him. A man who knows what he wants and how to get it. But how on earth did such a man fall for someone like Milly?"

Clarissa nodded. "The young ladies of Sheffield will be green with envy once they know he's taken."

Zoë said, "I can't say I'm sorry to see her go."

"No, she was starting to turn into Chinese fish," Lady Scattergood agreed.

They all looked at her. "Chinese fish?"

The old lady made a vague gesture. "Yes, you know, some Chinese saying about visitors becoming like fish— after a while they begin to smell."

They fell silent, reflecting on all that had happened.

"Does he realize, do you think," Lady Scattergood said, "that he's marrying a brainless widgeon?"

"He must, and clearly doesn't mind," Zoë said. "He's known her more than three years, after all."

"There's no accounting for taste," Izzy said.

"There's no accounting for love," Clarissa said softly.

"I predict Milly will become known in future for prefacing all her utterances with 'Thaddeus says,'" Zoë said.

"I suppose someone will inform Mrs. Harrington," Clarissa said after a minute.

"Thaddeus will have it all in hand," Izzy said. "He's that sort of man."

There was a sudden outbreak of yapping in the hall. Lady Scattergood glanced at the open doorway, stiffened, grabbed her lorgnette and made an outraged exclamation. "There's another one! What does Treadwell think he's doing, letting men into the house? That's the second one today! Has he completely lost his touch?" She pointed the lorgnette at someone just outside the door. "What the devil are you doing in my house, sirrah? Zoë, stay with your sis— The gels."

There was a scramble to put down teacups, but before the others could rise and see who Lady Scattergood was talking to, Lord Foxton stepped inside, moving carefully to avoid stepping on any of the small dogs swirling around his ankles.

Julian had decided on his course. It was a trifle drastic, but otherwise he could envisage only ever seeing Zoë in short visits, with her sisters lurking, ready to interrupt at a crucial time. And if he were to have any hope of winning her, he needed to get her alone so that they could talk.

He'd been a fool, he knew. He should have trusted her from the start, but being evasive, especially with women, had been a habit for too long. It had served him in the past. He'd always tried to keep them at bay and avoid being tied down, but now, when he was ready—more than ready; he was determined to commit—he was hoist with his own petard: she didn't trust him.

He'd been on his way to Lady Randall's house because, of both Zoë's sisters, he'd decided that Clarissa would be the most sympathetic to his cause—she was a romantic, he was sure. But passing Lady Scattergood's house knowing he would not be admitted there, he was surprised to see the door wide open and some fellow bodily lifting that pompous old butler, turning and dumping him on the steps outside.

Fascinated, he'd stopped the carriage at once and watched as the fellow stepped inside the house and the butler stood on the front step, trying to straighten his clothes and regain his usual impassive mien. With limited success. He then went inside, leaving the front door standing ajar.

That was enough for Julian. Shouting to his coachman to hold the horses, he jumped down and slipped inside the house, where he witnessed a fascinating scene. As things became clearer, he wasn't sure whether to laugh or swear. The fellow was taking some girl away, eloping possibly— she was off packing her things.

If there was a goddess of irony, she would clearly be having a good laugh at his expense.

He stood, watching from a quiet corner as the fellow ushered the girl out into a waiting carriage and they bowled away.

First the dogs and then the old lady spotted him. "What the devil are you doing in my house, sirrah?" she said, brandished her lorgnette. "Zoë, stay with the gels!"

Of course they all hurried toward the door and stared at him.

He swept them a deep bow, saying with a flourish, "Good morning, ladies. I see you are all dressed for an excursion. I presume that is your barouche waiting in the street."

"What business is it of yours, sirrah?" the old lady snapped. "I didn't invite you into my house and I don't want you here now. Get out! Shoo! Scat!"

"My deepest apologies, Lady Scattergood," he said smoothly. "I saw the front door was open and, perceiving there was some sort of disturbance inside, I was concerned for your safety and that of the ladies."

Zoë rolled skeptical eyes at him, confirming yet again— not that Julian needed any further confirmation—that she was the one for him.

The old lady snorted.

Julian continued. "I wondered whether Miss Benoît would be interested in a drive. It's a mild morning and the sun is out, though for how long is anyone's guess." The old lady scowled and opened her mouth to refuse, but he said quickly, "Naturally I have a very reliable chaperone waiting in the carriage to accompany us."

The old lady's scowl remained, but Lady Randall, after a brief silent exchange with her sister, Lady Salcott, stepped forward with a smile, saying, "That sounds delightful, Lord Foxton. I'm sure Zoë would enjoy it, especially seeing as you've gone to all the trouble of hiring a respectable chaperone. We were just saying we needed a break and were planning an excursion, weren't we, ladies?"

Zoë eyed her sister doubtfully. Julian hid a smile. Dear Lady Randall, so sweet, so gullible.

Lady Salcott gave him a sharp look, then nodded. "Yes, you go ahead with Lord Foxton, Zoë. Clarissa and I will follow in the barouche."

"Excellent." Julian bowed again. He'd bowed more in the last five minutes than he had in a month. "Shall we, Miss Benoît?" He offered her his arm, and she took it, her expression entirely skeptical. She knew he was up to something; she just couldn't figure out what.

As they stepped outside, Julian could hear the old lady upbraiding the butler for letting men into the house. The poor fellow was bleating excuses, but she wasn't having any of it.

He indicated his carriage, and Zoë jerked to a halt. "That's a traveling carriage."

"Yes, I know," he said apologetically. "But Grandmama arrived in town last night and she has commandeered the barouche for her own use. And I wasn't about to bring an open carriage, not after we were half drowned the other day in the park. Now, may I assist you?" He opened the door.

"Thank you, I'm perfectly capable of mounting a few steps," she said, still prickling with suspicion.

He opened the door. "Stay!"

She blinked, glanced inside, and suspicion was replaced by laughter. "This is your 'very reliable chaperone'?"

"Are you doubting his credentials?" he said with mock indignation. "He won't leave us alone for a minute, I can guarantee it. Not unless there's a rabbit in the vicinity."

Chuckling, she climbed into the carriage, where she and Hamish had an ecstatic reunion. Julian followed her in, blocking the view from any observers outside. He turned, waved to her sisters on the steps of the house and told the coachman to drive on.

The carriage set off with a jerk, and he dropped into the seat opposite Zoë, feeling very satisfied. There. It was done.

"You are shameless, you know." Zoë fondled Hamish's silky ears. "Bamboozling my sisters and Lady Scattergood that way."

"I know. I'm sorry." His blue eyes danced like sunlight on waves.

"You're not the least bit sorry!"

"I know. Sorry."

Zoë shook her head in frustration. Of course he wasn't sorry. He'd achieved exactly what he wanted. But she wasn't really upset. She did want to talk to him. She'd hardly had a wink of sleep last night, thinking about him, wondering and worrying about what to do.

She'd missed him dreadfully since she'd slipped out of the caravan that morning, and it didn't seem to matter how often or how firmly she told herself that he was no good and she'd be better off without him, it made no difference. Swindler, villain, liar, she wanted him, and that was the truth.

She glanced out the window and stiffened. "This isn't the way to the park."

"No, we're going the long way."

He looked so innocent she knew something was up. She narrowed her eyes. "Where are we going?"

"Ardingly."

"Ardingly? I've never heard of that. Where is it?"

"It's a delightful small village. There's an ancient, rather lovely church established, I believe, by some fellow who came over with the Conqueror. Then there's the remains of a Roman road that's even more ancient, of course, and—"

"Where is it?"

"Farther along this road." He waved vaguely.

She narrowed her eyes. "How far from London?"

He pursed his lips, thinking. "I'd say about forty miles."

"Forty miles! I don't believe it."

"It was an estimate," he said earnestly. "I could be wrong—rounding off, you know. Maybe it's only thirty-nine miles or even thirty-eight."

"Reynard! Stop prevaricating! Tell me why we're going to Ardingly."

"Oh, didn't I tell you? We're going to visit my sister, Dot. I told you about her, didn't I? She's married to Fred, and they live on a charming estate just outside Ardingly. The house was built in the late sixteenth century, and—"

"Why. Are. You. Taking. Me. There?"

He didn't answer for a moment, but his eyes were dancing with mischief and a smile quivered on his lips, as if trying to escape. "Isn't it obvious? I've kidnapped you."

She sank back against her seat. "Of course you have. I should have known you were up to something devious and disreputable."

"Nonsense. This is quite a respectable sort of kidnapping. We even have a chaperone." He chuckled, not the least bit abashed. "Mind you, when I saw that other fellow whisking that girl off to elope with her or whatever, I thought you'd be on to me in a flash. Ironic, wasn't it? Two of us planning the same wheeze from the same house on the same day? Luckily you didn't catch on. It was he who gave me the idea of saying I'd provided a chaperone. What a slow top, eloping with a girl and bringing a chaperone along."

She shook her head. "Honestly, will you never give a straight answer?"

"Seriously?" The mischief faded from his eyes. "It's been impossible to speak to you in London, not properly in the way I need to. So I'm taking you to my sister's place. Her presence will be sufficient to ensure it's a perfectly respectable visit, but knowing she will be entirely taken up with her two little boys and the new baby, she won't bother us at all. And Fred is too busy alarming the tenant farmers with his enthusiasm for experimental crops and agricultural innovations—in fact, he probably won't even notice we're there."

She was silent for a long time.

Eventually he leaned forward and held out his hands. For some reason unknown to her, she put her hands in his. "Vita," he said, his voice deep and serious, "if you want me to turn the carriage around and take you home, I will. We can be back in Bellaire Gardens in half an hour. Just say the word."

She hesitated.

"Nothing will happen unless you want it, I promise you," he said.

She bit her lip.

His long thumbs caressed her hands. "We need to talk freely and uninterrupted, and not in the small slivers of time your sisters are willing to allot us."

"They mean well."

"Of course they do, and I appreciate their good intentions, even though the actuality of it frustrates me."

Zoë sighed. She'd been frustrated, too. "How long will it take to reach your sister's place?"

"We'll be there in the afternoon, well before dark."

"Is she expecting us?"

"No, but she won't mind. Very accommodating and hospitable is Dot. So, do we turn around or not?"

She sighed. "No. But I'm not happy about your methods."

"I'm sorry."

"Stop saying that! You're not at all sorry."

He smiled. "You know me so well. But when a man is desperate . . ."

"Desperate? You?"

"Yes," he said seriously. "When I saw you'd gone that morning, leaving the caravan empty, I was devastated."

"Because of the painting I took."

He made an impatient gesture. "The painting was nothing—a minor irritant. It was you I missed, Vita. I searched Paris for you for several weeks."

"Really?"

"Of course I did. Don't you understand? I love you."

She said nothing.

"Dammit, Vita, you were a virgin! I thought when we made love that night that it meant something."

"It did," she said bleakly. "To me."

"It did to me, too. I've never felt like that before, not with any woman."

Could she believe him? She wasn't sure. He was so facile with words.

"And when I realized you'd gone, left me without a word and with no way of contacting you, not even a surname, I was devastated. You cut my heart out and took it with you."

She shook her head. She'd left her heart with him. He just didn't realize it.

"I gave up eventually. I told myself to forget you, that I'd meant nothing to you, that you'd diddled me finely." There was a short silence while she absorbed that. Then he added, "But I couldn't."

Zoë said nothing. It was how she'd felt too. She'd told herself over and over that he was a scoundrel who preyed on poor people, but it didn't make her feel any better. She missed him. He was a constant ache in her heart.

"After you left, it was as if my world had lost all color, a life painted in shades of gray. Then, when I saw the portrait you'd done of Grandmama, it was the first sign of hope, like new green shoots sprouting after a fire. So I went searching for you again, this time in London, still with practically no information about you. And then, when I saw you coming down the stairs at that party, glorious in green . . . I felt alive again."

She swallowed and gazed out at the landscape flashing past the window. She had no doubt of his sincerity. He might be twisty and devious in some matters, but when he spoke from the heart like this, she had to believe him.

But it wasn't so simple.

"I'll go with you to your sister's, but I'll need to send a note to my sisters and Lady Scattergood."

He smiled. "You can write to them when we stop to change the horses, and send the notes back with a courier. They won't worry then."

They probably would, but there was no point in saying so.

A short time later they stopped to change horses, and Julian took Hamish for a quick run while Zoë wrote notes to her sisters and Lady Scattergood. She explained her absence as an impulsive visit to his sister. She knew if she mentioned the word *kidnap*, her brothers-in-law, Leo and Race, would be following them posthaste, probably with horsewhips.

Julian made arrangements to have the notes delivered and also brought her a mug of tea and a custard tart.

The carriage set off again.

"Am I forgiven?"

"We'll see." She nibbled on the tart and sipped her tea. And then she stiffened as something occurred to her. "Julian, I don't have any baggage!"

He waved that off. "Don't worry about that. You'll manage. My sister isn't fussy about fashion."

"I'm not talking about fashion, I'm saying I have *no baggage*!"

He gave her a blank look. "So? You managed without baggage in France."

"In France I had *a bundle*," she said, exasperated, "containing a complete change of clothes, and . . . and various other necessities."

"You can borrow anything you need from my sister," said the clueless male.

"Won't she mind?"

He looked perplexed, as if she was making a fuss about nothing. "I don't see why she would."

It hadn't even occurred to him, she realized. "Did *you* bring any baggage?"

"Yes, of course. I had my valet pack a valise."

She breathed deeply and counted to ten. "Will your sister's clothes even fit me?"

His eyes ran over her, assessing. He frowned slightly. "I'm not sure. The last time I saw her she was"—he gestured—"very round, and you're not. Except in all the right places," he added hastily. "But I'm sure it will all work out."

He was hopeless, she decided. But she loved him anyway.

Chapter Eighteen

❧

The miles passed. For quite a while they were each lost in their own thoughts. Then Julian leaned forward. "So what is it that's stopping you, Zoë my love? What are you worried about?"

She just looked at him. She didn't know where to start.

"You know I love you, and I think you love me—no, don't say anything." He held up his hand. "You can't ask for love: it can only be given freely as a gift, so I'm not asking you. But can we talk about why you think marrying me is so problematic?"

She sighed.

"Your sisters like me. They'd be happy if we married, I'm sure."

"I know."

"And Lady Scattergood probably wouldn't approve, but—"

She huffed a small laugh. "Oh yes she would. As long as a few weeks after the wedding you left me and traveled to the other side of the world, sending back beautiful, exotic gifts until you died. It's her idea of the perfect marriage."

He laughed. "Well, she's doomed to disappointment, because if you marry me, wild horses couldn't make me leave you."

"Your grandmother would hate it, too," she said.

"Ah no, that's where you're wrong," he said smugly. "Last night when she arrived in London, she sent for me to deliver the usual rant about my finding a suitable bride and getting myself an heir."

"Well, an illegitimate half-French orphan is hardly what she would think is suitable."

"Trust me, when I present you as my bride, she'll fall on your neck with delight and gratitude."

"She won't."

"She will. I told her that I'd been in France, where I'd met and fallen in love with an orphaned, illiterate French maidservant who had been unjustly dismissed and who stole from me, but was very beautiful. I told her I wanted to marry her and that I was sure I could cure her of her larcenous habits." He grinned. "Naturally, she had a fit—steam was practically coming from her ears."

She couldn't help but laugh. "You are appalling, you know."

He grinned. "I know. But when I tell her I'm going to marry you instead of my light-fingered maidservant, she will be eternally grateful."

"No, she won't. She thinks I'm an impudent, brazen, insolent hussy."

"Ah yes, but you'll be an impudent, brazen, insolent *lady* hussy. In any case, I told you, Grandmama enjoys a good battle. It keeps her young. So, that's your sisters, Lady Scattergood and my grandmother sorted. What other barriers to our marriage have you dreamed up?"

"I haven't dreamed them up—they're real."

"I know, love," he said softly. "But let's bring them out

into the air and look at them in daylight. I find worries are worst when you keep them to yourself and brood over them in the dark of night."

He was right. She did spend a lot of time brooding at night.

"If I were marrying Reynard the wandering artist, it wouldn't be so hard," she began. "Although it would disappoint my sisters and Lucy. But I know how to do that, be that kind of wife. But a countess . . ." She shook her head. "It's not just that I'm illegitimate and was born in the gutter, it's that I don't know how to do countess things. It's different for Izzy. She was raised with Clarissa, as a lady, and knows how to do things properly."

"What sort of things?"

"Oh, how to run a grand house, manage servants, visit tenants, be a gracious hostess, entertain guests—"

"Stop it. You do know how to do that, and whatever you don't know, you'll learn. Every young wife, no matter what her station in life, must learn how to manage her household. And you already know how to deal with people from all walks of life. You think you don't know how to be a lady, but whatever Lucy Paton and your sisters may have taught you, none of it makes you a lady."

Zoë was confused. Had she spent the last three years wasting her time, then?

He continued. "I've known many a so-called lady—fine society ladies with all the airs and graces and accomplishments you can imagine—but the way they treat those who they consider their inferiors would make you cringe. You, on the other hand, must have learned all the important things from your mother. I'm not talking about your accent, I'm talking about kindness to others of all levels of society, I'm talking about loyalty to those you care about and a generosity of spirit that leaves me breathless at times."

She blinked and swallowed a lump in her throat. Did he really think that of her?

"Now, as to the so-called duties of a countess," he continued, "they vary considerably and depend very much on the kind of earl you marry. Your sister Izzy, for instance, married Salcott, a serious-minded fellow who is bidding fair to become a mover and shaker in the world of politics and government. Correct?"

She nodded.

"And yet this man, a well-known high stickler, punctilious in doing the right thing, and planning a serious political career, chose to marry an illegitimate, outspoken and unconventional woman—presumably the very last kind of woman an ambitious politician should marry."

"He loves her. And she loves him."

"Precisely, and that is more important than anything."

"But Izzy is an excellent hostess."

"I agree. She's intelligent and gregarious, and she will set out to learn whatever she needs to learn. As will you. But what about your other sister, Clarissa? My impression of her is that she's shy and doesn't enjoy large gatherings."

"She doesn't."

"And her husband, also an earl, has no political ambitions and is happy looking after his estate and adoring his wife."

She smiled mistily. "They are very happy together."

He reached out and took her hands. "And so could we be. I don't need a wife to impress others and further a career. I just want us to be together and be happy. And raise a family together. I don't intend to change my agreement with Grandmama, by the way."

Her brows drew together. "What agreement is that?"

"That I be the earl for nine months of the year and go vagabonding for the other three months, wandering and painting. We could do that together if you want—you, me and Hamish. I thought you enjoyed that life."

"I did."

"Well?"

She pursed her lips, thinking. "I want to be a painter."

He looked perplexed. "But you would be."

"No, a proper painter, not just a lady with a hobby."

"And I wouldn't have it any other way. I love painting, but I don't have half the talent you have. I promise you, if you marry me, I will do everything in my power to help you to further your talent and your opportunities."

"But I don't want to be 'the countess that paints' and have people say, 'Oh, isn't she clever?' I want to be myself."

"Z-B has already begun to make a name for herself. Being a countess should not make much difference, though admittedly, it might help you develop opportunities. But it's talent that counts in the art world. I should know." He gave a rueful smile. "My title will never get me accepted into the Royal Academy, because I'm simply not good enough. But your paintings might and probably will. The academy even accepts women—Angelica Kauffman and Mary Moser were early members—though it has to be admitted that most members are men."

They hit a pothole, and Hamish, who had been snoozing on the floor, his head resting on her feet, woke, scrambled to his feet and nudged her meaningfully. Glad of the respite from the questions that had been disturbing her peace of mind for weeks, she spent the next few minutes making a fuss of the dog.

Reynard—no, Julian—was right. When she'd been brooding over her worries, alone in the middle of the night, they'd seemed insuperable. But every single one of his responses made sense. So what was holding her up? Was it nerves? The fear and uncertainty of knowing that happiness was there, within reach? That all she needed to do was to reach out and grab it?

It was disturbing to think she was a coward. But marriage, especially to a peer of the realm, was a big step.

She'd told Milly, *Screw your courage to the sticking point and you'll not fail.* Lowering to think that Milly might have more courage than she.

The carriage slowed and turned down a narrow drive. Julian glanced out the window. "Ah, good, we're here. That's Dot and Fred's place."

At the end of a drive lined with trees, bare at this time of the year, the house emerged, a wide three-story sandstone building with an arched entrance from which two wings spread, with a line of gabled dormer windows on each side, and two large bay windows on the ground and second floors. Facing south, it would be wonderfully light.

"What a beautiful house," Zoë exclaimed. It was much bigger than she'd expected.

"Yes, it's not bad," Julian said diffidently. He was trying to hide his pride in it. She was stunned. He'd *given* this place to his sister and her husband. It was a magnificent gesture.

The front door opened and a footman ran down the steps to meet them. A butler waited in the entrance, and two grooms appeared from around the side to deal with the horses. The footman let down the carriage steps, and Hamish bounded out and hurried to the nearest tree while Julian assisted Zoë to alight.

"Julian!" A small, rounded, dark-haired lady emerged and bustled toward them, a huge smile on her face.

"Dot." He picked her up and whirled her around. Laughing, she exhorted him to put her down and introduce her to his lady friend.

"Dot, this is my intended, Miss Zoë Benoît. Zoë, my sister, Lady Strangham." Zoë shot him a glance.

"Your intended, Julian? Oh, this is exciting. Welcome, Miss Benoît, I'm delighted to meet you."

"I may have been a trifle premature," Julian admitted, intercepting a stern look from Zoë. "She hasn't exactly agreed yet."

His sister frowned. "But you've brought her here, un-chaperoned?"

"Yes, I kidnapped her."

His sister widened her eyes at him for a moment, then gave a merry peal of laughter. "Oh, Julian, you're incorrigible. Miss Benoît, you're not distressed by this, are you? You don't look distressed."

"Annoyed, perhaps, but not in the least distressed," Zoë assured her. "Thank you for your warm welcome, Lady Strangham, and I'm very sorry to have inconvenienced you."

She waved that away. "It's no inconvenience at all, I assure you. I love having visitors."

"You haven't heard the worst of it yet," Zoë said dryly. "Not realizing I was to be kidnapped, I brought nothing with me, just the contents of my reticule—a handkerchief and a few shillings."

Lady Strangham blinked, then laughed again. "Oh, how typical. Aren't men hopeless?"

"He seems to think you won't mind lending me whatever I need."

"I don't, of course, but whether I have anything to fit you is another matter. Perhaps some of my dresses from before my recent confinement will do, though they will have to be let down." She linked arms with Zoë. "Come inside and tell me all about it. And please, call me Dot. When people call me Lady Strangham, I always think they're addressing my mother-in-law."

She led Zoë into the house and called for refreshments to be served in twenty minutes. Two small boys came racing down the stairs, paying Zoë scant attention but hurling themselves joyfully at Uncle Julian, who swung the smallest one onto his shoulders and dangled the giggling older boy upside down for a moment before setting him on his feet again.

A nursemaid stood on the landing, halfway up the stairs, holding a squalling bundle in her arms.

"Oh dear, Bessie is hungry again," Dot exclaimed. "Do you mind?"

Slightly bewildered, Zoë said, "Not at all."

"Oh good, come with me, then. Julian can look after the boys. Boys, take Uncle Julian out to wherever your papa is. He will want to look over the farm. Perhaps you could start with the pigs." She darted a mischievous glance at her brother and laughed at his resigned expression as two small boys grabbed his hands and began towing him to the piggery.

"Come along." Dot took Zoë upstairs with her, and they followed the nursemaid into what was clearly the nursery. Dot started unfastening the front of her dress at once and said over the deafening sound of the tiny bundle's displeasure, "I'm feeding her myself, you see. I know it's terribly unfashionable and unladylike, and that I ought to employ a wet nurse, but I don't care. I love it." She sat in a chair, facing slightly away from Zoë, and took the baby. There was sudden, blissful silence. "Now," she said chattily, "tell me all about you and my scapegrace brother."

Which Zoë did. Relating her story to Julian's very receptive and warmhearted sister made her realize that somehow, their discussion of her fears had somehow settled them. And that what she wanted, more than anything in the world, was to be with him for the rest of her life.

Watching Dot with her sweet little baby daughter, she was also aware of a pang of envy. One day she wanted this for herself, too.

By the end of the day, Zoë felt almost as if she were already part of the family. Dot was lively, sympathetic and welcoming. Her husband was a tall, quiet man, quite content to let his wife take the conversational lead, unless it concerned farming, about which he was endearingly enthusiastic. The two of them were still clearly in love.

The children, too, were lively and happy. The boys had

firmly attached themselves to their uncle and begged that he come up and tell them a story before they went to sleep. Uncle Julian's stories were *amaaaazing*, they assured her. Zoë had no difficulty believing it, but she didn't go upstairs to join them.

Somehow her mind had settled. Julian was going to be her husband. She would accept his proposal tonight if they ever had a moment alone.

She had decided, and yet she was absurdly nervous.

She was fairly quiet during supper, which, luckily, wasn't particularly noticeable, as Julian and Dot were both very talkative. From time to time she felt his eyes resting on her, a question in them.

Finally it was time for bed. Dot accompanied Zoë upstairs to help get her settled in. Her maid had sorted out some clothing for Zoë, including a warm, long-sleeved nightgown in white flannel. Her bedchamber was cozy, with a fire burning in the grate and a large four-poster bed. Dot bustled around, closing the curtains and ensuring Zoë had warm water in which to wash, tooth powder and a toothbrush and anything else she might need, including books and a maid.

"Our bedroom is at the other end of the corridor," she explained. "The baby wakes in the night, but you shouldn't be able to hear her from here. At least I hope not. And Julian is right across the hall. I hope that's all right. Your door locks, of course."

Zoë thanked her again for her generosity and hospitality, which Dot dismissed with an airy wave of her hand. "I'd do the same for anyone my brother kidnapped," she joked. She wished Zoë good night and left her to get undressed.

The maid helped Zoë to undress and took the rest of her clothing away to be laundered. Zoë washed in the hot water, using a beautifully fragrant soap, then slipped into the voluminous white nightgown. She cleaned her teeth, then climbed onto the bed and waited.

A few minutes later she hopped off the bed, parted the curtains and peered out. A blackberry-dark sky with a bright scattering of stars and a crescent moon.

She picked up one of the books that Dot had left for her, climbed back onto the bed and idly flipped the pages, taking in nothing. Her ears were stretched for every little sound. Had he come upstairs yet, or was he still downstairs drinking and chatting with his brother-in-law?

She put the book aside, slipped off the bed and tried her door. Should she leave it ajar so he would see it when he came up to bed? Or would that be too brazen a hint? No. She was going to be brazen enough. Besides, it was letting in a draft. She closed the door and sank cross-legged on the rug in front of the fire.

Finally she heard him come up. His door closed. She waited a little while, imagining him preparing for bed. She swallowed, took a deep breath and knocked softly on his door. It swung open instantly. Julian stood there in just his breeches and shirtsleeves.

"Vita?" he said softly. She didn't say anything—her tongue was thick with nerves—but he held out his hand and she took it. He drew her inside, closed the door behind her and locked it.

"You're freezing, love. Come over to the fire and warm up."

But it wasn't the fire she needed to warm her. She put her hands on his shoulders and gazed earnestly up at him. "Are you sure about marrying me, Julian?"

His arms slid around her waist and he drew her against him. "More than sure. I love you with all my heart and soul and body, and I don't want to be apart from you ever again." His eyes blazed blue. "Does this mean you've made up your mind?"

She nodded. "There will be difficulties, but I'm sure we can—I can work through them."

"*We* will work through any problems together." He cupped her chin in his hand and kissed her softly, almost reverently, on the lips. It was a vow. She smiled, and his returning smile lit the room. He picked her up, whirled her around and they fell together, laughing, on the bed.

And then they were kissing, kissing, kissing. His mouth and hands everywhere, tasting her, caressing her, lavishing her with soft, sumptuous, silken kisses that fired her blood and melted her bones. She ran her palm down his jawline, reveling in the faint prickle of bristles under firm, masculine skin, enjoying the soft rasping sound it made.

He drew back. "I'm sorry, I didn't think. I should have shaved tonight."

"No, I like it," she murmured, and stroked her palm over his jaw again. "This is almost how I first met you, only you're not quite as bristly tonight."

"And you like it?"

She gave him a slow, sultry smile and brushed against him like a cat, breathing in the faint fragrance of his cologne. He hadn't worn cologne in France. She tried to decide which she preferred, the fresh, fragrant skin-with-cologne scent of Julian or the bare bold naked unadorned man scent that was Reynard. Both were incredibly appealing to her senses.

And then they were kissing again.

She couldn't get enough of it, of him. She felt not just desirable, but cherished, as if she were something—no *someone* precious.

She pulled off his shirt and ran her hands over his hard masculine chest.

"Hah! Two can play at that game, missy," he growled. He tugged at her nightgown. "What the devil *is* this thing my sister has dressed you in? It's practically a tent." He was floundering in its voluminous folds. "We might have first made love in a caravan, but I'm hanged if the second time is going to be in a tent!"

She laughed. "Oh, but it's lovely and warm," she purred provocatively, making no attempt to help him.

"You don't need this to keep you warm. That's my job." He finally found the hem. "Lift up," he said, and an instant later she was bare to the air and the nightgown had been flung away. "Ah, now that's how I prefer you to be dressed." And he proceeded to lavish her with . . . love. It wasn't just bed sports, it was love. Though as bed sports went, she was learning a lot.

They made love twice, and each time he took her to a peak where she arched and shuddered and then—shockingly— screamed. Just exactly like a wild vixen. And then collapsed, boneless and euphoric.

"I'm glad we're in the other wing of the house," she told him after the first time, when she'd been lying in his arms, dreamy and sated. "I wouldn't want your sister to hear that."

He laughed and proceeded to show her that she wasn't nearly as tired as she'd thought.

They made love again in the morning, and when they went down to breakfast, Dot gave them a knowing look and a big smile. Zoë tried not to blush, but she felt it heating her face.

"Let's get married," Julian said after breakfast.

Zoë gave him a quizzical look. "I thought we'd already agreed on that."

"Yes, but I mean now. Today. I have a special license with me."

"Today? You mean here?"

"Yes, in the village church if you like. It's quite ancient and rather lovely, as I think I mentioned." He gave her a hopeful look.

"I am not getting married in the village church, no matter how ancient and lovely it is," she told him. "My sisters and Lucy would be so disappointed if they missed my wedding. No, I will marry you at St. George's in Hanover Square with my sisters and their husbands and Lucy and Gerald and Lady Scattergood if we can get her there—and your grandmother as well as your other wives and their children."

"Other wives? What's this about other wives?" Dot had overheard them, and Zoë left it to Julian to explain his three wives. When he'd finished, Dot thumped him on the arm. "You are atrocious!" she told him.

"I know. I'm sorry," he said without the slightest sign of contrition.

❦

They stayed with Dot and Fred and the children two more days, spending the days walking and talking—with each other mostly, but also with Dot and Fred. She liked Julian's family very much.

And every night and each morning they made love, never the same way twice, but always gloriously satisfying.

Lovemaking with Julian wasn't anything like she'd expected. Sometimes it was intense—pure, raw passion—and at other times it was joyful and playful with conversation and laughter. And each morning she woke thinking she couldn't be any happier. And every day he proved her wrong.

Then on the third day, it was time to return to London and face the music.

❦

Drop me off at Clarissa's," Zoë said as they neared Bellaire Gardens. "I know she'll want to talk to both of us, and Lady Scattergood might not let you in the house."

But when they got to Clarissa's, they found Izzy and Leo as well as Lucy and Lady Tarrant gathered in the downstairs sitting room, looking worried.

"What's going on?" Zoë asked after she'd embraced everyone.

"Clarissa is having the baby."

Zoë glanced around. "What, now? Where is Race?"

Izzy pointed. "He's up there with her."

"In with Clarissa? When she's having the baby?" It was quite unheard of in Zoë's experience. Men simply weren't allowed in a birthing room, not unless they were a doctor. Or unless they were there to say goodbye. No wonder everyone looked so serious. Was Clarissa expected to die? She didn't know how to ask it.

But Izzy understood the silent question in her eyes. "No, there's nothing wrong—that we know of. Race has said from the beginning that he was going to be with Clarissa throughout her labor."

"Really?" Zoë glanced at Julian, who looked uncomfortable. She looked at Leo. "Did you—?"

"No," he said hastily. "I didn't."

"I wouldn't have allowed him in anyway," Izzy said. "I have no desire for anyone to see me in that state. But Clarissa is different. Race has been in there all this time, wiping her brow and holding her hand and doing whatever she wants."

"How long has it been?"

A scream rang out, and they all fell silent, listening.

"Long enough," Izzy said. She got up and paced the floor restlessly.

After a few minutes, Leo caught her hand and drew her down beside him. He rubbed her back soothingly and tried to distract them. "So, Zoë, how was your visit?" he asked, but another scream rang out, and they all fell silent again.

Tension filled the room.

They heard a door upstairs open and close. Someone was coming down the stairs. They all ran out to the hall, and looked up to see Race coming unsteadily down the stairs. A high, thin wail floated down. The baby.

"Oh God," he said. His knees appeared to give way and he plonked down halfway down the stairs. "It's over. It's all over."

They gathered around the foot of the stairs. "Race? You

mean—? Is Clarissa—?" Izzy faltered. Her skin was chalky gray.

He looked up. "Oh, no, no, she's fine—tired, but otherwise all right. Very happy. They're just cleaning her and the baby up. She was so brave, so strong. I had no idea . . . So brave. All you women . . . so strong."

There was a universal sigh of relief. The upstairs door opened again, and a nurse appeared on the stairs, carrying a small bundle, which was no longer yelling. "Lord Randall? Would you care to hold your daughter now?"

Without waiting for a reply, she came down the last few steps and placed the baby in Race's arms. "Oh God," he murmured, staring down at the bundle in his arms. He loosened the swaddling clothes a little and a tiny arm emerged.

In wonder, Race touched the little starfish hand, and it closed around his finger. "Look at her," he said brokenly. "Have you ever seen such a perfect little person? My daughter. Look at those little hands, those perfect tiny fingernails. It's a miracle. She's a miracle. And my Clarissa is a miracle. And alive." He looked down at them, his eyes full of tears. "We have a daughter."

Chapter Nineteen

The preparations for Zoë and Julian's wedding went on apace. Over the next three weeks banns were called at St. George's. Julian had been adamant that he could not possibly wait any more than three weeks to make Zoë his wife.

Zoë felt the same and had been prepared to wear one of her elegant French dresses for the wedding, but as it turned out, her sisters had already commissioned a wedding dress for her from the House of Chance. Miss Chance already had her measurements, and all there was left to do was the hem.

It was gorgeous, Zoë thought when she saw it, creamy white, in heavy silk that fell beautifully, quite plain with a hint of lace at the sleeves and hem.

There was also a beautiful, delicate, quite improper, almost-sheer silk-and-lace nightgown with a matching dressing gown. Zoë couldn't wait to wear it for Julian. Though she had no doubt it would go the way of every other nightgown she had worn for him.

They went together to break the news to his grand-mother, Lady Bagshott.

He told her, in all solemnity, "I've given up all hope of finding my little French maidservant, Grandmama. And knowing how much you want me to marry, I decided it was time, so I have asked Miss Benoît to be my countess, and she has accepted." Before his grandmother could say a word, he added, "And knowing how much you liked and admired Miss Benoît when she was painting your portrait, I knew you'd be delighted with my choice."

There was a short silence. Julian waited with an expression of such innocent expectance it sorely tried Zoë's self-control.

"Very good," his grandmother finally grated sourly. "Congratulations."

"There's only one small problem," he added. Zoë looked at him in surprise. "Miss Benoît has, as you know, been living with Lady Scattergood, but she, sadly, does not support our wedding."

The old lady stiffened. "What? Olive Barrington does not approve? How dare she? She always was a hoity-toity madam!"

He sighed. "I know."

Lady Bagshott glanced at Zoë and said reluctantly, "You are welcome to make your home here, in Foxton House."

"Foxton House?" Julian exclaimed. "You mean you'll move out and let us live here at Foxton House, Grandmama? How very generous of you. Naturally I will purchase another house in Mayfair for you to live in."

His grandmother's jaw dropped open. "But I didn't mean—"

Julian said smoothly, "Olive Barrington will be mortified, positively mortified when she learns how generous and selfless you have been to a new young bride—her protégée. What a comedown for her, to see you give up your home to make way for the new generation, just as you've always wanted. So magnanimous of you. Thank you, Grandmama."

Stupefied, Lady Bagshott goggled at him. But Zoë couldn't let it happen. She leaned forward and put her hand on Julian's arm. "No," she said. "No, we can't do that, deprive your grandmother of this house she loves so much."

Julian and his grandmother looked at her in surprise.

"Lady Bagshott must continue to live here. We will buy another house."

Bemused, Julian agreed. He kissed his grandmother's hand, took his leave and they left.

"Why did you do that? I had it all worked out," he said as they strolled arm in arm along the street. "The house isn't hers, you know. It belongs to me. She just took possession of it five or six years ago without so much as a by-your-leave."

"I know—and you really are atrocious, ambushing her like that." She chuckled. "Her face was a picture. But we really can't turn her out of her home." She shot him a sideways glance. "And since you were going to be buying a house anyway, I thought why not buy it for us."

He looked thoughtful for a moment, then nodded. "Very well. Any thoughts about where?"

"What about Bellaire Gardens or somewhere nearby? The gardens there are so beautiful." She added, "I was never even in a garden until Clarissa found me and took me there. I never dreamed such a place could exist. It's so beautiful, Julian. It's magic, even now in winter."

His face cleared. "Of course, I should have thought of that sooner. And you'll want to be near your sisters as well. I'll speak to my man of business this afternoon and put him onto it."

Five days before the wedding, when Julian called to take Zoë for their daily walk or drive in the park, he told her, "I have good news about a house. My man of business has learned of a house in Bellaire Gardens that the owner is willing to sell. For the last few years it has been rented by a widow and her daughter. However, both the daughter and the widow are about to be married, the widow to a marquess—apparently she's second cousin to a duke."

Zoë laughed and laughed. "I can't wait to tell my sisters this," she gasped when her laughter subsided.

He gazed at her, perplexed but smiling at her apparent delight. "What's so funny?"

"I know that house, though I've never been inside it. It's where Milly and her mother lived—the girl who went off with her betrothed the day you kidnapped me. And her mother is to marry the old spider. It couldn't be more perfect."

He shook his head. "If you say so. Well, if you approve, I'll tell my man to buy it, and we'll get someone in to refurbish the whole place. Best to have a fresh start with it."

She hugged his arm, almost dancing along beside him. "It's the most perfect solution. I shall have the gardens and my sisters and Lady Scattergood and Lucy for a while, and the Tarrants—oh, thank you, Julian. It couldn't be better."

"If you keep dancing and smiling like that, I'm going to have to kiss you in the middle of a public footpath," he warned her.

"How shocking that would be." She laughed and hugged his arm again. "Race had their house entirely refurbished before he and Clarissa married, and I believe Matteo, Leo's majordomo and general factotum, organized the complete redecoration of his and Izzy's house. They will know who to recommend. Oh, Julian, it's all turning out so well. When I left you that morning in France, I thought my heart was breaking and all my happiness was at an end. And now look at us."

"I don't need to look at us," he said. "Everyone else is doing it." And regardless of the people walking past, he bent and gave her a swift kiss.

* * *

Zoë and Julian's wedding day dawned cool but clear. Zoë was a little nervous—she had no idea why. This was what she wanted so much.

She'd bathed first thing in the morning, using a deliciously scented bath mix that Clarissa had made. The maids, Betty and Marie, helped her get dressed, arranging her hair beautifully and dusting a faint hint of rouge on her cheeks. Her sisters arrived then, Clarissa with flowers and a lovely red leather case containing all her best creations. Izzy brought a beautiful string of pearls, which were a gift from her and Leo.

And then it was time to go to the church.

Both Leo and Race had offered to give the bride away, but the choice was too difficult, so after some thought, she decided to ask Gerald, because he had housed and fed her for the last three years in Paris. He'd been touched and was delighted to accept.

"Ready?" Gerald murmured. She took a deep breath, nodded and stepped inside, pausing a moment to let her eyes adjust. The church smelled of beeswax and fresh greenery.

The pews were almost full. She glanced around in amazement. After Maman had died when she was a child, she'd thought no one would ever love her again. But look at her now.

All these people had come to be with her on her wedding day: Clarissa, who'd found and instantly embraced her as a sister; Izzy, who was practically her twin in appearance; and Lady Scattergood, who had ventured out of her house, despite her fears, just to see Zoë married.

The maidservants sat in the back row dressed in their best and all beaming at her. Betty, who had first discovered her in the orphanage, Joan, who had been chosen as a maid in Zoë's place, and Marie, the young Frenchwoman who had braved the vile Etienne and had the courage to accompany Zoë to London even though she knew no English and no one but Zoë. Such trust and loyalty. Zoë blew her a kiss, and all three of them blew one back.

Her throat filled with emotion. She continued down the aisle.

Small bunches of daphne had been fastened to the end of each pew, and as she passed, she caught the glorious scent. It was one of her favorites. Another wonderful Clarissa touch, she was sure.

There was Lucy, smiling and giving her a little wave. For the last three years she and Gerald had given Zoë a home and so much more—companionship, friendship and, finally, love. They might not be blood relations, but they were part of her family now. Lucy was sitting with Lord and Lady Tarrant, who had also shown her friendship and acceptance from the first day they'd met. She was so blessed in her friends.

On the groom's side, there were quite a few gentlemen— Julian's friends, she assumed. She spotted Lady Bagshott, resplendent in puce and gold, wearing an enormous turban. From time to time she shot a hostile glance across the aisle to where Lady Scattergood was seated. Lady Scattergood appeared to be utterly oblivious, but a small smile told Zoë she knew exactly what was happening and was enjoying every minute of it.

In the next pew sat an elegantly dressed lady with two much younger ladies. Julian's so-called "second wife," she assumed: his sister-in-law, the dowager countess, and her daughters.

Oh, and there were Dot and Fred! They'd made the journey from Ardingly. Dot, beaming, gave her a little wave. Zoë gave her a misty smile: she was finding it hard not to cry, it was all so lovely and moving and unexpected. The church felt filled with love.

And there, waiting in front of the altar, stood Julian,

magnificent in formal black, white and silver-gray, his blue, blue eyes gleaming. Julian, her soulmate, her lover and now her husband.

The last remnants of the cold ache of loneliness that had been part of her life for so long disappeared.

He held out his hand, she took it, and together they turned to face the minister. "Dearly Beloved . . ."

Chapter Twenty

The wedding breakfast was held in the gardens in a large marquee that had been erected there in case the weather turned. But it didn't.

The food was splendid—Leo and Izzy's chef, Alfonso, had prepared it all, and Matteo was everywhere, seeing that everything was smooth and well organized. A small string orchestra played and the champagne flowed.

Lady Scattergood had set up her court in the summer-house, surrounded by her cronies, enjoying the warmth of the enamel stove. In a corner of the marquee Lady Bagshott had set up her own, rival court.

Zoë and Julian chuckled over it. All was well in Bellaire Gardens.

Julian slid an arm around her waist. "Happy, love?"

"Very." She leaned against him.

"I thought we might go to Italy on our honeymoon. What do you think? Italy in the springtime. We can wander where we please, paint, explore and make love."

She sighed happily. "That sounds perfect. Would we go by boat?"

"Yes, by yacht. The Mediterranean is very beautiful. You would not believe the blue of the sea there."

She gave him a misty smile and gazed into his blue, blue eyes. "Oh, I believe it. And I love the idea."

"And by the time we return, our house will be ready for us to move in."

"Perfect."

Just then Clarissa, who had earlier gone inside to feed her baby, came out smiling and waving a letter. "This just arrived. It's from Milly. You have to read it."

Zoë took it and read:

Dear Lady Randall, Lady Salcott and Miss Benoît,

You may Wish me Happy because I am now a Married Lady. As is Mama, who liked my suggestion, and so has married the Marquess. We are now Reconciled, even though she would prefer that Thaddeus was Titled.

By the way, I told Thaddeus about that improper nightgown that you gave me. He says it sounds Intriguing and that he would like to see me wearing it. Men are strange, but he has mentioned it twice now, so please send it to me at the above address.

Yours truly,
Mrs. Thaddeus Henshaw (née Milly Harrington)

ABOUT THE AUTHOR

Anne Gracie is the award-winning author of the Chance Sisters, Marriage of Convenience, and Brides of Bellaire Gardens romance series. She started her first novel while backpacking solo around the world, writing by hand in notebooks. Since then, her books have been translated into more than eighteen languages, including Japanese manga editions. As well as writing, Anne promotes adult literacy, flings balls for her dog, enjoys her tangled garden and keeps bees.

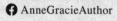

Ready to find
your next great read?

Let us help.

Visit prh.com/nextread

Penguin
Random
House